LateNightTalking

ALSO BY LESLIE SCHNUR

The Dog Walker

Leslie Schnur

LateNightTalking

ATRIA BOOKS

New York   London   Toronto   Sydney

ATRIA BOOKS

1230 Avenue of the Americas
New York, NY 10020

Library of Congress Cataloging in Publication Data is available

ISBN-13: 978-0-7432-8824-8
ISBN-10:   0-7432-8824-6

First Atria Books hardcover edition May 2007

10   9   8   7   6   5   4   3   2   1

ATRIA BOOKS is a trademark of Simon & Schuster, Inc.

Manufactured in the United States of America

For information regarding special discounts for bulk purchases,
please contact Simon & Schuster Special Sales at
1-800-456-6798 or business@simonandschuster.com.

For my parents, Milton Schnur and Myrna Schnur

And for Jerry, always

LateNightTalking

Morning Walk

There is something about Tribeca at five a.m. that is preternaturally romantic, Jeannie thought as she made a left onto Warren from Broadway, the *ca-thunk* of her Frye boots on the broken sidewalk echoing in the ethereal quiet, her fringed suede jacket protecting her against the cool morning air. An ellipse of lavender light sat like a halo over the city, the heavens above it cobalt blue. The streets were almost empty, hushed, except for a lone taxi and a van double-parked up the block. In less than an hour the morning rush would descend, but until then, this city of millions was at peace, dreamy and mysterious. And it was all hers. The cobblestone streets, the narrow alleys, the tree-lined squares, and the red brick buildings made her imagine ardent young lovers in their beds, made her aware of her own heart, full of possibility and desire.

She took this walk, rain or shine, five days a week, through the streets she loved. Only blocks from Ground Zero, this part of town was complex: historically rich, seedy, and chic, with ninety-nine-cent stores, designer furnishings, and trendy restaurants sharing a sidewalk. Its tragic, horrific past united the community, making it feel like a village, separate and apart from the rest of the city.

By the time Jeannie reached the corner of Hudson and Franklin, the preworkday hubbub was under way. She waved to Bill, who was unlocking the hefty padlock on the security gate at Ideal Dry Cleaners; to Tranh, who was sweeping the doorway at Jin Market; to her buddy Jonas at the counter of Socrates Coffee Shop. She bid a "Good morning!" to Esther, the tranny who religiously walked her two miniature white poodles, Marilyn and Marlene, up and down North Moore every morning at the same hour. She gave a buck to Stuart, the homeless guy who lived in the alley off Beach. These were the things she did every morning, the things that made this huge city feel like a quaint small town to her.

After her show, the long walk felt necessary, restorative. Tonight was a case in point. All those callers, all those complaints about all those idiots who behaved as if they never had a mother to teach them anything. And she certainly knew, as well as anybody, the effect of having a mother and then not having a mother. You have someone monitoring your deeds and then you don't, and you're on your own.

But something was going on in this beloved town of hers. Even with the crime rate down, rudeness was at an all-time high. Tonight she'd heard just a few examples: the woman getting a manicure who asked a young woman to lower the volume on her iPod—and then *she* was unjustly asked to leave the salon; the man who wouldn't give a pregnant lady his seat on the bus because it was her choice to get pregnant, and not his responsibility; the woman at the gym on the elliptical who'd cover her timer with a towel and repeatedly set it to zero, hoping nobody noticed that she'd far exceeded her thirty-minute limit; the guy talking on his cell phone while at the urinal in the office bathroom.

It was as if, like in those cartoons she saw as a kid, every person had a little angel whispering in one ear and a mini devil in the other, vying for control: be good, be bad, do right, do wrong, be considerate, be selfish, throw the wrapper in the garbage, just throw it in the street.

Someday, somehow, she swore to herself, she was going to devise a method to help the people with louder devils. Somewhere, someplace, her faith in the potential goodness of people, even when they're caught with their dick in one hand and their cell phone in the other, would be transforming.

A girl can dream, Jeannie thought as she entered her apartment building.

"Morning, Tony." She smiled at her night doorman, who had rushed from his perch at the desk to open the door. He had been sorting newspapers, getting ready to pass the baton to the morning guy. She could hear the radio that sat on the desk.

"Morning, Miss Sterling. Good show last night. Can't believe those people."

"You're telling me," she said, rolling her eyes.

He looked up at the sky. "But it's going to be some kind of day, isn't it?"

That was an understatement.

There's No Place Like Home

In her apartment, after throwing her bag on the kitchen counter, her keys too, Jeannie got herself a bottle of water from the fridge and sat at her dining-room table with the morning paper. This table was where she did her best thinking, sitting on the rigid old chair that was at the right of the table's head, where she could look out the windows at the Hudson River and beyond.

This view—the river before her, the endless sky, even that strange land called New Jersey way over there—was the reason she lived in this apartment. As far west as Manhattan would allow, as high as the building's limits, with walls of glass on three sides, Jeannie lived above and apart from the world below. It had cost her a minor fortune to buy this place, and thanks to her success at WBUZ she could afford it. But it had cost her in other ways too. It had become her refuge, her hideout, an excuse to stay inside. Once she was home, she sometimes had to force herself to go back out into the world.

After hours of dealing with the ethically challenged, with her crazy upside-down, inside-out lifestyle that usually included dinner twice a day—once in the morning when she got home from work, and once in the evening before she went to work—she relied on TiVo for her entertainment, which consisted of *Law and Order, Law and Order,* and *Law and Order.* She had to admit she enjoyed Regis and Kelly, except when Kelly wasn't on, and she never missed Ellen DeGeneres, believing that if there were any justice in the world, she would someday host *The Tonight Show.* This life of leftovers and TiVo and talk shows was the plight of the girl who works the night shift.

Not that her apartment was any more perfect than the world below. Her building was a knockoff of the Meier glass towers a few blocks uptown with their multimillion-dollar apartments. And like other designer knockoffs, this building looked like the original, until, upon closer inspection, you found its fabric flimsy, its stitching frayed at the edges. During storms, wind and water would seep in through the crevices of the metal beams that held the window panels in place. Then the bleached wood floors would stain, the corners of the ceilings would drip, and this so-called magnificent ode to modernism would become nothing more than any other shoddy postwar construction that plagued the city. And Jeannie would sit on her sofa wrapped in her favorite blue mohair throw, trying desperately to find protection against the storm outside.

Living the life transparent had other problems. The light that spilled in enlivened Jeannie's spirit, but she slept during the day, a detail she'd forgotten in her excitement when she first saw the apartment and made an offer right on the spot. So she had to work hard to keep the light out. It seemed a crime to shade the windows, so she wore a horribly froufrou, lavender silk ruffle-edged eye mask when she slept. And when that wasn't enough—on those glorious blue-skied New York City days when the sunlight's reflection bounced from one window to another and another, all the way from New Jersey and back, she would put up a temporary curtain, actually a thick wool blanket held in place by two small nails, making her chic modern apartment look a lot like the disheveled house she grew up in.

Not to mention that she couldn't just walk around naked. She got up from the table and made her way down the hall to her bedroom to strip from her jeans and sweater and put on her yoga pants and tank. She was on the seventeenth floor, so she couldn't be seen from the street below, and to the west was the river, but to the north and to the south were two other buildings with walls of glass just like hers. She didn't mind her neighbor to the north, another thirty-something woman who worked days like a normal person, but the one to the south was a potbellied movie or music guy, which she knew from his balding head and ponytail, as well as the bashes he threw that were sometimes still going on when Jeannie got home in the morning. Who knew that trying to live an open, sunlit, elegant lifestyle would be so fraught with concerns.

She was hungry and not ready for sleep, so she went to the fridge and got last Friday's leftovers from Gigino. It was only Tuesday, so they still had to be good. She opened the cardboard top, which had become soft and wet, stained red with tomato sauce, and stuck her nose close to the meatball. Not bad. She poured it into a bowl and heated it in the microwave.

Now, sitting high above the city of her dreams, the buzz of the TV in her ears, eating a reheated four-day-old meatball, she couldn't bullshit herself that her life was perfect. But she did have her priorities straight. She was as comfortable as she could be, given her upbringing, with her success. It wasn't NPR, but AM radio had its good points, like listeners and a steady paycheck. She lived well but not extravagantly, she donated a good portion of her income to those less fortunate than she, and on some days she even allowed herself to enjoy her most recent splurge, a Marc Jacobs bag.

And she was in it for all the right reasons. She truly believed the world would be a better place if people weren't so rude, if they'd say "excuse me" when they bumped into you, or stop talking in the movies, or stop spitting in public, or refrain from unwrapping candy in the theater. And she dreamed of that glorious day when people would turn down the volume on their iPods so that you couldn't hear them even when standing twenty feet away. On a noisy street corner. With a fire truck's siren blaring.

She was committed to making the world a more livable place, one annoying person at a time.

But love eluded her, and her longing was overwhelming.

She had had her relationships, her affairs, her flings, her dates and one-night stands. She'd been pursued, propositioned, and proposed to, but not once had she really been in love. She couldn't help but wonder if it was her own failing. Perhaps it was her upbringing. Though she couldn't pinpoint a moment when her mother had said anything specific, maybe she'd learned through osmosis, the silent legacy of the heart, what her mother felt—that love was a fallacy, that it simply didn't exist. Or how her father saw it—that love is overrated and that there's more to life, like having fun. Perhaps it was simply a matter of luck, or the lack of it.

Something happened to her when she observed couples laughing, touching, whispering intimately into each other's ears, their breath hot in each other's hair. Just last week at the black-tie fund-raiser for the Multiple Sclerosis Foundation, she had been wearing her Stella McCartney dress and her Jimmy Choo stilettos and feeling great in general, though her feet hurt like hell. She was at a table with a bunch of media types: a couple of dowdy female book editors from Random House, a self-important political blogger for *The Huffington Post*, and the funny, flamboyant editor of *Elle Decor*. There was also an older couple representing the foundation. Both doctors, the woman lovely, her white hair short, her diamond earrings flashing under the lights; the man bald, with a warm, open face. Something he said made his wife laugh and she threw back her head, fully enjoying the moment, her husband looking at her, laughing with her. Then, completely unconsciously, he raised his hand and took a speck of something from her hair. Not a word was exchanged. But with this one gesture, Jeannie became acutely aware of what she was missing.

Her disappointment was like realizing a flashing light in a

glorious night sky is not a comet nor a shooting star but just a jet bringing people from Topeka. Somewhere a comet was careening through a universe, but not Jeannie's.

She got up and put her plate in the sink and the empty bottle of water in the recycle bin, and got ready for sleep. In her bedroom the light was streaming in, so she got up on her desk chair and covered the window with the throw that had been on the chair, hanging it from the nails above the window that remained there for this very purpose. She climbed under her covers, placed the lavender mask over her eyes, and fell asleep with thoughts of installing a blackout shade and what to do about people who litter and whether she'd ever meet a man who would gently, lovingly, remove a foreign object from her hair.

STERLING BEHAVIOR

LUCE: *Quiet, people. Ten seconds. Stand by. Five seconds. Three, two, one. And we're live.*

JEANNIE: *Good evening, fellow insomniacs! You're tuned to Sterling Behavior on WBUZ, 660 on your AM dial, the number-one late-late-night talk show in the tri-state area and home of yours truly, Jeannie Sterling. Tonight I have an important issue on my mind. One that leads people to irrational behavior, and even to . . . violence. And that explosive issue is . . . bad driving. My question to you, dear listeners, is this: are bad drivers bad drivers because of their sense of entitlement, or are they just bad drivers? We're going to a commercial break but don't go away or to sleep. We've got some wrongs to right and we'll be right back.*

Better Late Than Never

"What happened? You cut it way too close tonight," said Luce, as she handed Jeannie a bottle of water.

Jeannie was still trying to catch her breath, having just made it to the studio about three minutes before her show was to air. She took a swig of the water, propped the bottle next to her mike, and pulled her long, wildly uncontrollable hair into a ponytail so it wouldn't get caught in the headphones, as it did so frequently.

"This guy, you wouldn't believe—"

Luce rolled her eyes and smiled. "Why do I have the feeling we're about to hear all about it?" With her index finger, she pointed to the mike, nodded, and said, "Three, two, one, and we're back."

STERLING BEHAVIOR

JEANNIE: *You will not believe what happened to me tonight. It's about ten thirty and there I am, standing at the corner of Hudson and Beach, trying to hail a taxi. It's almost pitch black, the moon hidden by clouds, barely a streetlamp, and I'm all alone.*

LUCE: *I love that area, where you live. All those old factories converted into apartments, all those super-cool bars and shops. Too hip for me.*

JEANNIE: *Everything west of Park and south of Sixty-sixth is too hip for you. Now where was I?*

LUCE: *You were setting the scene. It's late, it's dark, you're alone—*

JEANNIE: *Yeah, okay, so there I am, waiting and waiting on a dark corner for a cab to take me to my show here at WBUZ Radio* *near City Hall—where are all the cabs anyway? As a cabbie once said, "We're just like cops: you can never find one when you need one." So I've been waiting for maybe ten minutes now, and I have to be at the station by eleven thirty at the absolute latest to prepare for my one-to-four-a.m. gig talking to you, my loyal listeners, and I'm getting nervous and swearing to myself to make them pay for a car service. Don't you think that a girl who works the night shift—you listening, Harry?—deserves to be picked up so she's not standing alone on a dangerous corner in New York City?*

LUCE: *Yeah, Harry. And the same goes for her producer-slash-sidekick.*

JEANNIE: *But back to the dark and dangerous street. All of a sudden I see what looks like a tank coming right at me. The noise, the speed, it scares the you-know-what out of me, and it's barreling down the street, splashing water out of the puddles left over from yesterday's shower—fallout from Hurricane Igor, which blasted the Caribbean last week. By the way, thousands of you devoted listeners donated food and clothing for those people whose lives were left in rubble. Now that's Sterling Behavior.*

So now I see it's a Hummer, a military vehicle for god's sake, so huge, where you sit so high you can probably see Baghdad from its front seat, a car that should not be on the road—it's so big and gets maybe nine miles per gallon, and it's storming up the street with the speed and force of an entire army. The driver, naturally, is talking on his cell phone. While driving. Not only is that against the law in the state of New York, which is reason enough not to do it, it's also distracting and dangerous and wrong. I swear, someday I'm going to give out tickets for social infractions.

LUCE: *You didn't do anything foolish, did you?*

JEANNIE: *Well, I have to confess, even yours truly makes mistakes.*

LUCE: *Uh-oh. What did you—*

JEANNIE: *What did I do, you ask? Something very mature and productive.*

Turkey in a Hummer

"You turkey!" Jeannie yelled. "Shame on you!" *Now that really got him,* she thought, wanting to smack herself. What a self-righteous, idiotic thing for her to have done. But she just couldn't help it. At least she didn't call him a pig, her word of preference when it came to rude drivers like those who cut off pedestrians in crosswalks. Why couldn't New York adopt some of the principles of California? There the pedestrian is always given the right of way. This was just one of the ways New York differed from her home state, that and—oh, about everything else.

But when the Hummer screeched to a stop, "Oh no," was all Jeannie could say. It was dark and it was late and she was alone, and she knew from experience that trying to talk to people like this was futile and sometimes dangerous. It was one thing to talk from the secure world of the radio studio. Hell, there she could say anything she wanted. But the real world is a scary place.

The door flung open and the man stuck his head out, looking back at Jeannie.

Oh my god, he's gorgeous.

"All I really want to dooooo-ooo-ooo," he sang, loudly and badly, "is, baby, be friends with you."

And he's a moron. Though he gets one point for choosing Dylan to bastardize.

And then, as he got out of his car—if one could call it
that—he spoke into his cell phone. "Marshall, I've just been
called a turkey. Yeah! Right here on the street. A woman." She
couldn't help but notice him look her up and down. "Not
bad." And he paused again. "No, it's not Thanksgiving. No, I
am not wearing a feather boa." He then closed his phone
and put it in his pocket. "Did you call me a turkey?"

Oh shit, Jeannie thought to herself, her chest contracting,
making her an inch shorter, which was nothing in compari-
son to how small she felt for acting like a baby. She watched
him coming toward her. *Look at this guy. Look at how he walks*,
she thought. *Slowly, knowing exactly where he's going, knowing
you'd wait forever, if you had to, until he got there.*

She felt a familiar internal argument coming on. On one
hand, she couldn't stand men like this. They were arrogant
and ignorant and lacked good values, and their ethics were
up their asses. Not only did he drive this gigantic tank, he
was probably some stockbroker who insider-traded his way
into parties in the Hamptons. On the other hand, she
wanted men like this to think she was hot. And smart. But
they made her long legs seem not long enough, her hair
too wild, and her smile too broad. She could never live up
to their standard of beauty, of femininity. A man like this
would never appreciate her. And on the other hand—
though of course, there was no other hand—she fantasized
about meeting a man like this who was everything: brilliant
and compassionate, as well as exciting, sexy, powerful, and
masculine. Why couldn't she meet a man like that? Hell, besides the fact that he probably didn't exist, she couldn't
meet men at all. How long had it been since she'd even
gone out on a date with potential boyfriend material? Here
she was, living in the most exciting city in the world, with

a good job, an apartment to covet, and her college loans paid off, but she couldn't meet someone wonderful.

Of course, working the night shift didn't help. Who has time? Who else eats dinner at six a.m.? Who else sleeps from eight a.m. to two p.m. like a vampire and then walks around like a zombie? Only other vampires and zombies, and they seemed monstrous to her.

She looked up at the sky and noticed how the moon was finding its way through the clouds, streaking those surrounding it with a silver whitewash. And she looked again at the man coming her way, then at the black streets sleek and glassy with water. And she felt that old familiar tug of contradiction, of feeling insecure and yet powerful, of wanting to be loved for her mind, but desired as a sex object. How could one moment on a corner with a stranger raise in her a bucketful of doubts, as if it were pulled from a deep well forty feet below?

As he got closer, Jeannie told herself to stay focused. *Don't look him in the eyes, don't let those shoulders, that hair, his legs, distract you. Don't be shallow, for god's sake! See the whole person for who he really is, see his values, see his priorities, and not just someone you'd love to take home and make love to all night.* But that was exactly where her head went. To getting to her apartment door, him pushing her in, slamming the door shut, her taking off his jacket, his hands first on her face, pulling it toward him, now on her breasts, hers on his belt, his lips on her neck, on her lips, his tongue deep in her mouth as he pushed her against the wall, lifting her up, her legs wrapping around him, the wall as her buttress, pulling him tight against her, his hand pulling aside her panties, hers on his chest, his broad back, his ass, and then him inside her. *Oh my god.*

Nobody said being ethical was easy. But nobody said being ethical meant you couldn't have a vivid imagination.

STERLING BEHAVIOR

LUCE: *You're kidding. Turkey?*

JEANNIE: *Ugly but true.*

LUCE: *The only time I've heard you use that word is when you're ordering it on a roll with mustard.*

JEANNIE: *Yeah, I know, but . . .*

LUCE: *So why not something a little edgier? Like—*

JEANNIE: *Numbnuts? Your bad word of preference? I was trying to be nice! It's a word from my childhood.*

LUCE: *Well, at least you said something. As you always say—*

JEANNIE: *Personal responsibility can change the world? But there's being responsible and being an idiot.*

LUCE: *Speaking of which, can we get back to the guy in the Hummer?*

JEANNIE: *Okay, so where was I?*

LUCE: *You had just called the Hummer driver a turkey.*

JEANNIE: *So the door opens and out steps a man in a tux. The tie's loose, unfolded and hanging around his neck, his hair in his eyes, his eyes dark and shiny and deep. Mmmmm. He is, and I say this to make a point, to-die-for handsome. He resembles Cary Grant because of the tux, and Hugh Grant because he's caddishly adorable, and General Grant because of his Hummer. And I know I'm in trouble. I mean, he's yummy, except for the General Grant part.*

And even though he is definitely middle aged, he is a turkey who could ruffle my feathers any day. Or cook my goose. Or lay my egg. You know what I mean.

But here's something we women all know that cannot be reiterated too often: men have the capacity to be both cute and jerks. We must resist temptation and keep our eye on the ethical ball, so to speak. Look, here's a guy who drives an environmen-

tally irresponsible car; he's just come from a party, so it is possi-
ble he's driving it under the influence (and you know, loyal lis-
teners, how I feel about drunk drivers: lock 'em up and throw
away the key); he drives while talking on his cell phone; and he
has no respect for women. So what happens next? We'll find out
right after this commercial break. And then I want to hear from
you. I'll be taking calls, right, Luce?

LUCE: *At 777-246-3800. You're listening to* Sterling Behavior *on*
WBUZ, 660 on your AM dial, home of Jeannie Sterling, ethical
avenger. Don't go away or to sleep. Not yet. We've got some
wrongs to right and we'll be right back.

Devil in a Black Tux

But then, as Mr. Testosterone got closer, Jeannie got her
bearings, took a deep breath, and tried to bring herself back
to earth. She really hated face-to-face arguments. The safety
of the studio emboldened her to say what she thought, articulately and rationally, but in person, she became so con-
frontational that she always lost. Plus, people were crazy, as
she'd learned from experience. She recalled that night about
ten years before, the night she looked back on as her moment of truth, her spider bite. She'd been walking home from
her Wednesday-night Stanley Kaplan LSAT prep class—since
she was eight years old, the plan had been that she'd go to
law school to become an advocate for the poor and disen-
franchised—when she saw this guy walking on the sidewalk
in front of her drop a large brown paper bag. She picked up
the greasy, stinky bag and ran to him.

"You dropped this," she said, stopping him by putting her
hand on his arm. She lifted the bag to him.

"Go fuck yourself, you fucking c-word," he'd answered, though actually using the whole c-word, a word Jeannie hated so much she wouldn't even say it in her thoughts.

He followed her then, yelling more obscenities at her and forcing her to take refuge, in tears, in a liquor store, where a young clerk kindly offered to escort her home. He was cute and seemed smart and funny, but since she'd just learned a lesson about talking to strangers, she didn't dare ask this one in. The irony was not lost on her that here could be her Galahad, right on her doorstep. And neither was the anger that rose up in her every time she thought of that putrid garbage on the street, and her heart-stopping fear of the crazy bastard who threw it there, and the knowledge that you didn't have to be insane to be rude, that the city was filled with supposedly normal people who didn't pick up their dogs' poop.

That night she had a difficult time falling asleep. So she did what she always did when she couldn't sleep: she turned on her bedside radio and tuned it to *The Joey Reynolds Show* on WOR, featuring the lovable curmudgeon, New York legend, and self-proclaimed "Leader of the Royal Order of the Night People." On this particular night, he and his endearingly funny sidekick, Myra, had on a panel discussing the mayor's recent law prohibiting smoking in public places. Jeannie called to weigh in on the subject (you wouldn't need laws like that if people were more considerate) and the rest is history. Joey invited her to be on the show and she became a semiregular, until one night Harry Sommers at WBUZ tuned in, less to poach from the competition than to learn from it. But poach he did. He offered Jeannie a show of her own. *My own platform,* Jeannie had thought. *What a way to really make an impact.* She gave up her job at the law firm Skirball, Harrison and Nadel, where she'd been clerking to earn a much-needed paycheck before going to law school. Tommy, her best friend from college, introduced her to his old childhood friend, Luce, a recent grad who had been a producer at her college radio station. Jeannie set up the interview and Harry hired her on the spot. *Sterling Behavior* became a late-night haven for millions of sleep-deprived listeners and gave Joey Reynolds a run for his money. And Jeannie's plans for law school were tossed with that dirty old brown paper bag.

Now, with the Turkey in a Hummer coming her way, she considered running into the middle of the street and screaming *"Help!"* at the top of her lungs. But there he was, in her face.

"Shame on me?" he asked. "Is that what you said?"

Pulling her back straight and tall, using all the courage she could muster, she answered, "Listen, I could've called you something much worse. Like, hmm, I don't know, a, um, drunken . . . dickwad?" She had just heard a teenage kid yell that word the other day to a buddy on the street, and for some reason it came back to her now.

"Interesting word. But you just don't look like a 'dickwad' kind of girl. And besides, I am not drunk. I had one drink and—"

"Or even an ass—"

"No, that would've been over the top."

"Not to worry, I would never." Now that was a lie. "Asshole" was a wonderfully applicable word that she often used, though usually under her breath.

"I've only known you a moment, but I have a feeling you probably have."

Wow, he was something. She inhaled a heady cocktail of his cologne; his breath, with its hint of liquor; and his pheromones. Powerful and frightening. He gave real meaning to the term "handsome devil."

Mr. Mephistopheles looked at her now as if he were considering her as a potential receptacle for planting his demon seed. He studied her, from her eyes to her neck and her breasts, down her entire body to her legs, down those legs to her shoes. For Jeannie this seemed to endure for a lifetime, but she forced herself not to look away. She was not going to let him rock her world.

But then he smiled. In that smirky, smug, diabolical way she learned quickly was his.

Perfect teeth notwithstanding, she did not want to react in a dopey, girlie way. That was for dopey girls, not for an ethical avenger. But there was nothing she could do about the blood rushing to her face. *Shit, shit, shit,* she was thinking.

"You're blushing," he said, his dark eyes crinkling at the corners.

"I am not," she said. *Asshole.*

"Are too."

"Not." *What am I, ten years old?*

STERLING BEHAVIOR

LUCE: *We're talking bad driving tonight, and we have Becky on the line.*

JEANNIE: *Okay, hey there, Beck. You're on the air with Jeannie here on Sterling Behavior at WBUZ Radio, 660 on your AM dial.*

BECKY: *Yesterday I saw this guy crossing the street . . .*

LUCE: *So the sign said "walk."*

JEANNIE: *You need specifics?*

LUCE: *I just want to be sure.*

JEANNIE: *Don't make me have to kill you. Go on, Beck.*

BECKY: *Okay, so the man is crossing when and where he should, when a car turns in to the street and almost hits him. You know what the nice-looking pedestrian does? He spits on the car!*

LUCE: *I don't believe it. He spit?*

BECKY: *Twice!*

JEANNIE: *He spit two times, like a llama, right onto the car?*

LUCE: *Was there a fight?*

JEANNIE: *You sound hopeful.*

BECKY: *No, the driver stayed in his car, locked the doors, and drove away.*

JEANNIE: *He may have been a bad driver, but he wasn't stupid. He knew that the only kind of person who would spit on a car is probably a wacko. And you have to be very careful when it comes to wackos, am I right or what?*

Troll in a Pink Tutu

"Relax, would you?" said the Turkey in a Hummer.

Relax? Bite me, you weenie. Jeannie had been constantly told to relax or calm down, particularly by her mother, since she could remember, as if her enthusiasm was threatening, like an electrical storm about to zap the power out of the house. Maybe sometimes she was a little intense or overbearing, but she wasn't going to let this guy tell her so. She had to be brave. She let out a breath and took another.

"Listen, you," she said. And then, in the light of an oncoming vehicle that she so desperately wanted to flag down, run to, get into, and drive away in, she realized that there was something very familiar about him. She knew this guy or had seen him somewhere before. But here, on this street, in this light, she couldn't place him. Shit, she knew she knew him.

"Have we met?" She squinted her eyes and smiled. "Didn't you ask me out once and I turned you down?"

He smiled and raised his brows. "Now that's something I would've remembered."

"Yeah, you got very depressed. You could hardly function."

"Honey, I can't remember a time when you didn't depress me." He put his hands in his pants pockets and leaned against his monster truck.

"Well, you shouldn't be driving while talking on your cell phone." *Ugh,* she thought, hating herself for getting so serious.

"Aw. Back to reality? But we were having so much fun!"

"It's the law." *For crying out loud!* She couldn't stop herself.

"And you're the police? So why don't you just write me a ticket?"

Okay, she wanted to say. *Five hundred bucks for violating Social Infraction Code A22: feeling so entitled that you are above the law.* "And don't call me 'honey'!"

"Oh, so you're that kind of girl. Okay. Strike me dead if I ever refer to you as 'honey' again, *sweetheart.* And, as I said, I am not drunk."

"And I suppose you're not driving a Hummer either."

He turned and put a strong, beautiful hand on it and stroked it as if it were a thoroughbred horse. "It is great looking, isn't it?"

"It guzzles gas when we should be trying to be less dependent on Saudi Arabia."

He looked at her then, a sparkle in his eyes. "You know, you're right. I should be driving a hybrid—"

"Yes!"

"—Hummer! Yeah, I got to get on that."

Jeannie smiled and teased him right back. "You know, if

you were wearing some gold jewelry, had a little Sinatra playing on the radio, you'd look good in a Cadillac too. And
there you have it: the Hummer is the new Cadillac. You've
successfully taken us back fifty years. Now that's an era you
know something about!"

"Now you're getting personal," he pouted.

"Speaking of which, you know what they say about the size
of a man's car, don't you?"

Mr. Arrogant just smiled and said, "That it directly corre-
lates to how much fun his life is? You know what? Life is too
damn short. I'm climbing back into this Hummer, which, by
the way, is not just any Hummer. This is an über-Hummer,
the biggest, highest, loudest, heaviest, most gas-guzzlingest
and irresponsible Hummer they make. Ain't she a thing of
beauty?" He noticed Jeannie wasn't laughing. "Oh well. Some
things get lost on some people. Have a nice day."

Gag me, she thought. *Have a nice day? Where's he from,
Southern California?* She watched him walk away, watched
how he moved with such unbearable self-assuredness,
watched his shoulders swagger and his arms swing, watched
him climb into his Hummer effortlessly, watched him as he
leaned out to get the door and, as he did so, turned around
toward her and smiled that dazzlingly infuriating smile.

She couldn't stop herself. "Wait a minute," she called,
walking to his side of the car. His window was so high, she
had to stand on tippy-toes to get close. "If, in your mind, it's
okay to drive while talking on your cell phone, the law can be
broken just because you feel like it, what if . . ." She dug in
her bag for a moment and pulled out her keys. There were
several attached to a ring from which hung a three-inch troll
doll dressed as a ballerina, her arms out wide, her pink hair
standing straight up.

Mr. Sophisticated laughed at her. "And I can't call you 'honey,' *honey*?"

She almost began to explain that the key chain had sentimental value but stopped herself in the nick of time, though she couldn't help but notice how defensive she felt. "So, how would you like it if someone went right up to your big fat Hummer with her keys, and—"

"Careful. Careful there," he said, quickly climbing out of the Hummer and taking her by the wrist to pull her hand away from the side of the car. "You wouldn't want to do something you didn't—"

And in that action—her arm raised with the keys dangling from the pink-haired troll, his hand on her wrist to pull the potential weapon away, Jeannie pulling her hand back to free herself of his grip—a key, attached to that fuzzy-haired ballerina troll, hit the door, leaving Mr. Material completely pissed but not entirely surprised.

He looked at Jeannie, his eyes wide with horror, his hands on the door, feeling for a scratch, like one of those blind men with an elephant. And then he dug into his inside jacket pocket, making Jeannie uneasy. *What for, a gun?*

"Wait a minute. I just touched it. Hardly a touch at all. I'm sure it didn't even make a scratch," she said hopefully.

When he pulled out a pair of reading glasses, she sighed with relief.

As he put them on she teased, "It must be hard getting old."

He glared at her from over the rims, his brows up, his mouth down. And he turned to the car and examined it like a dermatologist would a freckled matron. After a few minutes, he found it. The key had left a tiny, semimicroscopic nick on the door, exposing a dot of silver metal below the black paint.

"You deliberately scratched this car," he said quietly, in almost a whisper, his index finger on the spot.

"It wouldn't have happened if you hadn't pulled me and— it's not a scratch at all. It's a nick. A tiny nick that nobody will notice—"

"You took out your keys," he said slowly, "with that midget in a tutu, and you scratched my car." Then he turned to her, his face in hers, his anger rising. "What's with you, lady? Are you on the wrong medication, or are you just a kook?"

"Kook?" She paused a moment in order to calm down. "Listen, I'll pay for half of the cost to repair—"

"And you feel that would be fair, do you? You know what? You're out of your mind, lady. Just get away from me. Okay?" And he got in the Hummer, slammed the door closed, and started the engine, gunning the motor a few times before driving off with a roar.

"And they're not 'midgets'! They prefer 'little people'!" she yelled after him, adding quietly to herself, "Only this is really just a troll in a pink tutu, to be specific."

Jeannie ended up walking that night and arriving at the station, looking bedraggled, just in time before her show was to begin.

STERLING BEHAVIOR

JEANNIE: *So, he blames me and calls me a kook.*

LUCE: *Well . . .*

JEANNIE: *Well, what?*

LUCE: *If the shoe fits . . . but we have Bob on the air.*

JEANNIE: *Then I'll ignore you. Hey there, Bob, you got a good driving story?*

BOB: *Yeah, just the other day I'm on the Long Island Expressway,* *and it's rush hour, and I got my two kids in the back seat—we're on our way to visit my mother-in-law, who's in a nursing home out on the island—and so I'm trying to get into the car pool lane to avoid all the traffic. But there's this Volvo station wagon with some Yuppie lady driver, and she's going too fast, then she's too slow and she won't let me in. It's like every time I try to get in, she speeds up. So I'm trying to cut her off and she speeds up and guess what the bi—*

JEANNIE: *Whoa there, Bob.*

BOB: *—woman does? She gives me the finger. And holds it up long and good for all her kids and my kids to see. Wassup with that?*

JEANNIE: *Okay, so Bob, you're a pretty special guy to visit your mother-in-law, I give you that. But you're not the best driver— sorry, but why risk it? You've got kids in the car, Bob, and you're going to play chicken? On the other hand, that woman sounds a little crazy to speed up so you couldn't get in and then flip you the bird. She earns a 7.5 on the Sterling Scale of Bad Behavior!*

[Sterling Scale sound effects: earthquake rumbling, crashing and sounds of destruction]

JEANNIE: *So, Bob, my answer to tonight's question—is it a sense of entitlement or are they just bad drivers?—me? I think the world is full of mean, selfish people, so I argue that people like you and your rude woman and my Hummer-driving guy have a sense of entitlement the size of Alaska. My friend Luce, who's much nicer than me—*

LUCE: *No, Jeannie, that's not really true.*

JEANNIE: *—and much more generous about people—*

LUCE: *But that really is.*

JEANNIE: *—would say you're all just bad drivers. And she has a point. For example, I spent a week this summer in the Hamp-*

tons, and oh my god, what terrible drivers they have out there. Luce would argue that since 90 percent of them are from the city, they don't drive much, so they're just plain lousy. But that logic doesn't work. Look at New Jersey drivers. They drive all the time and they're lousy. When you see a car with a Jersey plate, watch out, slow down, because it'll kill you.

I say people in the Hamptons are bad drivers because they think that because they're rich, they're special, and that laws don't pertain to them because they're above everybody else. Just like spoiled kids. And old people. Do you think because people have simply survived, they shouldn't have to say thank you, they should be allowed to cut in line, to shove? Have you ever flown on a Friday in the winter from La Guardia to Boca, Bob? Trust me, don't. You're taking your life in your hands. Same as on the road. Should they be allowed to drive, even when they can't see over the steering wheel?

LUCE: *My mother just turned seventy-two and she's still driving.*

JEANNIE: *Yeah, but people run faster than your mother drives.*

BOB: *My mom drives with only one eye.*

LUCE: *One eye? Where's the other one?*

JEANNIE: *And don't tell us she lost it in a—*

BOB: *—car accident.*

JEANNIE: *[a chuckle] Oh, that's terrible.*

BOB: *And she's eighty-two. And she lives in New Jersey.*

JEANNIE: *That's three strikes.*

BOB: *But you haven't met my mom, Jeannie. Oh yeah, I'll get her to stop driving. When moss doesn't grow on trees.*

JEANNIE: *That's who it was! My Hummer guy—the infamous Nicholas Moss, Mr. Entitlement himself.*

The Boss's Boss's Boss's New Boss

Nicholas Moss was doing exactly what he always did in the middle of the night. He was sitting in his boxers in his den, on his chocolate-brown suede couch, practicing Blake's hitches with his new arborist's rope, which held a carabiner on each end.

And he was catching up on his reading, an old issue of *Flying* magazine opened on the coffee table in front of him to an article on the pros and cons of Thielert diesel engines.

And he was watching ESPN on his fifty-three-inch flat-screen TV, which hung on the wall among his rock photo collection. He had original, signed black-and-white pictures of Elvis, Jimi Hendrix, and Jerry Garcia, but it was his signed Avedon of Bob Dylan, the one shot in Harlem in 1963 with Dylan's hands in his pockets, that Moss particularly loved, because of its innocence and hopefulness, the way he'd felt when he first started out. There was nobody he admired more, because of Dylan's poetic genius and the impact he had on an entire generation, two things Moss deeply coveted.

On the other walls, where there weren't bookshelves, there were the photos he'd taken himself while dangling three hundred feet high from a branch in the canopy of a redwood, in a forest up the coast from San Francisco where he did most of his climbing.

Nicholas Moss was a multitasker and always had been, ever since he was a kid and could chew gum, blow bubbles, ride a bike, and read Spider-Man comics while tossing a ball in the air, all at the same time. Being the only man he knew who could do so many things at once made him feel oddly in touch with his feminine side.

So he watched ESPN to get the latest baseball scores until he was so disgusted with his Mets that he turned off the TV and, with the same remote, turned on the radio to search for something good, some Traffic or Dylan or Kinks, something from his youth. Finding nothing, of course, he tuned in to WBUZ Radio, 660 on his AM dial, all talk, all the time, just as he did almost every night when he was home alone. There was something about this show *Sterling Behavior* that amused the hell out of him. The things people didn't learn as a kid about treating people with respect, doing unto them as you'd have them do unto you. And the host, that Jeannie Sterling, who listened politely in the face of idiocy and then spoke as if she were the final word on right and wrong. Where did these people come from, anyway? Not only New York City, that was for sure. Because—and this never ceased to amaze Moss—nowhere else in the world do so many millions of people live in such close proximity and not kill each other as frequently as New Yorkers do not kill each other.

Moss had been born and raised in New York City and continued to be the city's staunchest defender. Maligned and misunderstood, this city, his city, made him proud each and every day. And he knew it well, for he was born and bred in the West Village. Not the Village of bohemian dreams, of jazz and poetry, of intellectual writers hovering in smoky rooms around tables covered with glasses of watery scotch, but the Village of Irish and Italian workers, of butchers and greengrocers and barbers. His own father had been a city bus driver and his mom an office clerk for the local diocese. They had lived on West Eleventh Street, in a fifth-floor walk-up, in an apartment that was smaller than the room he sat in now.

He remembered weeks of eating potatoes when the bus drivers went out on strike, and of delivering groceries after school and on weekends to help pay the bills. And that wasn't easy, riding that bike, with its cart at the front, and then climbing with the bags up narrow stairways for a lousy fifty-cent tip.

With all the pressure on his folks to just make ends meet, they still had high hopes for him. Nothing less than a college degree was acceptable, in something that would get him out of the neighborhood, something exciting—like accounting. And so accounting is where it began, and capitalizing and investing is where it went.

It was important to Moss to give back to the great city of his birth. So, he'd built high-rises, an airline company, and some technology and transportation ventures too. But tonight he felt little generosity toward this fucking city. He'd had a hard day, trying to get his newest deal done—developing a hundred acres on the Brooklyn waterfront—while making everybody happy, from the environmentalists and nearby residents to the builders and the mayor's office. But he was used to conflict, and enjoyed negotiating so that everyone walked away with something. Maybe what was really bugging him was the experience he'd just had a few hours ago, with that lunatic on Hudson. That self-righteous, out-of-control, card-carrying—but very attractive, he had to admit—*bitch* who felt she had cornered the market on educating the masses about right and wrong. And then, who had the goddamn gumption to take out her stupid Kewpie-doll keys and scratch Marshall's Hummer.

Shit, Marshall was going to kill him, if he ever spoke to him again. Not that it was damage that couldn't be fixed. But the Hummer was Marshall's baby. He and Marshall had had one of their usual arguments about global warming (which Marshall felt was bullshit, that it didn't exist and was a political invention) and the Fed's new energy policy, when Marshall insisted Moss get behind the wheel of the Hummer and drive it so he'd know from experience that which he was condemning. Marshall was certain that he'd be won over and would never bother him again to get rid of it in the name of preserving the ozone layer and fuel economy. Besides, who was Moss to talk when he flew his private jet everywhere? So Moss agreed to take the Hummer for a drive, in the name of preserving their friendship.

And who the fuck was she, anyway? She was extreme self-righteousness personified *I mean, who,* Moss thought, *never behaved badly? Or did the wrong thing, out of sheer laziness? Or ignorance? Or just because it was fun? And who made her the judge?*

And worse, why, when she'd been out of his hair for hours, was she still pissing him off?

Then he heard Jeannie Sterling mention a Hummer. Wait a minute. He stopped everything he was doing and looked up, listening.

"Did you call me a turkey?"

Whoa there, Nelly. He put the rope down and turned up the volume, going from multi- to unitasking in a flash.

That's me she's talking about. She talked about his car and his driving and the things he had said. She accused him of having been drunk, which, of course, was not true and really pissed him off.

But the thing that bothered him most was the "middle aged" comment. He was not middle aged. Wasn't fifty-three the new forty-three? He would outlive his dad by decades, his dad who had died too young from too much alcohol, too much weight, too many cigarettes, too many stairs for his heart. Moss tried to move him countless times to one of his nice apartments in any one of his buildings, but there was no way his dad would go. Nah, he was going to live there, and die there, with Moss's mom at his side. And that's just what he did, died at sixty-seven, in the arms of his wife, who died just one year later. After a long, hard life together, neither could live without the other. That's what Moss wanted too. A lifetime of love. But given his age, and the fact that he wasn't anywhere near settling down, he might have to wait for love in the next life, if only he believed in that.

Yeah, yeah, yeah, all the other stuff she said was about right. But that "middle aged" thing got to him. Life as he knew it had no limits. Look how far he'd gotten in his "forty-something" short years. He hadn't come from money, like his colleagues in business. He didn't go to Princeton for under-grad and then Harvard for his MBA like his investment banker, buddy, and confidant, Marshall. Hell, he'd gotten to where he was—the head of his multibillion-dollar empire, with its planes, trains, real estate, and twenty-five-thousand employees—by sheer perseverance, with a little brains and a lot of luck thrown in. He'd spent a good part of his life strug-gling to get where everyone else he knew just started out.

But for crying out loud, what was making him so defensive tonight? A lot worse had been said about him in far more pub-lic places—like on prime-time network television. Here it was in the middle of the night and some Barbara fucking Walters wannabe on late-night talk radio, for Christ's sake, was talking about him. Why did he give a shit? Had he known that the lu-natic on the street who had called him a turkey and then tried to make him, of all people, feel guilty for driving a Hummer, and then scratched it, was Jeannie Sterling, the self-proclaimed ethical avenger, he would've said so much more.

But now he just listened. And as he did so, he got up and paced, his face changing with each comment, his hands flailing as if he were in discussion with her. Maybe he should call her. He picked up the phone.

"You hypocrite. Goddamn liar," he said aloud. "What about the keys, lady? You haven't mentioned the hairy, pink keys!" And when he saw himself reflected in the glass doors that led to his wraparound terrace—his face commingling with the lights of the city that stretched out before him, the Upper East Side across the park that lay black and expansive below—when he recognized the angry voice as his own, he stopped. He listened. He thought. And then he smiled. He had a better idea.

He dialed.

"Marshall, get me BUZ Radio."

"Moss, is that you? It's the middle of the night."

"Your point?"

Marshall laughed, in a sleepy, fuzzy way. "So what's the word, Moss?"

"I want to buy WBUZ."

"Yeah, you said that, didn't you? You're kidding, right?"

"You don't kid a kidder."

"What's this about? Did you hear something I haven't? Are they somebody's acquisition target? Did Ben say something about Clear Channel trying to buy it? Or maybe some major advertising contracts pending? I mean, it's just a fledgling station, privately owned, I'm pretty sure. Wha—"

"There's this girl . . ." He was immediately sorry he'd said that.

"No, no, no. Don't do this, Moss. You've never made a business decision because of a pair of—"

"And I don't intend to now. But she insulted your Hummer."

"Jesus, Moss, who the fuck cares?"

"And nicked it a little."

That woke him. *"What?* Where? How much of a nick?"

"Small, and I'll get it into the shop in the morning. I'll take care of it. Just get me the numbers and let's take a look."

"A nick? I'll kill her. But need I point out that you know nothing about media ventures? They're not your thing. You've done so well; why muck it up with media? You know those creative types, people who wouldn't know their bottom line from their butt. They think financial guys like us don't read, that we're beneath them, and besides, to get to the real point, your investment won't yield much, if anything. The margins, well, let's just say they're slim, okay? What do you think a radio station makes? It's not like the usual purchase, turnaround and tripling your money in three years. And you'd have a hell of a lot to lose. Radio has become molto expensivo. What's the point?"

"The point?"

"If it's not profit—and I mean the kind of profit you've known in the past ten years—what's the point?"

"Fun."

"You know me, Moss. Fun is good, but—"

"And revenge."

"Well, now you're talking my language. A goddamn nick!"

"So go."

"But not when it comes to investing millions of your money. Then the point should be about growth and turnover and yields."

"They're good too. Just get me the book on BUZ. And soon."

"All right, Mr. Moss. Done, Mr. Moss." Marshall was angry and hung up. And Nicholas knew it and felt bad. But he couldn't help himself. This was something he had to do.

As he put the phone back in its cradle, he heard: *"So, Mr. Entitlement . . ."*

He turned to face the luminescent photograph of the forest of towering trees that was almost as inspiring now as it had been on his first climb. "So, Ms. Jeannie Sterling . . . ," Nicholas Moss said aloud, finishing the thought in his head: *You ain't gonna know what hit you.* And with one flick of the remote, he turned off the radio and turned on the TV to VH1, where The Who was the focus of *Behind the Music. Perfect,* he thought, as he hunkered down into his couch, put his feet up on his coffee table, crossed his ankles, and clasped his hands behind his head. He smirked long and good and hard as he watched Pete Townshend smash his guitar into the stage floor during a concert at the Fillmore West in 1968, sending sparks into the thick, smoky air of the auditorium.

STERLING BEHAVIOR

JEANNIE: *So, Mr. Entitlement, and I won't mention his name again, since that wasn't very nice. You see? We all make mistakes. And I'm sorry I said his name before, but when I realized that the turkey in the Hummer was Nicholas—Oh god, I almost did it again! Oh gee, I'm sorry, I hope the radio police don't come and get me. Howard Stern, where are you when I need you? Anyway, thanks for the fun evening. I really learned a lot from you and from all of you out there. That's what ethical behavior is about,* *isn't it? It takes only two, not a whole village. So good night or good morning.*

This is Jeannie Sterling, ethical avenger, saying a little consideration can change the world and wishing you all Sterling Behavior.

Her Boyfriend's Back and She's Gonna Be in Trouble

"And you're out," said Luce, shaking her head in disapproval as she placed her antique hand-painted floral teacup into its matching saucer and looked up at Jeannie through the large glass window. Jeannie smiled then, and once she stopped giggling, blew her nose, and took a slug of water, she couldn't help but notice how adorable Luce looked tonight. A small Gucci logo scarf was tied around her neck, and she wore a crisply tailored shirt, short pleated skirt, and her ballerina "flats," as she called them, an homage to her Waspy background. She actually glowed, her cheeks rosy and her skin awash with shine, a smile at the edge of her mouth resisting, it seemed, an impulse to blossom into a full-blown one. Luce had always been that way: somewhat reserved, holding on to her feelings until there was proof they deserved to be shared. And only then would she allow them to slowly be revealed, never fully exposed, always under the cautious cover of self-control. Unlike Jeannie, whose feelings were on her lips, her face, in her eyes, her voice, her words, her attitude for the whole world to see, even if the world wasn't the least bit interested.

As Luce held the headset to her ear, still sitting at the console on the other side of the window with Joseph at her side, she looked at Jeannie, shook her head from side to side, and arched her eyebrows as if to say, "You're in trouble." She smiled then, but it was a smile as if to say, "You've gone too far." And then she actually moved her lips and said, "Nicholas Moss!"

Through the windows she could see Joseph take his hands from the board, throw his head to the side, lean back in his chair, spin it around, and yell, "Nicholas Moss! Fucking righteous!" Maybe twenty-three at most, Joseph was a master engineer, even though his T-shirts said things like IF YOU CAN READ THIS, THE BITCH FELL OFF, and his long, straggly, greasy hair said "wash me, please," and the tattoo of a boa constrictor slithering down his left arm said so much more than she wanted to know. He made Jeannie hope that rebellious customs skip a generation so that should she ever have a son, he'd rebel by playing golf instead.

Jeannie laughed, took her headset off, shook her hair out, and watched Luce through the glass. What was it like to be her? To wake each morning completely carefree, positive, not worried that you could have a brain tumor or that a bomb might go off in midtown or that someone you love might die today? What was it like to completely accept who you are, accept the world as it is, and just be content to be? What made Jeannie feel, each and every day, that she had to reflect, rescind, rethink, and reject the notion of "let it be" as an insipid mantra from the seventies?

Yet, as different as the two women were, they were truly best friends. The kind of friends who tell each other how much money they make and how much they weigh without lying even a little. And though Jeannie had gone to Berkeley and majored in political theory, and Luce had gone to Wellesley and majored in comparative literature; though they were worlds apart in sensibility, lifestyle, and worldview, Jeannie having been raised in a commune near Telegraph Avenue in Berkeley, Luce in the wealthy, white-gloved Upper East Side; and though Jeannie's bohemian life, with her teenage summers spent at a local Y day camp for underprivileged kids, was a galaxy away from Luce's—her summers had been spent at her mother's family retreat in Bordeaux, which resulted in Luce's sophisticated, cosmopolitan accent (which some felt was pretentious, but Jeannie accepted it because she knew that Luce didn't have a fraudulent bone in her body)—they were soul sisters. Even their upbringings, which were so different, were also similar in their effect. Luce's childhood was simple: everything was forbidden; Jeannie had had to navigate the dark and potentially dangerous waters of permissiveness. Luce was supposed to marry into the right family and have babies; Jeannie was to become an advocate for the poor. And neither was doing what was expected of her.

So when Jeannie moved three thousand miles away and met Luce, she knew she'd found a friend. And as they worked together at WBUZ, Luce became the yin to Jeannie's yang, their differences providing the fuel and fodder for talk-show banter and deep affection. They knew each other's moods and could almost read each other's minds, and though they bickered and argued and sometimes hurt each other in those small ways that friends do, they loved each other unconditionally.

But tonight something was up with Luce and Jeannie couldn't read it.

As Jeannie walked through the glass door that connected the studio to the control room, she asked, "Hey, so you want to get some breakfast?" though she didn't have to, since she and Luce had breakfast together every Wednesday morning at Bubby's. Sure, they'd been up all night, but they were always revved after the show, especially knowing there were three more to come. They felt like they were running on empty with a long way to go. Real sleep would come on the weekend.

"That was sort of stupid, Jeannie. You can't mess with someone like—"

"Nicholas Moss? Nicholas Moss?" Everybody turned to see Harry Sommers, WBUZ's station manager, galumphing down the hallway toward the studio, his voice booming over the early-morning din of arrivals and departures and vacuums, his steps shaking the thirty-six-floor building's very foundations. "You want to get us sued? Or worse?"

"What's worse than getting sued?" Jeannie asked. "And what the hell are you doing here this early? Your wife kick you out of bed again?"

"I'll tell you what's worse. Getting sued!" said Harry. "And I'm here at this ridiculous hour because I have to prep for this meeting today with our owners, speaking of getting sued. Our figures better look good to them. Or else."

"Harry, he won't sue. What could he sue for?" Luce defended her friend, though she wasn't quite convinced.

"Yeah," said Jeannie, "what? For being himself?"

"Yeah, a capitalist pig?" said Joseph.

"Laugh all you want," said Harry, "but trust me, if he heard your show tonight, and even if he didn't, we're going to hear about it. You don't go after somebody as powerful and scary as Moss without repercussions. And litigious? That guy is as litigious as I am big and fa—"

"Lovely," interrupted Jeannie, putting a hand on Harry's shoulder.

"That's what I meant. As litigious as I am lovely." And he curtseyed like a ballerina. He had the ability to make Jeannie and Luce laugh even as he was wringing his hands with worry or their necks with anger. Here was this guy, fifty-five looking like sixty-five, balding, fat, and a slob, his shirt coming out of his pants—his *beige* shirt, his *brown* pants—and totally adorable. His wife, with whom he had just celebrated their thirtieth anniversary, and his four kids out in Old Westbury were lucky to have him.

"Harry, stop," laughed Luce.

"Me stop! Tell your friend here to stop. She's gone too far this time, I fear."

"Aw, come on Harr, he was a pig and deserved what he got," said Jeannie.

"I agree," said Luce.

"Me too," said Joseph, putting on his leather jacket with the Harley insignia.

"And I agree with myself," said Jeannie.

"But if the station gets hit, you'll be the first to go," continued Harry, as he put a firm hand on Jeannie's shoulder.

"And what would you do without me? Huh?"

"You really want to know?"

"Yeah, I do." Jeannie crossed her arms, waiting for Harry's response.

"Celebrate," he said, crossing his arms in response to her.

"Me too," she replied, with all her weight on her left foot, tapping her right.

"Oh yeah? This place is all you have. Your entire life is within these walls. What would you do if you left?"

That was so true, it hurt. In her dark moments in the morning, after she showered and got into bed, alone and apart from the normal world around her, she thought about the lives outside, going to school, to work, to a museum, or to meet a friend for lunch, and when she got tired of staring at the ceiling, she'd pull her comforter up to her neck and turn to her left and see the unused pillows, the space for a warm, hard, and lovely man beside her; when she told herself to wake by three so she'd have time to run errands before everything closed and go to the gym, and she realized her urgency had only to do with stupid shit like getting cotton balls or going to the dry cleaner, or buying milk for her late-afternoon coffee, or swimming some laps, she knew full well how narrow and small her life was.

"What would I do? Have a real life, that's what!"

But she never seriously entertained leaving. There was something about having an excuse for her crappy life that felt reassuring.

Then Luce broke in. "Come on, guys, it's late and we're all cranky. Get out of here, all right? So we can close up shop."

Harry broke away from Jeannie. "But listen, seriously, no more Moss stuff on the air. We're already vulnerable—"

"We're vulnerable? What does that mean?" Jeannie responded.

Harry immediately seemed sorry he'd said anything. He looked down at his feet, his hands in his pockets. "All I mean is that we're the last privately owned station in the city, and *Sterling Behavior* is one of the very last live locals, and at the top of its time slot. I mean, you don't have Rush ratings—"

"But it's quality that counts, not quantity," said Jeannie.

"—and we just don't want to do anything to draw attention beyond our usual day-to-day."

"Would it be so bad if I got syndicated, for god's sake?" asked Jeannie. "Or, god forbid, a daytime slot?"

"And lose your independence? I just want to keep BUZ

running the way it's been running for the last twenty years, that's all. Nothing to worry about. Forget it. Just late night"—he looked at his watch—"early morning worries, that's all."

"We love you, Harry," said Luce.

"Sure you do. Now get out of here. I got a radio station to run."

"And I got to get me some Z's," said Joseph, as he grabbed his helmet, put it under his arm, and headed out the door.

Jeannie hooked her arm through Luce's. "And we got some egg sandwiches to eat." She could almost taste her two fried eggs on a roll, which she ate with the works—cheese and bacon—and which Luce always ordered plain, egg whites only, and ate with a knife and fork, separately from the roll. But as Harry disappeared down the hall, Luce broke away from her friend's embrace.

"What's up? You okay?" Jeannie asked her with concern. She tweaked Luce's cheek.

"I just can't have breakfast."

"But why? It's Wednesday. Come on, Spike knows you'll be late."

"I know. I just can't today, that's all."

"Hey, everything's okay with you two, right?" Jeannie looked at her friend with concern.

"Please. We're fine. He's just such a nerd. He's actually been building a computer from scratch, so that he can be 100 percent sure it's the fastest, best computer available."

"That Spike. He is one handy fellow. You're so lucky—"

"I am. And he is. It's not that—"

"So, what's up with you? You've been a little weird all night."

"Listen," Luce said, leaning into Jeannie, as if she were

going to whisper something in her ear. But she abruptly stood straight up, shaking her head. "No, no, I promised."

Jeannie's eyes narrowed suspiciously. "You promised? Who did you promise? What do you mean? Who—"

And then Luce stopped, looked over Jeannie's shoulder, then back at Jeannie, and then back over her shoulder.

Jeannie turned around and down the hall, walking toward them, was Tommy Whitney, a backpack slung over one shoulder; his light hair tousled and long, almost to his eyes; his khakis baggy and worn; a T-shirt under his button-down, which hung long over his belt; his hiking boots beaten to shit. And all the time his eyes kept shifting from Jeannie to Luce, then back to Jeannie. He smiled at her with that smile of his. Jeannie's face turned red, her lips curled up at their corners, and her eyes brightened and widened and warmed, as if they had just seen the sun go down over the Pacific.

Her heart started to pound so wildly, she was sure Luce would hear it. *Stop*, she begged to herself, *please stop. Do not give yourself away. Just this once.* She turned from her friend, for fear that her face, if not the beating of her heart, would betray her.

"I couldn't tell you, Jeannie," Luce whispered. "He asked me not to . . ." And then he was in through the glass doors.

Jeannie could feel her molecules rearrange themselves.

"Lucille," Tommy said. "Lucille Cunningham, thanks for keeping my secret." Then he kissed her twice, once on each side of her mouth. Jeannie watched him purse his lips, watched as they made contact with Luce's eggshell skin, watched as he pulled away and brushed his hair back with his beautiful hand. It felt like a century, standing there, watching and waiting for him to get to her, to see her, to acknowledge her. When, finally, he did, he said, "And her famous sidekick

Jeannie Sterling. Come here, you." He then gave her a kiss too. Right on her mouth, full and direct. Those lips of his, soft, firm, and full, right on hers. Then his arms were around her and she was waiting for another kiss—this time maybe open and deep and passionate, his tongue searching for hers— when he gave her a hug, rocking them both back and forth like the two old friends that they were. A hug! What is one to see in a hug except the bland expression that it is? He pulled back and looked at her with a smile.

She swallowed her disappointment and asked, "Have we met?"

Here's the thing of it: she was in love with her old friend. And she knew deep in her heart that he loved her too. Or should. Or would if only he'd let himself. She knew she was being stupid beyond belief. But she was convinced beyond the shadow of a doubt that they were meant to be together. Sure, he had a girlfriend, which made her feel like such a hypocrite, since she had a policy about not getting involved in any way with men in relationships. Sure, they had been friends since Berkeley, where they'd sit on the steps in Sproul Plaza and talk about why life sucked, how to get it not to suck, and whether life sucking was the real problem at all. And sure, they never, not once, slept together, unless you counted that marijuana-hazy night after the party at Dan's house when they were too bombed to make love but actually slept together slept together.

But if Tommy would only *admit it*, the incontrovertible truth was that she and Tommy were soul mates. And she didn't use the term lightly. She and Tommy were people who were about heart, and what's important, and living a life of value. Though it sounded like a goofy cliché, they were both passionate about changing the world, not that one's social consciousness was qualification enough for falling in love. But they shared a similar sensibility: Tommy on the front lines, writing articles that influenced politicians, incited activists, and actually helped to get food and supplies to ravaged areas; Jeannie working nightly to educate people about good and bad behavior, to empower them to be cooperative citizens and to act ethically in an unethical world. Sure, he was unbelievably adorable, in that energetic, boyish way of his, but it wasn't only about sexual attraction. No, this was about two people who belonged together because of their vision for the world, their hearts and minds and values. What a future they'd have, what a life.

Love had long been a theme between Jeannie and Tommy. Jeannie had dated several of Tommy's friends, had torrid affairs with a couple, had thought she was even, possibly, in love with one of them, had helped Tommy through countless heartbreaks and breakups of his own. Their friendship lasted through vomit (when polyps on her vocal cords were removed and the anesthesia had made her puke everywhere, he had held her hair back and whispered in her ear, "It's okay, Jeannie Beanie, it's okay"), through anger (when he forgot her birthday year after year), and through time (he was sometimes gone for months, often with little or no word during them).

The possibility that there might be a future for them as a "them" had become apparent only recently. Twenty-two days ago to be exact. It was like a thwack on the side of her head. Like a discovery of something so obvious it was ridiculous. She remembered the moment in detail: it was late in the afternoon on a sweltering hot Indian summer day, just after Labor Day. She had gone for a swim. The pool had been packed and she was pissed. With all the people at the gym in the afternoon, she wondered if anybody worked for a living. And how could they afford this gym, which had one of the few Olympic-sized pools in the city? They were there at this time to avoid rush hour, but now this was becoming a rush hour itself. If it kept going at this rate, rush hour would stretch from six a.m. to nine p.m. People overstayed their thirty-minute lane limit, they cut in line, and they hogged the towels and showers and steam room. Tommy had been away for two and a half months and she was missing him desperately. She walked home along the river, which sat brown and still under the hazy sky. The air was as thick as soup and she felt she might gag from not being able to breathe.

But when she had gotten home, an e-mail awaited her. Tommy was writing from Uganda, where he was reporting about boys violently recruited as soldiers. He sounded weary and frustrated, and yet his observations were as astute as always. But it was the end of the e-mail that brought time to a halt. The sun, an enormous red ball that sat in a sky washed with purples and pinks—the stunning effect of the smog—was setting over the Hudson. A Circle Line ferry was passing directly in front of her view, clogged with tourists who still lingered in the city and were trying to get some cool fresh air. Her fridge made a *crrrrick* as the ice maker went through its routine. The air conditioner's vent rattled and she reminded herself to have that adjusted. Her computer screen was dusty. A siren blared on the street below. And she read these words from the end of Tommy's e-mail:

> *Maybe it's because I'm living on little sleep, maybe it's because I've been here too long, but it's got me thinking. Why, Jeannie Beanie, has it never happened for us? How come we*

never fell in love? You know how I feel about you. Beautiful and so damned smart, a bit of a nut, but fiercely passionate. You always make me laugh and I love you like crazy and you've been huge in my life. I can hear you laughing right now at the thought of us together—there, just like that. But I need to ask, why not us? Why did it never happen? Just not in the cards? Or not the right chemistry? I don't know the answer, but I love you and miss you and hope to be home soon.

Yours, Tommy

She looked up from the screen and out the window, and her eyes filled with tears. Exactly. She shook her head side to side. This was exactly what was wrong with the world. Right here, this. You love somebody, he loves you. You could be perfect together. And yet, as if by some cosmic joke, you're just not. This—having the person right in front of your face, but for whatever reason, whether timing, or fear, or pheromones, he is unavailable—was deeply tragic and disappointing to her.

And unacceptable. *There is no way I am going to sit back and let something dumb get in the way of a Big Love,* she thought as she wiped her eyes dry and sat up straight. She was going to take this on as her grail and deliver the goods come hell or high water.

But, as usual, she avoided dealing with the real issues and e-mailed this back:

Thomas,
I love you too, even though I have no idea why you'd refer to me as a nut. Now shut up, go to sleep, and get home already. J
p.s. That "Jeannie Beanie" thing has got to stop.

Looking at him now, here, in the WBUZ hallway, Jeannie wanted to grab Tommy by his frayed collar and shake him and scream, "I'm the one. It's me you're supposed to love. It's me!" But now, as she watched him talking to Luce, his bright eyes glowing while he ribbed Jeannie with his elbow like an annoying brother, Jeannie knew that what Tommy said was the absolute truth. Jeannie was the sidekick and always would be.

Unless.

If only Jeannie could get Tommy's attention, cure his myopia, capture his heart, prove once and for all how perfect they were for each other. It wouldn't be easy, but it might be possible.

Jeannie Sterling was acutely aware of all the things accomplished in the name of love—wars waged, lives saved, mothers finding strength enough to lift a car, people sprinting at ten times their usual speed, mountains climbed, races won. In the name of love, the things people do. Just how far she would go, she couldn't be sure, but she had a strong sense that she could go the distance.

"Breakfast?" he asked.

"You guys go," Luce said, with a flip of her hand. "I'm pooped. But welcome back, Thomas." She gave him a kiss and turned back toward the studio.

"And say hi to that husband of yours," Tommy called after her. Then, turning to Jeannie, he said, "So, our old place? I've been craving breakfast there since the day I left."

"Only if you're paying," Jeannie said.

"Fine, if we're talking under ten bucks."

"You think you're still in a third-world country?"

"What, I'm not? Wait, what is this place? Am I in *The Twilight Zone*?"

"Yeah, the one with the pig faces."

"You got the operation! I knew there was something different about you." And he put the palm of his hand gently, softly, on her cheek. "Seriously, it is so good to see you. You have no idea."

She felt her head bend sideways, its weight resting in his palm. *Oh god, don't let it show. Don't give yourself away, not yet.* Tommy would be freaked out if he knew she was in love with him, and she'd have a lot of explaining to do to Luce. It was weird that she'd tell her best friend her real weight, but not whom she was in love with. But she felt she had to finesse this situation, prepare and plan and *then* pounce.

"Come on, you. Let's go. And, yeah, it's on me," he said. And he took her arm and walked her to her desk, where she gathered her things, and they were out the door.

You make your own life, her vagabond dad had always taught her. You make things happen. If you sit around and wait for things to happen to you, you could sit forever. If you accept that love finds you, that it's about chance or luck or fucking chemistry, you are nothing but a speck of dust on a computer screen. And that was not the life she was going to live.

Egg Sandwich, Hold the Ketchup

Kitchenette was packed. A tiny dive on Chambers, Kitchenette was a ten-table joint with the best breakfast in town. Everything was served with a fresh homemade biscuit and a cup of strong, good coffee. A little cheese from her omelet was now dripping from the edge of Jeannie's mouth, and Tommy reached over with his thumb and dabbed her there.

She blushed and said, "Eat your own breakfast. Hands off

mine. And by the way, where did you pick that up? Ketchup on your eggs? That's disgusting."

"A buddy from the *Post*. Mike, he always eats his eggs this way. So one morning I just tried it. And oh god, I found heaven."

"If that's heaven, take me to hell, please," laughed Jeannie, as she took another bite of her sandwich.

Then Tommy gulped his down, wiped his mouth with his napkin, and took a drink of water. He looked at her very seriously and said, "I missed you."

She finished chewing, and said, "Me too," unable to be clever or funny with him when it came to him and her.

"No, really, I missed you, Jeannie. I couldn't get you out of my head. I think . . ."

She put down her sandwich and looked up at him. "I thought about you too."

"That e-mail. When I asked you, you know . . ."

"You mean, why not, why have we never . . ."

"Yes. But you know"—and here he paused for what felt like five hours—"I wouldn't want to do anything to jeopardize our relationship. If I couldn't have you as a friend, life would be so, well, it would be plain ugly."

Jeannie wanted to stand on the table and scream, "Fuck friendship!" But she said, "Yeah, I so agree. We couldn't risk it."

Then Tommy put his hand on hers. "So. Hey. Life has a way of figuring this stuff out, you know? Besides . . ."

She imagined climbing over the table, sitting in his lap, and kissing him full and deep. But she said, "Yeah, we wouldn't want to do anything—"

"Good," he said, and gestured for the waiter to bring the check, doing that air scribble thing that Jeannie never liked, feeling it was disrespectful. "Besides," he continued, "Suzanne already doesn't trust you. She thinks you're—and this is hilarious—she thinks you're already secretly in love with me."

Jeannie was so embarrassed, so angry—whether with Tommy for fishing or Suzanne for knowing—she wasn't sure. "Well, be sure to tell her she has nothing to worry about."

"I'll tell her, but she won't believe me. How could she? She sees how you and I are together. Anybody would be jealous."

Especially Jeannie. Nobody could've been more jealous of the promise of her and Tommy than she.

Music of the Heart

God, it's great to be home, Tommy was thinking as he threw his backpack on the kitchen counter and inserted his iPod into the Bose docking station that Jeannie had bought him for his last birthday. Mahler's Symphony No. 9 played and Tommy sat on the couch to listen, a pillow behind his head, his feet up on the coffee table. It had been a long time since he'd sat within his own four walls, filled with his beloved books, in this handsome brownstone, in this civilized section of his favorite city in the world, and he took pleasure in the moment.

What a wild ride it had been the last few months. Foreign reporting for the *Times*, the long, lonely, often dangerous weeks in Africa, filing from some godforsaken places. The things he'd seen, the people he'd met, those children who had not a hope. He could not have stayed a moment longer. He'd felt the ground shifting with each day there and he'd had to leave, there was no choice. And now there was no looking back. Of everything he'd learned, nothing felt as ridiculously true as how unfair life can be, how arbitrary. It made him want to live life to its fullest, to feel, to love. He'd never thought of himself as a romantic, until now.

The change in him was imperceptible at first. Having lived a life of tremendous opportunity and accomplishment, the world was going to be his. That sense of great expectations was still very much a part of him, but now there was a sense of urgency too. Because there's just no knowing if there will be a tomorrow. So now, with his feelings for Suzanne waning and his love for Jeannie morphing into something altogether new, he so wanted to do the right thing, to not jeopardize this truly important friendship he'd had for how many years now. He was lucky to have a Jeannie in his life, a friend with whom love was unconditional. But he, too, wanted love of the symphonic kind, where the strings and horns and tympani converge, where one's heart soars to meet the high notes of someone else's.

Ah, to be back in New York. His city of wonder and challenge. There was so very much to accomplish. But first things first. He picked up the phone and dialed.

"Suzanne, I'm home," he said. "I missed you too." It was true. He had. But not like he'd missed Jeannie. Nowhere close. So, he'd set a time and a place to meet, maybe over lunch, and he'd tell her what was going on with him. He dreaded it, but he knew it had to be done. And done in person, not like some of his asshole friends who did it by phone or e-mail or text message. If he'd learned one thing from his dad, it was to do the right thing in situations like these. Don't prolong, don't bullshit or lie. *Do the thing in your heart and do it like a gent,* his dad had said. Or, as Jeannie would say, like a mensch.

He hung up the phone and turned to task number two: the getting of a new gig so he wouldn't have to travel so much. This life of his was taking its toll. He looked at himself in his hallway mirror. *Look at me, for crying out loud. I look a hundred years old.* Like his mom said last time he went up to the family's old country house in Connecticut for Sunday dinner, he wouldn't always have his boyish good looks. She was teasing, nudging him to find a girl and settle down already, urging him that time was passing quickly by *and then you're dead,* she'd said in that straightforward, no-bullshit Protestant way of hers.

He certainly was not a believer in any mystical, magical shit. But things did have a way of working themselves out. Here was this perfect confluence of things: he was getting older, he was sick of traveling to squalid, scary places for his job, and he'd fallen for Jeannie. As if the heavens had opened and a voice had said, "Okay, you. You've done your time."

He picked up the phone and made his next call, this time to his editor at the *Times.*

"John, how are you? It's Tom, back from the wars."

"Hey, Tom, good to hear from you. You did really good there. That last story, harrowing, brilliant. That's Pulitzer stuff, man."

"Pulitzer, huh? I was thinking Nobel."

"When the Yankees start winning again," he laughed. "Now that'll get a Nobel."

"Fucking Yanks. I'm gone a couple months and look what happens. The season begins, they're doing great, then what? They've already lost it."

"Maybe when you leave again, they'll start winning."

"Yeah, I want to talk to you about that. When can I see you?"

"Today, tomorrow. I need you to go to Pakistan."

Tommy felt his words like a punch in the gut. "That's not my beat. That's Will's."

"Will's sick."

"As in sick sick? Seriously?"

"Yeah. Hodgkin's. And I need someone I can rely on, someone like you, over there now."

"Jesus, Hodgkin's." He paused for a minute. Once again, the luck of the draw. Life was so precarious. And short. If you even lived that long. So he said, "It's funny, John. The reason I'd wanted to come in to talk was to ask you for a desk job. In town. I'm ready, you know?"

"We can talk about it. But right now, I need you out there. Just do this one, okay? Then we'll talk. I got to say, I never expected to hear this from you. I thought you were a lifer."

Tommy laughed. "Me too. I'm surprising myself."

"So I need you to go in a couple days, okay?"

"Yeah, I'll do my duty. I'll come in tomorrow and you can fill me in." And he hung up.

"Shit," he said aloud. "Flying fucking shit." What happened to all that stuff about confluence? It confluenced right up his ass, that's what.

Finally, now, at the ripe old age of thirty-eight, he could see his future. He could see marrying Jeannie, having kids with her, getting old with her. He could see them taking trips, laughing, arguing, crying together. He wanted his life, he wanted it with her. All these years feeling like she'd always be there, like he had all the time in the world, and then all of a sudden to have this acute sense of urgency disturbed him. *Jeannie*, he said to himself, *Jeannie, wait for me.*

Twelve Items or Less — or Else

Jeannie didn't see or speak to Tommy all the next day or night, making her mood flat and hard like the river below. She puttered around, she slept, she went to the gym and to work for another night of behavior madness. On the way home, she forced herself to stop at The Food Emporium for a few things. Normally she found food shopping to be one of life's necessary irritations. Today, feeling like the odd girl out, with Tommy's words about Suzanne ringing in her ears, she dreaded it. And this supermarket wasn't as bad as most in the city. It was relatively clean, it was well lit, and the aisles were even wide enough for two carts to get by without a fight. Though she only bought staples here, saving fruit and vegetables for Morgan's Market, this store was very popular, quiet only in the very early hours, when Jeannie usually shopped. But she'd gotten delayed by paperwork and then she'd stopped for breakfast at Bouley Bakery, so it was already after eight, and the place was packed with moms who'd just dropped their kids at school and nannies pushing strollers doing the family shopping. Lines were long, people were impatient.

If she ever got rich, really rich, Jeannie thought as she surveyed the scene, she wanted one wildly extravagant thing: to never, ever have to go grocery shopping again. She'd hire someone just to shop (and maybe cook a little), and checkout lines (and takeout) for Jeannie would be a thing of the past.

Jeannie took a look at her basket and counted her items. She had thirteen things, one over the limit. She wondered how bad would it be to get in the "twelve items or less" line, considering she was only one item over. She thought about taking one item out, but she needed everything—the milk, the eggs, the cheddar, the bread, the juice, and everything else. If she got in the express line, she was being the person she hated, but, surveying the checkout lines once more, she thought, *Shit, I'm going in.*

Unpacking her groceries onto the conveyor, she piled them up and then rearranged the pile so that maybe the cashier wouldn't notice the extra item. Then she heard the cashier's voice. "That's more than twelve, hon."

Jeannie looked up and smiled. The cashier wore bright red lipstick and had such long fingernails that Jeannie wondered how she worked the cash register, much less packed the bags, without breaking them. They were painted a deep purple with gold tips. "I know, but it's only one. And look how crowded it is. Please, would you let me through just this once? Please?"

"No can do," said the cashier, raising her chin, closing her eyes, turning her mouth down into a frown, and shaking her head, while waving the nails of her right hand in front of Jeannie's face. "You got to go to another line."

Jeannie could feel the heat rise in her face, could hear the thumping of her chest. There was no fucking way she was packing up her groceries and standing in another line.

"It's not like I have twenty items. I have one too many. And we're taking more time arguing about this than we would if you'd just check me out."

"It's the principle, baby!" the cashier yelled. "If I let you, I have to let everyone, and then where would we be? We'd be a regular line, that's where!"

This was a cashier to contend with.

"You have no idea how I would normally agree with you.

I'm just asking you, begging you. Please, just this once. I promise."

"Okay, honey. How about this: if it's okay with the people behind you in line, then I will accede to the majority," said the cashier, with a nod to the long line of people with baskets hanging off their arms.

Jeannie had to smile at how surprising people could be.

"No way," said a young man in a suit, about three people back. "That is bullshit." *Oh, shut up,* Jeannie thought.

"Go ahead," said an old woman, the first in line. "But don't do it again, honey." *Okay, Grandma.*

"It's totally rude, but what the hell," said a woman with a stroller that was blocking the aisle. *Look who's calling the kettle black.*

"She's got only one extra item, for crying out loud!" came a voice from the back. *Bless you, whoever you are.*

And so, with most strangers in line showing more mercy and generosity than she would if the situation were reversed, Jeannie said, "Thank you," and the cashier, Jeannie's doppelganger-in-principle, rang up her items.

The Setup

On the way home it began to rain, soaking her bags, which she put on the kitchen floor, puddles forming under them. Out her windows, a little red tugboat was pushing a barge up the river. A few birds trailed it, hoping for fish to emerge in the churning wake. The newly built condos of New Jersey sat rigid and tall on the river's far side like sentries watching over the city. Sometimes Jeannie imagined herself there, inside one of those apartments, looking to the city. She had become accustomed to being on the outside looking in, her face pressed against the glass. It was better that way than being in and not having a clue what to do there, or not knowing what it is you really want or how to get it. Jeannie was like that: everything looked better from the outside, because once in, she was still the same person.

She had always expected to be changed by something. By coming to New York, by applying to law school, by getting her show on WBUZ, by deciding not to go to law school, by moving from the funky little walk-up on East Twelfth Street that she adored to this cold and airy place. By watching her ratings grow. By going on the sporadic date, by being desired, being pursued, buying new clothes, changing her hair, falling in like over and over and over. By finding success and making money and learning to live the nocturnal lifestyle, leaving her conflicted by the need for sleep and the need to make it to the bank, or to a movie with a girlfriend, or to her favorite store in Nolita, or to anywhere before closing hours. By loving Tommy.

But she was never changed. Not in a meaningful way, anyway. She was, and seemed destined to always be, the little girl living in a commune, surrounded by people, who had to yell to be heard. The girl with the father with the heart—and life—of a gypsy, the girl with the earth-mother mom who tended her tomato plants with more care than she did her daughter.

You can take the girl out of her family, but you can't get the family out of the girl.

She let out a powerful sigh, as if the air had been pent up in her chest, pushing to find its way out, as she put the groceries away and wiped the water from the floor. It felt melodramatic to sigh like that, as if her life were so burdensome, as if she didn't have anything to be grateful for, that she immediately wanted to take it back, suck up the air and give herself a whack on the side of the head. *For god's sake, look at this place! Look at this life! Take account of your friends, your success, your achievements, your good work,* she told herself. *There is no moping allowed.*

Boy, she was buzzed, her heart tripping over itself, her mind still reeling from seeing Tommy and the talk about love and friendship and all that bullshit. She got a Diet Coke from the fridge and took a sip, thinking of all the people up and out, already at the gym, at work, well into their day. She considered getting herself to the gym for that salsa dance class she stumbled through now and then, but she was so physically exhausted that she'd never keep up; any dancing would have to be the merengue of her mind. She should be going to sleep and dreaming the dreams of bad girls everywhere.

Then the phone rang. *Tommy. Finally.* Jeannie rushed to the bedroom to pick it up.

"Eggs with ketchup? I'm still nauseous," Jeannie joked.

"Ugh. Nobody with a brain eats eggs with ketchup, little girl."

Unbelievably, it was her dad. Of course, Jeannie hadn't been little for twenty-something years, and she was hardly a girl, but that was how her dad always spoke to her.

"Hey Dad. How are you?"

There was silence on the other end.

"Dad? You okay?"

No response, but Jeannie thought she could hear a gasp of air.

Here it comes, the setup.

"Daa-aad. What's going on?"

He let out a long, slow sigh.

Uh-oh, something's up. Jeannie had heard this before.

"Come on, talk to me. What's the matter?"

"This is serious stuff," he said.

This has to be about money.

"What is it? What's going on?"

"I need to talk to you. It's important."

Another boondoggle.

"What? What happened? Where are you?"

"Out here."

He's so over-the-top.

"Out where, Pop? You're not living in a tent on the shores of Lake Tahoe again, are you?"

"I'm in front of your building."

Jesus Christ. He'd come in from California? On what horse?

"Dad!" And she called the doorman to let him in.

In two minutes there he was standing at Jeannie's door, carrying a beat-up old light blue Samsonite suitcase, the same one he'd taken from the set when he left the house for good. That was over twenty years ago. At least someone's claim of immutability and permanence was true.

The Shakedown

"We need to talk," said Louis Sterling, father of Jeannie, after he'd put down his suitcase, taken off his jacket, and used the bathroom. He now stood with his hands in his front pockets, his shoulders hunched ever so slightly, as if his seventy-four years were sitting right there on them.

He's still so handsome, Jeannie thought, looking at the color in his cheeks, the crinkles around his eyes, his silver hair, his meticulously groomed beard and nails, his perfectly pressed jeans, his blue plaid cowboy shirt and bolo, his shiny belt buckle with the etching of a bucking bronco, his polished cowboy boots. He'd started to dress like that years before. Not that he rode a horse, or worked on a ranch, or did anything remotely western. He was a Brooklyn boy, born and bred, who had escaped to sunny California when he was twenty. And now he'd become Cowboy Lou.

"You want a cup of coffee or something, Dad?"

"Nah, that's all right."

She knew what that meant: he was starving. Here was a man who never asked for what he really wanted but always got it. She went to the kitchen to make him an omelette. He moved to the counter and took up residence.

"When did you get in?"

"Just now. Took the red-eye."

"So what's so serious you needed to come all the way from Mendocino and tell me in person? Not that you're not welcome, it's just . . . ," said Jeannie as she broke an egg into a large glass bowl.

"Not like that." He came around the counter and grabbed the next egg right out of her hand. "Didn't I ever teach you anything?"

"Sure, Pop. The high art of the finagle." She watched him break two more eggs into the bowl using only one hand. It reminded her of his old tricks: pretending his thumb was cut in two, or playing a mean yo-yo, always the clown, anything for a laugh. He added a tiny amount of milk, some salt and pepper, and then whipped the hell out of the eggs using a fork.

"What are you talking about? I'm here on some very serious—"

"Dad."

"How about some toast? Got any bacon?"

Her eyes were hurting from being so tired and she rubbed her right one with the top of her wrist.

"Tired?" he asked. "Listen, we'll eat, we'll talk, you'll sleep, I'll stay the night, and I'm gone."

It was never that simple with her dad. But he finished breakfast, and over coffee, with Jeannie sitting and facing him and the river, the view making her work to stay focused on him and not on the barge or the way the sun hit the water, he said this: "I want to talk to you about my funeral."

That got her full attention. Her heart dropped to her stomach and her breathing got shorter. She put her cup down too hard, making the coffee bounce right out and onto the table.

She swallowed. "Okay, but why? Are you sick? Is there something—"

"Listen, I'm turning seventy-five this year. My oldest brother, your uncle Stan, died at seventy-four; my sister, your aunt Adele, lived to the ripe old age of seventy-six. We don't let ourselves get too old, us Sterlings. So, I figure—"

"You could live to be a hundred." *Please.*

"For what? To sit in a nursing home? That you'd have to pay for? Nah, not for me. But thanks for the offer," he added with a wink.

Jeannie smiled. He could be cute, but this whole conversation was very upsetting. This was her *dad.* And as absent as he had been through her life, she loved him. And yes, he was getting old, but in her mind he'd live forever. He had to. Who else was there?

"Listen, Dad, whatever you want, in terms of a funeral, I'll pay for. You know that."

"Well, I visited the Jewish cemetery where Stan and Adele

and their fat stupid spouses are buried in Pasadena, and they got room. And for twelve thousand bucks I get a nice funeral, a pine coffin that's just fine by me, and a plot. Oh, and a stone."

"What's the name of the place?" She got up and opened her kitchen junk drawer to fish for a pen and paper.

"No, I don't want you to spend your money like that. It's crazy! Those thieves. And in Southern California yet. You think I belong there—dead or alive? Besides, did you ever read that exposé of the funeral business by what's-her-name?"

"Jessica Mit—"

"Yeah, her. They'll kill you to bury you. So I went to the nearest veterans' cemetery, near Vacaville, just a few hours away. They'd give me a military burial, the plot, the stone and all for nine hundred."

"But Dad, if you want to be buried by Stan and Adele, do it. I can handle it. I'm lucky I can."

"And I'm proud of you. Look at my little girl." He leaned forward, his chest to the table, his arms outstretched across its width toward her, his hands reaching for hers. She took his hands in hers. "Are you happy, Jeannie?" he asked.

"Not particularly, Dad, not with this conversation."

"That's not what I mean. I mean, are you happy? Is life what you want it to be?"

Over her dad's shoulder, she watched a gull outside the window gliding on the wind from the river. *Can I come too?* she wanted to say to it.

"Dad, what's that got to do wi—"

"I mean, are you really happy? Why is that such a difficult question? You know if you're happy or not."

The gull just hovered there over his shoulder as if he too were waiting for her response. Shit, *she* was waiting for her response. *Make up something, for god's sake,* she told herself. *Don't plumb, don't delve, don't mine. Just say yes, dammit.*

But tears welled in her eyes.

"You come here to talk about your funeral, and now you ask me if I'm happy? Yeah, I'm fucking happy. Okay? Does that make you feel better? I have a good job, I get paid pretty well—I can pay for your fucking funeral, can't I?—I have friends, I go out, I go to parties, I even get laid once in a while. I'm happy."

The man of my dreams is right now, as we speak, having amazing sex with someone else. I work nights. I'm always exhausted. I have no life. And people behave just as badly as ever.

He sat quietly for a moment, waiting for her anger to subside, and then he asked, softly, "So why the tears, my love?" He waited for a response, and when none came, he added, "And why the fuck is my little girl using the f-word?"

Jeannie laughed and at that moment the gull flew away, swooping down toward the river. She wiped her face with the back of her right hand and contained herself. "So do the Jewish cemetery, okay? Now can we talk about something else?"

"You don't want to talk to your old dad, fine. But you listen to me. Getting happy is what it's all about."

"You used to want me to change the world."

"That too."

Jeannie laughed and her dad smiled.

"Which first? Getting happy or changing the world?"

"Accomplishing one will lead to the other."

"Thank you, Maharishi Yoda."

"You're welcome," he said, bowing his head.

"Can we get back to—"

"So I booked the vet cemetery. The price was right. And it's a done deal. All you'll have to pay is the nine hundred bucks."

"All right, if that's what you want."

"It is."

There was a long moment of silence, as if out of respect for his plan to soon be departed. Jeannie looked at her dad's hands in hers and fought back more tears.

"But that's not all!" her dad roared with enthusiasm.

Jeannie looked up, her tears sucked back in her head as if vacuum-powered by suspicion. *What now?*

"So I figure I saved you eleven thousand bucks."

Here it comes. How'd she let him get to her?

"And so, my seventy-fifth birthday is coming up and I know you'll want to do something. So I figure instead of a party or a dinner at some fancy restaurant where you'd give me a tie—"

"Now why the hell would I give you a tie?" Jeannie interrupted.

He ignored her. "—or anything like that, you could send me to Belize for a month or two."

The shyster! Jeannie's dad had retired at only fifty-five, with no savings, no benefits, nada, bupkes. Not that he'd had what one would call a career. He had been a salesman for a printing company, enabling him to drive up and down California, as well as into Reno, Portland, and Tucson, and set his own schedule. He could have done it until he was seventy, racked up some savings, and retired with some kind of cushion. But he quit. So that he could be free, which translated to living on Social Security and Jeannie's monthly installments, and whatever woman he was involved with at the time.

"Also, before I forget, can I sleep here tonight? My flight leaves in the morning."

Jeannie wanted to scream. Here was her dad, looking for reimbursement for his flights to New York and to Belize and back to California, which he'd bought with money he didn't have, hoping to cash in on some cash to last a month or two down there, knowing he'd get it all.

What was it about Jeannie that made her dad think he could take advantage of her like that?

It was because she let him take advantage of her like that.

"Sure, Dad, you can sleep here. If not here, where?"

"If not now, when?"

"Thank you, Philosopher Lou."

"Actually it was Rabbi Hillel. You got to give credit where credit is due."

"That's good of you."

"And one more thing. Let me go get it."

"What do you mean?"

"I have a little something. It's downstairs." And he was out the door.

Jeannie took the two minutes to clear the counter of dishes, put them in the dishwasher, wipe the counter, and putter in that way that distracts from all real kinds of thinking.

Then the knock on the door. And she opened it to find her dad holding a bright green leash that was attached to some kind of beagle or something. One eye was circled in brown; the rest of his face was white, like a cartoon dog face. His ears were long, floppy, and brown.

"Pretty cute, Pop." She kneeled down and scratched his head, the place under his ears. His tail wagged and his little pink tongue protruded through what looked like a smile. "Who's this?"

"This is Mouse. Mouse, meet Jeannie, my other child. He's

part beagle, and part basset hound, and part something else thrown in too. Got him at a shelter. Thought he's small enough to travel with, to live in an apartment. A nice companion."

"Never took you for a pet kind of guy, you, the wandering Jew."

"Never was. People can change, though. This I've learned over the years. People do change."

"Thought you said you took the red-eye. Put Mouse below with the luggage?"

"He's a *dog* for crying out loud, not a prince."

"It's dangerous."

"He's alive, isn't he? And stop criticizing. When he's *yours*, you can criticize." And he unclasped the leash, letting Mouse free to run around, explore, and pee on the potted white hydrangea in the corner of the room. Jeannie hated indoor potted plants, probably because she always killed them. She was never quite sure what was needed, more sun, less sun, plant food, more water or less, and the plants would eventually look scraggly, turn brown, and die. But hydrangeas and orchids, with their spectacular flowers, their architectural structures, were an exception.

Her dad looked at Jeannie and shrugged. "He's just marking. It's a dog thing."

"Yeah," Jeannie laughed, thinking of the funeral talk, as she retrieved a paper towel and the Windex. "Just don't leave him to me, Pop. Not a thing, please."

"What about my millions?"

"That would only be tax nightmare. Give it to charity." She looked at him, smiled, her face full of love.

"Gimme that," he said as he grabbed the towel from her and finished wiping the floor himself.

Quick-Change Artist

From the dais Moss could spot three men wearing toupees, another four balding with ponytails, and at least a dozen women with nose and/or boob jobs. And that was in just the first two rows of tables that filled the Beverly Hilton ballroom in Beverly Hills. It was a game he played to keep himself from nodding off while waiting for the dull speakers to finish, and to make himself look busy by pretending to be taking notes, when he was really tallying up his findings in neat columns like a scientist observing the mating habits of chimps. Then after they introduced him and presented him with his honor, he'd say a few words—and mean them—about the importance of their work, he'd thank everyone, and he'd take the humanitarian award, or the honorary PhD, or whatever award he was being given on this particular day in this particular town.

Not that he didn't appreciate that people appreciated his efforts. He just didn't see the need to attend these insipid black-tie functions that cost hundreds of thousands of dollars that could be going to the causes he championed and for which he was getting the awards in the first place. He'd tried to get out of them, and for a while he had been successful, but then his PR people said he had to comply if he wanted people to support the efforts and the politicians he threw his weight behind.

Tonight he was being honored by the Environmental Defense Fund. Other nights it was about feeding the poor, housing the homeless, providing quality health care for everyone. He felt that people should be able to pull them-selves up by their own bootstraps if they have to, but—and this he was passionate about—there are certain inalienable rights in a free society, like the rights to food, a roof over your head, and a doctor if you're sick. And it irritated him that for so many it was all about photo ops. It was his friend John, at the *Times*, who once said that some people created entire organizations just to make themselves famous. He had laughed at that comment, knowing John was right. But if it meant saving his beloved Pacific Coast redwoods from devel-opers, it was okay with him.

Looking out at the wealthy, glamorous Hollywood crowd, he felt like a prisoner. It was a funny thing. With all his suc-cess and money, he still didn't control his life in some impor-tant ways. If you want to do service, make a difference, you're shackled to the responsibilities that come with it, like at-tending these functions and mugging for the cameras. The more you give, the more shit you have to do.

Tonight it was bugging him more than usual. He had been distracted during the cocktail hour, barely able to make small talk, and now he was squirming in his seat, anxious and impatient. The station was on his mind. Making the deal with that quirky WBUZ was going quickly, with only a wrinkle or two to iron out. And he couldn't wait. There was something about it, maybe expanding his ventures into the entertain-ment industry, maybe that he'd done it on a whim instead of spending months poring over P&L's and ratings analyses, maybe that Jeannie Sterling, who got him crazy angry, got his blood rushing and his heart beating.

The applause broke his reverie and he looked out to see the entire ballroom of people on their feet. He looked to his right at the podium, and the speaker was gesturing to him. It was time. He rose, stood in front of the mike, looked at his notes, and waited.

He talked about responsibility, about how having money made it impossible to not act in behalf of things you believe in. He knew his audience, so he spoke about how people have to give back, that wealth and success should not be taken for granted. He spoke about the EDF and how important it was to protect the planet for the next generation and the ones that followed. He talked about his passion for climbing, for the redwoods, and how many acres had been lost since he began decades ago. And then he paused, looked out at the audience, crumpled his notes, and finished his speech.

"I was in New York this week and I heard two teenage girls talking. One said, 'Paris Hilton is what's wrong with the world.'" He paused to let the laughter subside.

"Then the other got angry and answered her with this: 'That's insane,' she said. 'Paris Hilton's not what's wrong with the world. Nazis are what's wrong with the world. The Ku Klux Klan. The genocide in Darfur. Intolerance and injustice. Poverty, ignorance, and plain old rudeness.'

"I wanted to grab that girl right there and give her a big, fat kiss." He paused for the punch line. "But I didn't want to get arrested." He waited again for quiet.

"There's been a lot of talk about the failure of empathy. That we don't care enough about others to stick our necks out for them. That we are unable or unwilling to imagine ourselves in their shoes. But those of us with the means, must. Maybe we can't eradicate war, poverty, or unemployment, or corporate greed entirely. But we can try. As part of the privileged few, it is our duty."

He got out of there quickly, had his driver rush to the airport, boarded his jet, and landed at his home in Napa Valley about an hour later. By eight a.m. he was up and out, his gear already in his jeep, and he was winding his way up Route 1, toward his beloved trees. By ten there he was, using his bow and arrow to shoot the rope over the first limb that jutted out over fifty feet up. And soon he was sitting in the canopy high above the world below.

He looked out over the Pacific and breathed in deeply, his chest expanding with the cool, clean ocean air. He let it out and felt empty. Something was missing. He knew what it was, but he didn't want to be dopey or sentimental. For crying out loud, he'd just said what he had to say at the dinner, he was buying a crack little radio station, his companies were flourishing, he had his friends, and here he was sitting in his favorite tree, his face against the wind.

But he had nobody to share it with. And all the money and the success, and even all the philanthropy and the redwoods, couldn't mean as much without someone who held his heart.

The House on Allston Way

Jeannie got her dad settled and walked down the hallway that was lined with photos to her bedroom. Though she was usually a photo slob, never organizing them into albums, throwing them instead into a box at the bottom of her front coat closet, these she'd specially selected to frame and hang because they were funny or touching or particularly revealing of the moments and people of her life. Though she rarely looked at them, she was always aware that they were there, hanging like ghosts in her periphery. But this morning, with her dad's surprise visit, it was the photo of her mom that stopped her.

There she was, standing on the porch of the big old house, rake in hand, from when Jeannie was about nine—she could tell by her mom's hair. Though her hairstyle had changed only once, its color marked the years like the rings of a redwood. When Jeannie was born, Harriet, which her mom insisted Jeannie call her from the moment she could speak, had long, straight black hair, which she always wore long and down to the middle of her back, with bangs cut short, straight across, like Joni Mitchell, who was their favorite then and Jeannie's favorite now.

"Joni was a poet, an innovator, a goddess," Jeannie would argue with Luce, or Joseph, or Tommy, or the guy she was dating at the time, or whoever would listen to her. "Damn it, name a lyric that compares to Joni's 'I wish I had a river I could skate away on.'"

Luce would answer, "I like Sarah McLachlan better," making Jeannie want to puke.

Joseph would say, "If she didn't write 'Stairway to Heaven,' she ain't shit."

Tommy would respond, "Yeah, but she's no Bono."

And Ray, a lawyer Jeannie went out with a couple of times, asked on their final date, "Who's Joni Mitchell?"

But it was the one thing upon which Jeannie and Harriet agreed: Joni Mitchell deserved a hell of a lot more respect than she got. And that if she had been a man, for god's sake, she would've gotten it. And she wouldn't have become so bitter and disillusioned, which had made her into a female Rodney Dangerfield. They spent many a night in the living room of the house, listening to the new Joni Mitchell album or the last Joni Mitchell album, maybe even dancing, until Ike or

Susie or Ted or Steve or Ali or Kirsten or any one of the people living in the house that night, that week, came in to join them. The dancing would continue and the pot would come out and Harriet would nod to Jeannie, and Jeannie knew that was her cue to leave. Though Harriet felt that if Jeannie were ever to take drugs or have sex, she'd rather Jeannie do it in the house than on the street, even Harriet had her limits in regard to permissiveness.

When Jeannie turned three, Harriet's Joni Mitchell hair began to turn gray, a direct response, it seemed, to mothering a toddler. By the time Jeannie was six, Harriet's hair was almost white. Until one day, when Harriet dyed her hair an unnatural orange-red. This act, by a woman who owned no makeup, who never shaved her legs or her underarms, seemed oddly out of character even to Jeannie's young mind, though it coincided with the arrival of Eddie, Harriet's boyfriend who stayed for two years, the longest relationship she would ever have.

Eddie was the only one of her mom's boyfriends, in all those years, with his long blond hair and kind eyes and the laugh of a hyena, that Jeannie liked. She actually had a crush on him. He could play a mean harp over strains of Cream, singing, "In the white room with black curtains near the station," and was the one who introduced her to Frank Zappa, and Captain Beefheart, and Big Brother and the Holding Company, the one who didn't make her feel self-conscious, as so many of the men in the house did. He was sweet and had thick, strong hands and made her laugh until tears found their way down her cheeks. Most important—and this was the thing she remembered most about him—he was concerned about her. He made sure she got up in time for school, had a good breakfast, did her homework, went to bed at a reasonable hour. The two years he spent in the house was a time Jeannie would never forget.

But then, one morning, she sat in the kitchen on her favorite old wooden stool, whose seat was smooth and worn, shaped by the butts that had sat in it over the years. Harriet had picked it up one Sunday morning at the flea market at Adeline and Alcatraz from an old black man with a white, grizzled beard who swore that it had been Huey Newton's and that probably every Black Panther had sat, at one time or other, on that stool. Harriet bought it for Jeannie because she felt sorry for her that she had missed all the important moments in postwar radical history. Jeannie was too young to have experienced the free speech movement, the antiwar movement, People's Park, the Black Panthers, and Woodstock. Jeannie felt bad enough about it already, and receiving the stool as a gift didn't make her feel any better. She grew up with the sense that she was born too late, that she was too young, that she'd missed all the momentous things, that everything great or important had happened already and she was here to live a life of aftermaths.

Sitting on Huey's stool, Jeannie had watched Kirsten, a woman living in the house at the time who wore long paisley caftans, make blueberry whole-wheat pancakes from scratch while Sam—a recent arrival who Jeannie didn't like because he never changed his overalls, making the smell, if you stood close enough, unbearable—made a seaweed tofu garlic shake in the blender. Eddie came in and Jeannie smiled at him, until she noticed his backpack slung over his shoulders, his down sleeping bag rolled small under it. He hugged her hard, holding her close and kissing her cheek, and told her it was time for him to go. He whispered in her ear, "You will have a wonderful life, my little one. This, I know." Her throat had tightened, her eyes filled with tears. He looked at her long and hard, brushed her hair from her face, and just like that he was gone. She'd gotten a postcard from him from Alaska about a month later. But she never heard from him again.

It made her wonder if nice men, like Eddie and her dad, always left. Or was this about her, she once asked Harriet. And in Harriet's completely self-absorbed, unconscious way, with her inability to reassure her daughter that she had absolutely nothing to do with the wayward men her mother chose, Harriet let out a bitter laugh and said, "Get used to it, honey. No man can ever love you enough to stick around. It's in their genes."

The next day, as if in some Shakespearean response to her wandering men's transgressions, Harriet cut her hair short, for the one and only time ever in her adult life, and dyed it a blackish purple, like Patti Smith's. It was an adulterous act, leaving Joni for Patti, and the last dye-job Harriet would get, too, which was a fashion statement in itself. For as Jeannie grew from a child into a young woman, Harriet let her hair grow long again, and as it did, the roots came in gray while the rest stayed black, as if the ends had been dipped in ink. Jeannie watched the two-tone hair change in proportion over the years. First, mostly black with a little gray, then half gray on top, half black on the bottom, then gray all over except for a two-inch band of black at the ends. By the time Jeannie was fourteen, Harriet's hair was Joni Mitchell–long again and it had turned a bright white. So Harriet had it cut one last time to trim off the black, any remnants of color completely gone.

And there she stood in the picture on the porch of the old Berkeley house on Allston Way, her rake in her right hand, in her baggy jeans, work boots, and white T-shirt, her breasts easy and free, unfettered by the confines of a bra. That was how Jeannie would always see her, frozen from her hippie days in the sixties until she died in 1990, just older and even more set in her ways. For Harriet, everything was black and white, just like her hair. Harriet loved things and hated things, adored people and despised people. There was no middle ground, no benefit of the doubt, little forgiveness. A mom like that is difficult to please and easy to resent.

Looking at her now, Jeannie wondered why, since she had inherited her dad's nose, his legs, his unruly hair, and his rootless dreamy heart, she'd failed to get any of Harriet's solidity, her sureness of things. Jeannie certainly felt confident about her own opinions on a wide variety of subjects (movies, books, politics, bad behavior), but in terms of Life and Love, with capital L's, Jeannie wasn't confident in herself. Judging others she shared with her mom; when it came to accepting who she was, or knowing what she wanted, she was on her own. Harriet always attributed it to Jeannie being a Gemini, and Jeannie would've loved to believe that, for at least there would've been an explanation.

The house was a typical three-story-high gray stucco Berkeley job, all straight lines, formidable, with a tile roof and large windows. It had probably been built in the twenties by someone who thought they could compete with the Maybecks and Morgans that graced the area. But as strong as the house was, the group did everything in its power to encourage its early decay. The shutters were peeling, their green paint shedding and exposing the gray wood below. The front door, painted a loud yellow, was covered with stickers of the MAKE LOVE, NOT WAR and WAR IS NOT HEALTHY FOR CHILDREN AND OTHER LIVING THINGS and BE HERE NOW variety.

The three wooden stairs leading to the decrepit porch were worse—broken and blistered, and you'd better watch out for the middle plank of the second stair, because your foot could go right through the thing and there you'd be, up to your knee in broken step, which happened to Jeannie more than once. Looking at the photo of the house brought the same feelings of apprehension it had every day when she got home from school. The faulty steps were simply a harbinger of what was inside.

But here in the photo it was summer; the garden that covered the small front yard was bursting out of its dilapidated fence. There, in that garden, Harriet toiled and took pride in the growth of things: huge cornstalks grew, but without producing one edible cob of corn, and huge sunflowers, sans their flowers, drooped over tomato plants that sat tomatoless on their stakes. Wisteria vines wound their way up the porch's beams as if they were holding it in place, but the wisterias themselves never bloomed. String bean, pepper, and daisy plants flourished, all interspersed in disarray, and all never producing one bean, pepper, or daisy. As lush and verdant as this garden was, so it was absurdly disorganized, which angered Jeannie then and angered her today. How could her mom—who spent almost every waking hour out there, planting and picking and hoeing and weeding—not see that if only she took more care to place and separate, to plan and map the small plot, to consider the individual needs of the various plants, perhaps fruit would actually grow, flowers actually bloom?

No wonder Jeannie was so unsettled and her generation so complacent, she thought, with the feeling that she was seeing something she had never seen before. They were raised by people who couldn't see the soil for the tomatoes.

Process was an end in itself; having goals, achieving success, or growing a green bean had no place in lives lived for the moment. And without grounding, a girl could get lost.

But it wasn't as if Harriet was totally irresponsible or wasn't at all concerned with Jeannie's welfare. It was just that Harriet felt passionately that a child should be treated with respect, be exposed to new ideas and people and experiences, that nurture beat the hell out of nature any day. Let a child live unfettered, her mind free to roam, her activities unthwarted by convention but governed by her own inner moral compass, and you will raise one hell of an open, spirited, and righteous soul. Jeannie went to school, had friends, excelled in the water at an early age, and even joined the high school swim team. But Harriet was very rigid in her permissiveness. No daughter of hers would wear makeup, or go to a prom, or join a sorority, or wear a diamond engagement ring, or be married in a white-gown-traditional-bullshit-sexist way (or get married at all, for that matter), or buy in to bourgeois expectations of her.

It was when Jeannie went to friends' homes that she understood what she was missing—her friend Lindsey's home, in particular. Lindsey lived in one of those old pink Berkeley houses, with a roof of Spanish tile, that hung on the edge of the hill leading to Tilden Park. Both of her parents were older, white haired, and retired. Her dad, his Eastern European accent thick with charm, was funny and warm, as if escaping the Holocaust as a child and losing most of his family made him so grateful to be alive that he enjoyed even the silliest pun, the grossest joke. Lindsey's mom had a similar history, but it had diminished her, made her shoulders hunch, her hands fold in judgment, her eyes harden in suspicion. But she had a huge heart, which beat under the layers of ice that had formed to protect it. Lindsey had a dog named Pookie, a sweet black Lab–spaniel mix; a kid brother named Eli, who was a pain in the butt; and a hill with a rose garden in her backyard. Jeannie so wanted to be there, and was there so frequently, that they treated her like part of their family. But instead of feeling lucky to have this home away from The House, Jeannie felt almost ashamed. She felt guilty for wanting this normal life, this life guided by parental expectations—early to bed, brush teeth, get good grades, go to college, fall in love, get married, have kids—that Jeannie had never known. So when Lindsey's mom would ask Jeannie about her home life, about if she ever saw her dad, if her mom had a new boyfriend, and how many people was it again that lived there, Jeannie's jaw muscles would clench, and she'd become defensive. And inevitably, Jeannie and Lindsey's friendship began to founder, as relationships that are laden with envy, competition, and unspoken feelings do.

Jeannie moved out of The House when she'd just turned seventeen, in October of her senior year of high school. She couldn't stand it anymore: the strangers in and out, the new faces, the lack of privacy, the mess, the parsley shakes. She couldn't stand seeing her mom deeply lonely and increasingly bitter. Looking at her mother, Jeannie saw herself. And the fear that she, too, would push people away, that she'd surround herself with many so she wouldn't be hurt by loving just one, propelled her up and out forever.

There was no final fight. There was no teary good-bye. Harriet knew it was time for Jeannie to go, perhaps even wanted her to go. To see the optimism and loveliness of a teenage girl, her girl, and know that in time hurt and disappointment would take their toll made her want to look away. She might have wanted for Jeannie a better life than she had

had, but she didn't believe it was possible. Jeannie got an apartment a block above Telegraph off Dwight, and could only afford it because she agreed to take on some management duties, including changing lightbulbs in the hallways and keeping the homeless hippies from People's Park out of their garage.

When Lindsey went to UCLA and Jeannie to Berkeley, the end of the relationship was clinched. And when Lindsey's mom died a year or so later, Jeannie did one of the things she would always regret: she failed to call Lindsey or send a note, or acknowledge her loss in any way. Perhaps she was secretly glad that Lindsey would finally understand how it felt to live without a mother's unconditional love, to never be able to go home again because there is no home to go to.

It was in Jeannie's junior year at Berkeley that her own mom died of cancer. Jeannie sprinkled Harriet's ashes out in the Pacific, just past the Golden Gate, courtesy of the Neptune Society, as Harriet had arranged. The others in The House on Allston left for parts unknown, and Jeannie gathered her mom's belongings and gave anything usable to the Salvation Army. Everything except the suede, fringed jacket that had been her mom's favorite, that Jeannie had worn every autumn since. After all these years of wear, it hung like a bag, worn bare in spots, where it was more like leather, shiny and smooth. But she loved it. It had history. It held memories and loss and the guilt of a child not appreciating that her mother did the best she could, given her own limitations.

When Harriet died, Jeannie received a letter from Lindsey that was surprisingly warm. She said she was saddened to hear of Jeannie's loss; she said she knew it must be terribly hard for her, because she had lost her mom too. She asked

Jeannie what happened, why she'd disappeared, how come she'd never called her when she'd heard her mom had died.

Jeannie wrote a pleasant but perfunctory note back and never heard from Lindsey again. Today, with the advantage of years, Jeannie knew how wrong she had been about Lindsey and her mom, how she'd completely negated the horrifying and tragic history that they lived with every day as if it were entwined in the threads of the Oriental carpets that covered their hardwood floors. She had backed off from their affection, had judged them harshly, without sympathy, just as her mother would have wanted her to.

"Mom," she said aloud, studying her picture, touching a finger to her mom's smiling face. Her heart tugged for the mother she never understood, who she couldn't please, who didn't live to see her daughter find her place in the world.

It was Harriet's death that changed Jeannie's relationship with her dad, who sat smiling on a little boat in Belize in her favorite photo of him on the wall. He'd gone missing when he and Harriet split up years before. But when Harriet died, her dad began to call more, to check in periodically, as if he felt some strange new responsibility as a dad. It pissed Jeannie off a little—*I mean, where the hell was he all those years?*—but she loved him as best she could and accepted the occasional contact and the paternal attention, however ambivalent it was. He could never fill the hole of moral arbiter that was her mother's, but he was fun to go to a movie with and it was nice just to know she had a dad at all, something that she did not take for granted.

That night, after she was dressed and ready for work and her dad was settled in his pajamas, Jeannie left him watching *Law and Order* on her couch with Mouse at his side, a bowl of mint chip ice cream on his lap, and a wad of dough in his pocket. They said their good-byes, for he'd have to leave early to make his flight out of JFK and would probably be gone by the time she got home from the studio the next morning. With a kiss on her dad's cheek, and a head scratch for Mouse, she walked out the door.

STERLING BEHAVIOR

JEANNIE: *Hello, fellow insomniacs! I'm in the mood for a Pet Peeve Rant. Luce, start us out. What's yours?*

LUCE: *Hmm, I have so many. Where to begin? I know. I just witnessed this yesterday: people who clip their nails in public.*

JEANNIE: *Totally gross. Do that in the privacy of your bathroom, please! You know what pisses me off? People who use their fingers at a salad bar.*

LUCE: *Disgusting. Not to mention unhealthy. How about the person who forwards your e-mail when you meant it only for him?*

JEANNIE: *Oh boy, e-mail ethics could take up an entire week. But here are my first two rules: one, never ever forward a personal e-mail unless you ask the sender first if it's okay. Feelings are hurt, gossip runs amok, wars get started.*

LUCE: *And your second e-mail rule?*

JEANNIE: *Never ever say something in an e-mail about someone you wouldn't say to his or her face. Because your e-mail will inevitably be forwarded.*

LUCE: *What else bugs you?*

JEANNIE: *Slow walkers. People, whether on the sidewalk, or at Costco, or getting off a subway, or wherever, who walk slowly. And you're in a hurry and you can't get around them. And sometimes they're walking four abreast. Or with strollers. It's a nightmare.*

LUCE: *My worst nightmare is people who throw their gum on the ground. This kills me. I hate to step in gum.*

JEANNIE: *Dirties your Tod's loafers?*

LUCE: *You're teasing me, Madame Frye boots, but nobody likes to step in gum. You know what Spike hates? Idiots who drive like they own the road. Tailgaiters. People who change lanes without using their blinkers.*

JEANNIE: *I hate indifferent sales clerks. Indifference means you plain don't care. About helping others, about doing your job. People should be fired for indifference.*

LUCE: *What about people who won't move over in a movie theater so that two people can sit together?*

JEANNIE: *People who talk in the movies. People who eat loudly in the movies.*

LUCE: *People who don't RSVP. People who do and don't show up or show up when they said they wouldn't.*

JEANNIE: *People who just show up, without an invitation, like my dad did today, expecting me to pay for his trip to Belize.*

LUCE: *Which I assume you did.*

JEANNIE: *Of course.*

LUCE: *So maybe your dad expects things from you because you always give him what he wants.*

JEANNIE: *Thank you, Madame Freud.*

LUCE: *That'll be two hundred dollars.*

JEANNIE: *Let's take some calls, already. Okay, hi, Carol, you're on the air.*

CAROL: *Hi, Jeannie. My pet peeve is people who don't pick up their doggie doodie.*

LUCE: *Hurray for Carol.*

CAROL: *But I have a politically incorrect story to tell you.*

JEANNIE: *That's refreshing. Let's hear it.*

CAROL: *Well, I was taking a walk last Wednesday. I had just bought a brand-new pair of Naturalizers, the only shoes I can wear anymore, what with my bunions. Getting old is no—*

LUCE: *Oh, you're not so old.*

CAROL: *That's sweet, dear. Now where was I? Oh, I was walking and I saw a woman ahead of me with a big yellow dog who was, you know, making a doggie doodie.*

JEANNIE: *Funny that this story is about dogs. I had a dog visit me this morning and after only three minutes, he peed right in my living room.*

LUCE: *Gross. I hope the dog's owner helped to clean it up.*

JEANNIE: *That would be my father—*

LUCE: *Well, you know what the good book says. Honor thy father—*

JEANNIE: *Now you're quoting the Bible?*

LUCE: *I'm just saying.*

JEANNIE: *—and yes, he did. Carol, did the woman with the dog pick up its . . . doodie?*

CAROL: *That's just it. She walked away, leaving the doggie doodie right there in the middle of the sidewalk.*

JEANNIE: *I hate when that happens. Picking up poop is part of the responsibility of having a dog in the city. You don't want to pick it up? Don't get a dog! That rates a six on the Jeannie Sterling Scale of Bad Behavior.*

[Sterling Scale sound effects: earthquake rumbling, crashing, and sounds of destruction]

CAROL: *I was very upset.*

JEANNIE: *I don't blame you.*

LUCE: *You were right to be upset.*

CAROL: *And for some reason on that particular morning I wanted to do something about it. I think you have influenced me, Jeannie, to do something when I see someone . . .*

JEANNIE: *Good for you.*

LUCE: *So, Carol, what did you do?*

CAROL: *I went after the four-legged culprit.*

JEANNIE: *Though you knew full well it was a two-legged one that was responsible for this bad behavior. A dog's got to do what a dog's got to do, right? That's exactly why a dog has a human: to clean up its . . . doodie.*

CAROL: *And then, because the light was red, they waited at the corner. At least they didn't break that law as well.*

LUCE: *You're so funny!*

CAROL: *So I walked as fast as these two old legs would allow and caught up with them. "Excuse me," I said, and the woman, who had been facing away from me, turned around and I realized she was blind.*

JEANNIE: *And the dog was a guide dog? Very interesting!*

CAROL: *So I just stood there for a minute thinking, She's blind. I mean, you make excuses, don't you? But shouldn't this woman, blind though she may be, be responsible for her doggie's doodie?*

JEANNIE: *Hmmm. I'm loving this!*

CAROL: *There was even a sign nearby that said* CURB YOUR DOG. *Well, are the blind exempt from picking up poop just because they can't read the sign?*

JEANNIE: *You certainly don't need a sign to know that some things—like lying, cheating, stealing, allowing your dog to poop on a sidewalk and not picking it up—are wrong.*

CAROL: *If being blind means you can leave your dog's pile of poop on the sidewalk, does it mean you can commit murder? Where oh where does it end?*

LUCE: *Well, I don't think that not picking up dog doodie leads to murder.*

JEANNIE: *[laughing] I don't know. In this city, it can, trust me, it can! But listen, Plato did say that a society that doesn't hold its citizens responsible for their actions will not thrive. So what did you do, Carol?*

CAROL: *I told the woman that she forgot to clean up her doggie's doodie. And you know what she said? She said, "You're kidding,* right?" And then she said, and these were her exact words, "Pardon me for living, but hello!"

LUCE: No!

CAROL: "Hello what?" I asked her. And she said, "Well, I am blind, or are you blind too?"

JEANNIE: Now that would've made me mad. She's exempt from good behavior, she can be rude, because of her disability? I. Don't. Think. So. What did you say?

CAROL: I told her I could see she was blind, but she could still train her dog to poop in the street or else she has to pick it up. And she said, "I don't see how that's possible, really." Then I asked her, "Do you feed your dog?"

LUCE: What'd she say to that?

CAROL: You won't believe it. She said, "What, I'm blind and cruel?" And then you know what she said?

JEANNIE AND LUCE: What?

CAROL: "Up yours."

JEANNIE: I can't believe she said that! But, Carol, you stuck your neck out and let this woman know, in your own charming way, how you felt about—

CAROL: But it wasn't going to change a damned thing. So I told her to go and fu [bleep] herself and the dog she rode in on.

JEANNIE AND LUCE: [full laughter]

A Date with Destiny

Jeannie needed to pee desperately when the break came, so she threw back her chair and almost ran out of the glass-enclosed studio, yelling, "Gotta go!", letting the door slam behind her, racing around the corner and down the hall— when she slammed right into Tommy.

He took hold of her upper arms, smiled, and said, "Just the woman I wanted to see."

Her breath caught in her throat. It took her a moment to respond. She looked down at the gray carpeting and then back up into his lovely eyes. "Hi. I wasn't sure, um. Well. What are you doing here? It's way too early for—"

"For nothing. Meet me after the show for coffee."

"I was worried. You know, you just got home and I didn't hear—"

"Just had to settle a few things. Anyway, I, there's so much I want—"

"Sure, okay, me too." And she smiled and pulled away, remembering her dad sleeping on her couch. She thought for a moment that maybe she should rush home after the show before he and his mutt left, but she'd already said good-bye, so it was probably best to leave it at that.

"It's important," Tommy said. "I need—"

"Okay, after the show." And she walked backward a step or two until she could delay no longer. She turned and made it into the ladies' room just as she was about to burst.

What the hell did that mean, she wondered, *"There's so much I want—"? What, "to say"? "To tell you"? "To do"? And what could he need, he of the perfect everything, from her? Why was he even awake at this hour?* It was her own damn fault, as usual. She hadn't let him finish a damn sentence.

Between Friends

Jeannie was trying to take off her headset when Luce came in through the glass door.

"Are you tangled again?"

"Shit, yeah, I hate this thing."

Luce walked around the table and began to painstakingly pull strands of Jeannie's hair out from the headset.

"Ouch!"

"Sorry. This is a mess. What did you do—mistake this for a hair iron or something?"

"Ouch! You're pulling."

"I'm *sorry*. But your hair is so ridiculous!"

Jeannie laughed and looked at her funny friend, and for a moment she thought she might cry. She felt her throat tighten and her brows furrow in an effort to keep back the tears. It wasn't just the stupid hair thing, though she didn't take this kind of intimate help for granted. It was that she loved her. And how many people throughout her life could she say that about? *Look at her,* Jeannie thought. She loved Luce's adorable outfit and the way she held her shoulders back and her head high. She thought her long smooth hair was beautiful, especially how it shone under the crackling fluorescent lights of the studio. She admired how Luce was so honest and earnest and without guile. She felt good knowing that Luce had Spike, who adored her with a passion unheard of in a man who can change a faucet. Jeannie loved how Luce made her laugh and was the perfect foil to her loud, silly, opinionated self. They really were Lucy and Ethel, as Harry liked to point out on a daily basis. She felt lucky to have a friend with whom there were no secrets, ever.

But there was something about Luce today that made her wonder. She seemed distracted.

"Is something going on with you? You . . ."

Luce turned to Jeannie, paused a moment, shook her head, and said, "Nah, I'm good. Nothing unusual."

"You sure?" Jeannie asked.

"Yeah, I'm fine."

Jeannie just looked at her.

"Jeannie, I tell you everything," Luce said. "And there's nothing to tell. I just have a lot going on. Spike's got some new business, so he's been busy, and we're thinking of renovating the apartment a little, and my mom's birthday is next week, and I haven't been sleeping so well. I'm just a little tired."

"That must be it," Jeannie said, but she wasn't sure.

They had been silent for a minute when the knock on the studio door startled them. Tommy burst in, a motorcycle helmet under his arm, another dangling by its straps from his fist. "And there they are! Luce, Luce, Luce, how the hell are you? We haven't had a chance to catch up. And Spike? How is that guy? Hey, I have an idea. Let's the four of us have dinner. What do you say?"

"That'd be fun. Definitely."

"Good," Tommy said. "I'll set it up."

"Okay, now get outta heah," Luce said with the accent of a don.

Jeannie hugged her and said, "I'm here, always, if you need me."

"There's nothing! Would you go already?" said Luce.

And Jeannie left with Tommy, looking back to her friend over her shoulder as she went through the door.

Someone to Watch Over Her

They climbed onto Tommy's Vespa and sped through the early-morning streets as they headed toward the Hudson. The air was brisk as it blew in her face, but the rising sun cast its gold between buildings so that it landed bright and vivid on the street below. She clung to Tommy, her arms around his waist, her cheek against his leather jacket, and tried not to think about her dad getting up and getting ready to leave. She shivered as if it were March already, that terrible month in New York when you are so sick of the cold that you start wearing lighter jackets out of sheer optimism, when all of a sudden six inches of snow drop on the city as if it's somebody's idea of a cosmic joke.

They arrived at the Empire Diner, but decided to take a walk first. Easier to talk that way than face to face.

They walked east, away from the river. It was only September. There were many warm days ahead. Still, nothing could shake the chill that jammed into Jeannie's muscles. Nothing, that is, until, as if reading her mind, Tommy put his arm around her and held her close. She leaned against him, her shoulder fitting perfectly under him, the side of her body up against his. They walked in sync, briskly, with long strides, holding tight, through the western edge of Chelsea, past old warehouses that held art galleries and real estate offices. People were going to work, getting off buses, coming up from the subways, getting out of taxis.

Jeannie noticed an idiot riding his bike on the sidewalk. *What's with that?* Jeannie argued to herself. *You ride a bike in the street and you walk on a sidewalk, or you're bound to hit someone. City streets not safe enough to ride in? Get a car!* Then she saw a young woman toting a large leather bag filled with papers, looking chic in tight jeans, a short black leather jacket, and a long knitted scarf, take a last sip from her cup of coffee, throw it toward a garbage can, miss the can, see the cup miss the can, and continue walking. Ooh, that pissed Jeannie off, but given her present circumstances, that Tommy was here and walking beside her, she decided not to do anything or to even mention these transgressions she witnessed. She would Be Here Now.

"I broke up with Suzanne," he said, playfully bumping his shoulder into hers. Then he took her hand in his. And then he stopped and turned to her, and with a hand on her cheek, he kissed her.

What was happening was like a dream. The people on the street had suddenly vanished. There was no sound except for Tommy and Jeannie's own breathing. He pulled her into the narrow, dark alley a few feet ahead. Back doors of stores, of restaurants, lined both sides. He pushed her up against the wall and looked at her long and hard and said, "Jeannie, it's our time now."

Shut up, she was thinking, her heart pumping right out of her chest. *Stop it right now. Don't flatter me, don't kiss me. Don't lead me down a path—or an alley—where I'll lose my way and get hurt.* He was so close she could smell him, she could feel his heat.

But he ignored her silent pleas, and this time he leaned into her, pushed her hard against the wall, his body against hers, his mouth on hers. She felt his tongue inside her, his hand down and up the side of her body, then on her breast. Her skin tingled, her head reeled, and she held him tight to her, felt the hard cold wall behind her, felt his hardness against her pelvis, breathed in his hair, his skin, clutched his back as if to save herself from falling.

The alley was dark, but Jeannie, her neck arched, her chin thrust upward, could see that the sky above the low buildings had turned blue in the light of day. She could not stop kissing him, her hand now on his chest, down his stomach, to the front of his jeans.

"Home," she whispered, her lips against his ear. "Come home with me." She paused, remembering. "No, wait, my dad might still be there."

"Better yet," he said, "come with me."

"Where? Your place"—she kissed him—"it's too far—"

"No, come with me. You'll see."

They could hardly pull apart enough to walk, but a block or two more and they were at the Maritime, a chic boutique hotel where Jeannie had had drinks only recently in the dark lobby bar. While Tommy signed for the room and gave his credit card at the reception desk, Jeannie brazenly put her hand on his ass, then ventured between his legs, making him jump and let out a loud "OHHH—sama bin Laden!" at the confused clerk, and five minutes later they were inside, taking off each other's clothes, Tommy first digging in his pocket for a condom.

Later, after making love and sleeping a couple of hours, then making love again, this time slowly, completely, they lay in each other's arms.

"Oh god, what have we done?" Jeannie said.

"Did we fuck it up, or what?" Tommy answered, stroking her hair.

"You think so? Already?"

"Well, what do you think?" he asked.

"I think it was, well, surprising," Jeannie said.

"Now why would you say that? Didn't expect it to be so good, huh?" he teased.

She paused for a moment, thinking. "I didn't expect it to be so . . . physical. I knew we had the friendship thing down. But, jeesh, the sex. As if this was meant to be all along."

Tommy didn't respond and Jeannie got a little nervous.

"Shit," she said. "I didn't mean—"

"I have to tell you something," he said, sitting up and looking at her intently.

She steeled herself against the whack that was sure to come.

"I'm leaving again."

Her stomach fell. "What do you mean? When?" she responded, raising herself up on her elbows.

"Tonight. Late flight."

"But you just got home. We just—" She rolled onto her back, hating to hear herself whine.

"I'll be back soon. A couple weeks, I hope."

"Where this time?"

"Pakistan."

Jeannie was silent. She got up and walked to the window. A chimney across the street blew black smoke in the blue sky. An old woman sitting on a bench below was feeding about a hundred hungry pigeons with a loaf of bread. A man in a business suit, walking and talking on his cell phone while smoking, took one last drag, then threw the butt down. *What, the city isn't dirty enough?*

"Dangerous."

"No more than everywhere else I've been lately. Don't worry about me. It's you—"

"Hey, no need to worry about me, mister," she joked.

"No, Madame Superwoman, I won't," he laughed, as if he'd expected this exact response. He got up and went to her at the window, put his hands on her shoulders, and turned her around to face him. "But I do need to, don't I?"

Yes, please. Let someone worry about me. "No, of course not. What do you mean?"

"What I mean is, Jeannie, let me. Just a little. I want to," he said.

For a moment she couldn't breathe. Her eyes burned. Her throat tightened. Her heart felt as if it would burst, as if all the blood in her body was rushing to that one muscle she couldn't control. Jeannie turned back to the window to see a whorl of leaves circling above the street, then lifting high into the air and blowing away. There were several plastic bags tangled in the branches of the trees. Funny how on a windy day, ordinary garbage was transformed into kites.

"Jeannie," he said, taking her into his arms and kissing her, "this has taken us too damn long."

"Listen, you," she said, kissing him, "far better late than never." And she put both her arms around him and there in front of that window in their hotel room in the middle of the day, with all the litterers, the cell phone talkers, and the sidewalk bike riders, Jeannie found love.

Mouse Trapped

When she got home, there were no traces of her dad's visit and the apartment seemed open and airy. The afternoon light streamed through the windows, making the colors of her living room seem softer and faded. She threw her keys with the pink-haired troll on the counter, put her bag on a stool, and headed down her hallway toward her bedroom. She was exhausted and needed to get some sleep before her show tonight, but with Tommy on her mind, with her body all yummy and sore from the morning, there was no way she'd sleep now. Her adrenaline was running rampant through her like a roller coaster, her heart pumping against her chest like a ping-pong ball off a goldfish bowl, her mind a tilt-a-whirl—the ride that made Jeannie throw up as a kid—

like a veritable carnival of turmoil. She'd go for a swim first.

Halfway down the hall she could hear the snoring. Oh no, had her dad missed his flight? Was he taking a nap? That really pissed her off. He never did get to appointments on time, show up when he said he would. But not wanting to wake him, she walked on tiptoes to the guest room door and stuck her head inside. The room was empty, her dad's Samsonite luggage gone. The only other room left, besides the bathroom (which was not an appropriate place for snoring), was her own. Why would her dad fall asleep in her bedroom? Hell, with her dad, anything was possible. She peeked in hesitantly, afraid of what she might find. And there, lying on the bed, was the horrible truth: snoring hideously, with his mouth wide open and tongue hanging out one side of it, was Mouse.

"No!" she screamed, waking the poor mutt, who in one split second raised his head, looked at her, got up on all fours, and spun around three times before jumping off the bed and running directly to her, his front paws now on her stomach.

No, this can't be happening, thought Jeannie. And then she saw the piece of paper stuck to the dog's collar. She struggled with Mouse for a moment to free the note, he thinking it was a game, his tail wagging, a growl coming from deep in his throat, making it harder for her to get it. At last, it came away in two pieces. She laid them out on her bed, trying to connect the torn edges, and read:

> Dear Jeannie,
> I need you to take care of Mouse while I'm gone.

Jeannie looked up, her hands shaking, her eyes tearing. "Nooooooo," she wailed, making Mouse think, apparently, that this was the beginning of a duet, because he joined in with a howl. Jeannie immediately stopped, glaring at the dog. He stopped too, jumping up on the bed. When she sat and continued to read, he curled into a ball and put his head on her leg.

You didn't think I could take him with me, did you? That would've been cruel. So I leave him for you, just until I get back. Because you never had a dog as a kid, because you always wanted one, because I just had a feeling you could use one right now. And because I never gave you a gift over all these years. Mouse is the best one I could find.

If this mangy mutt was the best, she was afraid to think what would be the worst. She went back to the note.

Be sure you walk him a few times a day and remember to feed him too—a cup of dry at night mixed with a little wet and warm water and a biscuit or two in the morning.
I love you, baby. Hasta la vista!
Your father,
Louis B. Sterling
P.S. Just in case you were wondering, I adopted Mouse from the Animal Rescue Shelter of Santa Rosa. I knew you'd never forgive me if I bought a designer dog. If you have any questions about Mouse, call them. 707-565-9000.

"Fuck fuck fuck!" Jeannie yelled, making Mouse howl again. He jumped off the bed and ran into the kitchen, turned around, his paws slipping on the hardwood floors, and ran back into the bedroom and up onto the bed, like a crazy dog. His front paws were forward and his chest was down, his rear was sticking up, his tongue out, his tail high, like a dog wanting to play, Jeannie figured. She reached out to him and off he went, running like a squirrel, and then came back. But this time he had her beautiful Marc Jacobs bag between his teeth.

"You drop that now!" she yelled. And then, with the inexperience of a person who's never had a dog before, she pulled on the other side of the bag to wrest it from him.

A game. He thought this was a game, and he tugged back and moved his head side to side, yanking on that bag as if it were a rabbit he'd hunted in the woods.

"Stop! Please, Mouse, stop!" She let go, but he shook that bag. The contents flew around the room, her BlackBerry here, her sunglasses there, her notebook, her iPod, her makeup kit, her wallet and its cards all over the place, and Jeannie was sure the crazed canine's bicuspids must've pierced and ripped it by now. *You see? That's what you get for spending so much money on a goddamned purse,* she thought. *It all comes back to bite you in the . . . bag.*

Mouse was overcome with doggie delight. He growled a "come and get me" and wagged his tail furiously.

"I'm going to kill you. Drop that right now, or I. Will. Kill. You."

He must've seen the anger in her eyes. But his stubborn nature, his hunter's ways, and his little stinker of a personality joined forces to make him run around the bedroom and curl up under the desk with Jeannie's bag under him for safekeeping, one of the handles in his mouth to chew.

Oh shit, she thought. *This is all I need.* She picked the ex-contents of her bag from the floor, put them in a pile on her chest of drawers, and then fell onto her bed, exhausted. Lying there, staring at the ceiling, she saw herself with

Tommy up against that wall in that alley, a moment in her life she knew she would never ever forget for its hot, romantic, life-altering quality. Mouse jumped up on the bed and sat on her pillow right next to her face. He scratched his ear with his right rear paw, shaking the bed. Then he yawned. And then he farted.

He looked at her as if to say, "I'm yours."

She looked back and said out loud, "No, you're not. Don't even think about it."

She figured she'd better take the dog for a walk before she hit the pool. She put on sweats and sneakers, grabbed a baggie, and leashed the excited pooch. *Down the elevator and out, to the pier, to the pier,* Mouse seemed to say as he pulled her. But it took a while to get there, for Mouse stopped to pee at every bush, garbage can, and light pole. With his nose to the pavement, he zig-zagged along the sidewalk, until finally he found the right place to poop. So what that it was in the middle of a crosswalk on the West Side Highway, or that the late-afternoon rush-hour traffic was coming right at them as she stooped to pick it up in her little plastic bag. Beggars can't be choosers; at least he did it outside. It was a successful walk all around until, while on the pier, Mouse found something that must've smelled delicious, because he rolled around in it and came up smelling disgusting.

Shit. Exactly. Luckily her sleek bathroom had a stall shower in addition to a tub. For this dog hated the water and it took eight attempts to get him in and keep him there before she got that stuff washed off of him for good. Or at least until the next time he went for a walk.

Normal World vs. Gym World

At six p.m. Jeannie was at the gym and had to open at least five lockers before she found one empty. *Goddamn it, why do people not use locks, for god's sake?* she wondered. *Aren't they afraid their stuff will get ripped off?* It's certainly not out of consideration for others, since a locker without a lock usually means, in the Normal World, that the locker is empty. But in Gym World, you open it, find it full, and have to open another and another before finding an empty one. *How rude,* Jeannie thought. She should steal stuff from these people just to teach them a goddamn lesson.

Normally a small annoyance for Jeannie, today it was magnified. She was still reeling from Tommy's touch, from the lovely words spoken, and then having to say good-bye. She'd spent last night making funeral arrangements for her very much alive father, and the afternoon wishing they were for her guest dog. Not as important, but enough to add insult to injury, her beautiful and expensive bag had been torn to smithereens, and last but not least, her bathroom was soaked and covered in dog hair.

So the swim was important. As she stripped to her underwear, then took off her panties and put on her Speedo to her waist, she watched the women around her parading around naked. There was a woman drying her hair at the mirror who was in her jeans and shoes but topless. Jeannie couldn't help but notice the rose tattoo on her right breast. There was another, entirely nude, having a conversation about her son's Little League coach with another woman who was fully dressed. In Gym World, women are not as concerned with

nudity, like the women in the house on Allston. Perhaps she
was uncomfortable with nudity because she grew up among
bare breasts and even the occasional apparent penis. It
wasn't as if everybody walked around naked, but an unconscious carelessness pervaded. Doors were left open, a towel
was dropped, a phone was answered in haste by someone
half dressed. There was nothing ideological about it (nudity
as a rebellious act against the trappings of bourgeois life and
all that other bullshit). It was the times. It was the place. Permissiveness hung over the house like a dark storm cloud on a
hot summer day.

Jeannie pulled the Speedo's straps over her shoulders and
noticed another Gym World characteristic: people were slobs.
The place was a mess. A Pilates mat class had just ended, so
there was clothing on the floor, benches were covered, and
there was nowhere for a woman to sit. There was a girl,
midtwenties, certainly old enough to know better, who had
left her stuff everywhere while she went to dry her hair, as if it
were okay to throw shit wherever she wanted. Her bag was on
the floor, opened, with a shirt halfway out, her socks on the
floor next to it, her pink pod on the bench with her shampoo
and her *Us Weekly*. She was even using the rest of the bench
for towels, totally oblivious to the people around her.

Jeannie watched her for a moment at the mirror, blowing
her hair. She was wearing tight, low jeans that revealed the
top of a lavender thong, and a matching lacy bra. Her hair
was long and curly and she was taking great pains to bring it
under control, to smooth it, straighten it, pulling a little hair
at a time with her brush, wrapping it down and under and
around the brush, placing the dryer just so in this painstak-
ing way, taking longer for each wrap and roll than Jeannie
took with her whole head of hair.

Finally, to the pool. With each step up the stairs and down the hall, the chlorine smell grew stronger. Now this was a smell Jeannie found intoxicating, powerful in its ability to transport her back to college and her mornings spent swimming laps in the Berkeley pool with its Grecian columns and Moorish tiles. Mornings spent in the cool blue water instead of writing papers on Hobbes's state of nature or why Daniel Bell and all the other neocons could go to hell.

But here, with the smell of chlorine rising with the steam off the pool's surface, the water glistening underneath the glass ceiling and walls that faced the Hudson, Jeannie was in heaven. The sun blazing from the east, on the far side of the city, sent its rays through streets and alleys, then onto the turquoise pool, which sparkled as if strewn with glitter.

Luckily, the pool was not overcrowded. There was only one person in each lane, and one lane was even free. It was on the side, nobody's favorite except hers, because here she had only one other swimmer to contend with. While most swimmers didn't choose the side because of the backwash, she preferred the wall to a person with a wide frog kick. She dropped her towel at the pool's edge and hopped in. The water was cold this evening—or perhaps the chill in her heart cooled the water. She pulled her hair back in a tight ponytail and put on her cap, one of those snug, head binding ones in black, tucking her hair in. With both hands, she tugged on her Speedo under her butt. Then she splashed her left arm first, using her right, with water; then her right, using her left.

Then the plunge. Down straight and a strong kickoff, her arms out straight ahead, the water soft and clear and cool, her body shooting lean and forceful through the water like an arrow.

Then the wall, the turn, the kickoff, and back, her breath now in sync with the rhythm in her head. Every time she swam, regardless of what was on her mind, she cried. Her tears always came and commingled with the water, as if the physical effort allowed her to relax just a little, releasing all the hurt and sadness and disappointment that welled inside her. Her life with men sucked, plain and simple. There seemed to be one kind that haunted her: those, like her dad and Tommy, who came and went, love not enough to make them stay. Of course there was the other male in her life, Mouse, whose love for her, already at 100 percent, she was unable to return.

She felt the water. Body straight, feet fluttering, torso twisting, right arm back, left forward, right coming up, head moving to the right, a breath, then down, air expelled, bubbles, and arm in and ahead as left goes back, all the while the ankles churning, the water yielding to her. The complete and pure action of the body in motion, in the cool, serene blue of the water.

And then, once the rhythm kicked in, once the breathing was in its groove, came the fantasy she had with each and every swim: to fly. With each stroke—right arm out, then in, left arm out, right elbow bent, chin to the side, and breathe—she felt herself soar. Funny how the water made her dream of the air. Like the M. C. Escher print of fish transmuting into birds that had hung in the old house in Berkeley, so was Jeannie transmuted. She swam and got her rhythm and then rose out of the water, her arms turning to wings, busting loose, out through the ceiling and directly into the sky, leaving the gym and the rude people in the dressing room, leaving her show; Harry's threat of its demise; the return of Tommy; her father's funeral plans; making love to

Tommy; Mouse, the stinker; Tommy's departure. The longing in her heart served as propulsion, the fear she'd never live her life fully forced her wings to open, and her desire to love spread them like an eagle and lifted her high into the evening sky.

Up up up, her nose to the wind, her eyes closed, her body held taut to achieve the correct aerodynamics, her chin thrust up and out, she flew. Tonight, straight ahead north to the George Washington Bridge, left over the river, right at New Jersey and north up its palisades, those dramatic, beautiful cliffs an ironic ending to a state you'd never want to go to except, perhaps, to outlet shop.

Dysfunctional Family Values

When she returned to the dressing room forty-five minutes later, she was shocked to find the same young woman still at the mirror. She was applying her makeup—another task that took Jeannie two, maybe three, minutes. A dab of tinted moisturizer, some under-eye concealer, a tiny bit of blush, lip gloss and mascara. All of which she'd taught herself well into her twenties. But this woman had a regimen that included those kinds of makeup items that Jeannie bought when she'd gone in to buy a lip gloss and never used: an eyelash curler, lip liner, eye shadow, glittery pressed powder.

Part of Jeannie felt very superior to the stupid woman at the mirror: she'd been there for almost an hour. Life is short. There's so little time to go to a new movie with friends, much less spend this much time every day doing your hair and makeup. But she also felt a twinge of jealousy, of resentment. Nobody in Jeannie's upbringing had taught her how to use makeup, and sometimes, but only when she thought about it, it saddened her that her mother hadn't been interested. But that wasn't entirely correct: it wasn't that she was not interested, she was disinterested. She felt makeup was unnecessary, that women should be as nature intended, that the only purpose to makeup was attracting men. And men like that weren't worth it. Jeannie's mother had never worn makeup and would have been very disappointed to see Jeannie wearing it today.

Watching the girl at the mirror carefully apply her eye shadow, Jeannie remembered that day when she had been about to turn sixteen and her aunt Lily, the wife of her dad's brother, had come to visit. Aunt Lily was staying at the Claremont Hotel, high up in the hills, with its day spa and its bar that overlooked the entire Bay Area. She dressed the way Jeannie imagined everyone in Palm Springs dressed: matching blouse-and-pant sets, riotous color, coordinated shoes and bag. She had gone to San Francisco to shop for the day and when she came over that night, she handed Jeannie a small bag from Saks Fifth Avenue. Jeannie was excited. Only rarely did she venture into the city to shop; her clothing beat was Telegraph Avenue, with the inexpensive embroidered Mexican blouses and Indian sandals that had now become so popular and cost a fortune. Maybe in the bag was a blouse like the one Lindsey wore, a gift from her mom, a paisley-printed silk top with long flowing sleeves.

Jeannie took the bag into the living room, away from the kitchen where Harriet was, as if she instinctively knew she'd object to its contents. She sat on one of the worn sofas that lined the room. She was excited. She had never been to Saks, had never owned anything from a store like that. She opened the bag slowly, pulling away at the pink tissue paper that filled the glossy gray bag. And there, at the bottom, were little boxes of cosmetics. She took them out one by one. There was lipstick and eye shadow and mascara and concealer. There was powder and eyeliner. All from a company called Estée Lauder.

Jeannie looked up at her aunt and forced a smile. This was Aunt Lily's way of challenging Harriet's ideals. She knew, and she knew Aunt Lily knew, how Harriet would feel about this gift. There was no way Jeannie was going to be able to enjoy it.

Aunt Lily said, "Every girl can use a little makeup, hon. How will you get the boys to notice you without a little color in your cheeks? You're such a pretty girl, too. All you need is—"

"Boys will notice her because she's smart and funny and kind and cares about the world. Not because she's fake and painted."

Jeannie turned to see Harriet standing at the doorway and became flushed with rage and humiliation. She would have done almost anything to be able to steal away to a bathroom, lock herself in for an hour, and try on the makeup. Or, even better, to ask Aunt Lily to show her how to apply it. But she could only hear Harriet's words, see Harriet's face, and she felt compelled to stick up for her.

"You should've asked me first, Lil," said Harriet.

"Asked you? You would've said no and deprived your daughter of yet another thing every other teenage girl in America has."

Harriet's voice rose. "Deprived? You have no idea what deprived is. I—"

"Stop it, both of you!" Jeannie threw the bag at her aunt. "Take it back. Take it all back. Yeah, and if boys, as you call them, only like me with makeup, then they can fuck themselves." Jeannie ran out of the room and up to her bedroom, slamming the door behind her.

Later, after Jeannie's tears had dried, Harriet appeared at her door with the Saks bag in her hand. "You did good, Jeannie. It's always right to be honest. Here, your aunt wanted you to have this to return. You should buy yourself something you want." She handed Jeannie the bag. When she left, Jeannie went to her bedroom mirror and looked at herself. She liked her face enough, but what would her eyes look like with a little liner, her lips with a little gloss? *But in this bag is what I want,* she thought. She hated herself then, but not as much as she hated Harriet.

A week or two later Jeannie ventured into San Francisco to Saks with Lindsey and returned the bag of cosmetics, never allowing herself to try them. Even when the saleswoman asked if she'd like a complimentary makeup session, Jeannie declined.

She and Lindsey went to the juniors department and Jeannie bought the same blouse Lindsey's mom had gotten for her, but in a different color so that it wouldn't appear that Jeannie was a total copycat.

But when she wore that blouse to school the next day, Jeannie felt shabby. It didn't fit right, the color was off, the seams were itchy. It just felt wrong. She hung it in her closet and never wore it again.

Goodbye, Hello

When Jeannie got home, Tommy was sitting on the bench in her lobby under the painting of the number 540, her building's address, his duffel and messenger bag on the floor at his feet.

She was thrilled. "Don't you ever call?" she teased. "We have a device commonly known as the telephone."

"With you, for some crazy reason, I can't plan, do what any normal person would do. And I couldn't just leave, like that. After this morning."

Then he was up and holding her. He kissed her hard on her mouth, which he opened with his own. Forgetting Ahmet, the evening doorman who sat at the desk, forgetting where they were, forgetting their own legs, there was nothing for them at that moment but the kiss, fervent and wet.

"You see?" Tommy said, turning to Ahmet. "I told you I knew her. Next time, you might listen when somebody like me—"

"What happened?" Jeannie looked from Ahmet to Tommy.

"Nothing. Typical doorman . . ."

Jeannie liked Ahmet, found him to be only helpful, and smiled at him apologetically as they got into the elevator. As the door closed, Tommy kissed her again.

"Your flight . . ."

He looked at his watch. "I have forty minutes before I have to catch a cab."

Jeannie smiled. "It'll do."

They barely got inside her apartment and they were on each other again. That is, until Mouse came bounding in, howling, and was on them too. He was up on his hind legs, his front paws wrapped around Tommy's legs, his hips a-humping as if he was joining the fun.

"Come," said Jeannie. "I know a place where we can be alone." She took Tommy's hand and led him down the hallway to her bedroom. Of course, Mouse followed, and it wasn't until they cornered him on the bed and she pulled him by his collar that they were able to kick him out and close the door behind him. He scratched and hit the door and whimpered, but they ignored it.

Afterward, Tommy got dressed quickly. "I have to go," he said.

Jeannie threw on a big T-shirt over her panties. "I know."

He came to her then. "No, really, I have to go. I don't want to, you know. Maybe for the first time ever."

She stroked his cheek. She held his hand. She put a palm up onto his chest.

"I want to be here with you. This is huge for me, Jeannie, to feel this way. Me," he said with a croaky laugh, "me, the Pulitzer whore. Yesterday I would've done anything. Today, look at me."

He kissed her gently, his lips soft and full on hers. He put his hand on the back of her head, cupping it, feeling its weight as she leaned into him. "It feels like overnight, but this has been happening to me over the last ten years. I must have been waiting for you."

She couldn't help it. Her face scrunched up into that hideous lump of lines and frowns that it made when she cried, and the tears came. "I love you, you know." Her stomach lurched, the fear of what she'd just said rising. "I'm sorry, I'm such a—" She waved her hands as if she were swatting away a bee.

"Me too," he said. "You know I do."

"So go. And come back already, would you?" she sniffed, smiling.

He leaned over her and kissed her. She could hear his footsteps down the hall, could hear Mouse bark, following him to the door, heard him pick up his messenger bag and his duffel. She heard the door open, then close, and Mouse's nails tap-tapping on the floor to her room. He stood in the doorway and sat, looking at her with a cocked head.

"Come," she said. "Come here, Mouse." And this time he did. She scratched his ears and he rolled onto his back, so she scratched his chest. It was as if he knew exactly what she needed: someone here, someone now, even if this someone was a canine.

Luce. Jeannie had to tell her. She sat at the edge of her bed and picked up the phone. When nobody answered, she decided not to leave a message. Better to tell her in person where she could see the excitement in her face.

Grand Theft Taxi

Moss stood at the mirror and put a comb through his hair, then his fingers through it to mess it up a little. *Not bad*, he thought, and he buttoned and then unbuttoned the second button on his brown suede jacket, which was really more like a shirt, under which he wore a black T-shirt. He decided to forgo his usual work shirt and jeans, or the requisite suit, which he hated, thinking he should appear authoritative without being intimidating.

This was the fastest buyout he and Marshall had ever accomplished, and though there were still legal details and FCC sanctions outstanding, the deal was going down, and he wanted to tell them himself before it got out and they read it in the *Times*. He couldn't wait to see the look on her face, and the thought of it put a smile on his that spanned ear to ear. *Life is good.*

A few minutes later he was out the door, heading uptown

to the studio, and forced to deal with the number-one aspect of city life that, according to Madame Sterling, was rife with bad behavior: taxis. His Prius was still in the shop. He had taken Marshall's Hummer to get its nick un-nicked. And he didn't feel like calling for his driver. Hell, he'd be normal and take a taxi.

When the elevator arrived in the lobby, Moss walked slowly through it, appreciating its stone, glass, and cherrywood simplicity, like an ode to Frank Lloyd Wright. This lobby was the very reason Moss had bought in this building and he never failed to appreciate it. *The little things*, he thought, *that are essential to one's life.* Moss was greeted by Isa, his favorite doorman, a tall, good-looking Albanian immigrant.

"Your car's not here, Mr. Moss. Want me to call—"

"Not taking the car tonight, Isa. I'll be taking a cab."

"Let me get it . . . ," he said as he loped toward the lobby doors and opened one, letting Moss through.

"You know what? I'm going to get it myself." He put his hands in his pants pockets and looked up at the sky.

"Beautiful night, isn't it?" Isa stood right next to him and stretched his neck upward as well.

Moss looked at him, curious as always about the scar that crossed his neck ear to ear. *Must've been from the war,* Moss thought. He imagined the violence, but never asked.

"You sure I can't get you the taxi?" Isa asked.

Moss turned to him, taking a couple steps backward. "Nah, but thanks. And hey, how's the baby?"

"Sleeping, eating, you know. Living the life."

"Good for him. And good for you. Hey—what'd you find out about going back to school?" Here was this guy, a dentist in his own country, comes to the states for a better life, hell, for life itself, and the best job he can get is doorman without a few more years of dental school.

Isa shook his head. "Too expensive. Maybe in a few years. Maybe."

"Well, we get to keep you, anyway. Lucky for us."

"You have a good one, Mr. Moss," said Isa.

Moss started to walk toward the corner, then turned back to Isa. "You know what? Why don't you get the applications to the schools you're interested in. I'll hook you up with someone at my company. We might be able to help."

"Thank you, sir," Isa said with a grin. "Yes, thank you."

And Moss sprinted to the corner, making a mental note to get one of his guys on this, to get Isa the money. At least he has a family. Someday, sometime, someway, Moss'd like a family too. He'd have a zillion kids. Having grown up an only child, it was not something he'd want to perpetrate on anybody. But it sure as hell wasn't as if he were some young kid who had his whole life ahead of him. If only—but just as he reached the street, a taxi was passing by. Up went his hand and it screeched to a stop. He ran to reach it, and as he did, he saw a woman a block ahead with her arm raised and then on her hip, her body posed in anger.

She yelled at him, "That's my taxi!"

Too fucking bad, he thought to himself. Not that he didn't care, but hell, there was the survival of the fittest thing, not to mention that life happens and he was there first. He climbed in and tried to ignore the woman as they passed slowly by, but with one glance, he realized the woman was Jeannie Sterling herself. Twice in one week. Someone who he'd never seen before. Only in a magical village like New York City.

Shit, she was something. Her hair in the moonlight, that

pissed-off expression on her face, the way she reeked of personality just standing still. He turned to her, smiled through the window, and waved. She seemed to behave this time, and didn't call him a turkey. But he could see a word form in her mouth, could see her lips move, as if the woman could not help herself. There it was on her lips, a simple three-letter word: pig.

Moss yelled out, "Stop!" and, as a second thought, added, "Please, I just need a minute." He flung his door open and stuck his head out, looking back at Jeannie.

"Well, well, well, now I'm a pig? From turkey to pig in a week. Now that's one hell of a metamorphosis."

"Oh Christ, it's you again."

"'Christ' is good. You can call me Christ. It's a whole lot better than 'pig.'" He saw a tiny beginning of a smile form on the corner of her mouth, and then he watched her fight it away. *Stubborn, isn't she.*

"Hey mister, you in or out?" asked the driver.

"This'll only take a minute," Moss answered.

"You stole my taxi," Jeannie said to Moss. "He stole my taxi," she then said to the driver.

"Which is something I am sure you've never, ever done."

"That's right." She looked down at her feet, kicked at a cigarette stub on the ground. "Not intentionally, that is."

"Hmmm. A 'not intentional' theft. Interesting. Is that like 'I didn't mean to shoot the guy even though my loaded gun was in his face'?"

She was silent for a moment and then she said, "Sometimes you have no choice."

"Hey buddy, we leaving tonight?" asked the taxi driver.

"And sometimes you make a mistake," she continued.

"That I can live with. Come on. I'll drop you." He smiled,

saw her hesitate, and added, "It's okay. Get in. You'll be waiting a long time."

She walked very slowly toward the cab, her lips pursed in
amusement, her eyes sparkling as if delighted by this amazing coincidence, as if enjoying the stall.

"Can you believe this one?" said the cabbie. "She's got all
the time in the world."

"Some people, right?" answered Moss. "Hard to fathom."
He watched the wind from the river blow her hair behind
her, the flimsy material of her blouse beneath her open
jacket pulling across her breasts. She was so not his type—
what's with those beat-up old boots and those old jeans and
the way she throws her arms when she walks?—but something about her struck him like a punch in the gut.

"You lied on air," he said as the taxi pulled away from the
curb. "And besides, you don't really own this taxi. I mean, it
isn't really yours, is it? The medallion isn't in your name, or
am I wrong?"

He saw her raise a brow and her smile spread across her
face. "And what're you doing slumming, anyway?" she asked.
"Where's that tank of yours?"

"Getting a touch-up," he said, raising his brows.

She knew very well what he meant. But she continued, "So
how come you don't have a car and driver?"

"You haven't answered my question: do you own this taxi?"
He leaned toward her.

She rolled her eyes upward as she shook her head. "I saw it
before you were even on the street. I flagged it and it flashed
me."

"It flashed you, huh? Hmmm, interesting." Ugh, he hated
stupid double-entendres, but this woman brought out the
worst in him. Then he said, "But it could be argued, could it

not, that since the taxi does not have your name on it, you do not actually own it, and therefore, it isn't yours, per se."

"What are you, a lawyer?" she teased.

"For that matter, one doesn't really own anything, does one, because there's no conclusive evidence that we really *exist*."

"Hmmm, a lawyer-philosopher! So let's talk Kierkegaard. I flagged the taxi, the driver acknowledged me, so it is my taxi for the next ride. He said so in his classic essay 'God and Taxis,' written in 1835, I think it was."

"That doesn't sound like Kierkegaard to me. You're probably talking about Nietzsche. Because Kierkegaard said in his 'Treatise on Name-Calling and Life on the Farm' that calling someone a pig, or a turkey, or a barnyard animal of any kind, is not very nice."

"It may not be nice, but since when is pursuing justice about being nice? I just have an acute sense of justice," she said.

Did she know how ridiculously self-righteous she sounded?

"Lady, I'm not arguing whether you're acute or not. You're definitely a-cute," he said, and winked his most obnoxious wink at her. He could be just as obnoxious as she. He'd prove it.

"You are unbelievably shallow," she said with a *tsk*.

"You have no idea. I bring new depth to the meaning of shallow," he said.

"Ha!" she belted out loudly as she turned her head away in a lame attempt to hide the smile that blew him away. *This woman.* But then she must've realized she hadn't told the driver where she was going, because she said, "Oh, excuse me, I'm going to Broadway and—"

"Vesey," Moss interrupted.

"You know where I'm going?" she asked.

"Of course I do, Ms. Jeannie Sterling, so-called, self-appointed ethical avenger. And don't you have to be there soon? It's after ten."

"Yes I do, thank you very much, Nicholas Moss, self-proclaimed real estate mogul and ladies' man, if you do say so yourself. And you do. All the time, in every interview you give."

"Hey, I can't help it if women—" But he stopped himself because even he thought he was going too far.

They rode in silence the rest of the way across town, she looking out her window and he looking out his. And when they got to City Hall, he could've gotten out with her, but he wanted to savor the surprise, to prolong the joke. So he said good-bye and she thanked him, and everything was completely banal and polite. No strident pronouncements, no name-calling, no teasing or obnoxious attempts at flirting.

That will come later, he thought. *That will definitely come later.*

Love Me, Love My Husband's Butt Crack

Jeannie checked in with the night guard, as she always did. "Hey, Moses. How're you doing tonight?" She signed the log: date, name, time of entry, floor she was going to.

"Just hanging," he said.

I bet you are, thought Jeannie, *like a horse.*

He smiled as if he knew her thoughts.

Moses, the nighttime security guard at 220 Broadway, was hot. Just sitting there in his uniform, sipping on a cup of coffee, watching whatever sport was on TV, just like every night, leaning back in his chair, his feet up on the desk behind the chest-high counter, a copy of *Car and Driver* magazine opened on his thighs, he was a sex god, pure and simple. Some guys just have it. He looked at her long and languidly, his dark eyes simmering with confidence. "You?"

"Me? I'm fine. Like always." What she wanted to say was *How about we take an hour, go upstairs, sneak into the program director's office, and fuck our brains out?* There's nothing like having had recent amazing sex to make a girl feel sexier.

"Glad to hear it. And if ever you're not, I'm always here, Jeannie, if you need me."

"Thanks, Moses."

"I mean it."

Is he thinking what I'm thinking?

He must've read her look, because he smiled. Then he said, "Take elevator three, okay?"

"Yup, see you later," she said as she walked through the lobby to the elevator bank.

"Good show!" he yelled after her.

The elevators, except for number three, were shut off for the night, as were half of the lights. She wondered what this lobby looked like during the day, when all eight elevators were running and people filled its walls. Now, it was eerie and quiet, only partially lit.

Up on the eleventh floor it was empty as always. The reception area, behind the glass wall with the red logo for WBUZ RADIO, 660 AM was still messy. Cups half-filled with coffee sat on the tables, newspapers were piled on a chair, and bits and pieces of paper were on the floor. Detritus from the day. Jeannie could hear the hum of a vacuum that would be back in the cubicle area by now but had yet to make it this far.

She picked up the phone on the wall. "It's me," she said, hung up, and heard the latch on the door that led to the inner sanctum.

The fluorescent lights were blinding and the speakers deafening in the hallway that held the studios. Larry Longfellow, the controversial criminal attorney, was live on air and ranting about the recent shooting by cops of a kid in Brooklyn. As she passed his studio, Studio A, she could see him through the glass windows, past the engineering booth. She waved, and he waved back, without a beat missed in his rap.

The next studio, Studio B, was home to Dr. Susan Bittman, Jeannie's nemesis if there ever was one. The studio was dark, of course, since Dr. Bite Me, as Jeannie so maturely referred to her, held the highly coveted daytime slot of seven to ten a.m., drive time. And why? Because her show was about sex and relationships. Good and bad behavior got you two a.m., love and blow jobs got you mornings. And a normal life. And a commensurate salary, as her vast supply of Manolos illustrated.

Jeannie told herself to stop being a baby. Her time would come. Hopefully while she was still able to get around without a walker.

It didn't work. The only thing that made Jeannie feel better about Dr. Susan Bite Me was that her butt was bigger than Jeannie's.

Studio C was Jeannie's. And when she got there, Joseph was already setting up and yelling something about the playlist, and Luce was at the computer, reading e-mails for changes to spots, things like that. Joseph was working the board to test the mics, sound levels, and timers. He was wearing a T-shirt that said ONE TEQUILA, TWO TEQUILA, THREE TEQUILA, FLOOR.

"Hey, gang," said Jeannie, peeking her head through the open doorway into the engineering area, outside the studio. It was set up like a studio within the studio, with glass on both sides—to the hallway and to the studio itself.

"Speak of the devil. So, Jeannie, when're we changing the goddamn bumper? I hate this goddamn music," Joseph complained. "It's about the stupidest—"

"Hey, Jeannie," Luce said, not moving her eyes from her laptop screen, "I'm late with the commercial . . ."

Jeannie ignored them both. "You will not believe who gave me a ride tonight."

"Okay, who?" Luce said, still buried in her laptop.

"Come on," Jeannie whined.

Luce looked up. "Well, whoever it was, you sure look great tonight." She narrowed her eyes. "What's up with you?"

Jeannie rolled her eyes. "First guess. No? Okay, Nicholas Moss."

"No way. That's funny."

Jeannie was silent, thinking for a moment about how she was going to get Luce out of there to tell her about Tommy.

Luce went back to typing. "He's cute, isn't he?"

"Who?" Jeannie asked, wondering if she meant Tommy, as Joseph turned in his chair.

"Who," Luce answered sarcastically.

"What?"

"Moss! We're talking about Nicholas Moss."

Jeannie let out a sigh, shaking her head. "He's obnoxious. He's old."

"Not so old," said Luce, raising one brow. "You've had older."

Jeannie smiled, raising a brow. "And younger."

"Ladies," Joseph interrupted. "Please. Do I tell you about my love life? Do I get all personal and intimate in here?"

"Would you?" asked Jeannie.

"Please?" asked Luce.

"You don't have the time or the guts to hear about my love life. It could fill books. It could break records."

"Yeah, for animal husbandry," said Jeannie. "Luce, can I talk to you for a minute?"

Without looking up from her screen, Luce answered, "Sure, go on, I need to finish—"

"Lu-uce. Please," whined Jeannie. This time Luce turned to Jeannie to see her nodding toward the door, her eyes imploringly wide.

"Let me just fini—"

But Jeannie grabbed her by her pink cashmere sweater and took her out into the hall. Joseph could see the two women talking through the window but couldn't hear a word.

"Okay, so what's so important?" said Luce, crossing her arms and leaning on one foot, like an elementary school teacher.

"Luce," Jeannie said breathlessly, "Tommy and I. Well, we . . . Tommy and I slept together and we're, well—"

"Excuse me. You what? When? When were you going to tell me?" Luce grabbed Jeannie's arms. "Was it fun? What happened? I want details, woman. Details!" She was in Jeannie's face. "You vill talk. You vill tell me everyzing, or else!"

Jeannie looked over her shoulder to see Joseph at the studio doorway, but she continued, "Okay, well first we walked, then he kissed me. Right on the street, against a wall. Oh god, Luce, it was—"

"Whoa there, lady. I do not want to hear about this," said Joseph, his hands over his ears.

"Hello? Nobody invited you."

"Methinks we have a prude in our midst," Luce teased. "You embarrassed? Huh?"

Jeannie walked up so close to him that she could see the individual hairs growing out of his long sideburns. And she whispered, "You don't want to hear about his tongue down my throat, his hard body, and I do mean hard in every sense of the word, rubbing up against my—"

"Stop! Please. I'm outta here," said Joseph as he turned back in to the studio, letting the door close behind him.

Larry Longfellow's voice was booming out of the speakers, "What we need is a police force better trained and prepared for . . ."

"So tell me," said Luce. "Everything that happened, every single detail."

"Oh god, Luce. It was amazing. It was beautiful. And it was, mmm, well, you know, perfect. Except one thing."

"Uh-oh."

"He's gone again."

"You mean he gets you in bed and says, 'Sayonara, Ms. Sterling'?"

"You know his work. He has no choice."

"I know. But I care about you. And I love Tommy, you know I do, and I love you with Tommy, but . . ."

"What."

"You deserve to be loved, Jeannie. By someone on the same continent."

Jeannie let out a big sigh, as if accepting her man-fate.

"But don't you ever wonder . . ."

Jeannie didn't have the patience for Luce to gather her thoughts.

"Wonder what? Come on, Luce, you're making me crazy."

"Wonder, I don't know, about the stars?"

Jeannie was about to wrap the fucking computer around Luce's scrawny neck. "What the hell does that mean? The stars!"

"Don't get mad. I didn't want to talk about this. You asked me to talk about this."

"I can still get mad."

"Not really, you can't. You have to listen and be open-minded."

"Okay. I'll be open-minded. So what's this star shit?"

"That's open-minded?"

Jeannie just looked at her.

So Luce spoke very slowly and carefully, and said, "I guess I'm talking about fate. What we're in for in our lives. How things happen. It's funny—" She stopped herself.

"You can say that again," said Jeannie, thinking of Tommy.

And then, Luce said, "You, Jeannie, deserve more than you ask for. You should feel as entitled as the entitled people you hate."

"Aw, Luce," replied Jeannie. "Not everybody is you and Spike."

"You think me and Spike are perfect? I know it may seem that way, but we have our differences. I mean, I married a man who likes to, well, how do I put this? To putter. Look at me. I wear Prada. He wears a tool belt. And when he's on the floor fixing his computer, you can see his butt crack. It's a very sad thing. But this is not about Spike and me. This is about you falling in love with a great guy who happens to have a job that takes him away. A lot. For long periods of time."

"You think Tommy's too good for me, don't you?" Jeannie couldn't understand why Luce was being so negative.

"Jeannie! I'm going to shoot you. I just want you, once, to

think about your needs. Tommy is special. Hello? Who's known him longer? I played Capture the Flag with him when I was a kid, for god's sake. I'd just love to see you in a relationship with someone attainable. Here. Now. In the flesh. Besides, come on, you know Tommy. A different girlfriend every week."

At another time, on another day, Jeannie would have appreciated Luce's loyalty and would've given her a hug, and Luce would've blushed and gotten defensive, saying this was just what good friends do—they watch each other's backs and tell the truth. But today, given that the relationship had just begun a minute ago, and that Jeannie was high as a kite and all those wonderfully cliché things one feels when one falls in love, and also that Luce was cutting very close to the bone, Jeannie felt her blood rising, the anger, the resentment, welling in her throat. "Just because you have Spike doesn't mean I can't have someone. In your eyes, nobody is for me. Am I that weird? That unlovable? You know what? Forget it."

"That's not what I was saying. I just think you might have to talk to Tommy, not now, I mean I know it's all new, but if—"

Joseph peeked his head over the wall of the cubicle. "Ladies, we're on in ten minutes. You might want to familiarize yourselves—"

"Shut up!" Jeannie and Luce yelled in unison. Then they just stood there, looking at each other.

Finally, Luce said, very quietly, "That's just it, Jeannie. You deserve to be loved. In a thunderous-applause, a-million-stars-in-the-sky kind of way. And I'm certain Tommy loves you like that. Or else he's a baboon."

Jeannie laughed at her friend's silly choice of words. Then she said, "Okay, truce? At least for tonight?"

"Truce," Luce said.

"Okay," Jeannie said.

"Just one thing," Luce said.

"Jesus, what now?"

"You, who are so brave in so many ways, are such a wuss in the love department. What happened to you to make you so afraid to tell someone what you need?"

"Our relationship—or this new part of it—is about five minutes old! I should tell him what I need?" Jeannie couldn't tell Luce how she really felt, that, whether five minutes or five years, it was difficult for her to actually tell a man she cared for what she wanted.

"Eight minutes, ladies!" shouted Joseph from down the hall. "Let's go, already! And don't embarrass me."

Stranger in a Strange Land

Harry met Moss the minute he walked through the WBUZ doors. He'd been jittery all night, anxious about Moss's arrival. How was he going to tell everybody? How was he going to convince them that they wouldn't lose their jobs, especially when he couldn't convince himself? Of course, it was early in the game: the offer had been accepted, but that was as far as the deal had gone. There were many miles to go before they slept, or were canned, or however the poem goes, thought Harry.

Harry warmly offered his hand. "Mr. Moss, good to see you again."

Moss firmly took Harry's hand in his. "It's Moss, or Nick, but no 'Mr.,' please. Makes me feel so damn old."

Harry laughed, folding his arms over his belly. "Know what

you mean. Every year I keep getting older. I don't understand it. I just know I don't like it."

Now it was Moss's turn to laugh. And the two men continued to walk the hall.

"Hey, so this is our humble abode. Want to meet some folks? Jeannie's about to go on the air, but—"

"Let's save Jeannie for last." He smiled. "I wouldn't want to interrupt the show."

"And, uh, Moss, nobody knows yet, about you, that is."

"Well, now's as good a time as any, right? Let's do this thing."

The two men, one tall and lean and dressed elegantly, his black slacks fitting so well they seemed made for him—and probably were—the other short and round, his brown slacks bunching over his ass and hanging low under his stomach, were an unlikely pair. Harry introduced Moss to Sue, an assistant; Marla, a booker; and Jenna, producer of *The Larry Longfellow Show,* drawing a hush of surprise and fear from them when they heard he was the new owner of the station. When Moss was introduced to Larry himself, Larry made it clear that he was angry that the station had been sold without one word to their big moneymaking stars.

"What the hell is going on out there?" asked Jeannie through her mike from her inner studio.

Joseph and Luce turned, and Joseph said, "Not sure." Then he looked at the clock on the wall and said, "We have a minute, let me check."

Joseph made his way through the crowd toward Harry. He was introduced to Moss, and shook his hand and said "No shit!" when he learned that Moss had bought the station.

"You gonna keep us in our jobs? Or you feeling like we need some change here?"

"Hey, you guys do great. I need time to look things over but I can't imagine any big changes occurring in the foreseeable future."

"Interesting concept, 'foreseeable future,'" said Harry. "If the future was foreseeable we'd put the psychics out of business."

Moss put a hand on Harry's shoulder. And Joseph returned to the studio. There was less than a minute to airtime.

"So what's going on?" Jeannie said.

"Joseph, tell us," said Luce.

Hell if Joseph was going to give it away. But he did smile. "You ready? We're on in forty."

"Joseph! Come on!" said Jeannie. "This is unfair. What the hell is happening?"

From the studio, Jeannie still couldn't make out the hubbub in the hallway. People were shaking hands, laughing. There were some nervous faces. The commotion was distracting, and it pissed her off when she was in the middle of a show and something was going on down the hall.

Then she saw him. There, in a sliver of a view through the crowd, she spotted Nicholas Moss. *What the hell,* she thought, *was that guy doing here?* Her heart pounded against her chest like a drum sounding a beat of warning.

"Luce, look. It's Nicholas Moss. There, see?"

"Oh my god," said Luce. "What's he doing here, buying the station or something?"

"Yeah, right," chuckled Jeannie.

Both women turned to Joseph in unison, but he just smiled and said, "Twenty . . ."

She turned to look at Moss again, who just at that moment saw her. Their eyes locked. He smiled, and then he winked.

"The asshole winked at me!" she said, throwing her head back in frustration, hitting the frame of the *Sterling Behavior* poster, which was about half the size of Bite Me's. "Shit," she said aloud, rubbing the back of her head.

Joseph was already giving them the hand, his fingers counting, three, two, one, " . . . and we're live."

STERLING BEHAVIOR

JEANNIE: *Tonight's topic . . . bad behavior at the gym. Have you ever noticed how there's Gym World and there's Normal World, and how different the two are? I mean, in Normal World, would you get naked in front of complete strangers or leave a mess in someone else's living room or not lock your car if there were valuables in it? Would you park in front of a fire hydrant or steal an old lady's purse? I'm talking metaphors here.*

LUCE: *Well, you might get naked in front of a stranger, I mean I wouldn't, um, not now, anyway, being married and everything, not that I was ever really into strangers per se, but you know what I mean.*

JEANNIE: *But a room full of them?*

LUCE: *Okay, Jeannie, I think this is a topic that touches people's nerves, because the phones are going crazy. Sally's on the line.*

JEANNIE: *Hi, Sally, Jeannie Sterling here.*

SALLY: *Hello, Jeannie. I'm calling from beautiful downtown Bayonne; I mean, it's not really beautiful, I'm just kidding arou—*

JEANNIE: *You're up late for a gal from Jersey.*

SALLY: *It's the only time I have to myself, Jeannie. With three little ones and a husband who acts like a little one . . . like just the other day—*

JEANNIE: *But you digress.*

SALLY: *I do digress! All the time! That reminds me of when—*

JEANNIE: *Sally, you're digressing again . . .*

SALLY: *I think it's from being a full-time mom. You go nuts. I mean, my oldest is always telling me that I talk to myself.*

JEANNIE: *I talk to myself and I don't have kids. But, tell me, what happened at your gym that you'd like to share with us tonight?*

SALLY: *I work out at the local Y, which has a pretty nice gym in it. Plus it's got a playroom for the kids, which is pretty convenient. The kids get to read and color—*

LUCE: *It is so nice when they provide services like that!*

SALLY: *It would be impossible for me to go otherwise. My kids aren't in school yet, but—*

JEANNIE: *Sally? Where are you going, Sally? Stay with us!*

LUCE: *You have three kids under kindergarten age?*

SALLY: *Eighteen months, three, and four.*

JEANNIE: *Yikes! You have earned the right to digress!*

SALLY: *Well, we wanted three kids. We just didn't intend for them to happen so quickly. I only met my husband when—*

JEANNIE: *Sally . . .*

SALLY: *Okay, so here's what happened Now remember this is a Y and it's nothing fancy and there isn't a ton of equipment. So I like to begin with fifteen minutes on the bike and then do another thirty of elliptical. And every morning—well, not every morning, because I only go to the gym on Mondays—*

JEANNIE: *Sally . . .*

SALLY: *—yes, right, so this old woman—well, she's not so old, maybe sixty or so, which today, in the scheme of things—*

JEANNIE: *Sally!*

SALLY: *Sorry, sorry. So, she puts her towel and her bottle of water and her headphones on an elliptical machine and then she goes into the dressing room . . .*

JEANNIE: *She "claims" a machine and walks away? For how long?*

SALLY: *I clocked her at twelve minutes.*

JEANNIE: *Completely unacceptable. But, let me ask you this: were other ellipticals available? Or was she claiming the last one? Because it does make a difference. It is a nuance but an important one. If there are other machines available, her bad behavior isn't unethical because it doesn't exclude someone else from using the machines.*

SALLY: *Sometimes it's the last one, sometimes there may be one or two others available. But it's the principle! I mean, who the heck does she think she is? Why does she think it's all right for her to put a machine out of use for over ten minutes when they are in such demand? Not to mention that there is a sign that says "30 Minutes Maximum on Each Machine."*

JEANNIE: *So, she puts her stuff on the machine, walks away, and then gets on it for thirty minutes, and thereby actually uses it for forty. Where does she go? Do you have any idea?*

SALLY: *I think she goes to the bathroom and then chats with everyone on her way there and back.*

JEANNIE: *Ooooohhh. A gym chatter. Don't you just hate them?*

LUCE: *Come on, Jeannie. You're saying you've never stopped to chat with anyone at the gym?*

JEANNIE: *Of course I have. To say hello. To make a date for a real chat. But let me take a moment here to be clear about something in case you weren't sure. I. Am. Not. Perfect. Even I have done some of the foul deeds we've discussed on this show. I have never claimed to be 100 percent Sterling-behaved all the time. I mean, I called that guy, you-know-who, a turkey!*

LUCE: *Uh-huh.*

JEANNIE: *I'm more like 98 percent Sterling-behaved.*

LUCE: *And I'm Uma Thurman.*

JEANNIE: *So, Sally, have you said anything to the rude woman who hoards the elliptical?*

SALLY: *Well, last week, I, well, I, um . . .*

JEANNIE: *It's okay Sally, we're all friends here. You can tell us.*

SALLY: *Well, I cursed her.*

LUCE: *You mean you swore at her?*

SALLY: *No, I mean I actually cursed her. I told her she would die an early death.*

JEANNIE: *You mean you put a curse on her?*

LUCE: *Really?*

JEANNIE: *You're kidding. What did she say?*

SALLY: *Nothing. But I think I scared her. I haven't seen her since.*

JEANNIE: *Maybe she died.*

LUCE: *Jeannie!*

JEANNIE: *Well, maybe the curse worked.*

LUCE: *Maybe it's time for a commercial. Thanks, Sally—*

JEANNIE: *Yes, thank you, Sally, for speaking up against rudeness. Now that's Sterling Behavior.*

LUCE: *And we'll be back in a few minutes.*

Full Frontal

It had taken more self-control than Jeannie could muster to stay focused on the show, what with Moss walking around and being introduced to everyone by Harry. By the time Jeannie swigged some water and took off her headgear, Harry and Nicholas Moss had entered the studio. Moss was being introduced to Luce, whose back was to Jeannie, but after introductions, Luce turned her head to Jeannie and silently mouthed, "Oh. My. God," her eyes wide, her brows raised. Then he was talking to Joseph, Jeannie could see beyond the glass. Moss had his hands in his pockets in that way of his and apparently said something that cracked Joseph up. Now Joseph seemed to be giving him a tour of the console.

Then they were at the interior glass door of her studio, where she was pretending to be busy with something, anything. And in walked Harry and Luce and Mr. Nicholas Moss.

Harry said, "And this is the famous Jeannie Sterling, host of our very successful talk show on—"

"Rude behavior," said Moss. "Yes, we've met." He stuck his hand out to shake hers.

She accepted the offer. "Nice to see you again, Mr. Moss."

"You know each other?" asked Harry. Then he remembered. "Oh yes, your Hummer."

"Not my Hummer, Harry. It was my—"

"—gigantic Hummer that you were driving. Does it matter who pays the bill? Still rationalizing," said Jeannie.

"Still a kook," said Moss.

"Jeannie, I have something to tell you. Moss—"

"—doesn't grow on trees!" said Jeannie with a goofy laugh, too loud, too self-conscious, and too alone.

"Well, this one might. Jeannie, Moss is the new owner of WBUZ."

Jeannie blinked. Joseph hit his thigh with his palm. Luce gulped. Harry demurred. Moss smiled. Jeannie let out a yelp. She immediately covered her mouth with the palm of her hand. She felt naked standing there, unable to clothe her feelings, to cover her embarrassment, to cloak her fear and anger. This jerk, this turkey in a Hummer, was now her boss.

Satan's Spawn

Getting into her apartment elevator, Jeannie felt relieved to have the entire weekend ahead of her to catch up on sleep and errands, and to go through the seven stages of grief over the sale of WBUZ. She was already at anger, but she had a long way to go before acceptance.

She could hear the howling as the elevator passed the fourteenth floor. She thought it sounded like Beethoven's Fifth—*yelp yelp yelp howwwwwwl, yelp yelp yelp howwwwwwwl*. By the time she got to the seventeenth floor, the canine symphony had reached its crescendo, making Jeannie sure she would receive an eviction notice or at least a stern warning from the co-op board. But the minute the elevator opened on her floor, the pianissimo must have kicked in, because the howling turned into a whimper. By the time she'd slid her key into the lock and the door clicked open, the concert was over. The dog was eerily silent. She carefully, slowly opened the door and there, jumping up on her, was Mouse, her new beagle/basset/something mix, or as she would come to think of him, her Dog From Hell.

The smell hit her like a ton of bricks. And there it was, poop on her shiny wooden floor, and in the corner, her beautiful white wall tinted yellow with a puddle of pee below. First she yelled at Mouse and then she grabbed some paper towels, picked up the poop, and dropped it in the garbage, as Mouse watched her from the comfort of the couch. Then more paper towels and Windex and the place was cleaned. She looked at Mouse lying there in a ball, his head stretched up on the arm of the couch as if waiting for a massage—or the guillotine. What was her dad thinking? She was going to kill him when he got back. If he came back. The thought that he might not return at all got Jeannie a little panicky. There was no goddamn way in hell she was keeping this vile mutt. Why would a single girl want a dog anyway? Having one is a huge responsibility. You have to walk it, feed it, keep a schedule. It curtails your freedom. You need to plan, to be home at specific times or hire a dog walker. There's no spontaneity in that. And look at this dog. Now walking to the hydrangea, digging in its dirt, and back to the couch, with something hanging out of his mouth. *What the hell is that?* As she approached him, he ran away.

"Come here, Mouse," she said. "Come here, boy."

He took a few steps toward her.

"That's it, fella." She saw it then: what he held between his teeth were the panties she'd worn yesterday. The worn panties that had been thrown in the hamper to be washed were now covered with dirt and in his mouth. "That's gross," she said. "But at least someone wants to get in my pants." It was a Hanro thong. "Mouse, give me those right now." The softest cotton in the world. Obviously Mouse agreed. He turned and bolted. "Hey, wait a minute, you!"

He ran to the hydrangea and proceeded to dig in the dirt again, this time to rebury her panties. At least he didn't insist on a fresh pair.

I'm going to kill my dad. He could've brought her a little Coton de Tulear, like her friend Liz's, all cute and fuzzy. But no, he brings her this little stinker.

Her mind segued to Moss, another male she wanted to kill, another stinker. Who knew what he had planned for the station, but she was sure she could kiss the comfort, and more importantly, the independence of her little show good-bye.

And now this dog. Luckily, she remembered that her friend Liz said she had the greatest dog walker on earth. So she waited until eight a.m., when she knew her friend would be up and getting ready for a run, and then gave her a call.

"All dogs need training," said Liz, with a yawn, when she heard about Mouse. "Isaiah will change your life."

The only life-changing Jeannie needed was a dogectomy.

"Isaiah?" she asked when the deep voice answered the phone.

"That would be me," he answered. "And with whom do I have the pleasure of speaking?"

"Hi, my name is Jeannie Sterling. I'm a friend of Liz—"

"Not *the* Jeannie Sterling? The one with the talk show?"

"That's me."

"Girl, you are my hero. You want your dog walked? I'm your man."

"But I must warn you: this is no ordinary dog. This is a devil dog. He is terribly behaved. He pees and poops in the apartment, he howls, he chewed my beautiful new bag, and he stole my . . . my underwear and buried them in a house-plant."

Isaiah laughed.

"You laugh, do you? What, may I ask, is so funny?"

"It's weird, right? That you, General of the Good-Behavior Brigade, should own a dog like that."

"I'd laugh too, except the smell of Windex mixed with dog pee is making me nauseous. I really need your help, Isaiah. More than dog walking, I need a dog trainer who is experienced with exorcisms."

They decided on eleven that morning for Isaiah to come by and meet Mouse.

"But do me a favor, first," said Isaiah. "Call the shelter where Mouse is from and get his history, okay? Find out as much as you can. Where he's from, how long he was there, whether he was hanging out in purgatory or made it all the way to Hades and back."

Since it was too early to call California, and since Mouse had recently peed and pooped—right in the safety of her own living room—she figured he could wait for his walk and she'd feed them both. First a cup of dry for him, the stuff her dad had smuggled in his Samsonite. And a couple eggs, scrambled, with a little cheddar, for her. He gobbled his down in about three seconds flat. She never had a chance with hers. When she turned to put the egg pan into the sink, Mouse climbed on a stool and then on the counter—on all fours—and ate the eggs right off the dish.

"Okay, you! That's it!" Jeannie cried, shooing him off the counter. "We're going out."

Jeannie took him over to the river, where so many others were walking their dogs. She was pleased to see Mouse get along with other dogs so well, his tail wagging furiously and his nose sniffing lots of doggie butts. Spending time in a shelter must have socialized him well. He peed a little but didn't poop, of course, because he'd already done that this morning.

Their only mishap occurred between Mouse and a big boisterous Lab that was being walked with one of those retractable leashes. The dog's human, if you could call her that, since she was more Neanderthal in brain capacity, had let the dog out a hundred feet and the cord was tripping people and other dogs, blocking the path. Jeannie just wished she had a pair of scissors with her. She knew what she'd do.

By the time they got back, Mouse was tired. He jumped up on her couch, clawed at it several times, and curled up in a ball. She called the shelter.

A girl with a squeaky voice answered. Jeannie asked to speak to someone who could give her information about a recently adopted dog that was now living with her in New York. She was put on hold.

She looked at Mouse, wondering if he could sense what she was doing, if he was aware that she was pissed, that she had no intention of keeping this hog of a hound, that she was outraged by his behavior and offended by his bathroom habits. But there he was, lying on her beautiful, expensive couch, licking his privates. When she saw that he was licking the couch as well as his balls, she realized that her instinct to buy Ultrasuede, which she had been told was virtually indestructible, had been right. A zillion short white hairs were all over the couch too. "Shit," she said aloud.

"No, not you, sorry about that." Someone had finally come to the phone. "I'm just watching my new dog shed all over my beautiful sofa."

"That's what dogs do, hon. Unless you get the kind that doesn't."

"Yeah, well, next time I'll make sure I do my homework before someone dumps an adopted dog on me."

"Hmmm. A sarcastic New York City girl. You called for information? What is the name of the dog and the person who adopted him?" She had a deep Southern twang.

"My dad just adopted him. Lou Sterling." She liked being called a New York City girl. Made her feel like a true native instead of the California expat that she was.

"Oh yeah, I remember, a nice older gentleman. Said he wanted a dog for his daughter. That's you, huh? Well, you got yourself one nice dog, don't you? A little dirty perhaps, that Mouse." She pronounced his name with two syllables, like My-youse.

"Dirty? What do you mean—"

"Well, he would sometimes do his business in his crate."

"Yeah, well he did it in my apartment today."

"And then roll around in it."

"That I was spared. Today. I thought he was housebroken." *Did she say that Dad had adopted the dog specifically for me? The rotten, no good—*

"He is, but he's also a little high strung, and probably a little scared to be back in a new place."

"What do you mean 'back'? He's been adopted before?"

"A couple of times, I think."

Jeannie couldn't believe this. She had a dog that human families had adopted and then returned. "What happened? Why—how old is he?"

"He's about two years old, a basset/beagle mix."

"I'd really like to know what happened."

"Well, one time there was another dog and they didn't get along. Wasn't Mouse's fault."

"Okay . . ."

"Next time, we found him wandering the streets out here. The family was too permissive. We took him back."

"Yeah . . ."

"One time—"

"There's another time?"

"—this nice young couple took him to the city, but they traveled a lot and then they had a baby, and, well, it just didn't work out."

"I can relate."

"And then—"

"You're kidding."

"—another time there was a death in the family and they just couldn't keep Mouse anymore."

"Maybe he was responsible."

There was a roaring silence. "And another family just wouldn't take the time to train him."

"That's five! Any more?"

"That's all I'm aware of, hon."

Jeannie looked over at the couch and saw the dog hop off

and run to the window, yelping at the bird on the other side, running back and forth, his long ears flying behind him like wings, as if he were a bird himself.

"He is pretty cute though," she confessed.

"Yes, he has that," said the Southern belle on the phone.

Jeannie's built-in alarm system went off. Bells were ringing, gongs clanging, sirens wailing. *As in, not one thing else? Or, as opposed to everything else?* "He has that? What the hell does that mean? Have I got myself a psycho dog?"

"No honey, you've got yourself a wonderful hound dog who needs consistency, a good amount of patience, and a lot of exercise. You up for that, doll? This dog just needs a commitment, that's all. He's had some bad luck. But all he needs is a whole lotta love."

Jeannie watched Mouse chase the bird that was hanging there in the sky, floating on the breezes from the river. He was going crazy, running right a few steps, then up on his hind legs, his front paws on the window, then left and back again, the whole time howling and barking so loud she had to go down the hall to be able to hear Miss Priss on the phone.

"And how'd he get this name, Mouse?"

"Mouse? His name isn't Mouse. Why, that's a silly name for a dog. His name is Mouse."

"Excuse me, I'm not understanding. His name is not Mouse? But you just said it was Mouse."

She laughed a cute little Southern belle laugh, like the tinkling of wind chimes that Jeannie wanted to tear off with her fangs and bury in the bushes.

"It must be me. I always forget I have an accent. His name is Mouse, M-Y-L-E-S. Mouse."

"Do you mean Myles? His name is Myles?"

"That's it, honey, Mouse."

Now Jeannie had to laugh, making Mouse or Myles or whatever the hell his name was turn, look at her, and run down the hall to sniff her pant leg and then jump up on his hind legs for a pat on the head, which Jeannie gave him.

"Though he could also be called 'Nose,'" she continued, "since his whole thing is about his nose. He's a hunter, you know."

"Yeah, he's already proven himself," Jeannie said, thinking of her torn panties buried in the hydrangea.

"So, you clear on everything, hon? You got yourself one wonderful dog. Just get a trainer if you need one. Don't be afraid to ask for help."

"Thanks," said Jeannie, hanging up. *Ask for help. Five fucking times. It's as if this dog doesn't want to be adopted.* She narrowed her eyes at Mouse and said, "You trying to get sent back to the shelter? Well, over my dead body, buddy. You're mine now. So watch your ass." Jeannie wasn't one to shy away from a challenge.

Then she said, "But I can't call you Myles. Way too preppy. I'm going to stick with Mouse."

Maybe what she needed was more information. She turned on her computer and went surfing for background on Mouse's breeds. Even after she learned that he was smart and stubborn, that he howled and hunted, she decided she'd keep him until her dad came home. Then, if he didn't take him back, she'd elevate the returns to six.

Of course Jeannie was angry that the shelter and her father weren't more conscious of his breed and what it predicted about his behavior, and what it said about his needs. This dog should be living on a farm, with acres to run and squirrels to chase. Dogs' breeds said much about their needs and personalities; everybody knew that. She had always espoused on her show that nobody in America, or at least in a city or suburb or anywhere with a population larger than two, should own a pit bull. Wasn't she the one who always said that a pit bull or even a pit bull mix might be "cute" today, but would bite your face off tomorrow? Didn't she rant about that couple she'd met walking by the river with their pit bull and their toddler and how the mom had said, "Oh, but he's so gentle and loving and protective." And how Jeannie had thought she should be brought up on child abuse charges? That the dog was genetically predisposed to be aggressive, that no matter how much love or care you give it, a pit bull is a pit bull is a pit bull.

So why had she ignored her own principles of biological determinism and decided to keep this dog that 1) howled (and could get her evicted), 2) hunted (and therefore had inherited terrible food behavior that was almost impossible to change, since it was a self-rewarding behavior—"Sure, I'm getting yelled at for being on the dining-room table, but hell, this hummus is pretty good"), 3) was fiercely stubborn and intelligent (the worst duo in dogdom), 4) was independent and for whom loving and being loved was not a given but had to be earned (for this, she could've gotten a cat), and finally 5) might have been starved or abused as a puppy, which could explain his terrible manners (though what would explain the panties in the hydrangea, she wasn't sure).

Because he was cute. He had that. And Jeannie had a terrible habit of falling for cute. So she spent the weekend walking the dog and training the dog and feeding the dog and walking the dog and cleaning up after the dog and walking the damn devil dog.

Taking It Up a Notch

It was silly, but he wanted to do it. He rarely got so involved and he knew he'd pull back right after this, but he wanted to be at the meeting himself, if only to get a better picture of how it worked. And maybe for himself too. Because there was something wild, something energizing and nutty about the radio station that turned him on. Not unlike the trees he climbed. Unsteady, unyielding, and so unpredictable that you had to be creative to deal. So all week he'd been making the rounds, talking to the staff of the top five shows, to let them know what he expected of them.

And tonight it was *Sterling Behavior*'s turn. Harry had told him this was a first. Normally, if Harry had something to say, he'd just come in and say it. And normally, Moss would've let Harry do it how he wanted to. He didn't usually have the time or the interest to deal at this level. But this time, he wanted to say it all himself. And it had absolutely nothing to do with that Jeannie Sterling. Nothing.

Normally, he'd be off in his Gulfstream G550, his beautiful jet, to Napa, where his private airstrip led right to his home, a hacienda-style farmhouse that sat in a lush, warm, sun-filled valley, surrounded by his vineyards. Just over an hour from his favorite, secret tree-climbing place about ten miles up the coast from Mendocino.

But tonight here he was, in the offices of his favorite acquisition. By the time he arrived in the conference room, if that's what you'd call it, given that it was the size of a shoe box and about the same color as one's cardboard, everybody was there, all four of them—Harry, Joseph, a couple of marketing people from the station. Everyone, except Madame

Sterling and her friend Luce. *Now that's a funny duo,* thought Moss. *The hippie and the debutante.*

"So, Harr, we expecting Jeannie? Tonight, that is?"

At that moment the door opened. Jeannie and Luce were obviously in the middle of a conversation. Jeannie was giggling as she said, " . . . let's just say he's got no hang-ups. Anything goes, *everywhere—*"

"Really? Is that a promise?" Moss said, smiling.

He swore she blushed, and then, as expected, she ignored him, taking a seat at the far end of the table.

"So, Harr, what's this all about?" she asked.

"Listen, Jeannie, be nice, okay? We're going to talk about what we've been doing and maybe we'll hear from Moss about what's on his mind."

"Jeannie's always nice," said Moss.

"Except when she's not," said Joseph with a laugh. Did his T-shirt really say MY OTHER RIDE HAS TITS? Over it he wore a blue jean jacket covered with Harley patches, its arms cut off at the shoulders.

"Nice shirt, Joseph. Dress specially for the meeting?" Jeannie said.

"Hey, that's why I got my fancy vest on," he answered.

Moss shook each person's hand. To Luce, he said, "You feeling okay? You look a little . . . um . . . green."

"Something I ate, I think. Oysters at dinner, or leftover sushi, earlier today."

"Well, I hope you feel better soon. But try not to throw up during the meeting, okay? I get a little nauseous when someone throws up."

"I'll try," she said with a smile.

When he got to Jeannie, he took her hand and said, "Nice show last night."

"Thanks. Nice to know you actually listen to it," she said, pulling her hand back.

"You know I do."

"Yes, that's one thing you've made clear."

"That's good," said Harry, "so you know what we're doing here and how—"

"And you ought to push it a little further."

"What do you mean, 'push it'?" asked Jeannie.

You'd have to be deaf to not hear her voice rise an octave, see her jaw working. *Good*, thought Moss, *she's nervous.* "Let it go a little further," he said. "Open it up. Bring in experts, meet the people, go out on the street, I don't know. Push it. The ratings—"

"Are sky high," said Harry. "Why mess with a good thing?"

"Because they could be higher, Harr. They've been where they've been for a year, or more. I'm not saying they're not good. They're good, very good. What you have here is a pretty hot show that could be a scorcher. Jeannie, you don't seem like the complacent type. So why not try something new? Take it up a notch."

"Take it up a notch? Ah, the old American Heritage Dictionary of Business Clichés. Like 'pushing the envelope' or 'twenty-four/seven' or 'raising the bar.'"

"Now Jeannie," said Moss, "your defensiveness is showing."

"Come on, Jeannie," said Luce. "You know you've wanted to do something new. You're bored. Now you're being given an opportunity to—"

"What, push the envelope?" She glared at Luce, knowing she was right, but feeling betrayed by her friend at this moment right in front of Moss.

She turned to Moss. "Okay, boss. You want pushing? Notching? Ratings? Just watch me. I'm there, twenty-four/seven."

Was he a total asshole to think she was cute when she was pissed? He couldn't stop himself from smiling. "Would you relax? I like what you've been doing, just—"

"Would you please stop telling me to relax? This is relaxed!"

"Yeah, you ought to see her stressed," said Joseph.

She turned to him and narrowed her eyes. She was so obvious.

"It's a beautiful thing," said Joseph, "poetic, really." And he sang, while strumming his air guitar, "Lady Evil, evil/She's a magical, mystical woman."

Moss smiled, first in agreement with Joseph and then smugly at Jeannie. Only Black Sabbath could've said it so well.

"I'll think about it," she said.

This is going to be fun, thought Moss.

Shrink to the Stars

He's done it again. He's made me want to kill him, she thought as she let her apartment door close hard behind her. She wasn't sure, precisely, what it was—his clothes, his posture, his power? She hated everything about him. Must be her aversion to authority, she figured. Though there was nothing authoritative about how he'd been dressed tonight: casually, in jeans and a T-shirt with a denim shirt over it, with its sleeves rolled up. And hiking boots, for god's sake. And what the hell was that woven stringy bracelet around his wrist? Looked like it had gotten wet way too many times. Color faded, threads hanging off. As if he thought that dressing like this made him more like the people.

But then again, who am I to talk? she thought, as she threw her fringed jacket on the counter. The apartment was dark, quiet. If the sun was up, it couldn't be seen behind the layer of clouds that coated the sky.

But when Mouse ran out to meet her, she squatted down low to scratch his ears and say "Hey, boy" softly. *The things you tolerate when you have a dog,* she thought. A minute ago, he had been a disgusting foreign four-legged creature. Now he was licking her on her face, and she was welcoming it.

Thank god it was the weekend again, because she had so much shit to do today that she just wanted to lie down and watch TV. Pick up dry cleaning, buy some groceries, drop a Bluefly.com return at the post office. The everyday duties made her feel lonely. This was the meat of her life, the potatoes of her existence. Dull, expected, rote.

Bullshit. It wasn't that. It was that she felt completely alone, coming home with nobody there to talk to about the idiocy of the staff meeting, to make fun of Moss with, to dream with, to hold. She had only herself and there was no love in that.

Her affair with Tommy had lasted a night and a day. And now he'd been gone for over a week. In that shadowy area where memory meets insecurity, she couldn't be certain it had really happened at all. Perhaps she had conjured it to fill the emptiness.

She checked the kitchen answering machine for calls. There were two. First, Isaiah, saying he'd given Mouse his morning walk, as they had agreed since she knew she'd be late. Okay, at least that was covered. And Luce, calling to say that she couldn't make it all the way home, and the minute she'd gotten out of her taxi, right on the corner of Madison and Seventy-second, she threw up and felt ever so much better. But not to call, because she was going to sleep.

The image of Luce, in her little tan Tod's, wearing her beige cashmere sweater set, standing on Madison Avenue in front of Ralph Lauren with its Aryan mannequins in the windows and puking her guts out, amused Jeannie. Normally she didn't laugh at her friend's expense, so she felt a twang of guilt. But Luce felt better getting it out of her system, and so did she.

So Jeannie went to her room and turned on her computer, hoping for an e-mail from Tommy.

And there it was. She let out an audible sigh of relief.

Hey Jeannie Beanie (I know you said not to call you this, but too goddamn bad. Didn't someone once say old habits die hard? A wise man.) Sorry it's taken so long to write. Tough to get a line out. Tough here. The worst. But I think of you, of us, and I can work, I can sleep at night.

She answered him with words of encouragement and silliness, and then turned on the TV and sprawled on her living-room couch. *The Early Early Show* had on a psychologist who was talking about how to get your spouse to make the bed, or pick up his underwear, or have sex more often. And a light-bulb went off over Jeannie's head.

STERLING BEHAVIOR

JEANNIE: *Tonight we have a guest in our studio, the preeminent psychologist Dr. Matthew Richards, author of the new book* The Gentle Art of Persuasion: How to Get What You Want from Others by Getting Others to Give You What You Want.

LUCE: *Catchy title. I like that getting and giving and wanting stuff—*

JEANNIE: *I'm happy when you're happy. So, Dr. Richards, good evening. Thanks for joining us so late—*

DR. RICHARDS: *Thank you for having me here. I enjoy your show very much.*

JEANNIE: *I found your book very interesting, but I have to say I'm a little skeptical about how you propose we deal with people who are being rude. You say we should flatter and cajole—*

DR. RICHARDS: *What I'm saying, Jeannie, is that to get someone to stop behaving rudely, we need to treat others with the same respect and decency we'd like from them in order to get them to be sympathetic to us.*

JEANNIE: *Okay, so I'm sitting in the waiting room at my gynecologist's office and there's a woman popping her gum. What do I do?*

DR. RICHARDS: *You say quietly to her, "Excuse me, it sounds like you're really enjoying your gum, but I'm a little nervous about my appointment, so if you wouldn't mind, could you please stop popping it? I'd so appreciate it."*

JEANNIE: *So I kiss her butt, lie, and beg.*

LUCE: *I'm always nervous at the gynecologist. It wouldn't be a lie to me.*

JEANNIE: *You mean I can't just be honest and straightforward and say, "Keep your mouth shut or toss it, would you? I don't want to hear you chewing."*

DR. RICHARDS: *[laughing] I think it's far better to say something that requires her compassion for your situation. If that requires a little white lie, so be it.*

JEANNIE: *Okay, one more example before we take calls. You're leaving the bank and you hold the door open for someone who walks through as if you weren't there, without saying "thank you" or acknowledging your existence in any way.*

DR. RICHARDS: *You might want to ask yourself why you need the* "thank-you." Can't you hold a door open just for the pleasure of it?

JEANNIE: Come on, doc, nobody holds a door for the "thank-you," but it's lousy when you don't get one, am I right, people? You feel like a nonperson, performing a service, like a robot. As if the person expected the door to be opened, as if people were always doing that—and who knows what else—for them.

DR. RICHARDS: The "I feel" system would have worked in that situation.

JEANNIE: You mean "I feel this when you do that"? You're suggesting I talk that way to a complete stranger?

DR. RICHARDS: That's right, Jeannie. Couples therapists have long used the "I feel" system as a tool for expressing feelings. "I feel lonely when you don't talk to me over dinner, honey." When you take responsibility for your feelings, your partner won't feel as criticized or attacked. And a stranger will respond too.

LUCE: Oh, you mean I shouldn't just yell at Spike, "You are such a slob!" when he leaves his tools all over the house? Ohhhhh!!!

JEANNIE: Very funny.

DR. RICHARDS: So Jeannie, what would you say to the woman who walks through the door you're holding without as much as a nod?

JEANNIE: Hmmm . . . how about "I feel like ripping your head off and stuffing it down your neck"?

DR. RICHARDS: It's tough, Jeannie, I know. But how about, "Excuse me, but I feel embarrassed that I held the door open for you and you didn't even acknowledge me as a human being."

JEANNIE: Doc, I'm sorry, but there is no way I'm going to talk to a stranger like that. Hell, I wouldn't even talk to Luce like that!

LUCE: Maybe you should.

DR. RICHARDS: Yes, Jeannie. If you treat people with respect, if you tell them how their actions make you feel, if you encourage their

good qualities, like compassion and sympathy, they will rise to
the occasion.

JEANNIE: *Or they'll remain the selfish, badly mannered individuals
they are. Well, loyal listeners, the phone lines are open and we
want to know what you think. Can bad behavior be changed by
telling people that their actions make you feel sad? Or by using
a little white lie to get their sympathy?*

LUCE: *We have a call, Jeannie, from Gabe.*

GABE: *It's a matter of life and death, Jeannie. Dr. Richards, my
mom—*

JEANNIE: *How old are you, Gabe?*

GABE: *Eleven.*

JEANNIE: *Wow! Shouldn't you be asleep? Why are you up so late?*

GABE: *Because I have this mom who yells at everybody and I'm worried, and I saw on your website today about Dr. Richards being
on the show and I wanted—*

JEANNIE: *Okay, Gabe, but promise me that after you ask your question, you'll go to bed. Don't you have school tomorrow?*

GABE: *Yeah. It sucks.*

JEANNIE: *Yeah. I know. But you have to go. So, one question, then
to bed, okay?*

GABE: *Okay. Dr. Richards, my mom yells at everybody—people in
cars who don't let us cross the street, people on cell phones, people who litter, taxi drivers who go the wrong way, people who cut
in line at the grocery store, lots of people. And I'm worried she's
going to get beat up one day. On the way to school every day we
see these big kids and yesterday one threw his bottle of Gatorade
over the fence onto the grass at the Museum of Natural History
and my mom yelled at him and he called her a f [bleep] b
[bleep]—*

JEANNIE: *Whoa there, mister!*

GABE: *—and then he said she'd never have yelled at him if he* *wasn't black and she said she didn't care what color he was and she bet his mom would be mad to see him do such a thing, and that he wouldn't do that in his own front yard. I thought he was going to punch her in the face. And we see him almost every day on the way to school. What should I tell my mom to do?*

JEANNIE: *First, tell your mom she's my hero.*

DR. RICHARDS: *But let's give her some real tools for persuading someone to do what she wants before she gets someone angry. Okay, Gabe? The next time she sees that kid throw a bottle, she should say, "That looks like fun, but I know you don't mean to litter the lawn, so why not try to get it in that trash can?"*

GABE: *They'd just laugh at her and say what they meant to do was to kick her lily-white ass.*

LUCE: *Hello? Don't we bleep "ass"?*

DR. RICHARDS: *You need to trust me on this, Gabe. I think I know the most effective methods to persuade people—*

GABE: *Trust me, doc. You're going to get my mom's face bashed in. Those kids need to act tough and seem cool and my mom needs to mind her own business.*

DR. RICHARDS: *Gabe, I have years of experience with this and I guarantee—*

JEANNIE: *Doc, I have to agree with Gabe.*

LUCE: *We have a Miriam on the line.*

JEANNIE: *Hi, Miriam.*

MIRIAM: *Hi, Jeannie. She also tells taxi drivers how to get where they're going and she gets mad if they're driving too slow and if they're driving too fast. My dad thinks she's going to get shot one day.*

JEANNIE: *Wait a minute, wait a minute. Who's "she"?*

MIRIAM: *My mom. Gabe's mom.*

JEANNIE: *You're Gabe's sister? Talking about the same mom?*

MIRIAM: *We're twins. And our mom is insane.*

JEANNIE: *She sounds awesome.*

DR. RICHARDS: *Okay, Miriam. Let's talk about the taxi.*

MIRIAM: *Just the other day, the taxi was going slow, and we were late. And my mom said something like, "Can you drive like you care about getting us where we want to go?"*

DR. RICHARDS: *What about "Excuse me, my daughter is worried she'll be late for school. Could you please drive a little faster?"*

JEANNIE: *Obviously you haven't taken too many cabs in the city, Dr. Richards. Miriam, what do you think that driver would say?*

MIRIAM: *He'd either say something like, "You want fast? Take a subway," or "You want fast? I'll show you fast," and then he'd speed to scare us.*

JEANNIE: *Hmmm, I wonder. Wait, that's it! Thank you, Miriam and Gabe. You've given me an idea. We're taking this to the streets. That's right. We're going to see what works and what doesn't when it comes to kicking bad behavior in the butt. Details to follow on tomorrow night's show.*

LUCE: *But let's take a break now for a station ID. You're listening to Sterling Behavior on WBUZ radio, at 660 on your AM dial. And we're taking more calls at 777-246-3800.*

And So It Begins

"That's it!" Jeannie was excited as she took off her headgear. "We'll do a 'man on the street.'"

"I'm listening. Please explain," said Luce.

"You know, catch people doing bad stuff. Catch them in the act and confront them."

"To do what? Embarrass people?"

"Teach them a lesson. A kind of 'Candid Ethical Camera,' without the camera. Moss wants ratings? We'll give him ratings. Get Harry and Joseph. I want this to be a covert operation. I want to be invisible. Unseen, unheard. Think we can start next week?" Jeannie hadn't been so excited about her work in a very long time. She was about to burst, this idea was so damned good. For so many reasons.

Call from Abroad

Sitting at her dining table, making notes about the new show while eating leftover roasted chicken, with Mouse panting (begging) heavily at her side, drool dripping from his mouth onto the napkin in her lap (now she knew the real purpose of putting it there), his front paws up on the edge of the table until Jeannie yelled a loud, firm "off" (which she had to do every thirty seconds), she watched a tugboat pushing a barge upriver, heard a siren on the street below. Fall was in full bloom now; the trees in New Jersey were gold and red, glittering in the rays of the rising sun.

How long had it been since he left? Almost three weeks? Would he remember what it was like to make love to her? Would they take up where they left off or would he feel regret for what had happened? Maybe it was one of those once-only things . . . maybe he had second thoughts, maybe he . . .

Her mouth was full when the phone rang. She didn't hesitate because it just might be him this time.

"Herro," she said, trying to chew and talk at the same time.

"Jeannie." It was him. It was Tommy. Static filled the silence.

"Where are you?" she asked, with a painful gulp, the kind you feel in your chest for five minutes afterward.

"Charles de Gaulle. Waiting for my flight to New York."

"You're coming home!" It was as if he had heard her heart's longing from the other side of the planet.

More static, but she thought he said he was thinking of her or had thought something about them, or something that would keep her up all night worrying.

" . . . and I'll see you tomorrow." And the line went dead.

Wait, she thought, *just wait until you hear what I'm doing. You're going to love it, Tommy. You're going to love me.*

STERLING BEHAVIOR

JEANNIE: *Hello, loyal listeners. Tonight we're doing something completely different. You're going to hear something we taped earlier—an on-the-street experiment in human behavior, Sterling and otherwise. What you'll witness actually happened at about ten p.m. tonight. With me were Luce, who's here right now, of course—*

LUCE: *Hi, everybody.*

JEANNIE: *—and our engineer, Joseph, who made sure we were inconspicuous. We each wore a hidden mic, so people wouldn't know they were being taped. And if we were a little concerned that people thought we were nuts, talking to ourselves, we just had to look around—*

LUCE: *We were just like everybody else, looking like lunatics talking on cell phones with Bluetooths. Or do you say Blueteeth?*

JEANNIE: *Exactly. So here we go, taped earlier tonight in front of the Loews movie theater on Broadway at Sixty-eighth Street, on the Upper West Side. [taped segment begins] Luce and I are standing in front of one of the busiest movie theaters in Manhattan and one of the better-managed ones. There's never a line because the movies are scheduled so well, there's freshly popped popcorn and plentiful bathrooms.*

LUCE: *That are usually disgustingly filthy.*

JEANNIE: *But you rarely have to wait—even in the women's.*

LUCE: *And what more can you want from your moviegoing experience?*

JEANNIE: *Yeah, hmmm, let me think about that. How about no people talking during the movie? Popcorn and a Diet Coke for under twenty bucks? No commercials?*

LUCE: *Now that's pressing your luck.*

JEANNIE: *That's for a future* Sterling Behavior. *Tonight we're here near Lincoln Center, with Barnes & Noble, Pottery Barn, Banana Republic, Starbucks, and Victoria's Secret all within two blocks of one another. Chain store USA, an urban outdoor mall.*

And it's Thursday night, so it's not crazy crowded but it's busy, with people going in and out of this thirteen-plex. What we've done is this: we've placed an empty soda can on the sidewalk right outside the revolving doors, and we're going to see how long it takes for someone to pick it up and throw it away. What I want you to think about is this: what would you do in this situation?

LUCE: *Pick it up before someone trips on it and breaks a leg, I hope.*

JEANNIE: *Me too. But very soon, two movies will be over and a whole lot of people will be exiting the theater, adults and teens alike. One movie is the new George Clooney, the other is American Pie Four—*

LUCE: *I think it's five, actually.*

JEANNIE: *Okay, five. Obviously it's for younger people, so we'll have a good span of ages.*

LUCE: *Very scientific. I bet on the kids.*

JEANNIE: *I bet on the old folks. A woman over fifty. A mom. Twenty bucks?*

LUCE: *Ten.*

JEANNIE: *Ten? Ten's child's play. Fifteen.*

LUCE: *Ten. It's not even right, is it, to bet on the goodness of others? We shouldn't be betting anyway. I wonder if it's within the broadcast—*

JEANNIE: *Okay, ten it is. All right, here they come. There's a woman. She sees the can, but look, she steps aside to avoid it. And here comes, I don't know, how old is that kid, Luce?*

LUCE: *Looks about seventeen, eighteen, I guess. Oh, pick it up, please pick it up.*

JEANNIE: *Nope. He kicks it! That's right, kicks the can into the heel of an older man walking with a woman. That man looks behind to see what hit him, sees it, and continues walking. Now look, one woman, now another, just stepping over the can to avoid it.*

LUCE: *To be fair, would you want to pick up a can that someone drank out of? Full of germs and saliva. Yuck.*

JEANNIE: *Yuck it may be, but still, it's only right. Uh-oh, look, a guy, maybe in his forties, just tripped over it, is now looking at it, gets his bearings and stands there, chatting with his friends. But he doesn't pick it up! Will nobody pick up the can? Oops, there, it's kicked again by a woman who sees it and walks the other way.*

LUCE: *This is making me very nervous, Jeannie.*

JEANNIE: *You worried someone'll trip? Ot that you'll lose ten bucks? Let's wait—*

LUCE: *One more minute.*

JEANNIE: *Two.*

LUCE: *Ninety seconds.*

JEANNIE: *Done. Now wait. Look. Okay. We may have something. Look at that.*

[a pause]

LUCE: *You need to describe what you're seeing, Jeannie, for our listeners at home.*

JEANNIE: *Yes, okay. Sorry, listeners, I'm not used to this. There are* two couples, older, like, I don't know, late fifties, early sixties. They've gathered around the can. They're talking, they're discussing the movie they've just seen, I imagine. One of the women looks down and sees the can. Will she pick it up? She looks like she's considering it. Wait, nope. They've walked away. I am depressed, Luce. Will nobody pick up the can? Is there not a soul who sees it there and will bend down and toss it in the trash? I am despondent. I don't think I can go on—

LUCE: *Come on, Jeannie! Be optimistic. Look.*

JEANNIE: *I don't want to.*

LUCE: *Jeannie, look!*

JEANNIE: *Loyal listeners, three teenage girls have just come out of a taxi and are entering the theater, when one trips on the can—*

LUCE: *And almost falls.*

JEANNIE: *Well, look at the height of her heels. Hello? I'd trip in those without a can to do it for me! But it's her friend who has picked up the can and is now holding it between her thumb and index finger, so as not to get dirty, I imagine. Now she's walking toward the trash. I am elated. Let's go meet her.*

LUCE: *You owe me ten.*

JEANNIE: *And you'll get it. When she drops the can in the garbage. Let's talk to her. Um, hello. May I speak to you for a minute? I am Jeannie Sterling and I have a radio show called* Sterling Behavior. *And we're taping right now as we speak. Can I ask you a question? This may be aired later.*

GIRL: *Really? Cool.*

JEANNIE: *First, what's your name?*

GIRL: *Lisa.*

JEANNIE: *Hey Lisa, do you have a last name?*

LISA: *Yeah.*

JEANNIE: *Well, Lisa, do you wish to share it with us?*

LISA: *Not really. Do I have to?*

JEANNIE: *No, Lisa, you don't have to. Just thought it would be fun to have your name mentioned to eight million listeners.*

LISA: *Not really.*

JEANNIE: *You know, you've been part of a field experiment in manners. You see, we planted that soda can on the ground there and waited to see how long it took before someone picked it up and threw it away. And you, my dear, did it.*

LISA: *Yeah, well my friend almost fell tripping on it and—*

JEANNIE: *What are you doing? Lisa's foraging in her pink Roxy duffel-shaped bag, like she's looking for something.*

LISA: *Would you hold this for me, please?*

JEANNIE: *Sure. She's handed me the can and—*

LUCE: *Hey, what are you doing?*

LISA: *I'm lighting a cigarette.*

LUCE: *Oh no. How old are you? Does your mother—*

JEANNIE: *Do you mean you picked up the can to use it as an ashtray?*

LISA: *I'm sixteen, and no, my mother has no idea. She'd kill me!*

LUCE: *Smoking will kill you.*

LISA: *So they say, but we're all going to die anyway, right? Seriously, I'll stop. When I get married. Definitely before I have kids.*

LUCE: *You're too young to get married!*

LISA: *Don't I know it. Are you kidding?*

JEANNIE: *What will you do with the can when you finish your cigarette?*

LISA: *Throw it in this garbage can here.*

LUCE: *Promise?*

LISA: *Promise.*

JEANNIE: *Well, dear listeners, we are presented with a quandary. A young woman picks up the can, and thereby does the right thing. But, the reason she picks up the can is for her own selfish, not to mention unhealthy—*

LUCE: *And illegal. She's underage.*

JEANNIE: —*purposes. Interesting. We will be taking calls right after this commercial break. I'd like to know what you think about what we witnessed here on Broadway earlier tonight. Let's hear from you at 777-246-3800. You're listening to* Sterling Behavior *on WBUZ radio at 660 on your AM dial.*

Caught Ya!

Jeannie was buzzed. It was as if she had consumed three iced grande skim lattes in a single hour. Her chest was pounding, her temples throbbing, her veins pumping with adrenaline.

How many calls had come in? Hundreds. How many calls had she taken? Not enough. The phone was ringing off the hook from the moment they finished the tape until the end of the show three and a half hours later. It was clear that "watching" people who didn't know they were being watched was titillating to listeners. And then judging their behavior, with the "what would you do?" aspect—making people search their souls for how bad or good they would be in the same situation—was fun. You become a witness to bad behavior, as well as judge, audience, and voyeur. It was a reality show featuring the worst traits of people, with listeners able to feel higher than thou. Whether this was its own kind of bad behavior was a question in the back of Jeannie's mind, but she didn't want to go there. She liked the excitement, the potential, the promise of getting noticed—by her bosses, by other stations who might want to woo her away, by her fans, and by the one person she so wanted to impress.

She felt like a teenage girl with a crush. *Tommy, can you hear me? Can you feel me near you?* The Who was blaring in her head when Moss walked in.

He knocked on the edge of her cubicle wall. She swiveled in her chair to face him. His ratty, stringy bracelet was hanging there on his dark, hairy wrist. Not the accessory for his perfectly cut suit and his crisp dark shirt.

"Nice show. Well done." He smiled.

She fought it with all her might, but his compliment was important to her, made her feel proud. She smiled back.

"Nice bracelet," she said. "And thanks. Amazing response. The calls."

"You like it? It's Cartier."

"Really?" She stood to get a better look. "Looks more like vintage day camp."

"You know, that's exactly right. You are a true fashion maven."

"Let me guess: it's from the seventies. You bought it on Telegraph Avenue."

"Look who's talking. And no, this," he said, as he spun the string around his wrist, "was a gift."

"From who? Fan mail from some flounder?"

"Fan mail . . ." he laughed. "You could be the poster girl for 1972."

"I like the seventies. Sort of my decade, spiritually speaking."

"Hence the Frye boots," he said, looking down at them and then lettting his eyes roam slowly up her body like a plow on a snowy hillside. "And everything else. Even the *Rocky and Bullwinkle* reference. I knew there was a reason we—"

"But back to the show," she said, changing the subject with a look as if to say "Your obnoxiousness is noted."

"You'll do it again. The person on the street thing."

"Why are you here, anyway? Shouldn't you be in Frankfurt

at some meeting with other captains of industry? Can't you rely on Harry to do your bidding?"

"That's a helluva lot of questions. Let me try and answer them for you. A, I like it here. B, I'd rely on him to run the country, if I could. And C, so when can I expect to hear another on-the-town segment?"

"Soon." Compliment aside, she sure as shit didn't want him telling her what to do.

"Soon is good. Sooner is better."

She tried to be nice, but she couldn't. "Buy us today, sell us tomorrow. Is that the plan?"

"That is not the plan."

She looked at him skeptically, folding her arms as she leaned against her desk.

"I need you to trust that I have your best interests at heart."

"My best interests, huh?"

"Listen, sarcasm doesn't suit you. You're much more of an in-your-face kind of girl."

"Girl, huh? Nice."

"There it is again."

"So let me ask you this: what should we call it?"

"Call what, lady without a segue?"

"My mind too quick for you?"

"Just need some notice about where we might be headed."

"I'll spell it out each time, okay?" And she proceeded to do just that, very, very slowly, enunciating each word as if speaking to a two-year-old who spoke only Urdu. "So, back to my show. The radio show. We were talking about doing more candid person-on-the-street segments, like we did tonight. Are you following?"

Moss smiled, his eyes crinkling at the corners, raised his brows, crossed his arms over his chest, crossed one leg in front of the other, and leaned against the cubicle opening. *He is actually pretty sexy. An asshole, but sexy.*

"I feel it would be beneficial—a word that means 'good'— if we name the segment of the show where we go out live on the street. Something like 'Candid Camera' or 'Eye on You' or something. It has to be catchy and—"

"'Caught Ya,'" Moss said.

"Caught me what?"

"Caught ya not being too quick." He turned, shaking his head in exaggerated disappointment, and headed down the hallway toward his office.

"Hello?" she asked, following him.

"No," he replied, still walking.

"Goodbye?"

He stopped and turned to her. "What's this, 'Who's On First?', *Caught Ya*, the name of the show."

"*Caught Ya?*"

"Ah, she understands."

"Not bad."

"Good."

"I'll think about it," Jeannie said.

"Do."

"Okay."

"Tomorrow."

"What?"

"I'll spell it out: see you t-o-m-o-r-o-w," said Moss, walking away.

"You forgot an R," said Jeannie, to his back.

He spun around, and with a smile, said, "I must've missed that day in school."

She laughed then—*That's my joke!*—and touched her hair. Shit, she always did that when she was flirting. Was she flirting? With him? Now? Here? Why? "Okay," she said curtly, "but it's tonight. You'll see me tonight."

He hit himself in the forehead. "I just cannot get these crazy hours right. Okay, then. Have a good *day*. See you to*night*." He turned and walked a few steps. Stopped, then turned back to her. "You did good, Jeannie. Really good."

She looked at him, her face flushed with embarrassment and pleasure, a quick flash on Tommy and what he'd think of all this. "I know. It was good, wasn't it?"

"*You* were good. *You* were amazing. There's something about you that just . . ." He walked back to her, stood close. He noticed how her hair was lighter on the top, sun streaked, and dark underneath, changing colors many times on its way. *Like her,* he thought, *deep and complicated, just like her.*

Oh god, don't look at me like that. She noticed how her chest was lifting with each breath. "Yes? Just what?" she demanded. "Say it. That just what?"

That moves me, he thought. "That makes you perfect for your job of judging others," he said.

"Hmmm. I think I'll take it as a compliment." She smiled.

"Good," he said as turned on his heel and walked to his office doorway. "Have a good night, or morning, Jeannie."

She watched his back and wanted to blow poison darts into it. "You too, boss."

"Yeah, I will. Hey, you know, can I drop you? I have my car and we're headed in the same direction."

She hesitated. This felt a little weird, them getting all chummy. But then she figured it couldn't hurt to be chummy with the boss. "Well—"

"Ach," he said, hitting himself on his forehead. "If only I didn't have this . . . this thing." *Shit.* He wasn't going to mention it.

She narrowed her eyes. "Let me guess. Breakfast at the Four Seasons? The Grill Room, of course."

"Actually, today? It's at 21." He looked at her with narrowed eyes. "How'd you know?"

"Your suit. And besides, I have a suspicious mind. You *are* selling."

"Why, you buying?" he said, walking into his office. Then he turned to her. "You don't trust anybody, do you? I am not selling the station. Not right now, anyway."

She followed close behind, in case he was trying to escape. "What's that mean, 'not right now'? You mean soon? You mean when you turn it over for the most bucks to the highest bidder, who will inevitably be some corporate player who couldn't give a shit about the people here, much less the show, and will lay off everyone and make *Sterling Behavior* a softened daytime psychobabble talk show, like that large-butted Dr. Bite Me bitch? You ask me to trust you?" she asked.

She looked around his office. She had never been in here before. "My god! A man who is so neat? Where is all your stuff?" There was not one thing on his desk except a paper-weight, which was a hard, plastic rendition of a balled-up tax return, and a laptop.

"Hey, what's that?" she asked, as she walked behind his desk to the large black-and-white photo on the wall.

"Redwood canopy," he said, now standing next to her, his hands, as usual, in his pockets, as he stared at the photo. "Took it myself."

"From the canopy? You climbed up there?" She was still upset.

"Yeah. And would you stop yelling at me?"

She breathed in deeply and let it go. Dropped her voice to

almost a whisper. "I like the black-and-white. And the fog in the trees. How'd you get up there?"

"Rope, harness, carabiners, throw-weights, slingshot, patience. And a helmet. It's not hard."

"Sounds hard. It's high."

"You ever been to the California redwoods? They're tall. The tallest trees in the world. These happen to be north of San Francisco near—"

"Point Reyes?"

He smiled and looked at her. "You've been to Point Reyes?"

"Only about a hundred times. I'm from Berkeley. Spent many a summer hiking to the lighthouse. Swimming at Drake's Beach."

His eyes crinkled with his smile. "Well, this shot wasn't taken at Point Reyes, but it's close, a little more north, just north of Sonoma."

"It's beautiful."

"Yes, it is."

Then she turned to look at him, to see his face full-on. "So you climb trees?" she asked, now quiet.

"It's a hobby. Safer than race car driving, right?"

"Is it?"

"Trust me. All I know is I couldn't not climb trees. It's something I do."

"And take pictures."

"Yeah, but it's the climbing that's important. The pictures just record, as best they can, what I see when I'm up there. But"—and here he turned to the picture—"there's no way they can capture the chill, the mist settled in the trees, the smell of the wet bark, the sound of the ocean beyond, and the wind in the branches. I just take the pictures to remind me of the whole thing."

She paused and looked, trying to smell, to feel the cold, to hear the breeze. Then she looked at him. More than the beautiful photo, more than his unusual hobby, what really moved her was the light in his eyes, the dreamy quality of his face, as if he was seeing something beyond the trees, outside of this everyday existence. She felt the bitter tug of jealousy; she wanted that. Perhaps this Moss guy had more soul than she gave him credit for. She turned on the heel of her Frye. "You are something," she said.

He watched her as she walked out. *Boy oh boy, you are too,* he thought.

She knew he was watching, because when she turned to take one last look at him that morning, as he stood there proudly in front of that photo, his eyes were on her.

Power Breakfast

There would be a time soon, he thought as he sat in his office behind his Knoll table, in his beautiful, custom-fitted Aeron chair, when he'd have to do something about that girl. Something wild and explosive, something unpredictable that would rock her world. And not only because he wanted to spin her, throw her, uproot her like a tornado, but because he wouldn't be able to hold himself back any longer. Every time he was with her, standing next to her, down the hall from her, hell, in the same zip code as her, he had to stop himself from pulling her to him and kissing her, feeling those lips, seeing those eyes up close.

Ah, shit. He was her boss, for Christ's sake. That really wasn't a big deal, but she was difficult. And he hardly knew her. Though that was bullshit, because he was sure he knew her. But she was probably involved with somebody. And she was a goddamn psychotic who carried a ton of baggage on her shoulders. How could he, who dated who knew how many interesting women—models, actresses, CEOs, judges, for crying out loud—let himself be attracted to this oddball neurotic misfit? Who the fuck cared? His mom would say what she said when he was a kid: that he was being open-hearted, that he was too sensitive for his own good, that he needed to build a wall around his heart so that he wouldn't be hurt so easily. But that was years ago. He'd learned a lot since then, but he still hadn't learned, yet, how to love and let himself be loved. Not yet, not now, not today.

That's why he climbed. He looked at the photo again and was amazed at life's coincidences, that she had actually come from somewhere near the Northern California coast. His home away from home, or rather, his spiritual home, the place he really hung his heartfelt hat, the place he was born to be. Except when he was in New York, where his business life seemed to fix him like Krazy Glue. So he was stuck, living in two worlds.

As he walked out, he passed her cubicle on the way, noticing all the crap on her desk. What a slob. Piles of papers, stuff everywhere. Magazines, articles torn out of the newspaper, shoes under her desk, books, notes, and unopened mail. Hadn't she heard of feng shui? How could she work, how could she even think in this clutter?

Not that this place had any feng to shui about. He looked out over the island of cubicles, at the gray walls, the dull beige of the cubicles, the stark fluorescent lights that floated above, and smiled. Even in this mess of a place, with its gray dingy wall-to-wall that was filthy after twenty hours of use a day, even with the smeared glass walls that separated hallway from office, inner studio from outer, there was life. There was a spark and electricity. He took his hands out of his pockets and put them on the cubicle wall, flung his head back, and breathed the rancid, stale air. *It's good to be the king,* he thought, *the king of a wacky empire.* For the first time in his business life, he liked what he'd bought. It was a place full of quirky people, big ideas, fast talk. He, of the deals and money and turnovers and draws, was happy here. Or as happy at work as he could imagine being.

I wish, he thought, *I was climbing, one foot on a limb, another dangling below me, my ass in a harness, a hundred feet off the forest floor, halfway to heaven.*

But he had a breakfast to get to, he realized, looking at his watch. Marshall would be pissed if he was late. And there was no way he was going to sell. Hands back in his pockets, standing straight up, he walked out with a wave to Dave, the morning custodian, who was vacuuming the hallway.

At 21 a half hour later, he sat with Robert Shaltow, owner of Clear Channel, and Marshall, his buddy and business adviser, eating fruit and a bran muffin, and trying hard to listen to Bob's pitch. On the wall behind Bob's head was a painting of a woman in a red riding outfit on a horse, which Moss kept trying not to look at, forcing himself to stay focused on Bob's eyes. To at least pretend he was listening. But he kept going back to that painting. Something about it, he wasn't sure what, reminded him of her. The woman in it didn't look like her, but something in the painted woman's eyes, some fury mixed with fear, or perhaps a sadness, made his heart reel like it did whenever he was with her.

Then Bob asked, "So what do you think? I think there's something here to explore, don't you?"

"Definitely, don't you agree, Moss?" said Marshall.

Moss knew he wouldn't sell, but he wanted to grow the station, to make his money back and more. And she was the key. Nobody there had that kind of potential. And he wanted to keep her challenged, and that would mean pushing her forward.

"Yes," he answered, "yes, guys, I think we do. We certainly have things to explore." He wouldn't sell, but he had other plans.

Breakfast at Bubby's

Jeannie and Luce got the same window table for breakfast at Bubby's every week. On Wednesday, their usual day, Luce had a doctor's appointment (just her annual, she'd said) so their breakfast was postponed until today, Friday. Suzi, their regular waitress, dressed in her camouflage capris and the three-inch-high espadrilles with the ankle ribbons that she wore year round, brought them coffee.

"No coffee for me today," said Luce.

"Hello?" said Jeannie.

"Just trying to cut back. Had a cup already at the station."

The women ordered and Luce looked out the window. She'd been off coffee completely for three months, but Jeannie hadn't noticed. Typical. So self-involved. She hadn't noticed Luce's morning sickness either. Soon Luce'd have to tell her because she'd be showing, but for some reason she just couldn't bring herself to do it yet.

What was that about? she wondered. Why couldn't she tell her very best friend that she was pregnant? That she was feeling delighted and scared and like shit and exhilarated all at once? That she and Spike were already fighting about where they'd live and whether public or private school was better?

Because Jeannie just wouldn't get it. She'd get critical and think Luce was throwing her career down the toilet. She wouldn't care. Jeannie had never been a baby person, which was evident from all the stroller comments on the show, all the crying-baby jabs. And Luce, in her estrogen-drunk state, couldn't deal with Jeannie not being thoroughly 100 percent behind her. *It was okay,* Luce rationalized. *One person can't be everything for you.*

"You seem distracted," said Jeannie.

That's an understatement, Luce was thinking. "Would you stop saying that to me? I'm fine."

"Okay, okay, but I assume you'd tell me if something was bothering you."

"Jeannie," she whined.

"So Moss wants to name the new segment *Caught Ya!*"

Thank god she changed the subject, thought Luce. "I like it. It's the content I'm worried about."

"Yeah, me too. I don't think I've ever been so excited and so scared about something."

Hello, me too, thought Luce.

Their food came and they ate, making small talk, catching up on Jeannie's dad and dog, Spike and shopping, and Tommy.

"He's coming home today."

"You'll see him?"

"Yeah, I hope so, I think so."

"So have fun."

"I just hope he hangs around for a while."

"And if not?"

Jeannie shrugged. "Then not. It's okay, I have a life."

Luce knew she was dissembling. "Be careful," she said, accepting the check from Suzi with a smile. "Trust your instincts. Nobody is worth losing yourself over."

"Thanks, Luce. *As if.*"

And they proceeded to fight over the check.

The Sometime Dad

Jeannie got home that morning to find Isaiah, the dog walker, in her apartment.

"This dog is a trip, lady," he said as she walked in the door. He was in the process of feeding Mouse, who was standing on his hind legs and hopping around the kitchen like a rabbit, following Isaiah's every move. "You know, I'm pretty good at the training thing, but this guy's almost impossible. Bad food habits are self-rewarding. He climbs on the table, ends up with a bagel. How do you stop that? Not to mention that he loves to roll in shit. I had to bathe him this morning. I think I left your bathroom pretty clean, except for a couple of towels. Those people at the shelter—it is unconscionable that they didn't tell you about his problems."

Isaiah's indignation warmed Jeannie through and through. A fellow justice seeker. With that, in addition to his waist-long dreadlocks and his six foot six, 140-pound build, Isaiah was one in a million. The pride he took in his work, his concern for the animals and their treatment, the injustice he felt when dog walkers were maligned—Isaiah was her ethical counterpart in the dog-walking world. He'd even formed a dog walker's union, so he was one of those rare people who put action where their mouths were.

"Oh, and I found him chewing these when I came to pick him up," Isaiah said, and he held up between two long and skinny fingers yet another pair of torn and soiled panties that had clearly been chewed, buried, dug up again. She took them from Isaiah, awkwardly, for they were her underpants, after all.

The buzzer rang from the lobby. Mouse howled. Jeannie picked up the phone.

"You're kidding." She turned to Isaiah and leaned against the front door. "Send him up." She hung up the phone. "It's my dad. But he's supposed to be in Belize!"

She hadn't had a chance to shower, to brush her teeth, or even to ditch the dirty panties. So with them in hand she waited at the door, with Mouse howling and running back and forth from his bowl to the door and Isaiah putting on his backpack.

There was the knock. She opened the door and there stood her dad.

"Jesus Christ, Dad, what's going on? Are you okay? I thought you were in Belize. You couldn't call first? You—"

"Can I come in? I'm a little tired from the flight."

Isaiah held the door for him.

"Dad, this is Isaiah, a trainer and dog walker for Mouse. You know—Mouse. He's the dog you forgot to take with you when you left."

"Hello, Isaiah. Hope you got him to stop using the apartment for his business."

"Oh yes, sir, he's done with that. Now if I could only get him to stop getting on the kitchen counter on all fours and eating Jeannie's leftovers. Girl, you might want to cook once in a while. Maybe that would scare him off human food for good."

"Thanks for teasing me like that in front of my dad, the very dad who once gave me a copy of *The Settlement Cook Book*. You know what the reading line is on the cover of that book? I'll never forget it: 'The Way to a Man's Heart.'"

"It was a good basic. What's the problem?"

"With that, I am out of here," said Isaiah. "Good to meet you, Mr. . . ."

"Lou."

"Lou. Enjoy your stay."

And the two men, who stood a foot apart in height and miles apart in sensibilities, shook hands, and Isaiah was gone, the door closing behind him.

Jeannie's dad turned to her and said, "Now that's tall. You two having sex?" He had that aggravating twinkle in his eyes but he looked haggard and tired.

"Daa-aad," she said, taking the Samsonite case from him and putting it against the wall, next to the door. She helped him off with his jacket, canvas with a leather collar, like a rancher's.

"Can I have a glass of water?" he asked, and sat on a stool at the kitchen counter.

"Water we have," she said, and got him one.

He swigged the water down in two gulps. "Thirsty. Hey Jeannie, mind if I go lie down a little? I'm just a little tired."

"Sure, go, you show up out of the blue when you're supposed to be in another hemisphere and you want to take a nap," she answered.

"Glad to see you too," her dad said as he made his way down the hall.

"But I'm glad you came back for Mouse!" she yelled after him.

As her dad slept, she did too. By the time she woke, her

dad was up, watching TV with Mouse on the couch next to him.

"So how you feeling, Pop?"

"Better. Ate your leftovers from Gigino—not a bad meat-ball—and even had the energy to take the dog for a walk. Nice day out there."

"Yeah, yeah," she said, as she ground beans for her coffee. "Now what are you doing here, Dad? Didn't you say you'd be away, what, two, three months? What happened?"

"Didn't like it. So I came home."

"What do you mean, you didn't like it?" She narrowed her eyes and looked at him. "Belize is your kind of place. Beach, bikinis, boats, beer. What's not to like?"

"Bugs. Lots of them. And hot. I got a little sick—"

"What do you mean 'sick'?"

"I mean, I, well, you know, it was hot, for god's sakes. I don't like it so hot."

"So you're okay otherwise?"

"I'm okay."

He said it in a way that made Jeannie worry. "But what? What aren't you saying, Dad?"

"I could use a cup of coffee. And a Danish."

She laughed. "Coffee we got. Danish, well, I'll make a run to the deli."

"How can you not have a Danish? In this city of all cities, where Danish are available on every corner of every street, in every run-down soda-pop joint."

"So is crack."

He laughed. "Yeah, well, do you remember how I used to go into the city on Sunday mornings and buy Danish from Sol's? An hour for a Danish. That's before California had much of a Jewish population. Couldn't even get a bagel.

Today, a bagel store on every corner. Of course, it's got nothing to do with Jews. It has to do with Sara Lee and the
co-opting of all things ethnic. It's why there'll never be a rev-
olution in America."

"Because of Sara Lee?"

"When everything subversive becomes adopted into the
general culture, you get complacency. But can we get back to
Danish? I used to get the best for you every Sunday morning.
Don't you remember that?"

"When you were around, you mean."

"What's that supposed to mean?"

"It means you used to go to the city to buy Danish when
you were around. Which wasn't very often."

He looked out the window in thought. Then he turned
back to her and said, "Hey, your father taught you everything
you know."

"Really."

"Yeah, like, hmmm, like how to yo-yo."

She smiled now. "True. Walk the Dog."

"Rock the Baby."

"I could never get that one! You were good."

"I was the master."

"Really. Let's see." She opened a drawer in the kitchen, the
one reserved for junk: pencils and rubber bands and tooth-
picks and screws, scotch tape and batteries and a hammer
and a flashlight and . . . a couple yo-yos, which Luce had gotten her for her birthday last year, knowing her secret hobby.
"Show me."

She handed him the bright green Duncan, keeping the
red one for herself. He put his on his middle finger, she put
hers on hers, and they proceeded to impress each other with
their deftness and cunning. Father and daughter, with the

same long legs and longing in their hearts, the same wild hair and the same jaunty stance, the similar yearnings and dissatisfactions, yo-yo'd together side by side like a vaudeville act of long ago.

"Walk the Dog." His hands moved like he was still thirty. She wasn't quite as fast or fluid. "Now Around the World. And now, drumroll please, the pièce de résistance—Rock the Baby."

She stopped and watched him and applauded. He bowed to her and said, "Now you show me." And he partially sat on a stool, his weight still on a leg extended to the floor. And she did. Though her Rock the Baby was nowhere near the showstopper that his was, she got through it.

"Pretty good," he said, obviously pleased with his daughter, and himself.

"What else?" she asked.

"I don't know any others."

"Not yo-yo tricks, things you contributed to my life."

"So many things! I was a huge influence."

"Dad, you were hardly there."

"Bananas and cream! Remember?"

"Old Russian recipe. Take a banana, slice it, add a few tablespoons of sour cream and, oh, about a ton of sugar."

"Not a ton. Three teaspoons. It was good. You can't say it wasn't good."

"It was good, Dad. What else?"

"Was I really not there? Is that how you remember it?"

"Dad . . ."

"I just didn't know how to be with you. Your mother, she didn't make it easy."

"So what if it wasn't easy? I was your daughter."

"You still are, so you better behave!" He shook a long index finger at her.

Jeannie smiled, but said nothing, waiting.

"I taught you some other things too. I know I did." He paused, thinking. Then he snapped his fingers. "How to eat an egg salad sandwich."

"With muenster cheese," she said with a smile.

"Nah!" he yelled. "That's sacrilegious. Where'd you learn that?"

"I've always eaten it that way."

"No. No. No. Did I say 'no'? With mustard! M-U-S-T-A-R-D! You must've heard me wrong. All those times, ordering egg salad with mustard, did you think I said 'muenster'? You were a kid. How'd you know from muenster?"

"Maybe because eggs with mustard is disgusting, Dad. Tell me something else. Something that has nothing to do with food, thank you very much."

"It's good with mustard," he said softly. "You should try it." He thought for a while. Then he slapped his knee. "How to tell a joke."

"I don't tell jokes, Dad. I can't even remember them. What you did teach me about joke-telling is how to tell the same one over. And over. And over."

"Okay, okay. Let me see. Why you should never gamble." He looked at her, his eyes twinkling.

"Ha!" Jeannie laughed that guffaw of hers. "Now that was a lesson!" One Memorial Day weekend, when Jeannie was around nine years old, she, her dad, Harriet, and Amy, Harriet's best friend at the time (yet another short-lived relationship, since nobody could live up to Harriet's standards), had taken a trip to Las Vegas. Her dad had awakened everybody at three a.m. to get an early start, in the dark of night; they piled into his blue Chevy, its trunk stuffed with sleeping bags and backpacks and supplies, and drove down through

California on Route 101, a main artery through the agricultural center of the state. They passed Castroville, the artichoke capital of the world, and had breakfast in San Luis Obispo, where they visited the mission. Harriet and Dad had argued about whether they should take a side trip back up Route 101 to San Simeon, the ostentatious palace of William Randolph Hearst. Harriet felt that stepping even one foot there was paying homage to the bourgeois, racist, anti-Semitic fascist, and that going to Las Vegas was bad enough. Jeannie's dad thought it would be educational, that you should see everything whether you agree with it politically or not. But Harriet won, and instead they turned west and cut through The Mojave National Preserve and slept in the desert for one night.

Lying there on her back, the moonlit shadows of the strange gnarly Joshua trees stretching across her sleeping bag, Jeannie felt very small. The sky was huge and bright with layers of stars, more stars than she had ever seen in one sky. Some felt so close she could touch them, others so far that she felt left behind.

"Do you know, Jeannie, that there are more stars in the sky than there are grains of sand on all the beaches in the world?" said her dad from his sleeping bag.

At first Jeannie didn't believe it—not that her dad wasn't trustworthy with this kind of information. But, the idea that the sky went on forever, that what you saw wasn't anywhere close to what you'd get, that it was vast and unimaginably deep, was difficult to comprehend. Was there a star meant for her or was she destined to be bound to the craggy desert soil? That was the first inkling Jeannie had that she was a romantic, that her dreams were as big as the sky, her hopes as vivid as the twinkling dots above, her yearnings as powerful as the light from the moon. She had no idea then (and little now) what, specifically, those dreams were, but she could physically feel their tug deep in the center of her chest.

They arrived in Las Vegas in the morning, found a campground, showered, changed, and went into town. It was only the late seventies, so the Bellagio, MGM Grand, and New York, New York hadn't been built yet. But Caesar's Palace was plenty big and flashy. With her nose pressed against the glass, Jeannie watched the people pull the arms of the slot machines over and over, feeding them with quarters, pulling the arms, and feeding them again. Her mom was lecturing her about the disease of gambling, which, like liquor or heroin, was addictive and worse than smoking pot, when her dad dug into his pants pockets and pulled out his change. He said, "I'm going to play these two quarters. And that's it."

Harriet yelled at his back, as he went through the revolving doors into the gold-leaf-gilded pillared lobby with its thick carpeting and velvet walls, "Just look at this place, Lou. The house always wins!"

He chose a slot machine near the sidewalk windows so Jeannie could watch, since she was too young to be allowed on the gambling floor. The first coin he lost. The second, with one strong pull, hit the $2,500 jackpot. Bells clanged, sirens wailed, and lights flashed. Her dad turned to them, his fists raised high in the air, his smile triumphant. Jeannie laughed. Harriet shook her head and said, "Unbelievable." And they celebrated with a lavish dinner at the Sands. Over dessert, her dad said, "But your mom is right, honey. The house, 99 point 999999 times, wins. Or these monstrosities"—and he gestured broadly to the room—"wouldn't be here." He gave her a wink. "But it's pretty fun to win."

As if they had arrived at the exact same point in their memory at the exact same moment, Jeannie looked at her dad and he turned to look at her. "That was funny. Your mom—"

"Oh god. Even she had to laugh. Though it took some convincing to make her feel comfortable spending the money."

They were silent for a minute or two, both deep in memory. Then Jeannie said, "So what else?"

And her dad replied, "Ain't that enough?" When he saw her face, he turned to the window, his hands in his front pockets, and said, "What poor really is."

"Oh yeah. How could I forget?" She looked out the window too. The sky had turned gray and dull, the river a solid streak of steel. One rainy Saturday afternoon—she remembered it was gloomy and chilly, a day much like this one—when her dad had been there three solid months, making her feel like perhaps, this time, he was staying, making her feel stupidly secure, almost to the point of taking his presence for granted, the way a child should think of her parent—he and Harriet were in the living room, reading, when she burst in dripping wet. She had just been at Lindsey's house, where she'd taken a ride on Lindsey's shiny blue new bike. Jeannie's had been a hand-me-down from Patrick, a boy a few years older than Jeannie who had lived with his mom in the house for a while. "Lindsey got a brand-new bike. It wasn't her birthday or anything."

"You have a bike," Harriet had said, barely looking up from the newspaper she was reading.

"It's old! It was what's his name's, that stupid kid. Why can't I get a new bike, a bike of my own, like everybody else?"

"What's wrong with the one you have? Besides, we can't afford it."

Jeannie cried, "I wish we weren't so fucking poor," as she stomped out of the room.

But she didn't get far, because her dad had gotten up from the chair where he'd been reading, his face red, his nostrils flaring, and in a booming voice he'd said, "Poor? I'll show you poor." He went and grabbed her by her arm. "I should wash your mouth out with soap. But first, get in the car!" He dragged her out the front door into the rain.

She remembered Harriet calling after them, "Louis, don't."

They drove to East Oakland, he at the wheel, she right behind him, down High Street toward the bay, down below the highway, where old rickety wood houses sat in squalid fields next to warehouses surrounded by barbed wire. "Poor?" he boomed. "That's poor." And out of the window she saw two little kids, an older girl, ten maybe, and a small boy, playing in the rain, in their yard that was ragged with weeds and enclosed by a metal fence.

She remembered wondering where their mom was and if she knew that they were outside. She wondered if they had a dad, or even a sometime dad like hers. She doubted they had bikes, even rusty old ones like hers. So she began to cry, as her dad railed from the front of the car, and she didn't stop until they got home. She cried because she felt ashamed, because there were poor, really poor, people who lived only twenty minutes away. She cried because she was scared that her greedy, stupid self would send her dad away again.

And it did. Or she forever thought that was the reason. Because only three days later, her dad packed his things into the same piece of Samsonite luggage he carried today, and left in his battered Chevy, never to live with her again. He had hardly said good-bye. Just, "I can't live here anymore. Your mom and I, well, life is too short. And I just, well, I have to go. I'll be seeing you, Jeannie. I will. I love you, you know," a kiss, and he was gone. She would see him again, of course, once or twice a year, at a restaurant, at a park, never in his home or hers. For a couple hours, sometimes half a day. Sometimes they'd talk, sometimes just eat or walk.

Thinking of it now, her throat became full and tears welled in her eyes. Not for those poor kids or out of shame, but for the dad she had only sometimes, when he felt like it. She cried because, today, with all the money she could ever need, knowing she could never know what it was like to be poor like that, she could relate to those kids who played that day in the mud and chill. It wasn't the money she'd been after, it wasn't only the new bike. It was warmth, an arm around her, a heart beating for her, feeling loved and cherished. What would it have been like to be raised like Lindsey or Luce, with a dad who considered her his princess?

"You're not crying," her dad said as a statement of fact.

"Nah, just thinking. So," she said, wiping her eyes, taking a deep breath, "how long you staying, Pop? A day? Two?"

"Well, I was wondering if, this time, I could hang around a while. Get to know the city. See my little girl at work. Get to know her too."

She turned to look at him. *Shit, you've got to be kidding. Now you're interested?* But there he was, already sitting down on her couch, putting his feet on her Noguchi coffee table and turning on the flat-screen TV that hung on the wall. Making plans to stay.

"Nice couch," he said. "A little lumpy." He was feeling for something behind where he sat, in the crack between the seat and back cushion. "What the hell?" he asked as he pulled out a pair of panties, barely identifiable, all chewed up and torn to shreds. He held it up and said gleefully, "Glad to see my baby's having some fun!"

"Mouse! You have got to stop stealing my underwear!" She had yelled at the dog in her angriest voice, but he just looked at her, tail wagging, as if she'd just said, "Want a treat?" *Not too bright*, she was thinking.

"Well, don't let your old pop cramp your style while I'm here. I sure wouldn't want to do that."

"Not to worry. Trust me," she answered, as she put on her sneakers for the walk to the deli to get a cheese Danish for her dad.

"Oh, and would you fill this prescription, honey, while you're out?" He dug into his pants pocket and handed her a piece of paper. "It's nothing, just a little something the doctor recommended."

He must've noticed the face on her, full of concern. "Don't ask. I'm old. You take medicine when you're old."

"You're not old. Shut up."

"Don't talk to your father that way. Thou shalt honor thy—"

"Yeah, yeah, yeah. But have you been to a New York City drugstore recently? You have no idea what you're asking of me, do you? You are asking me to risk life and limb, to be treated in a subhuman way, to be humiliated by untrained clerks and indifferent cashiers. In other words, you're asking me to go to hell and back."

"So don't go. And don't get my blood pressure medicine."

"Daa-aad."

"It's nothing, I tell you. Just a little beta blocker. And while you're there, would you pick up a little gas-blocker too? That food in Belize, please."

Parting Sky

Out the front doors and onto the street on the gray, rainy autumn afternoon, she put up the hood of her black slicker and pulled its string tight around her face. She never carried an umbrella, on principle: she always lost the expensive ones, the cheap ones broke in only a gentle wind, and it was just another thing to carry. So she stood for a moment under her awning and steeled herself against the wet and cold to come, and tried to tell herself that her dad really was okay, that he just hadn't liked Belize, that he was simply tired from his trip, and nothing more.

And then she saw Tommy. Parking his Vespa across the street, his messenger bag slung diagonally across one shoulder to the opposite hip, his khakis baggy, wrinkled, and wet, his leather jacket dripping, he took off his helmet and shook his head, ran a hand back through his hair. It felt like an hour to Jeannie before he looked over and saw her standing there. He smiled and ran to meet her, and she to him, and there in the middle of the street, Jeannie threw her arms around him, pressed her face to his.

"Jeannie," said Tommy, the rain falling onto his face as he kissed her.

A car honked, making them jump. *What, you can't wait one goddamn minute?* Jeannie thought as Tommy took her by the hand and ran with her to the sidewalk in front of her building.

"Were you going out? I know I should've called. I was going to, but . . . can we go upstairs?"

She shook her head. "My dad. He's back. I was on my way to get him some breakfast." Then she looked at him with concern. "How are you? How was it? Are you okay? Did you get everything you needed?"

"Just glad to be home. I'll tell you all about it. Let's go to my place, okay?"

"I can't. He just got here." She saw Tommy's disappointment and didn't try to hide her own. "Today's not good. Maybe later?"

"Come on, Jeannie, come with me. It's only your dad. You'll see him later."

Only my dad? She struggled for a moment with what was right. She shook her head. "I have to be here for him."

"What about me? What about us? Jesus, Jeannie. You have no idea what it was like—"

"I'm sorry. I want to. Don't make this hard. How about later, before the show?"

"Shit, I can't. I'm having dinner tonight with my editor at the *Times*. I asked him for a desk job. Full time, on this side of the Atlantic, in New York City."

"You mean . . ." Her heart flew. And immediately plummeted back to earth. She felt guilty—she wouldn't go with him now, and yet here he was, trying to be near her. And she wanted him close, but not at the expense of his career.

"Wouldn't that be something?" he said, and kissed the corner of her mouth. He nuzzled her ear with his nose.

"It would," she said, "but only if it's right, and if not, I'll still be here. You won't get rid of me without a fight." She kissed him, putting her hand on his cheek.

"I know you're not making me do this. I'm making me do this." He kissed her again, brushed her hair away from her face. "Tomorrow morning, then, after the show. I'll know more by then anyway. And I'll have showered," he said, smiling.

"And now I'm off to do battle at Duane Reade." She turned

and walked two steps before she felt him grab her wrist and pull her back to him.

"Wait a minute, you" he said, wrapping his arm around her, its length circling her waist. He kissed her. Long and deep and fervently, with the urgency of a teenage boy. There they were, two old friends, kissing in the chilly afternoon on the sidewalk of a cobblestone street. Then, all of a sudden, the air grew warm around them and the rain stopped. Jeannie opened her eyes and looked up at the sky, and then over Tommy's shoulder toward the river.

"Look," she said. Above them, it was blue, but right over there, just across the street, the rain continued to fall. How funny that a cloud, with its fuzzy, amorphous edges, could be so abrupt in its effect that there was no rain here, and yet there, twenty feet away, there was. *There's alchemy in that,* Jeannie thought. She and Tommy looked at each other then, and felt very special, like two deer in the woods, huddled under a tree but protected from the raging storm, as if they'd found a greater shelter in each other.

One more kiss, one more time Jeannie buried her face in Tommy's neck, smelled his scent and breathed in deeply, memorizing it until the next time they were together. Tommy put on his helmet, adjusted the strap under his chin, revved the bike's motor, headed north. Then she turned away and walked east, into the city.

Debts and Threats

By the time Tommy got to News Café on Eighth Avenue that night, every booth was taken, every stool at the bar filled. It seemed like the entire staff of the *Times* was there getting sustenance to make it through until deadline. Tommy let his eyes adjust to the darkness and then saw John at the bar. When he approached, John stood and motioned to the back.

"Let's go to the rear. Less noise. Fewer ears."

They sat, ordered a couple of beers.

"It's really good to see you, Tom. I don't have much time, so let's get to it. You did good, by the way, in Paki. You know, you could do it from anywhere. You know your stuff, you do the research, you get in deep. It's all good. I don't see why—"

"I'm tired. I want a life."

"Yeah, tell me about it."

"And I'm involved with this—"

"Ah, so that's it."

"No. Yes. I guess it is. And I've paid my dues. I want a local job. Editor, City Hall, something close."

John let out a deep guffaw. "You covering City Hall. You'd go fucking crazy. Give me a break. Why don't we just give you obits? Or social shit?"

"John, I'm serious. I've done this for fifteen years and I'm tired. And I deserve it."

"No question you deserve it. But—"

"And you owe me."

"I owe you? You're kidding, right? I've handed you every plum in the last five years. You wouldn't be who you are without me. It's you—"

"I'm not going to argue," Tommy said, shaking his head. "I appreciate everything you've done for me. Now I want to do something different. What's so hard?"

"Can't do it. I'm sorry. You're too good. Even if I wanted to, shit, I just can't. You make us look good. You're perfect right where you are." He laughed again. "Maybe if you weren't so good, then you'd get what you want. Nothing like that kind of irony, right?"

"If I weren't so good, you wouldn't have had the time to write that book of yours, would you?" Tommy looked directly at John and then, in the silence, he looked down at his beer. Thumbed the condensation on the glass. "I may have to go somewhere else then."

"You mean like a weekly? Because there ain't no daily going to pay you like we do."

"So, okay, a weekly. I'll give Whitaker at *Newsweek* a call. And besides, I don't need the goddamn money you're paying me."

"Must be nice to have a trust fund. And don't threaten me, rich boy."

"That's not what I meant." *How'd this get so ugly?* Tommy wondered. He stood, dug in his pocket, and threw a twenty on the table. "Here, let the trust fund pay." And he walked out.

STERLING BEHAVIOR

JEANNIE: *Good evening, fellow insomniacs! You're listening to Jeannie Sterling, and this is* Sterling Behavior *at WBUZ, 660 on your AM dial. Tonight we're proud to bring you* Caught Ya!, *our own radio reality show, where you witness bad behavior as it actually happened. Tonight, the Line Police. We have reports from a Times Square movie theater and a New Jersey gas station. And then we'll be taking calls at 777-246-3800. I'm here with our extraordinary engineer, Joseph, who's dressed in another of his whimsical T-shirts. This one says, in huge block letters,* I'M HOME. TAKE ME DRUNK. *I guess he wants to be inconspicuous! And Luce, who you all know.*

JOSEPH: *We're ready to go, Jeannie.*

LUCE: *That's my introduction? Joseph is extraordinary and I'm, well, someone to take for granted? Or as Dr. Richards taught us to say, I feel sad when you diss me like that.*

JEANNIE: *You're kidding, right? But okay, with us is Luce, my best friend and our terrific producer who is here making it all happen.*

LUCE: *Thank you.*

JEANNIE: *Yesterday we visited a movie theater in Times Square. The following is what occurred there. Okay, Joseph, let 'er roll.*

[taped segment begins]

JEANNIE: *Hey everybody, here we are in front of the Loews cineplex on West Forty-second Street. There's a line around the corner. Must be opening night for Matrix four, or is it five?*

JOSEPH: *It's actually a prequel to Matrix one.*

JEANNIE: *That's too confusing for me. Well, now that they're taking tickets and the line is beginning to move, will people try to cut the line, actually forgo the line completely by walking in from the other side of the door? Let's go up and see.*

LUCE: *Look, I think you're right.*

JEANNIE: *Hey you! Hey guys! Two young men in their late teens just walked up and are trying to give their ticket to the doorman. Hey, hey you! There's a line! See it? It's there, goes all the way to the corner and wraps around Eighth Avenue.*

GUY#1: *Yeah, okay, we see it. But we came the other way and—*

JEANNIE: *And you have to get in line like everybody else.*

GUY#2: *And who made you the line god? Why don't you just smite me?*

GUY#1: *That's cool, man. "The line god." Sweet.*

JEANNIE: *Don't either of you feel that it's just plain wrong to cut the line?*

GUY#1: *Nah. I feel like it's survival of the fittest.*

GUY#2: *Yeah, survival is right, man. Let's get our seats.*

JEANNIE: *Wait a minute, you. You and those attitudes of yours are getting a ticket for committing social infraction AB-negative: no cutting lines. That's a fine of twenty bucks, which we will donate to the Hurricane Relief Fund.*

GUY#1: *You can suck my twenty dollar di [bleep], doll.*

GUY#2: *Or as Obi-Wan said, "What the fu [bleep] be with you."*

GUY#1: *He didn't say that. Did he?*

GUY#2: *I know. I just gotta get rid of this chick.*

GUY#1: *She's sort of a hottie though, isn't she?*

GUY#2: *Yeah, but so high maintenance.*

LUCE: *Jeannie, this is not working. They just don't take this getting-tickets-for-social-infractions thing seriously.*

JEANNIE: *You're right. We're going to have to take it up a notch, as they say. Do something they can't ignore. Any ideas, loyal listeners? This is Jeannie Sterling talking to you from Times Square on WBUZ Radio, 660 on your AM dial. When we come back, we'll be paying a visit to New Jersey.*

The Plan

"I want you to listen to this," said Moss, as he turned up the volume of his Bose speakers with the remote and leaned back in the red leather Mies sofa in his office on the thirty-eighth floor of Moss Enterprises, at Fifth and Fifty-seventh. "She's really something." He had to hype, even if it was true, because it wasn't easy getting Robert Shaltow up to a meeting this late at night. Marshall was there too, also revved, jittery, his crossed leg shaking with impatience.

Shaltow looked at the folder in his lap. "The numbers look good."

"Good?" said Marshall. "They're excellent. And growing. If

there was a moment for a show to fly, this is it for Sterling."

"Okay, she's back. Listen." He wondered if his enthusiasm was giving him away. Or did they believe, as he always had, that he was all business all the time?

STERLING BEHAVIOR

JEANNIE: *We were at a 7-Eleven in New Jersey earlier tonight, acting in the role of bad behavior watchdogs. Not like my dog, thank you very much—*

LUCE: *Your dog is a little stinker.*

JEANNIE: *Excuse me? I resent that. I prefer to think of him as . . . the devil incarnate.*

LUCE: *But he is very cute.*

JEANNIE AND LUCE: *He has that!*

JEANNIE: *No, tonight we're the line police. In the last segment we heard two guys rationalize cutting in line. Now we're going to witness what I call line abuse. Here, from earlier this evening: [taped segment begins]*

JEANNIE: *This busy 7-Eleven in Lyndhurst, New Jersey, has six pumps for gas. But it's rush hour and they're all taken. Cars are in lines on both sides of the pumps, waiting for the next available pump. Sadly, three of the six cars at the pumps are empty, devoid of people, who must be inside buying a Slurpee and potato chips. So what we have here are empty cars taking up gas pumps while people wait in line. How rude is that? You get gas, you pay, you move your car, and, then and only then, you shop. Or else you're a pump hog.*

LUCE: *Or Fritos.*

JEANNIE: *What?*

LUCE: *They could be buying Fritos. Not everybody likes potato chips.*

JOSEPH: *Or cigarettes, for that matter. Or beer. Or a Snickers bar.*

JEANNIE: *Okay, okay. Now, did you know that New Jersey is one of the last two states in all of America that doesn't allow self-service gas? Here and in Oregon, you can't pump your ride! Wait, wait wait— here comes a driver of a pump hog. Hello! Mister, can I have a word?*

MAN: *Sure, lady.*

JEANNIE: *You realize all these cars are waiting to get gas and you were in the store for over five minutes while your car sat here in front of a pump?*

MAN: *Yeah, and your point?*

JEANNIE: *You should get gas, pay the attendant, and—*

MAN: *Piss. I had to take a piss.*

JEANNIE: *Thanks for the details, but couldn't you have moved your car first?*

MAN: *No, I pissed while the guy pumped. And then I decided to get a Slurpee. So I go in and kill two birds with one stone.*

JEANNIE: *But why not move your car and park over there, and then, you know.*

MAN: *Because I didn't want to. That's why.*

JEANNIE: *Well, I'm giving you a ticket for violating social code number 75839482746, or hogging a pump. Next time, be more considerate, would you?*

MAN: *Lady, [tearing paper heard] you can take this ticket and shove it right up your ass.*

WOMAN: *Hey you! Yeah, you there!*

JEANNIE: *Me?*

WOMAN: *Yeah, lady, you. Stop littering, you hear? Use a garbage can. You must be from the city, because only those kind of people would litter like that.*

JEANNIE: *It wasn't me—*

WOMAN: *And would you move away from the pump so someone can use it already? How rude can you be?*

The Deal

"Okay, let's do it. I think people would love to see this as it's happening," said Shaltow. "How does she look, by the way? We'll have to be sure the camera takes to her."

"Not bad," said Marshall. "If you like that type."

Moss just said, "I think it'll work."

"Then we have a deal?" asked Marshall.

"When Bob says 'Let's do it,' consider it done, Marshall," replied Moss. "So when can we begin, do you think?"

"She's an unknown," said Shaltow, "but I'd put her on the air during February sweeps. If it's something we believe in."

The two men waited quietly for him to decide. Marshall kept his eyes on him, but Moss looked out the window at the night sky. The stars were unusually visible, undimmed by the lights from the city.

"Done," Shaltow said, finally.

"Partners. I've been looking forward to this, Bob," said Moss, putting out his hand.

As the two men shook, Moss wondered how Jeannie was going to feel about moving to television. She'd be pissed, he was sure, that the decision was made for her without her involvement. But she was going to love the possibility of becoming a star. That he knew.

Ethics 101

"And there she is, woman of the streets. What did they call you? 'High maintenance'? It's as if they'd known you forever," said Moss, as he walked into her studio.

"They also called me 'hottie,'" she said breathily.

"It was good," he said.

"It was okay." Jeannie took a swig of water. She took off her headphones and shook her head to loosen her hair.

"What do you mean? It was funny, it was great."

She turned to him, her eyes ablaze. "I mean, what's the point? People are idiots. Always were. Forever will be. The only person who got reprimanded for behaving badly was me, for god's sake."

"Listen to you. You've been dreaming of a way to get people to actually do the right thing rather than just talk about it. So this time, it backfired a little. You'll figure it out. Maybe you need to push it more. To really get in people's faces and embarrass them a little."

"Ah. So you want me to humiliate them? The ends will justify the means, it's okay to be bad to be good, and all that shit."

"Oh. Okay. We're having one of our philosophical arguments."

"Well, as Aristotle said in his 'Treatise on Shushing and the Republic,' how far do we go? Total humiliation or just mild exploitation?"

"That's not what I meant, and you know it. And since when are you so high and mighty?" He sounded angry and frustrated.

"And with that," she said, with a glance to the clock on the wall, "it's time to go home."

"That would be good."

"Good."

"Good." And Moss walked out of the studio, leaving her with Luce and Joseph, who were wrapping up business.

So when Moss turned up in her cubicle a few minutes later with his jacket on and picked up hers, and said, "Come. Walk with me," she was more than surprised. She felt the musty gray wall-to-wall she stood on slipping out from under her.

"I can't, my dad . . ." Of course it was Tommy she was going to see. But she looked at her watch and realized he wouldn't be up at six a.m.

"Come," he said again, with a tilt of his head this time, sweetly, imploringly, as if it was important. "You need some perspective."

"Oh," she said, "and you're the one to give it to me, not to be disrespectful, oh boss, sir."

He smiled and nodded, acknowledging her lousy attempt to kiss his ass. "Somebody has to, so it might as well be me."

He held her old brown suede jacket up for her, as if it were a princess's velvet robe, and she put her arms in it; then he lifted it up and onto her shoulders, leaving his hands there for a tiny moment, but long enough for her to feel their strength through the old suede. He stood behind her, letting her walk first through the glass doors into the hallway, past the receptionist, to the elevator bank. When the elevator arrived, he put his hand on the small of her back, pushing her gently into it. Only her father had ever treated her this way. When she was growing up she felt it was sexist and patronizing. Now, as a grown-up, it felt sexy and protective. She stood a little taller, held her shoulders back, and walked as regally as she was being treated.

Outside in the early-morning air, it was still dark. The days had gotten shorter, now that winter was approaching, and the streets looked strange, with only a few early birds bustling to jobs, all under cover of the night. He didn't say a word as they got into a black sedan parked out in front of the building.

"I want you to see something," he said. "Hey Rog, let's go," he said to the driver.

What, the Hummer showroom? His darkroom? Who knew with this guy? she thought.

She turned her head to look at him, this stranger, at his profile as they drove. His strong nose, his jaw unshaven, dark, flecked with gray. That soft place where his neck met his ear, the way his hair was long over his collar, the way his jacket fell on his shoulders. The way he sat, perfectly comfortable. This was a Man, with a capital M. There was something old-fashioned about him, something so masculine and retro. He made her think of a button she'd seen recently at one of those cute gift shops stuffed with overpriced upscale junk on Hudson. It showed the head of a man from an illustrated ad from the fifties, and it read: BEING AN ASSHOLE IS ALL PART OF MY MANLY ESSENCE. She made a mental note to herself to get it for him for his birthday if they were still working together and speaking to each other.

They were driving north, up through Central Park, along the park drive that wound its way up the East Side. The sun was rising, its light finding its way through the trees. The old, iron streetlamps were still on, but the grand apartment buildings on Fifth Avenue were silhouetted against the brightening sky. Jeannie glanced over at Moss to see that he, too, was watching night became day.

Then the road wound its way to the West Side and they found themselves on Central Park West, heading north.

"How far uptown are we going?" Jeannie asked. "I think I need an oxygen mask. The air is getting thinner."

"Quiet. We're almost there."

"I forgot my passport. They're strict at the Canadian border."

"You downtown snob. Be patient."

When they arrived at 100th Street, the car pulled over.

"We're here," said Moss.

When they got out, Jeannie could see they were at the top of a hill. Who knew this flat sea-level city had hills? Below were rolling grass knolls and a pond covered with ducks. Here, right in her city, was a piece of earth she had never seen before. They headed down the paved path, toward the pond. A weeping willow was growing out from the water. A small waterfall leapt over rocks until it fed into the pond, crossing under their path. Carved wooden benches stood on wood-chipped pathways that wound like hiking trails near the pond's edge.

They were silent as they walked. Moss held Jeannie's elbow. She thought it odd and old fashioned, but felt its support and allowed herself to lean into it. Mallards floated on the water, which was green and opaque. Flowering bushes surrounded the perimeter, as did trees whose leaves were pure autumn—burnished gold, deep red, and even maroon, a color that seemed as out of place in nature as the deep blue sky above. A yellow blanket of leaves covered the sloping hill.

By the time they reached the opposite side, past the stone steps, past the arched bridge where a stream coursed its way north through lush, dense shrubs, reminding her of places in

Big Sur, the sun was up, its light pouring through the sparse leaves that remained in the trees, making them appear translucent, neon colored, their veins dark and deep within them.

What a place. What a surprise. Jeannie knew that uptown was foreign to her, but she never expected it to feel like another world. It was dreamy and enchanting, this place, with the light, the trees, the vivid colors, the strange man taking hold of her hand in silence.

As they headed back to the car, Moss said, "Special, isn't it."

"I never knew this existed," Jeannie said, but she was confused. Why had he brought her here? What did he want from her?

As if he heard her thoughts, he stopped, turned to her, held her arms, and pulled her to him. She almost forgot herself, almost thought he was going to kiss her, almost raised her chin, almost kissed him, when he said, "Don't you get it? Everything in time. Will your show change the world? Of course not."

She felt like a fool. "But—"

"Will it influence people? You bet your butt it will."

She struggled to gather herself. "I don't know. I don't think—"

"I think you won't know what hit you. I think your star will rise so fast we'll have to keep you tethered to the earth. Even the money will come."

"I'm not interested."

"In what? In getting rich? Even more successful than you are now? Bullshit. I know where you live. Just because you wear that old jacket and that beat-up old bag that looks half chewed—"

"It is. It was. My deadbeat dog."

"Don't think I'm not aware how expensive it was originally. And that's okay. You are allowed to be happy, to make money, to spend it—as long as you are saving some too, of course. What's wrong with that?" He looked at her then and saw the look on her face. "Oh, wait a minute. Don't tell me that you're one of those."

"What's 'one of those'?"

"You live well, you make a lot of money, but you don't allow yourself to feel good about it. If you feel truly uncomfortable with all the money, give some away. There are a lot of people who could use what you've got."

"Oh, and I need you to tell me that. What the hell," she finally asked aloud, "do you want anyway? Why did you bring me here?"

"What do I want?" he repeated. Then they got into the car, in silence. Finally, he turned to her. "I want you to fly."

"This is about selling, isn't it."

"Oh, shut up, for crying out loud."

She couldn't help but throw her head back and laugh.

As the car made its way back downtown through the park, Jeannie felt something turning, plates shifting. It was a subtle force, but after that walk, she was tuned to her heart, and though she couldn't identify the station or the song that was playing, she knew it was meaningful and melodic. *Everything in time*, he'd said.

Chinese Staircase

What the hell was that, Moss was thinking as the car made its way down through the park. *To bring her up there, to take hold of her like that. Jesus fucking Christ.* He kept his head turned away from her, but there was no way he could help but feel her sitting beside him, the space between them alive with energy. *This is exactly how it starts.* And he knew damn well how it would end. He fingered the string bracelet on his wrist, feeling it between his thumb and index finger, remembering its original texture, now worn smooth and fragile.

A year had gone by since he'd last seen Rosie, the one real love of his life. And almost six since he'd broken up with her mother, Celia. He thought he loved her too, but he couldn't give her the time and attention she needed, that any relationship required. He tried to tell her, and himself, that it was a particularly busy time, what with his new venture that the *Journal* had branded "insane." (It *was* pretty crazy, Moss remembered with a smile, to try to run the New York State Lottery and give every cent of the profits to charity. But he figured with his success rate, if a couple of his "insane" notions didn't make it, at least he brought some attention to the issues.) But he knew in his heart if he'd really wanted to make a place for Celia in his life, he would have. He also knew that he would've walked away earlier if it hadn't been for Rosie.

Rosie was only ten when Moss had stopped seeing Celia, but nobody spoke truer words to him before or since. There are maybe three people, if you're lucky, in your life who change you, Moss felt. And Rosie was one.

"Why are you so mean to my mom?" she had asked him at the end, when Moss and Celia were already past the point of no return, when words that never should have been spoken had been. Of course he hadn't been mean, he just hadn't been *there*. Always distracted by the new venture, the wild idea, the taller tree.

One day, during that sweltering last summer after Rosie

returned from a four-week stint at a camp in the Berkshires, Moss had taken her to Coney Island for a Nathan's with sauerkraut and mustard and a ride on the Cyclone. Resting on a bench, looking out to the Atlantic, Rosie turned to Moss and said, "I made something for you at camp." She dug in the pocket of her shorts and pulled out what looked like a bracelet made of string. It was a bright turquoise blue, much like the ocean before them, woven with neon green into a pattern that she told him was called "Chinese Staircase."

"Here," she said. "I want you to wear this and never take it off."

"Never *ever*? It's going to get pretty funky."

"Moss," Rosie said, "you have to trust me on this. This bracelet is your only hope."

He smiled and said, "Okay, now tell me what you're talking about."

"You have to wear this bracelet until you get a girlfriend. Then and only then can you take it off."

"I get a girlfriend every other day," he laughed, then caught himself. "Not like your mom, of course, who has been a lot more than a girlfriend to me."

"No, I mean one you love. And I mean it. One you really really love. Like in the movies. Like, you know the Greek myths? There was this guy, Pygmalion. He was a sculptor and couldn't find anybody to love, so he sculpted the perfect woman. And his love for her brought her to life. That kind of love. Crazy love."

"Pygmalion, huh? Impressive."

"I'm going into the fifth grade, Moss. There *are* other things to read besides Harry Potter."

"Yeah, but Pygmalion, that's big. Some people go a lifetime and don't find that kind of love."

"That's why you have this bracelet, Moss. Boy," she said shaking her head, "don't you get it? You have to believe. Because it sure won't happen if you don't believe it will."

"You getting woo woo on me? If I believe, it'll happen? Then how come the world isn't perfect, huh? How come there are poor people, how come you're short, if all I have to do is believe?"

"Don't change the subject. And I'm not short. I'm a kid. Now," she said, taking his hand, turning it palm up and tying the bracelet around his wrist, "you have to promise to wear this forever and only take it off when you fall in love in a Pygmalion kind of way. And if it breaks or tears before that, you put it back on. Now promise me."

"But Rosie honey, why? Why is this so important to you?"

"Because you should have a happy life," she had said to him.

He laughed. "How old *are* you? Eighty-eight?"

"Close."

He put his arm around her shoulder. "You know what would make me happy? If I had a little girl like you one day."

"I know," she said. "But you won't. Because there's only one me."

"Truer words were never spoken."

"Now promise."

And he did, and six years later, he was still wearing the damn piece of string. It had lost its color and had torn off a couple times. It was frayed and ugly and he didn't give a shit. He risked a quick glance at the woman sitting on his right, beside him in the car's back seat. She was turned away, her hair a rocky stream over her shoulder, cascading down her arm, over her breast. One hand was clenched on her thigh, as if she were holding on for dear life. *Rosie*, he thought, *I have a feeling, if I'm not careful . . . I might have found my Galatea.*

That was their last day together, at Coney Island, except for a short visit here and there when he could get down to Miami, where Rosie and her mom had moved shortly after. Sitting on that bench, he had pulled her to him and hugged her tightly and said, "I love you, Rosie. And I promise to wear the bracelet until such time that—"

"It won't be long, Moss, if you just stop being a baby and let it happen."

He took in a deep breath of air as the taxi left the park and entered the shadowed streets of midtown. *This time, I don't think I have a choice.*

Love, Sex, and the Public Library

By the time she got to Tommy's it was already ten a.m. It had been at least a year since she'd been here, when he had people over for drinks for his thirty-seventh birthday. He lived on the top floor of a brownstone that his family owned on East Seventy-fourth off Madison, in the same swank and strangely clean Upper East Side as Luce. His brother and his family lived on the second and third floors and his grandparents lived on the parlor and first floor, which had access to a beautiful garden that burst with tulips and lilacs in the summer. She didn't know if Tommy had to pay rent for the apartment and she never asked. His money situation was out of bounds in terms of discussion. All she did know was that she had been uptown twice today and Tommy's uptown was a whole lot different from Moss's.

Where Jeannie lived, in Tribeca, there was wealth, to be

sure, but for the most part it was new money from media and the dot-com phase. But here, there was more than wealth, there was history. Families with names, entries in *The Social Register*. Before Jeannie came to New York, she hadn't a clue that class really existed in America, and she'd never even heard the term "nouveau riche" before, because in California that's all there was: new money. The west was the new—relatively speaking—frontier, so it was a fairly level playing field in terms of class. It was only when she came to New York that Jeannie saw class distinction in action, and the height of it sat on the Upper East Side.

Tommy, of course, was of legitimate, deeply bred, highly protected Old Money. His family, the Whitneys, had a long and white-bread—as she teased him—history in the United States that went back centuries to the first Europeans on American soil. Her dad's family had come here in steerage on a freighter through Ellis Island, Tommy's on the *Mayflower*.

He must've still been asleep, because she had to ring his doorbell several times before he buzzed her in. Up the three flights to the fourth floor, following the green carpeting with the leaf motif, the striped wallpaper, the dark mahogany banister carved with leaves and flowers. His door was toward the front of the building. When she reached it, there he was, holding the door open for her. Standing there in only his boxers. His hair disheveled, his bare chest tanned and broad, his legs muscular. A sleepy, sexy look in his eyes and half smile.

She walked in past him, put down The Marc Jacobs That Mouse Chewed, as Jeannie had come to think of her bag, took off her jacket, and heard the door close behind her. She turned. And he was there, waiting.

Without words, without the kind of conversation that normally made Jeannie feel comfortable, with no discussion of any kind, Tommy took her face in his hands and kissed her. He pulled her sweater over her head and threw it on a chair. He kissed her again and backed her into the bedroom. His hands were on her neck, her shoulders, her breasts, as they fell onto the bed. Slowly, sensually, he crept down her body until his knees were on the floor, and he removed her boots. When he saw that she was wearing no socks, he laughed out loud and touched her feet, held each one and kissed her toes, remembering how she'd never worn socks since he knew her. What had she said? "They make me feel claustrophobic." He raised himself onto her enough to unzip her jeans and removed them too.

Now, finally, in only her bra and panties, Jeannie rolled over on top of him. She sat up and removed her bra. He held her breasts, his thumb moving over and across them, and she rolled her head to the ceiling. And now it was her turn to find her way down his body.

They made love and made love again. She slept a while and woke up to find him at his computer, working. She went to him from behind and kissed his neck. It was already after three, the afternoon sun slipping between the slats of his wooden shades.

"I'm starved! You?" Tommy asked, kissing her. He stood, put on his boxers, said, "Come on!" and left the room. As she grabbed a shirt from his closet, she heard the fridge open and imagined him standing there in the glow of its light.

"Your choices are grilled cheese, cheese on grilled bread, or pan-fried cheese bread," he called.

"Hmmm. Too bad you don't have any cheese," Jeannie responded. She came out to a freshly made pot of coffee. She poured herself a cup, stood on her tiptoes to kiss Tommy on the back of his neck, and went into the living room, which opened to the kitchen. One side was brick walled. The other was lined with books, from floor to ceiling. Mostly nonfiction—history, politics, war, and biography. Some fiction too, classics as well as contemporary stuff.

From a top shelf she pulled *In Our Time*, the collection of Hemingway's Nick Adam short stories, and held it up for Tommy. "This is how we met. Remember?"

He smiled. "How could I forget? You were sitting in the back row of that huge lecture hall. There had to be five hundred people in there that day, all wanting to kiss Loewinson's butt, and you start to mouth off about Hemingway being a sexist pig. I had to meet you. If only to find out who the big-mouth was. And the rest," he said with a wave of his spatula, as he turned back to the stove, "is history."

He had only said "hi" to her that day. But the following weekend at some party, while she stood alone swigging a beer, checking out the guacamole and chips, the onion dip and brie cheese on the dining-room table, he had appeared right next to her and said, "I prefer Fitzgerald myself."

She'd turned to him with a faint smile, and her brows pursed in the way they always had since she was a kid, whether she was upset or teasing or playful or angry, leaving her with three creases that screamed for the Botox treatment Luce said one day she'd have to have. She said, "Bourgeois white boy. If we're talking twentieth-century American lit"—for that was the class they were taking— "I go for Steinbeck any old day."

"Mediocre talent, writer of soap operas."

"Oh, shut up."

"No, you shut up."

And their friendship was born. Both just okay students,

she because she worked twenty-five hours a week to get by and saved the writing of papers until the last minute, he because he was the editor of *The Daily Californian*, the college newspaper. They shared friends and spent much time at movies, at coffeehouses, at parties, sitting on the steps of Sproul Hall.

And look where we are now. She looked at Tommy's ass, as seen through his boxers, at his legs, his strong back, and considered for a moment bagging the grilled cheese and getting him back in bed, but she realized that she was hungry too. Besides, she needed to know what happened. She sat at his dining table, which was cluttered with books, newspapers, and his laptop.

"So, how was dinner with your editor?"

"You know how these things go. It may take a little time, but it'll happen. He's not too keen, but he'll come around."

"He must be surprised."

"Yeah, but things change." He closed the fridge and, with a pack of American cheese in one hand, he turned to her with a smile. "Don't they?"

Fucking A, she said to herself, as she opened a weighty history of China during the Chiang Kai-shek regime. "Doing some light reading, huh?" she asked, thumbing through it.

Tommy had been watching her. "Excellent book," he said. "Really well written, fascinating."

Jeannie was about to close it when she noticed PROPERTY OF THE NYC PUBLIC LIBRARY stamped on the inside front cover. Then she turned to the back and saw it there again, with the checkout card as well.

"Buy this at a library sale?"

"I got it at the library, yeah."

"I love those sales. I've gotten lots of great books there."

"Well, to be honest, I didn't actually get it at a sale, per se."

"What do you mean?"

"If you have to know, I took it. What kind of bread? Wonder or raisin?" he asked, holding a loaf in each hand.

"I don't understand."

"I mean, how would you like your grilled cheese? On white or raisin?"

"That's not what I mean. I mean, you just took the book and never—"

"Yeah. I checked it out and didn't return it."

"Well," she laughed, "you're sure going to owe one hefty fine."

"Wanted it for my own. To study. To have on hand. It's a terrific book. And there won't be a fine."

"Why no fine? You exempt or something?" She laughed at the thought.

"I'm just not going to pay it."

Her eyes widened. Thinking he was teasing, she teased back. "So you're stealing it."

"Not really. Though I suppose you could look at it that way. Okay, I'm going traditional and using Wonder." This time he held up a spatula.

"Come on, you. This makes no sense. You checked it out and never returned it and you're not planning to ever return it?"

"Yeah, but I paid for it, in a manner of speaking."

"How did you pay for it?"

"Taxes. My tax dollars."

"You're joking, right?" *Please*, she thought, *please be goofing around with me.*

"Not really. No," he said with a shrug. "I pay taxes. Some of that money goes to the library. So I figure I can take a book now and then and we're square."

She could feel the blood rise to her face and her voice rise right along with it. "That is the stupidest logic I have ever heard. Not to mention plain wrong and unethical. And, oh, did I mention, illegal?" She could feel her muscles, which were sore from their lovemaking.

Now he was angry too. "Fuck it. You're over the top, you know? You're going to make a big deal about this after the amazing morning we just had?"

"I'm sorry, I just . . ."

He came around the counter and kissed her. "Good. Come on," he said, nuzzling her neck.

"But one more question."

"Jeannie!"

"Is this the only book you've stolen?"

"I do not consider it stealing. But if you're asking if this is the only book from the library I've kept, yes, it is, except for maybe one or two others."

"So, you're only a petty thief."

"Jeannie, calm down, would you? Everybody does it."

"No. Not everybody does it. Most people, I'd venture a guess, have never done it. And do you know why? It's stealing. And stealing is wrong. And besides, if everyone jumped off the Golden Gate Bridge, would you?" Ugh. Was she turning into her mother?

"Jeannie, I pay my taxes. And I don't have to. I could lie about my income like everybody else. But I count up my earnings, report the truth, and pay the taxes. I mean, I don't pay for this place and have no idea how my folks handle taxes on this, but I report all my income. I bet most people you know don't do that."

"But stealing books from a library? By your logic, it would be okay if you walked into the public elementary school up the street to steal the kids' art supplies. Because you wanted to." *And his parents are still paying his rent,* Jeannie thought, *just like he's a child.*

"Yes, I could."

"And so could everyone else for that matter."

"Hey, if everybody would do it, taxes wouldn't be so high. You would have to pay for each library book you checked out. Lower taxes, put money in the hands of the people."

How quickly Jeannie's memory of the morning had faded, the luscious sex now a distant shadow. She had some coffee, took a couple of bites from her sandwich, got dressed, and left quickly without looking Tommy in the eyes.

Talk about taking after my mother, she thought as she hailed a cab to get home. One thing. He does one thing she doesn't agree with and he loses points. It wasn't as if he made a habit of keeping books. So Jeannie vowed there and then, on that chichi street corner, with Issey Miyake, Michael Kors, Christian Louboutin, and Yves St. Laurent in sight, that she'd give the guy a break, she'd keep her heart open, she wouldn't make this into a bigger deal than it was and wouldn't judge a book by its cover.

Money and Mint Chip

But acceptance of someone's faults was a more difficult process than she realized. Disappointment, the kind that sucks the air out of you, was exactly what Jeannie felt as she left Tommy's apartment, rode downtown in the taxi, went up the elevator, scratched Mouse's head when he jumped on her, found her dad napping on her couch, and took a shower. She knew she was making too big a deal of this, but she couldn't shake it. The water wasn't quite hot enough, the soap wouldn't lather sufficiently. She found her room chilly, and even when she lay in her bed—not necessarily to nap, though some sleep after her sleepless morning would've been good—she could not get warm. Eventually she found that the only thing that would soothe her was rationalization. Strategy is everything in the fight between heart and mind.

Nobody's perfect, she told herself. People are complex. If they weren't they wouldn't be interesting. The world would be a bore if everyone agreed on everything. If she wanted someone who felt exactly the way she did about everything, she could get a fucking robot, right? Or a goddamn mirror.

Right.

So later she had dinner with her dad, who immediately guessed where she had been and what she had been doing. "You're looking like you had a nice afternoon, Jeannie. All flushed and rosy. Good for you."

When she just smiled and whined, "Da-ad," he tried to guess who the lucky camper was.

"Your boss?"

She furrowed that brow again and said, "Now why would you ever think that?"

"It happens all the time. Besides, he's rich, good-looking . . . yeah, he's a little old for you, I think, but what the hell. I certainly am no one to talk—"

"Stop right there, Dad. I don't want to know, thank you very much. What do you know about my boss anyway?"

"Please. He was just in the *Times*, like he is every other day."

"Well, it's not him."

"Then who? Tell your old pop."

"Remember my friend from college, the writer? I think you met him a couple of times."

"The Wasp. Rode a little motorbike. Him?"

She took a bite of her linguini with clam sauce, having rolled the pasta around her fork a couple of times. Mouse was under the table, standing with his muzzle up against her leg, waiting for something, anything, to fall into her lap. "I like him, Dad." She didn't sound convincing, she knew.

"I don't know," he said, shaking his head, as if he heard the hesitance in her voice.

"What do you mean? We've been friends for years. That's a good basis for a relationship, right?" She paused, then hit herself on the forehead. "Why am I asking you?"

"Hey, your old pop knows a trick or two. I've had my share, don't you worry. It's just that, well, I'm not sure I'd think anybody is good enough for you."

"Dad."

"And besides, he's from that very rich family—"

"Don't hold that against him. Having money is not necessarily a bad thing, you know."

"That's only part of it."

"What else?" *He couldn't possibly know about the library books. So what,* she thought, *is bugging him?*

"He has a penis."

"Oh Christ."

"I think I'd hate anybody with a penis for my little girl."

"You'd rather I be a lesbian?"

"It's a thought."

"It can be arranged," she answered, raising her brows. "You just hate that he's from money."

"As long as he appreciates you."

"Can I ask you something, Dad?"

"I'm an open book."

Funny choice of words, she was thinking. But she continued. "Did you love Mom?"

"Ach, what's the point, Jeannie? It was a long time ago."

"Dad, come on. Answer me. Did you love Mom?"

He pushed himself up from the table and walked to the window, with Mouse following at his heels. There he looked out over the river to the lights beyond. "Did I love your mom."

Time went by slowly, and it felt like forever before he answered. Wasn't yes or no easy enough?

"Yes. I did. I loved your mom."

Her throat tightened. This was exactly what she wanted to hear, but "no" would've been so much simpler. "So what happened?"

"I screwed it up, excuse the language."

"How? Did you—"

"Yeah, I messed around. But that's not what did it. That was later."

"So what was it?" He'd had affairs, she'd found out long ago. It hurt her then, it hurt her now, but she didn't want to get caught up in that.

"I . . . well. It's hard to say."

Jeannie waited as patiently as she could. Her pulse beat in her ears. She was afraid of what was coming next.

"I was a bum. I couldn't find something that stuck. My family, your aunt and uncle, were both successful. Me, I never made much money. I only had a couple things going: my charm and my good looks." He shrugged, smiled, put his hands in his jeans pockets.

He'd said it like it was a joke, but she knew there was truth to it. "So what are you saying? Mom didn't care about money."

"No, but she cared about everything else. I could never . . . you know. Your mom, I couldn't give her what she wanted. You know those high standards of hers."

She walked to the window and stood next to him, her arms crossed over her chest as if it were cold inside. And in almost a whisper she asked, "So she dumped you? Is that what happened? She dumped you?" Jeannie had always assumed he had walked out on them, but of course this made so much sense.

"Yeah, the dame dumped me," he said with a thick, hood-like accent. "But"—and now he turned to her and put his hand on the back of her head, stroked her hair—"I never stopped loving her. And I never stopped loving you. I just couldn't come back much. You know what babies men are. And I am the king of baby men everywhere."

"I thought . . ." Her voice trailed off as the tears came now, and Jeannie didn't try to stop them. "I thought," she said, with a catch in her throat, "that you didn't love me."

"*What?* Only with all my heart. Every waking minute of every day."

"I think I saw you twice a year."

"I know. You look so much like her, you know," he said.

She turned to face him. "Really? I don't see it."

"Not the hair, not your coloring, and she sure didn't have gams like yours. That stuff you got from me. But your eyes, the way about you, something in how you walk, definitely your laugh."

Jeannie was silent, trying to remember Harriet laughing, and she couldn't think of a single time.

"Ah, the past is the past. Let's have some mint chip."

And the two of them, father and daughter, sat side by side on her couch, eating ice cream while watching that morning's *Ellen* on TiVo, with Mouse curled up in a ball at their feet. There was something about the ice cream, the moment, sitting there with her dad and his dog, that made her want to sit there forever. This was what was missing in her life: feeling completely comfortable. It was so simple that she couldn't believe it was so special. Maybe her bar was set particularly low or, perhaps, feeling at peace and easy with someone was a measure of love, the highest standard to achieve.

It's a Bird. It's a Plane — No, It's Sterling Behaviorwoman

One night the following week, Moss was getting anxious waiting for Jeannie. Where the hell was she? He'd asked her to get in by eight p.m. so that he could talk to her before this thing he had to go to. Yet another thing. He was so sick of fucking things, he wanted to kick something. It was already 8:20. He was sitting in his office, trying to read through some cash flow reports his CFO had sent him, when Harry came in.

"She here yet?" Moss asked.

"Any minute," Harry answered, shaking his head. "I don't know, Moss. You think she'll like it?"

"You tell me. You have the history and the relationship with her. You think she'll go for it?"

"I do. If only to prove—"

Then she walked in, and Moss's breath caught in his lungs. She always did that to him, knocked him out as if he'd fallen from a thirty-foot-high limb, like he did last summer. "Glad you could make it, Ms. Sterling," he said, sarcastically.

Jeannie thought he looked very handsome tonight. He was wearing a dressy dark suit, beautifully tailored, Armani or something, with a crisp white shirt and a Sulka tie. *Hmmm,* she thought, *I wonder where he's going. Some party or maybe a date.*

"I'm sorry I'm late. My dad—"

"Why don't you shut that door so we can begin? Harry and I need to talk to you."

Jeannie looked from one man to the other and saw her life flash before her eyes. She got nervous, so she joked, "No last rites? No last meal? Hmmm, what would I order? First, mussels and fries from Schiller's, then a hot fudge sundae from Serendipity."

"Me?" said Harry. "A sack of Slyders from White Castle and a dozen Krispy Kremes, glazed. Oh, and a Bud."

"Harr, no question, that would be your last meal. Because if the injection didn't kill you, the cholesterol would," Jeannie said.

Moss tried to get a word in. "Listen, Madame Mussels—"

"What about you, Mr. Moss, sir? What would your last meal be?" asked Jeannie.

"—I want to congratulate you," he continued, ignoring her question.

"Why, thank you," she beamed, and looked from Moss to Harry and back to Moss, Harry standing there with a stupid grin, his arms crossing over his fat stomach, Moss half sitting on his glass desk, his hands holding its edge, a typical look of self-satisfaction on his face. When neither man said anything, she spoke. "Can I ask for what?"

"*Sterling Behavior* is moving to television."

"You're kidding." Her excitement was unmistakable. "No way! Television?" Her eyes glistened, her face brightened, and her smile, well, it slayed him.

"We're not. We've made the deal. It's local for now, but if it works, national is the future. Clear Channel is producing and distributing."

"And," said Harry, "you're going to love this—it's on five to six p.m., in the evening. One night a week."

"No!" Jeannie imagined herself going to bed in the darkness, waking up at eight a.m., eating breakfast, being a normal person.

"The street stuff will be prerecorded," Harry continued, "but you'll be live in a studio, narrating the video, taking calls."

"Loving those hours."

"Not so fast. You'll be working like a dog, running through the dailies, editing, writing your copy. The hours may change, but there are going to be a hell of a lot more of them," said Harry.

"So this is what your talks with them have been about," Jeannie said to Moss. "You're not selling? Or is this all a prelude to selling us off?"

"Yes, no, and hopefully it'll prevent a sale. Nothing like success to help you fend off the unwanted advances of others."

"So what happens to the radio show? You give my time slot away?"

Harry answered, "You can't do both."

"What happens if this doesn't work? I'm out of a job?"

"Everything is a gamble," Moss said, sitting on the edge of his desk or table or whatever the hell you wanted to call it.

"You want to stay where you are forever? Remember what Plato said about 'forever': there ain't no such thing."

"What about Luce? Does she know?"

"You're the first," said Harry. "She'll be on board if you are."

She shook her head. "I hope so." Nothing specific had happened, but whatever was going on with Luce that she wasn't discussing gnawed at Jeannie.

"But not as producer," said Harry, who saw Jeannie's look, so he continued, "We need someone experienced with television. We're going to bring in someone. Luce will still be your sidekick."

"Not even AP? She won't be happy."

"I know," said Harry, "but she doesn't have the experience, even for assistant producer."

"She can learn."

"We don't have that kind of time. Luce is a pro. She'll understand," said Moss.

"I don't know," said Jeannie. "She's already—"

"What did you do, piss her off?" teased Moss, unaware he was treading where angels fear to go. "Just you being you?"

"I didn't say she was angry with me."

"Uh-huh." Moss smiled.

Jeannie wanted to choke him to death, but she ignored the impulse and turned to Harry. "She's good at her job," Jeannie said.

Harry shrugged, put his hands in his pockets. "Nobody said she's not. She's just . . . well . . . between her lack of hands-on experience and her condition, it makes me nervous."

"Her what? Her condition? What are you talking about?" She looked from Harry to Moss and back.

"Oh shit. Oh *shit!*" He slapped himself on his forehead. "I thought she'd told you by now. She told me she was going to tell you."

"By now? How long—? What?"

"She's pregnant, Jeannie."

It all made sense now. No coffee, the throwing up. "How long?"

"She's got to be at least four months by now."

Jeannie turned away so they couldn't see her face. "You both knew?"

The silence was deafening. *Luce is pregnant. And everyone knew but me.* She felt as if she'd been punched in the stomach, the wind knocked out of her. *Why wouldn't she tell me?* Jeannie wanted to sit and put her head between her legs, but she willed herself to keep standing.

"Joseph too?"

"Just us," said Harry.

"I'm sure she was waiting to surprise you," said Moss.

Right, that has to be it, you idiot.

"Listen, Jeannie, I'm sure she has her reasons," said Harry. "But you see, for this change, we need someone who knows the ropes. Sure, Luce is a fast learner, but her TV experience is minimal, plus there's no promise she'll even be here, so the learning curve may take more time than we have. Maybe after she gives birth, when she comes back. If she comes back. Who knows what the future holds?"

"Yeah, who knows?" Jeannie shook her head, thinking, *I could stand up for her, I could threaten to walk out if they don't keep her in the job, I could say something, anything, in Luce's behalf. Yeah, well, fuck her.* She took a deep breath and said, "So, when do we begin? When do we air?"

"We're going to have to move on this to make February

sweeps. We'll need to plan where and what to shoot, which I'm thinking Joseph can do, what with his background, and to edit we'll be using the studios downstairs," said Harry. "This has to be discussed with Joseph, but I figure we'll keep it simple, use a handheld to make it look raw and real. We want it to be done without the victim knowing."

"The victim?" asked Jeannie.

"It's doing what you've been doing, but we're going to see it in action. We set up a little vignette. You get into people's faces. They get to rethink their behavior," said Moss.

"It's more like on-air humiliation, right? It's getting even. You want me to be Charles Bronson for the behaviorally challenged?"

"We want you to be you, for Christ's sake, Jeannie," said Harry. "We don't want you to humiliate people. They could be me or you or Luce or her mother, after all. Consider it your opportunity, Jeannie, to just nip that bad behavior in the bud. To do what needs to be done, within what's right and, of course, the law, to stop it. It's what you've wanted all along. Right?"

She had a momentary flash of being dressed in tights, leotard, cape, and boots, a huge red SB emblazoned on her chest, flying through the New York City night, her hair blown back behind her, swooping down on Moss, picking him up, then carrying him off into the night sky and dropping him, headfirst, into the Hudson.

"Definitely," she said, her eyes flashing. "When do we start?"

Bitten in the Ass by Dr. Bite Me

"So, you excited?" Moss asked her, as he walked her down the hall to her studio.

"You following me?" she answered. "And yes, I have to admit, I am."

"So what's the matter? And don't forget I own this place. I can walk wherever I'd like. For no reason whatsoever."

"Nothing's the matter." She wasn't going to give him the pleasure of knowing how upset she was about Luce. She turned to him and narrowed her eyes. He smelled delicious. "You going on a date or something?"

"Now, why would you think that? Just because I'm dressed like this? Don't I look good?" He stopped and looked at himself in the studio window. "I look good, don't I." He straightened his tie, put a hand through his hair. Then he turned to her. "Luce should've told you. But she must have her reasons."

With a quick turn and a fling of her hair, which she knew hit him in the face, she opened her studio door. She was not going to talk about Luce with him.

"Careful there, with that hair of yours," he said, following her inside. "It's a lethal weapon."

"So who's the lucky girl? Let me guess: she's rich, she's dumb, she's twenty-two."

"Sounds good. You must know her." And then, there was Susan Bittman, Dr. Bite Me herself, at the studio door. "Ah, and here she is now. You look lovely tonight, Susan."

"Thank you, Nicholas. Ready to go?"

Jeannie felt her jaw drop and her eyes open wide at the

sight of the überpop doc, with her stupid little dress and her little beaded evening bag and her strappy sandals and her hair and her face and her smile. Rich, yes, but in no way was she dumb, and she certainly wasn't even in the vicinity of twenty-two. She was dating Moss? Moss was dating her? They were dating each other? It all seemed so wrong. She saw Moss smile at Bite Me and pull her toward Jeannie with a palm at her back. That very same palm Jeannie had felt the day they walked in the park. The two-timing palmist! Jeannie felt her color rise, her heart beat harder, a sweat break out on her forehead. She came out from behind her desk.

"Hello, Jeannie. Lovely to see you. It's been a while. I think since last year's Christmas party, wasn't it?" She put out her hand with her long red nails.

Of course she'd bring that up. She'd been the fucking star of the party. WBUZ had just wooed her away from her Minneapolis station and she was an overnight hit. Jeannie had watched her from her corner, entertaining Luce and Joseph and a couple of others with snide, offhand comments about Dr. Bite Me, her stupid show, her tight outfit. She moped and drank a little too much and got a little wild, and all in all acted like a spoiled brat. "Funny, I don't remember," she said, taking Bite Me's hand.

"Perhaps that's because you had had a little too much to drink. I can't imagine how else you could forget—"

"Hmmm. Very interesting," interrupted Moss. "I wish I had been there. But we really have to go." He looked at Jeannie then and nodded.

Jeannie nodded back, acknowledging that he'd just saved her butt by butting into his date's dimwitted story.

"Well, have a good night, Jeannie," said Moss, as he palmed Bite Me's back.

She smiled at Moss, then right at Jeannie. "Yes, it was so nice to see you again. And I'm glad to see your little show has found an audience."

Jeannie would've said something, anything, but there was Tommy, walking down the hall toward them with a big bouquet of flowers in his hand. He was wearing a black jacket and jeans, dressed up for him. He looked amazing. Talk about perfect timing.

"Jeannie Beanie," Tommy said.

Fuck, Jeannie thought, blushing. Not in front of her boss, for crying out loud. But then Tommy put his arm around her waist and kissed her in a way that no one could confuse as immature.

"Interesting," Moss said, crossing his arms. "Jeannie *is* biologically human, after all. She mates just like the rest of us."

Jeannie rolled her eyes. Introductions were made; the two men shook hands. Tommy shook Bite Me's hand warmly as she complimented him on his recent series of articles in the *Times,* and then he turned to Jeannie, holding the flowers out to her, and said, "These are for you."

"How nice of you. Flowers! Pretty, too. And roses," Moss said, leaning over to smell them. "Heck, Jeannie, what a guy," said Moss, full of feigned enthusiasm, looking back and forth from Jeannie to Tommy.

"I just wanted to see you," Tommy said to Jeannie. "I couldn't wait until after the party."

"He couldn't wait," said Moss, raising his brows. "Wait a minute. You're going to the party for John Hesselman's new book, aren't you?"

"Yeah. You?"

"He's an old friend from way back," said Moss.

"He's my—"

"Your editor at the *Times*, right? Small world, that I should be friends with your boss, don't you think?"

This is not going well, Jeannie thought. She looked at Tommy and kissed him again, knowing that Moss's eyes were on her the entire time. She turned to him and scowled.

"Everyone's going to a party but me. I guess someone here has to work for a living."

"Poor girl," said Moss. "Let me know if you need to borrow this." And he pulled the small, silk handkerchief from his jacket's breast pocket, dabbed his eyes as if to dry his tears, and then pretended to blow his nose in it.

Tommy laughed; she punched his arm. He pretended he was hurt. She kissed him playfully. And then he kissed her. Of course Moss noticed every detail of the exchange between the two lovebirds, but damned if he was going to give her the pleasure of letting her know. So he did everything in his power (which normally was estimable, but tonight it nearly failed him) to ignore it and walked away with Susan, his hand on the small of her back.

"Have a good show, Jeannie," he said, turning back to her as they made their way down the hall. "See you at the party, Tom."

"Yeah, see you there."

Still in Tommy's arms, Jeannie watched them leave and thought she saw Moss turn his head, but she quickly turned away, so she couldn't be sure. She told Tommy the news about the TV show, about her excitement and how disappointed Luce would be at not producing, said they'd talk later at dinner and, with a final kiss good-bye, he left for the party at Buddakan.

Jeannie was both relieved and sorry he'd be unable to hear her show tonight. Because it was going to be all about him.

STERLING BEHAVIOR

JEANNIE: *You're tuned to* Sterling Behavior *and we'll soon be on the street again, but tonight we're in the studio, and the subject is love.*

LUCE: *Love? Hmmm, interesting.*

JEANNIE: *Is love always unconditional? Should it be? Should you forgive people you love who do bad things?*

LUCE: *Like what? I'm assuming we're not talking about murder or something like that. Or like, um, I don't know, like . . .*

JEANNIE: *Like, a friend who keeps something important from you, or a friend who, let's say, checks out a book from his local public library, and if he likes it, if he feels he'll read it again or refer to it, he never returns it.*

LUCE: *Does he pay for the book? Pay the fine?*

JEANNIE: *No fine, nada, bupkis.*

LUCE: *That's terrible. Library books are meant for everyone. If he keeps them, then someone else cannot read them. It's stealing, pure and simple.*

JEANNIE: *Well, that's the funny part. He doesn't think so.*

LUCE: *Oh, come on! This guy is a total jerk, Jeannie. Is this someone we both know? Because I'd—you know, this is way more offensive than most things we deal with, like cutting in line at the movies.*

JEANNIE: *I hope you're listening out there, library book thief.*

LUCE: *Because that's just rude behavior. This is theft of public property. Our libraries have enough trouble as it is. Never enough funding, dealing with censorship. This guy is actually stealing our tax dollars!*

JEANNIE: *That's exactly his point. He claims that because he's a tax-paying citizen, he has a right to the library books. He feels he actually owns them.*

LUCE: *That is about the stupidest thing I've ever heard. By that logic, he has the right to steal a garbage truck! Or even medicine from a hospital or milk from a public school cafeteria. How can you be friends with someone like that?*

JEANNIE: *That's precisely my question. Are all your friends perfect?*

LUCE: *Helloooooo?*

JEANNIE: *You mean me?*

LUCE: *But even you don't steal from a library, for god's sake.*

JEANNIE: *But should we remain friends with people who do things we feel are wrong? When is friendship unconditional? People are complicated. What if he volunteers in a soup kitchen or an old-age home?*

LUCE: *I doubt that a person who feels that paying taxes gives him the right to keep a library book would volunteer for anything. Except maybe getting votes out for the Libertarian Party.*

JEANNIE: *Well, let's hear from you people out there on the subject. You're listening to* Sterling Behavior *at WBUZ, 660 on your AM dial. And we're taking calls right after this commercial break.*

Fessing Up

"It's Tommy, isn't it? The library thief."

Jeannie almost spit out the gulp of water she had in her mouth. She had to will herself to stay calm. "No way. Why would you—"

"I just wouldn't be surprised."

"Why not?"

"Don't forget I've known him a long time. He's a good guy, he's a wonderful guy, but as you just said, nobody's perfect."

She seems to be covering up something, thought Jeannie. "What do you mean?"

"Nothing specific, I just have a feeling he's not above pushing the boundaries and rationalizing it. He's ambitious, and talk about entitlement . . ."

"What about you? You're from the same neighborhood, so to speak."

"But our families are so different. My folks were all hard work and limitations, the Puritan ethic. His were about competition and expectations."

Jeannie was silent then. She hadn't meant the neighborhood comment so literally. She took another drink from her bottle of water and leaned back in her chair. The Tommy she knew was compassionate, diligent, caring. She thought of their night together, his body, her pleasure, their lovemaking. Okay, so he could be rude to a waiter. And he kept one or two library books.

"Tell me," she said. "What you're not saying."

"There's nothing specific," Luce answered. "I'm just not surprised."

Was Luce not saying something else she knew? *You lie about one thing, you can lie about many,* thought Jeannie.

The two women were silent for a moment, neither saying what was on her mind. When they saw Joseph giving them a two-minute warning, Luce broke the silence.

"So what was the meeting about?" Luce asked.

Jeannie had been dreading this moment. "What meeting?"

"Come on, the one right before the show, with Harry and Moss."

"The show is changing. One of those corporate things. To make more money. You know."

Joseph stood at the glass and mouthed "one minute."

"Changing how? Come on, Jeannie. Tell me."

"Harry's going to talk to you."

"Jeannie!"

"Okay, okay. Luce, we're moving to television. Like a reality show for bad behavior."

Luce stood, waved her arms, covered her mouth. "Oh my god! When? How?" Then she sat. "Gee, I don't know much about producing a TV show."

"And it's going to be on at five . . . p.m. We won't have to work all night."

"I'm producer, right?"

Jeannie hesitated.

"I'm not?"

"No. But Luce—"

"AP?"

Jeannie shook her head. "You said it yourself, didn't you? You don't have the experience."

"Jeannie," started Luce, whose eyes had grown dark and who sat now, slumped into her chair, "you fought for me, didn't you? You told them how important I am to the show?"

You didn't tell me you were pregnant, but I should fight for you?

"Well, I . . ."

"You didn't, did you," said Luce.

Then there was Joseph's voice and she turned to see him on the other side of the window, counting with his fingers. "Ten, nine, eight . . ." His T-shirt read FUCK YOU, YOU FUCKING FUCK.

Exactly, Jeannie thought. *Exactly.*

STERLING BEHAVIOR

JEANNIE: *And we're back. This is Jeannie Sterling talking to you tonight about love and friendship. Can we, should we, remain friends with people who behave badly?*

LUCE: *Jeannie, we have some calls. I have a Mike on the line.*

JEANNIE: *So, what do you think, Mike? If you have a friend and he does something that you don't agree with, you dump him?*

MIKE: *There are bad things and then there are bad things, you know? Eating with your elbows on the table is one thing—*

LUCE: *Not to me, Mike. That's grounds.*

MIKE: *—keeping a library book is another. It says something about the man, Jeannie. If he can steal books from the public library, who knows, he could do almost anything. Where does he draw the line? That guy's working with a broken moral compass.*

JEANNIE: *But nobody's perfect, right? Mike, isn't there anybody you know, who you like, who has done something you find reprehensible?*

MIKE: *Well, Jeannie, this girl I know, and I won't name names, will buy a dress, wear it to a party, and then return it to the store for a full refund.*

JEANNIE: *I hate that. It's totally unacceptable.*

MIKE: *She argues that it's okay because she's returning the dress in the same condition she bought it. And besides, she says, why should a flimsy piece of fabric cost three hundred dollars? It's not right, so she considers what she does justice.*

JEANNIE: *Tell her she's full of it. You wear it, you own it. That's the shopping covenant. And that price argument is ridiculous. Let her shop on sale, on eBay, at the Salvation Army. Nobody forces her to pay that much for a dress.*

LUCE: *I wonder, Mike, if you should dump your friend. If Jeannie should dump hers. By being friends with people like that, aren't you implicating yourselves in their acts?*

JEANNIE: *But Luce, we'd all be pretty lonely if we couldn't love somebody who made mistakes.*

MIKE: *I think Luce is right, in principle. But when you care about someone, it's not so black-and-white, you know?*

LUCE: *But if a friend doesn't stick up for you, what kind of friend is that?*

JEANNIE: *Or if a friend lies to you, can you still be friends?*

MIKE: *Sounds like you guys need a break.*

JEANNIE: *You said it. You're listening to* Sterling Behavior *on WBUZ radio. We'll be right back.*

House of Love

Florent was relatively quiet, just like Jeannie knew it would be on a Friday morning at 4:30 a.m. The burnt golden haze of the restaurant still lingered, along with a few diehard cigarette smokers hanging outside the front door, but the throngs of beautiful people dressed in black had gone home. She imagined them, only two hours before, standing three-deep at the bar, others seated huddled together, laughing, gossiping, necking, the waiters with their white aprons carrying trays of Moules Frites and Steak Frites and Tartare with Frites over their shoulders. Now there were several empty tables, and a languid hush hovered in the air.

And yet, it was still difficult getting the hostess's attention. One look at that tall, cool blonde in a short, black sheath who was giggling in whispers with a waiter, and Jeannie knew she didn't have a chance in hell, that a man would do so much better. Tommy hadn't arrived yet, so Luce asked Spike.

"Go ahead, honey. Try," she said.

"If she gives us a hard time, there's a little place around the corner. And it has an added bonus: the food is good," Spike said, his arm around Luce. He was wearing a dark sports jacket, an open-collared shirt, blue jeans, New Balance tennis shoes. His prematurely gray hair was cut short, framing his thin, handsome face. If Jeannie didn't know him, she would assume he was some kind of middle manager for an insurance company.

"Ha ha, you're so funny," said Luce. Her hair dazzled under the lights, its blonde shimmering gold, like the little bag she carried.

He approached the sacred podium. First he had to work to get the hostess's attention, then he said something that made her laugh and the three were seated.

They ordered a bottle of wine and perused the menu. Talked about anything but the TV show. When the wine was poured, Luce, of course, declined with some lame excuse about feeling tired.

Jeannie was taking a sip of the Sancerre when she saw Tommy walking toward them. He looked tired, pissed off. "Fucking hostess," he said when he reached the table. "I've been outside waiting for you guys. She didn't realize you were here already. Hot but dumb." He leaned over and kissed Jeannie, then Luce, and shook Spike's hand.

"A little harsh, don't you think?" asked Jeannie. *Not to mention gross, but one thing at a time.*

"Haven't heard Tommy on the Regular People, huh, Jeannie?" teased Luce.

"What's that mean?" asked Jeannie. "What does she mean?"

Tommy sighed. "Luce has always felt that I'm a snob, old-fashioned."

"You know, smart begets smart, and people are in the positions in life they deserve to be, and the help is the help is the help," said Luce.

"You don't really think that," said Jeannie. "How could you when you've seen all you've seen? Who knows better how circumstances can define you?"

"Exactly," said Tommy.

"Uh-huh," said Luce.

"Anyway, how was the party?" Jeannie asked, wanting to change the subject, sensing that to stay on this one would reveal more than she wanted to know. "Anybody interesting?"

"You know, another book party, another room full of people who think that reading a book review is the same as reading the book itself."

"You're in some mood," she said.

"And my boss has his new book out, but I'm still working as a grunt. A little jealous, I guess."

"Yeah, but you're here, at least. And not somewhere on the other side of the world."

"That is true," he said, and kissed her. "But he's still an asshole."

So with Jeannie secretly seething at Luce, and Luce openly upset with Jeannie, and Tommy angry at everybody, they ordered and ate and talked. Jeannie looked around the table, thinking that her friends were as closely connected as if they had grown up under the same roof, just like family. Luce was Jeannie's best friend, and Tommy was Jeannie's boyfriend, and he and Luce were old childhood friends, and Luce was married to Spike. *How small is the life we live,* Jeannie marveled. Maybe it's because the world is so damn wide and seemingly unnavigable that we intentionally bring all the far-flung materials of our lives together to build a protective enclave. Maybe that's why she cherished her dad even when she resented him so. Maybe that's why she tolerated Tommy's library behavior. Maybe it's why she tried not to expect much from him in terms of his being around. Maybe it's why she'd eventually forgive Luce, she hoped, for lying to her. Jeannie wanted her house of friends and family to shelter the love and intimacy her mother's house never had.

Tommy turned to her, took her hand. "I'm sorry. I'm here. And happy to be. Now what did I miss? Hey, let's toast the new show," Tommy said, raising his glass. "To Jeannie."

Jeannie cringed at his insensitivity.

"Yes, to *Jeannie's* new show," said Luce.

"And honey, to you too," said Spike, lifting his glass. "You're still an important part of it."

Luce looked at him appreciatively and smiled. There was no show between them, not an ounce of falsehood. Luce didn't care that Spike was semigeeky. And Spike just smiled when Luce changed her mind about her order three times. But it was more than that; he was caring, sweet, protective, and there for her. When she dropped her napkin, he picked it up. When they discussed the new Supreme Court justice selection, they discussed it as if each didn't know how the other would think. Each was actually interested in what the other would say. They liked each other, accepted each other, and, it was clear to see, they loved each other. And now they were making a family, at the expense of career and who knows what else.

I want that. Way beneath the surface of being in love is love itself. Not an original idea, but a revelation to Jeannie, who was clueless about that kind of love. When she looked at Tommy, though one of her hands was holding his and the other was on his shoulder, all she could think was that in her house of love, the roof was secure, the walls were holding, but the interior structure—the electricity, the plumbing— needed repair.

And when she looked at Luce, whom Jeannie was unable to confront because she was so hurt by her secret, she knew the foundation was cracked.

STERLING BEHAVIOR

JEANNIE: *I'm sure you've all heard that* Sterling Behavior *is moving to television. The show is called* Caught Ya! *and you can catch it beginning February fifteenth on Thursdays at five p.m. on NY1, the city's first news station. Tonight is the final broadcast of* Sterling Behavior *from WBUZ Radio. It's a sad thing, to end the show after ten years, but it's exciting too. We're not mourning a loss, we're celebrating a new beginning. And passion is what it's about, isn't it? Feeling strongly about things, doing your part. That's why tonight's topic has special meaning for me: Indifference. People who don't care. Indifferent sales clerks. Indifferent restaurant hostesses. Indifferent anybody and everybody.*

LUCE: *Like what, Jeannie?*

JEANNIE: *Don't you just hate it when you're greeted at a restaurant by a tall, beautiful woman in a black dress who could care less that you're there? She just keeps talking to the other tall, beautiful hostesses as if you don't exist.*

LUCE: *Or when you go to Staples—*

JEANNIE: *They're the worst! Nobody knows where anything is. And nobody cares. I hate it when the staff is untrained.*

LUCE: *And rude! Every time I go in that store, I swear it's going to be the last. But where's a girl to find number-two pencils? Or computer paper? Or multicolored stickies?*

JEANNIE: *It's the same with drugstores. You can sum up hell in one word: Duane Reade!*

LUCE: *That's two, but who's counting.*

[Sterling Scale sound effects: earthquake rumbling, crashing, and sounds of destruction]

JEANNIE: *For those of you listening from outside the city, Duane Reade is a drugstore chain, like Longs or Walgreens, that has a store on almost every block of the city. So you're almost forced to shop there. Need shampoo? Cotton balls? Band-Aids? Toothpaste? This is where you go. Because you have to. Because there's almost nowhere else. Just like Staples. And the staff has no idea where anything is, and they don't care. Completely unhelpful. Just the other day I had to ask three different clerks where the Dramamine was.*

LUCE: *For motion sickness? Since when—*

JEANNIE: *It's not for me, it's for my devil dog, Mouse.*

LUCE: *Mouse gets motion sickness? How do you know? Take him on a Caribbean cruise?*

JEANNIE: *Took him in a taxi to the vet. Threw up. Took him home. Threw up. In the taxis.*

LUCE: *[laughter]*

JEANNIE: *It's not funny. Guess how much it cost me in tips?*

LUCE: *I have a call, Jeannie. Jennifer's on the line.*

JENNIFER: *Hi, Jeannie. Hi, Luce. It's not only Duane Reade or Staples. Take stewardesses.*

LUCE: *You mean flight attendants.*

JENNIFER: *I guess, the distinction being that stewardesses were well trained and had work to do. Recently I had a flight attendant who was so mean. She could care less about our comfort, but she sure as hell cared about the rules—her rules.*

JEANNIE: *What did she do?*

JENNIFER: *She yelled at people! You couldn't get up, you had to keep your shade closed, you could hardly talk. She was so strict. Scary strict.*

LUCE: *Was she old, with a wart on her nose and a broomstick?*

JENNIFER: *No, she was actually beautiful, stunning really. The bitch.*

JEANNIE: *A stunning stewardess bitch.*

LUCE: *Thanks, Jen. We have a Lindsey on the line.*

JEANNIE: *Hey, Lindsey.*

LINDSEY: *Hi, Jeannie; hey, Luce. I think indifference is actually very passive-aggressive. It's like saying "whatever."*

JEANNIE: *I hate that, don't you? When people behave as if they have no responsibility. Or it's out of their control. All not true. Right, Lindsey?*

LINDSEY: *You're right. In principle, that is.*

JEANNIE: *Okay . . . what do you mean?*

LINDSEY: *A long time ago—and I mean twenty years ago—I had a very good friend who used to play at my house, who would sleep over and hang out. She was like a sister to me and a daughter to my folks. Her family life was difficult, so being at my house made her feel better.*

JEANNIE: *How lucky for her to have wonderful parents like yours to reach out to.*

LINDSEY: *I'm not saying things were perfect. We were sometimes jealous of each other—*

LUCE: *Like all girls, right?*

LINDSEY: *I guess. I mean, she'd want my clothes, I'd want her hair. She'd want to have a so-called regular family; I wished I could live in her commune.*

JEANNIE: *Um, wait a minute . . .*

LINDSEY: *But even with the competition and envy, we loved each other, or so I thought.*

JEANNIE: *Lindsey? Is that you? Are you in New York?*

LINDSEY: *And then my mother died. It was a few years later. My friend was away at school. But you know what? I never heard from her. She didn't come to the funeral or to our house to mourn with us. She didn't even call. Or send a note. Nothing.*

JEANNIE: *Lindsey, I'm sure she had her reasons.*

LUCE: *But she couldn't just make a call? What reason could there be? Maybe you weren't as close as you thought—*

LINDSEY: *Obviously not. It broke my heart. It really hurt. I had thought we were such close friends, and then—*

LUCE: *Talk about indifference.*

LINDSEY: *See how indifference can hurt just as much as a slap in the face?*

LUCE: *Friendship is a very delicate thing. We've talked about that here, just recently, right, Jeannie?*

[silence]

LUCE: *Jeannie?*

[silence]

LUCE: *Okay, we're going to take a break now. You're listening to* Sterling Behavior *at WBUZ 660 on your AM dial, and we'll be right back.*

Clean Hands, Warm Heart

"Where?" Moss checked in with Luce first, and that was all he needed to ask. When he entered the ladies' bathroom, he could hear sobbing, sniffling, and the occasional blow of a nose. He bent down to see if Jeannie was in one of the stalls. Sure enough, there were those boots.

"Hey. Come out."

She sniffled loudly. "What're you doing in here? This is the ladies' room. Why aren't you on a date? Or flying your jet to Bora Bora? Don't you have a multinational corporation to run or something? Don't you have *anything* better to do?"

He rolled his eyes and leaned on the door of the stall. "Come on out."

"No. I like it in here." A loud nose-blow.

"What's going on? You did good. We have to screen better. We—"

"She was right."

"She's not right," said Moss.

"Yes," said Jeannie, softly, her voice catching. "I was a wimp."

Moss said nothing, allowing her time to go on.

"Not just a wimp. I wanted to hurt her. I must've, even though it wasn't conscious. But how do you ignore a friend in a situation like that unless you want to hurt them?"

"Jeannie. Nobody's perfect—"

"If I hear that one more time . . . I will kill someone. I swear. That's no excuse."

"Listen, we all hurt each other, sometimes intentionally, sometimes not. Luce not telling you about her pregnancy hurt, didn't it? You have to tell her, Jeannie. You need to let Luce know you know how much she's hurt you. That's what's bothering you most, I think."

"Yeah, yeah."

"And you and Lindsey, that sounds complicated—"

"Bullshit, bullshit!" Luce and now Lindsey; this all felt too much. "Nothing's that complicated. Her mom died, for god's sake, and I ignored it completely. This is twenty years ago and it still hurts her and haunts me." She stopped to blow her nose. "But why would I expect you to understand?"

"Oh, it's come to that, has it? Come out and argue with me face to face."

"I don't want to."

"Then I'm coming in."

"Wha—"

Moss went into the stall next to Jeannie's, put the toilet lid down, stood on it, lifted himself onto the wall that separated the two, swung one leg over, then the other, and sat there on top, like a kid in a tree. He looked down at Jeannie, who was standing, arms crossed in front of her chest, looking up at him.

"You're very difficult, you know," she said with a smile.

"People in glass houses . . ." he answered.

She turned and walked out of the stall to a sink. He jumped down and followed her. She turned on the water, rinsed her hands, and tried to get soap out of the dispenser. But, as usual, it was broken, so Jeannie banged and banged it. She could see Moss in the mirror watching her.

"What?" she said. "Want to be sure I wash properly? Does nothing in this world work the way it should?"

He just smiled as he pushed up the sleeves of his cashmere shirt, revealing his forearms, which were surprisingly muscular and tan beneath a covering of dark, fine hair. There was that faded old string bracelet on his wrist. Now by her side, so close that she could feel the space between them, he lifted the top of the dispenser, put one hand in it, and, with his fingers, scooped out the gooey pink soap. With his other hand he took one of hers, held it palm facing up, and wiped the soap in it.

And then he washed her hands. Calmly and deliberately, carefully and sensually, he massaged her palms, he put his long fingers between hers, he encircled her wrists and rubbed the pulse point below her hand with his thumb.

Her eyes stopped burning, her heart found its beat, and though embarrassed as hell by this intimate gesture, from this man in particular, she felt woozy at his touch. She watched him through the mirror, but only once did he look up from her hands, and when his eyes met hers, she quickly glanced away.

After he rinsed the soap off them both, he turned off the water, ripped a couple towels from the dispenser, and handed them to Jeannie. She used them to wipe her eyes and her hands, then she blew her nose and tossed them in the garbage. Then he walked her to the door.

He opened it and there was Harry, waiting for them.

"Harry," said Moss. "Good show tonight."

"Thank you, Moss," said Harry. He looked at Jeannie.

She sniffed.

"Jeannie," Harry said. Then he looked back at Moss, who continued down the hall toward his office. And then he smiled. He put his arm around Jeannie's shoulders and guided her back to the studio.

So-Called Best Friends

Luce entered the studio and closed the door behind her. She cut the sound that projected into the outside booth and the hallways, and sat down at Jeannie's desk, facing her.

"What just happened? Was that your old friend Lindsey from California?"

"She's right. I blew her off."

"Well, that's a surprise."

Jeannie's defensive hackles stood straight up, like Mouse's did whenever he ran into that pit bull on the pier. "What the hell does that mean? I'm a good friend. I've always been there for you. We've been like sisters, though I never had a sister, so what the hell do I know, but we're like family."

"Yeah, and like with family, we tend to take each other for granted."

"What's that supposed to mean?"

"Oh, come on, Jeannie. You're so self-centered. Everything is about you. You're moody, you ignore me, you never credit me on the air for something good I did or said."

"Is that the reason? Is that why . . . ?"

The color in Luce's face washed away. "Why what?"

"You didn't tell me?"

Luce said nothing, got up, walked the four steps to one wall, then the four steps back to the other. It wasn't a space meant for pacing, but Luce did the best she could with what she had.

"Who told you?"

"It doesn't matter. But it could've been anyone, right? Because everyone knew but me."

"I was going to tell you. I wanted to be the one."

"But why now and not four months ago? You're already four months pregnant, right?" She looked at Luce's stomach. "You're not even showing. Are you eating okay?"

"I'm fine and I am showing, but not with clothes yet." She sat. "Look, Jeannie, I wanted to tell you. When I first learned, months ago. But I couldn't."

Luce looked down, put her hand on her belly.

"So tell me why you didn't tell me. Something like this, if it were me, you'd be the first. Even before the father! I'd call you from the doctor's office. I'd have taken you with me to the doctor's office."

Luce shook her head. "I don't know."

"You've really hurt me."

"I thought you wouldn't be excited. I thought you'd be upset. You know how you are."

Jeannie sat in silence for a moment, looking at her hands

and how pink and dry they were; they were normally olive colored. Was it the chill in the air? Or the fact that she'd been clenching them so tightly?

"How am I?"

"Judgmental. Critical. Listen to yourself, how you rant on about strollers and babies in restaurants. Please!"

"But don't you think I'd be excited for you, because it's you?"

"I wasn't sure."

Jeannie stood, put her hands on her desk, leaning toward Luce. "So why not try me? What were you afraid of? Even if I was an asshole who couldn't get excited for you, I was going to find out anyway. I mean, at some point, you are going to look pregnant."

"I was going to tell you before then. I was."

"For months you've been lying to me."

Luce didn't respond.

"You should've told me, regardless of how you imagined in your fantasy-addled brain I'd react."

"I know. But you and I, well, we're complicated. You know? Sometimes honesty's overrated. Why do I have to explain that to you—you of the ethical bullshit?"

Jeannie was angry now. "Ethical bullshit? If that's how you feel, why don't you just—" But she stopped herself.

"Just what? Quit? Don't worry, it has crossed my mind. And now—"

Jeannie looked at Luce and sat down. She would always love this woman, right or wrong. Sure, they'd have fights, even hurt each other, but they were like sisters, like family, where love is unconditional and forever. Or so she'd heard.

"And now what?"

"Now there's a reason."

Don't quit, please don't, thought Jeannie. "Well, do what you have to do," she said.

California Girl

When Jeannie got home that morning, her dad and Mouse were out on a walk. Jeannie was relieved because she sure didn't feel like dealing with them. Her dad had been there so long, she couldn't even remember what it was like to live alone anymore.

There was a message on her answering machine from Lindsey. *Oh shit,* she thought, as she removed her boots. What was this, *A* fucking *Christmas Carol*? First Luce and now this. Was every mistake in her past coming back to confront her?

Jeannie called her back and they agreed to meet for lunch at The Odeon.

Lindsey looked older, Jeannie thought, worn, with deep furrows between her brows and long frown lines on either side of her mouth, a good ten years older than she was, as if her cares had marked her for life. Her hair had grayed and she'd made no attempt to dye it. She wore a wrinkled, baggy shirt-and-pant outfit, typical Berkeley, made of something like linen or hemp, some material otherwise used for working with farm animals. Her shoes were of the sensible, ugly variety, beige and flat, with laces. She was thinner than she used to be, which, in her case, given her dour aspect, was not a good thing.

"Are you in New York for fun or on business?" Jeannie asked.

"Montessori conference. Just here for a few days."

She looked at her watch and then up directly into Jeannie's eyes.

"So, why didn't you contact me when my mom died?" asked Lindsey. "You didn't even send a note, much less come to the funeral."

"I don't know."

"You must know. You had to have a reason. My mom loved you. You were part of the family."

"I know. I don't know."

"Jeannie, you have to know. I want you to tell me."

"I couldn't face it, face you. I just wasn't big enough."

"Not big enough? What the hell does that mean? That's bullshit."

"I mean, it was too much, your mom dying. Your perfect family, your perfect mom. She was always so critical about my mom, you know?"

"So you were glad my mom died?"

"Of course not!"

"But you were angry with her."

"Not with her."

"With me, then."

Jeannie was silent.

"What did I do to hurt you?" Lindsey was almost pleading for a response so she could understand.

"It wasn't you. It was me."

"Always has been."

"Really? I wasn't a good friend? Ever?"

"You were fun. Everything about you was exciting and we certainly laughed a lot. I'll never forget. But when I needed you . . . remember when my dad got sick? You were gone. You disappeared."

Jeannie sat silently, looking out into the large open room,

with its dark red leather banquettes, the mahogany bar with the gold embellishments, the stone pillars. The bored waiter leaning against a table as he took an order. The man at the table in the corner biting into his croque-monsieur.

"And it wasn't as if my life was perfect. Or my family was always happy."

"When wasn't it? Besides your dad being sick, when wasn't your family perfect?"

Lindsey sat quietly, in thought, her chin in her hand. Finally, she sat up and said, "It was, I guess. Almost perfect, anyway. Don't forget, though, we had a history. You can't ignore that. My mother's experiences during the war made her who she was, and made me who I am. We are our mothers' daughters, I guess."

Jeannie let out some of the air she'd been holding in since the beginning of this conversation.

"But it's no excuse. You were a shitty friend," said Lindsey. "I was really hurt by you."

"Look, I want to show you something," Jeannie said, picking up her bag, which sat next to her on the banquette.

"What happened to that?" Lindsey asked. "Looks like it was mauled by a tiger."

"Close. Chewed by my dog, Mouse, himself." Jeannie dug through it and pulled out the troll-with-the-pink-hair key chain. "Look." Its hair was tangled and dirty, its naked body darkened by pen marks and smudges.

Lindsey laughed. "Me too," she said. And she dug in her backpack and pulled out one with remnants of lime-green hair, filled with keys. "It got some gunk in its hair and I had to cut it." But it still had its original purple felt dress.

Jeannie laughed. "Are we idiots? Or what?"

"Do you remember when we got these?"

"You saved my life that summer. I was so lonely, so every day when you got back from day camp, you'd call and I'd come over. We'd walk to the variety store—"

"It's still there, by the way, only the penny candies are a quarter now."

"—and we bought each other these stupid trolls."

"So, what happened?" asked Lindsey. Her face scrunched up in sadness.

"I don't know," said Jeannie. "Life, I guess. Life happened."

"Yeah, it sure did. Look at me," she said, turning in the banquette to the narrow mirror that lined the wall, "looking a hundred years old." She turned back to face Jeannie. "But look at you."

"It's the genes," Jeannie responded offhandedly. "Did you ever marry? How's your brother?"

"He's good, a doctor, married, two kids. But, me, well, I live alone, I teach preschool. I doubt I'll ever meet anyone. My folks, they were too protective, I think. And now, well, you see. My perfect family. Who's good enough to replace it?"

Jeannie put her hand on Lindsey's and held it tight. Funny, she thought, that both of them suffered from the same thing. Maybe that's why they had found each other long ago. Two girls who clicked because neither could carry the burdens of her family alone. But together they had been formidable.

They finished their meal, paid the check, laughed as they recalled their first hitchhiking episode, the first time they smoked a joint, the boys they dated, and then Jeannie helped Lindsey get a taxi to take her back to her hotel.

"Be in touch, okay?" Jeannie said as the two women kissed goodbye. But she knew Lindsey wouldn't. Jeannie felt for her and wished she didn't have the weight of her mother's history on her shoulders.

"It was great seeing you. Come visit," said Lindsey as she got into the taxi. "You want me to drop you?"

"Nah, I'm going to walk." Jeannie waved as the taxi drove uptown and then made her way home, deep in thought.

Cast of Thousands

There had to be thirty people working on *Caught Ya!* in the tiny studio at New York One. There was a technical director, an assistant technical director, a lighting designer, an assistant lighting designer, and an assistant to the assistant. There were sound people and script people. There were people to get coffee and people to get supplies. There was the producer, and the associate producer, and the station executives. There were Harry and Jeannie and Luce and Joseph, trying to keep control. And there was Moss, keeping a low profile, now often working out of his corporate offices or traveling to LA to finalize a new deal or attend another meeting. He hadn't been around much since *Sterling Behavior* stopped broadcasting. And Jeannie missed the teasing, the arguments, the banter. She missed him.

After two months of preparation, the show was almost ready to air. Autumn had flown by; winter, with bone-chilling winds off the Hudson and record low temperatures and high snowfalls, had descended upon the city. Christmas and New Year's had come and gone, celebrated, as Jeannie usually did, with a small group of friends, except for the few holiday parties she attended. Sometimes her dad came along, proving to be an able dancer and a charmer, but more often than not he preferred to stay at home with Mouse. And, for the first time in a long time, she had a real

boyfriend. Tommy was in town full time now, though sometimes he wouldn't leave his apartment for days, hunkered
down there, working hard. But when he wasn't working, and
when Jeannie's schedule allowed, they spent much of their
time together, making love, seeing movies, listening to
music, hanging with friends, and being in a real relationship. Some of the intensity was gone, which Jeannie attributed to their settling in as a couple. Though, sometimes,
when lying next to him in bed, his breathing a soft regular
rumble, she had moments of clarity and admitted that perhaps the lack of intensity had to do with her. That it was
she who wasn't one hundred percent committed. She felt,
yet again, on the outside looking in, instead of being in
deep. Sometimes, in those moments, her mind drifted to
Moss—holding her in the park, washing her hands, gazing
at his redwoods, the teasing, the sparring, his eyes, his
hands, his ass, for god's sake—and she wondered if she was
using her thoughts of him to distance her from Tommy. Or
if something real was happening between them. The
thought did cross her mind, but she chose to ignore it.

She had to. There was the show, which hadn't been simple
to produce. First there was the weather to contend with. The
video stings had to be planned (as much as they could be
planned, given that you couldn't know in advance how people would react) and written, shot, and edited. The live show
in the studio needed a script. It was thrilling for Jeannie in
that wonderfully scary way that tosses your stomach and
makes breathing a conscious act.

Luce was growing and gorgeous, and even in her disappointment she was helpful with the show, pitching in any way
she could. Jeannie and Luce were being more than civil; they

brainstormed ideas for bad-behavior stings, they talked about Spike and Tommy and Mouse and Lou, and even her pregnancy. But there was a deep wound where their hearts used to be, and nothing, it seemed, could heal it.

CAUGHT YA!

JEANNIE: *Good evening and welcome to* Caught Ya! *I'm Jeannie Sterling and this is my friend and partner in crime, Luce Cunningham. Many of you have heard my radio show,* Sterling Behavior, *on WBUZ-AM Radio. Tonight, for the very first time, we're on television, coming to you in a live broadcast. Consider us your Bad Behavior Patrol. Whether it's inconsiderate cell phone use, or bad driving, or not picking up your dog's poop; whether it's littering, stealing taxis, cutting in line, or just being rude, we'll catch you. To make the world a more livable place, one annoying person at a time.*

LUCE: *And then we'll be taking calls from our studio.*

JEANNIE: *So let's begin. Winter in New York is a beautiful time of year. And there's almost no place as wondrous as Fifth Avenue and Rockefeller Center.*

LUCE: *Don't you just love it? The skaters, the shoppers, and in February, a time for sales.*

JEANNIE: *A time to push, to cut and be rude. So here's what we did: I was dressed in a uniform specially designed for this show.*

LUCE: *You look good in uniform. I like your hair up and out of your face. What's that BBP across your back stand for?*

JEANNIE: *Bad Behavior Patrol.*

LUCE: *Looks official.*

JEANNIE: *So I can patrol and give out tickets for social infractions. Let's see what happened. Okay, here we go. This is Fifth Avenue,* the shopping mecca of the city, where Prada is on one block and the Disney store is on the next, where Cartier and the NBA Store share a corner. Fifth Avenue, where mass merch meets designer mayhem.

I'm walking the beat. It's beautiful out, cold but sunny and dry. Joseph, our ace photographer and engineer, is following behind, carrying a small mini-DV camera, and we're both rigged with mics. The sidewalk is crowded with shoppers, businesspeople, couples, kids, and dogs, like that little one there, with the pink sweater and silver lamé collar.

LUCE: *Pretty cute.*

JEANNIE: *I never thought you were a dog person, especially for a yappy little white dog in clothes.*

LUCE: *I'm talking about the Chanel coat the woman's wearing. Not to mention her Louboutin boots.*

JEANNIE: *But look at that leash. It's one of those retractable ones, and she's got it out ten feet. It's dangerous, sure to trip someone. Watch what happens . . . I approach her and . . .*

JEANNIE AS COP: *Lady, excuse me.*

WOMAN WITH DOG: *Hello, officer.*

JEANNIE AS COP: *I'm sorry, but you'll have to pull in that leash. You're going to trip someone.*

WOMAN WITH DOG: *But Paris loves the freedom.*

JEANNIE AS COP: *Does she? Is that why you have her dressed in a sweater—because you're concerned for her canine instincts? Then find a dog run. This sidewalk's way too crowded. I'll need to see a picture ID, please.*

WOMAN WITH DOG: *What for? I'm on my way—*

JEANNIE AS COP: *For walking your dog without considering people around you. For thinking you and she own the sidewalk.*

WOMAN WITH DOG: *And, officer, since when is that against the law?*

JEANNIE AS COP: *Here you go, it's a fifty-dollar fine.*

WOMAN WITH DOG: *That's insane. That's absurd.*

JEANNIE AS COP: *No, that's . . .* Caught Ya!

LUCE: *That was fun! Look at her face!*

JEANNIE: *Something I've always wanted to do. Now watch this. See that fellow there standing outside Armani Exchange? He's probably waiting for his girlfriend who's inside shopping. He's chewing gum . . . now watch . . . he takes it out of his mouth . . .*

LUCE: *Oh no, he's not . . . he did!*

JEANNIE AS COP: *Excuse me, young man. Did you do what I think you just did?*

YOUNG MAN: *That depends.*

JEANNIE AS COP: *Don't be a wiseass, fella. Did you or did you not just throw your gum into the street?*

YOUNG MAN: *Yeah, I guess I did. What're you going to do, arrest me?*

JEANNIE AS COP: *No—*

YOUNG MAN: *That's a relief.*

JEANNIE AS COP: *I detect a hint of sarcasm. Which is pretty funny, since I am about to write you a ticket.*

YOUNG MAN: *You're kidding, right?*

JEANNIE AS COP: *Fifty bucks is no joke.*

YOUNG MAN: *You're f [bleep] kidding me. For what? For chewing gum?*

JEANNIE AS COP: *For littering. For throwing your gum in the street. So that someone can step in it. And there's a garbage can right over there. And over there too. You know what? On second thought, I'm going to charge you a hundred instead.*

YOUNG MAN: *Wait a minute. You can't do that. I don't believe this! Where am I, in Singapore?*

JEANNIE AS COP: *No, you're on . . .* Caught Ya!

LUCE: *Look at his face. He deserved it.*

JEANNIE: *And finally, watch this. We shot this one night in a movie* *theater on West Twenty-third Street. I'm in my uniform, in the women's bathroom. Joseph, obviously, can't come in, so we've rigged a tiny camera to my chest and I'm still wearing a wireless mic. The bathroom, as you see, is busy at this twelve-plex. People go into stalls and as they come out, I quickly go in to check if they've left the toilet seat clean.*

LUCE: *I hate sitting on a seat and getting all wet. It's disgusting.*

JEANNIE: *It really is . . . Now watch . . . most people are pretty good, but then there's this woman. Look at her, she's middle-aged, she's dressed nicely, she's washing her hands. And she's left the seat a mess.*

JEANNIE AS COP: *Excuse me, ma'am.*

WOMAN: *Hello, officer. Is something going on? I've never seen a police person in the ladies' bathroom before. Is there a rapist in here?*

JEANNIE AS COP: *I'm going to have to ask you to clean off your toilet seat, ma'am.*

WOMAN: *Excuse me?*

JEANNIE AS COP: *That was your stall, was it not? You left urine all over your seat.*

WOMAN: *What are you, the pee police? [she laughs]*

JEANNIE AS COP: *I'll need to see a photo ID.*

WOMAN: *Why, you going to call the toilet in? See if it's licensed? [she laughs]*

JEANNIE AS COP: *Very funny. No, I'm going to give you a ticket.*

WOMAN: *For what?*

JEANNIE AS COP: *For violating social code number 007, Failure to Leave Toilet Seat Clean for the Next Person.*

WOMAN: *Is this for real? Since when is there a law against that? You should never sit on the seat. You could get a disease! And why should I clean it when there's a woman stationed in here and paid to do it?*

JEANNIE AS COP: *Since you're on . . .* Caught Ya!

LUCE: *Jeannie, I have one question. Did anybody actually pay their tickets?*

JEANNIE: *They didn't have to. I was never going to take their money. It was all part of the setup. In exchange for allowing us to use their segment, we dropped all charges.*

Call from the Coast

"Jeannie, I have Moss on the line," said Susie, a production assistant of the most detail-oriented, pain-in-the-ass kind.

"Hey, Mr. Moss, sir," said Jeannie into the phone, excited to hear from him.

There was that voice. He wondered if she was sitting or standing, if her hand was in her hair, if her cheeks were flushed. "Harry emailed me the show last night. Love it. You're doing great. Keep it up. Actually—"

"Oh, here it comes."

"Don't be afraid to push it more. You're being too nice. I want to see—"

"Blood?"

"Jeannie, no, not what I was thinking. I want to see you do what every person would want to do in the same situation. A lady doesn't wipe her toilet seat? She gets a ticket, and then you let her off? No. She gets a ticket. She pays. After she wipes the seat. That's what we want to see. People doing the right thing."

"Okay . . ."

"We have a lot riding on this, Jeannie. First there's you. You have the potential to fly. And my partners, well, need I say more? They want this to—"

"And you?"

"Me?" He sighed. He wasn't going to let on how he couldn't stop thinking about her. "I want to be high in a tree somewhere overlooking the Pacific. Or the Passaic. Anywhere but here."

Her heart dropped. *But what about me?* "If New Jersey's an option, you must mean the existentialist 'anywhere,' don't you."

"But I have a job to do too."

"Okay, boss," she said, coolly.

"And Jeannie? You okay otherwise?" He paused. "You and Luce?"

She let out a loud sigh. "I don't know. We're working, doing the show."

"Can I offer my advice?"

"Could I say no if I wanted to?"

"Don't take what you have with her for granted. A friend like that is one of those once-in-a-lifetime things." *Like love,* he thought. "Very hard to replace. Try to work it out."

"Thanks, boss, I needed that."

"Sarcasm doesn't become you, Jeannie. And stop calling me boss!"

CAUGHT YA!

JEANNIE: *Welcome to another night of* Caught Ya! *This is our sixth week, and tonight we're going to try something different. We're tackling littering, but we won't be writing tickets. We're on Amsterdam Avenue looking for people who can't be bothered with finding a garbage can. Who knew we'd find a litterbug in a car? There, keep your eye on that black sedan. Watch. It stops at a* light, the door opens, and the driver drops the remains of his lunch right there on the street. Styrofoam container, chicken bones, and all.

LUCE: He was eating that in his car? Yech!

JEANNIE: So, there I am running up to him. I yell Caught Ya! I ask for his driver's license, I fine him and ask him to pick it up. And when he refuses to, I promise I'll run the tape, with his name and address, and here it is. Hasta la vista, Andy Schmidt of two-oh-two East Sixteenth Street. That's Andy Schmidt, litterer, who lives at two-oh-two East Sixteenth Street.

LUCE: Wait a minute, Jeannie. You want people to know where he lives? I don't know—

JEANNIE: And check this out. We're on Sutton Place, and watch that man. He exits his apartment building with a huge bag of garbage and leaves it on the sidewalk next to the garbage can.

LUCE: Now why would he do that? It's illegal. Besides, he lives in a very nice building on this fancy street. He has to have garbage pickup right from his apartment.

JEANNIE: And look what happens. A dog is sniffing around it and pees on it. And there you have it. The life cycle of litter. Now Luce, we have one more. Watch this. We're on Third Avenue. See that kid there in the red sweatshirt, in front of the deli? He's taking his time, unwrapping his Snickers bar, slowly, painstakingly. And then, he just drops it on the ground. Now, I was not needed to write a ticket or yell "Caught ya!," because see that little old lady? She shoves him, she scolds him, she says, "Caught ya!" and . . . he picks it up. It's catching on! If everyone did that we wouldn't need Caught Ya!

LUCE: And you'd be out of a job.

JEANNIE: So tonight, I want all of you watching to copy down the names, addresses, and phone numbers that we're providing you.

Then give them a call, write them a letter, do something to let them know how you feel about their behavior. Here they are: first, Charles Montgomery of . . .

Parental Disapproval

Jeannie's dad was drinking coffee and reading the morning paper at the kitchen counter, and Mouse was on her couch chewing her lacy black panties, when Jeannie walked in that morning in her bathrobe.

"Hey, Pop," she greeted him warmly. Then she went over to him and kissed him on the cheek. "So did you watch?"

"Hi, toots," he said. "I did." He sipped his coffee, went back to reading the paper.

"Please don't lavish me with praise. I don't think I could take it."

He finally looked up at her. "Jeannie, Jeannie, Jeannie," he said, shaking his head. "Didn't I teach you anything?"

"We already established that, Dad. Yo-yos, bananas and cream—"

"That's not what I mean. Your show."

"Yeah, wasn't that something? God, I was so excited when I got to ticket that guy dropping garbage out of his car. I mean it was exactly . . . we couldn't have written that better."

"Well, maybe it's just me, but . . ." her dad said, looking down at his finger, which was drawing circles in the coffee that had dripped onto the counter. "Actually, in the words of Gandhi, the master of nonviolent demonstration, 'It sucked.'"

Jeannie's mouth fell open and she put her two palms flat down onto the counter, hard enough to make a *smack* and make the counter vibrate. "What the hell are you talking about? It was everything that I could ever wish for. It was everything they wanted. It was perfect."

"You know the old saying: be careful what you wish for . . ."

"But Dad," Jeannie said, "did you see the look on those people's faces? I thought you'd be proud. I thought this was what you wanted for me. Success, fame, and most of all, finally accomplishing something."

"Jeannie, Jeannie," her dad said, putting his hands on hers, which still lay flat on the counter. "Fuck fame. And definitely not at the expense of others. I'm sorry if I led you to believe this kind of treatment of people would be right. It's not. And besides, what they're doing is not important. You think it matters that the kid threw his wrapper on the ground? It's bupkis."

"It's not nothing. It's the principle. That's what's important. Be courteous, be considerate, just be nice human beings, and trust me, life would be better," she said, pulling her hands away and turning her back to him. "If people need to be embarrassed in order to see how lousy they are behaving, then they are to blame." She took a mug down from her cabinet and poured herself some coffee.

"I am ashamed. At myself for not being a better father, because you should know better, and that's my job. And at you, because you should know better just because you are an intelligent, thoughtful adult."

First she felt the tightness of her throat, then the muscles in her face clenched into that terrible crying expression she made that altered every molecule in it, and then her eyes filled with the tears of anger and frustration, of terrible hurt.

"I'm not stopping. This will help people, the good people, and besides, I signed a contract." She waited a beat, then said, "Fuck the contract. I'm not stopping because I'm just getting started!"

"Even good people do bad things. Don't they? Even good people make mistakes."

She got a bottle of water from her fridge and took a slug from it. "I'm not stopping. I believe in this. And I'm sorry you don't like it."

The phone rang. It was Tommy. She walked down the hall for some privacy.

"Great show. Keeps getting better. Those idiots. Hilarious."

"You think so? Maybe it was too much. My dad thinks—"

"Nah, it was perfect. And then putting that guy's address and phone number up? You're going to ruin his life! Perfect."

She rolled her eyes. "I don't know." *No, it wasn't perfect.*

"Why don't you come over?"

"Not tonight."

"When?"

She let out a sigh. "Maybe tomorrow."

"Jeannie, you okay? We okay?"

"I'm just exhausted. This new schedule. It's hard to adjust to normalcy."

"Now that I can relate to. I love you, you know."

"Yeah, me too."

A Person Could Get Hurt

The next morning, it was bedlam in the studio. The phones were ringing off their hooks, and there wasn't enough staff to handle it all. People out there seemed overwhelmed and joyous that someone, finally, had taken bad behavior by the balls.

Luce was helping with the phones; Joseph was preparing

for another day of shooting. Harry was dealing with paper-work when the phone rang.

"Moss wants to see you, Jeannie. His office."

He's back, she thought, and surprised herself that she was so pleased. She smoothed her sweater down over her jeans and then ran her hands through her hair. When she walked in, he was sitting behind his desk, looking very serious, and asked her to close the door.

"Sit," he said. "Please."

She sat on one of the leather chairs facing his glass desk; he remained in his desk chair. *This is awfully official,* she thought, and she began to get nervous.

"That was some show last night," he said.

"Oh man, you should've been there! It was—"

"It was too much. You can't give people's addresses and phone numbers to millions of people."

"Why not? It's peer pressure."

"It violates their privacy. Someone could get hurt. I heard one guy had garbage thrown on his doorstep, eggs thrown at his windows. And besides, I don't think you want to humiliate people."

She stood. Her face was red now, and her ears rang. "Wait a minute. Wasn't it you who told me to get people to do the right thing? Now the phones are backed up. People are going wild for this. Finally someone is doing something. Fi-nally *I* am doing something. It's what you wanted. The ratings will be sky high, your ad dollars will quadruple, and besides, we might, finally, make a goddamn difference."

"Bring it down, Jeannie. We need to find the middle ground here. I want you to talk to people out there. I want it to be entertaining. And it will be, if it's just you being you. I do not want you to hurt them. Or berate them."

"Is everybody a hypocrite?"

He stood, angry now. "I don't know. Is everybody? Wouldn't you say that it might be a teensy-weensy bit hypocritical to treat people badly, without respect, in order to get them to stop treating people badly and without respect?"

"Please. Don't talk to me about means to the ends. We all know that asking nicely does nothing. You need to be in their faces. This is just what you wanted!"

He turned to look for a moment at his photo of the forest canopy. Then he looked up at her. "I just don't want you to get hurt. Or anybody else, for that matter. You have no idea how powerful you are."

And maybe that was the heart of it. Maybe Jeannie didn't realize that *Caught Ya!* was changing life—for her and everyone—in the tri-state area as she knew it. Or maybe she did.

Wish Robber

Spring was finally beginning to burst forth: the crocuses were in bloom, the grass was green again, trees were sprouting their leaves, and there was a clean feel to the air. Tommy came to the office to take Jeannie to lunch.

"Let's celebrate," he said. "What a show. What a reception. Everybody at the *Times* is talking about it." He leaned over to kiss her.

Down on the street, he took her hand and they walked for blocks, down Broadway to Chambers, the street of ratty but irresistible ninety-nine-cent discount stores filled with huge bags of unknown-brand candy, fake Bic pens, birthday cards with glitter that came off in your hands, plaid kitchen towels, closeout dishes and glasses, plastic flowers and Lucite picture frames, measuring cups and ruffly curtains and all kinds of must-have cheap stuff. Sometimes, maybe, Jeannie would find a gem, like a sketch pad or a simple black wood picture frame that would cost a buck and make her day.

"Look at all that crap," Tommy said, looking in the windows of Jack's 99-Cent Store, one of the best on the block.

"What? That's Jack's. It's awesome."

"Filled with shit from Hong Kong."

"If you're arguing that we shouldn't buy stuff because it exploits—"

"Nah. It's just that it's shit. Junk."

"Oh! I get it. You're a snob."

Tommy smiled and grabbed her hand and pulled her, running across Broadway toward City Hall Park. She loved the feel of her hand being held, the wind blowing her hair, someone pulling her, like they were young lovers. But when she looked at Tommy, there was a disconnect between her brain and her heart.

They had to walk around the low gray cement barricades that had circled City Hall Park since 9/11. But once in, Jeannie brightened, for the park was a triangular oasis in downtown Manhattan, where Broadway and Park Row and Chambers converged, with its old trees, its Victorian fountain, and its colorful history. Here, Washington and his Continental Army heard the Declaration of Independence read; two months later, when the British occupied the city, they imprisoned and executed hundreds of Americans right here under these trees. It was hallowed ground, this park, representing democracy and freedom, and it was lovely, one of Jeannie's favorite places in the city. From under the shade of a huge locust tree, listening to the lulling water of the fountain, you could watch the world go by: moms chasing kids on trikes, people in dark suits on their way to jobs, students at CUNY studying for a biology quiz, tourists who'd walked east from Ground Zero, hot dog vendors, empanada vendors, Big Apple souvenir vendors, poor people with their shopping carts overflowing with plastic garbage bags containing the bottles they would return for the nickel deposits, others like her with free time during the day—night-shifters, the homeless, the unemployed—an eclectic mix that represented all that Jeannie loved about this city, her city, the city that finally she had influenced, that was following her, for good or for bad.

And today, on this fresh spring day, she finally came *with* someone, and that someone was someone with whom she'd so wanted to be in love. Someone bright and beautiful, who held her hand tight and led her to this bench, with its scrolled iron arms and legs, its slatted wood seat and back that had a gold plaque that read IN LOVING MEMORY OF DOROTHEA SIMON, and beneath that the Walt Whitman words IF YOU BRING THE WARMTH OF THE SUN TO THEM THEY WILL OPEN AND BRING FORM, COLOR, PERFUME, TO YOU. *Someone had surely loved this Dorothea,* Jeannie thought, as they sat under a leaning tree, its leaves still unfolding, its branches alive with the jabbering of birds. Tommy put his arm around her and held her firmly as if he knew she might take flight at any moment like those birds in the tree above. From here they could view the plaza and watch life happening as if they were watching a play from eighth row center, riveted.

He then took his hand, turned her face toward his, and kissed her. His kiss was ardent, his mouth opening to hers, his hand now pulling her close, forcing her back to straighten, her head to fall back, her chin to rise up. She put her hand on his chest, to hold him less conspicuously but also to keep him at some distance.

"Jeannie," he said softly, as he pressed his lips against hers. "Jeannie," he said again.

Her name spoken in a kiss. *Oh god, what more is there than that*, she wondered. But if she could be honest about the moment, if she would only allow herself to see deeply into her heart, she'd admit how much more there could be. Like the passion she felt before learning where he stood on survival of the fittest, or on library books and taxpayer rights, before seeing Luce and Spike together and understanding what she and Tommy were missing, before Moss became a presence in her life.

She saw something out of the corner of her eye that made her break away. She turned to look out at the park, and there she saw a young man walking toward the fountain.

"What is it?" asked Tommy.

"Wait, something . . ." Her voice trailed off as she watched the young man. She wasn't sure what held her gaze. She liked the way his face was full of intent. The sun made his hair shine with light that bounced directly into her eyes. He sat on the low stone wall that circled the fountain and took off his shoes, then his socks. Then he turned 180 degrees and put his feet in, as if it were summer.

Jeannie watched the man walk around the fountain, first once, then again, looking over his right and left shoulders as if he knew what he was doing might cause suspicion. He put his hand in his pocket—or was it his pants?—and she thought, *Oh no, he's not going to pee in the fountain, is he?* And then he bent over to pick up something in the water. He looked at it and put it in his pocket. Then he bent again and again, and Jeannie realized what he was doing: he was stealing the coins that sat on the fountain floor.

Her heart plunged deep into the murky waters of discouragement. Bending down and then up, pocketing the change, sloshing slowly through the turbulent waters that bubbled in the fountain pool, he was stealing the coins people had thrown as they wished to win the lottery, to get married, for good health, for world peace, for love.

She couldn't stop herself. Someone had to do something. And that someone would be her. She stood up and yelled from her bench.

"Hey! You! Stop!" she said, so articulately.

"Jeannie, come on," urged Tommy, pulling her down next to him.

The man looked at her over his shoulder, then kept at his pursuit.

But she rose and walked a few steps toward the fountain. "Hey! That's not your money! That's not money to take!" She frantically looked around, but there was no cop, of course, and only a few heads looked her way. She turned to implore Tommy, "He's stealing the coins from the fountain! It's not right."

"Sit down," said Tommy, "what's the big deal? Let the guy—"

"It *is* a big deal. He's stealing."

"Not really. People threw their money there. They don't own it anymore."

"He's stealing their wishes! Don't you see?"

"Jesus, Jeannie. Sometimes—" He stopped himself.

"What? Sometimes what?" She could not believe he was actually defending this pig!

"Sometimes you're over the top, you know? You need to relax a little. It's really no big deal. And anyway, what do you expect from someone like him?"

"I expect from him what I'd expect from you." She looked at

him closely, into his eyes, and, for the first time, saw steel, hard and cold. Not one shred of texture or light in those gray eyes. "I should relax? Not a big deal?" *Don't you know me at all?*

Tommy, like every other New Yorker in the park, had, of course, seen almost everything, and this was nothing. So a young guy is an animal, so he's stealing coins from the fountain, so what else is new? But to Jeannie this was about everything she stood for. This was everything *Caught Ya!* was supposed to be. There was no law against this, no sign that said "No Stealing of Coins Allowed." This was simply wrong. People had made wishes, for god's sake, a woman had taken the time to dig in the bottom of her purse, a man in the bottom of his pants pocket, a kid had asked her mom for a penny, all for a wish. For a new bicycle, for a better job, for any job, for a nicer house, for a baby, for a sick child to be well, for a kinder boyfriend, for a fucking boyfriend at all. People had thrown the coins and they had hit the water with a little splash, had fallen slowly to the bottom, and the people walked away feeling that perhaps, just this once, their wish would come true.

This wasn't merely pick-pocketing or purse-snatching. This was robbery of a more spiritual kind. And though Jeannie believed that stealing wishes was a kind of karmic suicide and would bite the thief in the ass someday, she knew she couldn't rely on fate to deal with him.

She'd have to do something herself. And without her crew, her camera, her mic, and uniform to help her.

For here was this guy, this asshole, this guy who felt his need for, what—a cup of coffee? A pint of whiskey? A subway fare? A fix?—was more important than the wishes of others.

And here was Tommy not getting her, not sharing in her outrage.

Jeannie walked closer. She could hear Tommy pleading with her to come back. She was about ten feet from the Wish Robber now. Her anger bubbled over like the spray of the fountain as it spewed from the four corners of the pool around it. "What the hell are you doing?" she shouted. "You stealing the coins?"

He turned to her and she could see now that the face she'd thought was handsome from far away was pockmarked and worn, that his feet were, even in the water, visibly filthy, with long ragged toenails. He said, "Mind your own business, lady. And shut the fuck up, would you?"

"You thief! You wish robber!"

In her fantasies, a hundred people would join her in her verbal attack, sending him off into the shadows of the city. It would be a total vigilante spree, getting the bad guy to stop, making him see the error of his ways, making him feel ashamed and alone. But today her yells of reproach yielded one lone supporter. And it wasn't Tommy, who sat watching her from the bench where only a minute ago they were kissing. A black teenager, the crotch of his pants at his knees, his Knicks jersey large and baggy, his gold chains heavy on his neck, his big white high-top leather tennis shoes unlaced and opened, a black Nike backpack sliding off his shoulders, walked right up to her from across the fountain, one arm raised with his index finger pointing down at her. "You da man, girl. You da man!" And then, shaking his head, he said to the thief, "Fucking wish robber. Stealing some sick old lady's wishes. I oughta steal your ass! You motha fucka."

When the guy ignored him, the kid in the Knicks jersey walked right into that fountain, right up to him. The water was up to his knees, probably ruining his shoes, drenching his saggy-butt jeans. Jeannie watched the kid, a stranger who had jumped in there because of her; then she looked back at Tommy, still sitting on the bench, watching from afar like a spectator at a basketball game. She looked again at the kid sloshing in the fountain, who was getting soaked, and back at Tommy once more. Then Jeannie walked right into that fountain with the kid and approached the thief. The floor of the fountain was slippery, the water was cold, bubbling around her, soaking her jeans and her boots, even the fringes of her suede jacket.

"The lady said to stop," the kid yelled, to be heard over the cascading water.

"I heard the crazy lady," said the guy as he continued to pocket the change. His pockets were now bulging, his pants hanging from the weight.

"So stop that shit right now, man. And get your ass out of the fountain."

"Yeah," said Jeannie. "Yeah!"

The kid turned to her, surprised to see her there coming up behind, and said, "That's right, girl."

The Wish Robber stood there looking at the unusual duo and probably came to the conclusion that the sides were not balanced, because he turned around and walked until he hit the fountain's center column and climbed up on it. Then, as if he were in Hyde Park on a Sunday soapbox, he turned and yelled, "This is a public fountain! There are no laws here, no signs, no rules. This is a free country and I am free to pick up money that other people throw away. This is a free country! Fucking idiots!" Then he jumped down, climbed out of the fountain, found his shoes, and walked off barefoot, leaving a path of water behind him.

The kid got a good laugh out of that. He and Jeannie climbed out of the fountain and were rehashing the event and shaking their legs out, stomping on their shoes, which squished with water, as Tommy approached. He smiled at her, shaking his head. "Look at you. You're my hero."

Jeannie couldn't help but smile at the thought that she went after the bad guy without TV cameras, without a crew.

"Look at your boots."

She didn't have to. She could feel them seeping with water, her toes all wet and funky.

Then Tommy turned to the kid. "Hey man, nicely done."

"Got to do what you got to do," said the kid. But he went back to talking to Jeannie, pretty much ignoring Tommy, still reminiscing, still laughing, dealing with the water.

Then the kid turned to Tommy and said, "Your lady is something, man. She is all right." He smiled big at Jeannie, knocking her knuckles with a clenched fist.

Tommy laughed, looked at Jeannie. "Let's go, huh?" He put his arm around her.

She felt uncomfortable with it there but let it rest.

"And what about you, man? Sitting over there on the sidelines? What's up with that?" asked the kid.

The kid had voiced exactly what Jeannie was thinking.

"She didn't need me. She was in complete control," he said, giving Jeannie a squeeze.

Jeannie's heart raced, her eyes blinking in the sun. *I don't need you. That's the sad thing.*

"Well, I got to be going," said the kid, shifting his weight from one foot to the other and back.

"Hey, thanks," Jeannie said. "You did a good thing today. Not too many people—"

"Hey, nothing," the kid answered. "Can't let some asshole steal people's wishes, disappoint them, can we?" He glared at Tommy.

Jeannie felt a hollow at the pit of her stomach. *No, we can't,* she thought, *we can't.*

Hypocritical Oath

Jeannie came home that evening to find her dad's Samsonite suitcase at the front door, his jacket thrown over it and his carry-on beside it. He was sitting on his favorite kitchen stool, reading the newspaper. Mouse jumped up on her, barking, his tail wagging. She knelt to scratch him behind his ears.

Jeannie knew in her gut after their latest argument that this was coming. She threw her bag and jacket on the counter.

"You're leaving," she said.

"I am," he answered.

"Because you're angry with me?"

"That and because I've been here too long."

"I'm surprised you're even here to say good-bye. Usually you just go."

"Honestly? I didn't think you'd be home so soon. What'd you do, steal someone's taxi? Or beat up someone who stole someone's taxi and then steal the taxi?"

"You know I'd never do that."

"Jeannie, we all do that."

"Let's not start."

"You're right. I gotta go, anyway," he said, looking at his watch. "Mouse, come."

Mouse stood and waited for the leash to be attached to his collar.

"You're not taking my dog," Jeannie said.

"Oh, so now he's your dog? The only things you've done for this dog are feed him and get him that nice dog walker. I have never seen you give him even the slightest affection."

"You gave him to me!"

"Only for a while. To see—" He stopped himself.

"So this was a test? Administered by the great judge of love and affection. Nothing like a little hypocrisy, right, Dad?"

"Jeannie, I know my limitations. I know what I did and did not provide for you." Now he turned to her head on, his nostrils flaring, his eyes black with anger. "Do you have any inkling at all about your limitations? You want to talk about tests? Guess how you'd score on a test of your ability to love and to forgive? A goddamn F. That's what. And don't talk to me about hypocrisy. Your show—"

"That is so not true!" said Jeannie. But in her heart she knew it was true. She looked down at the floor and noticed the scratches in the soft wood from Mouse's crazy play, from his running back and forth from bedroom to front door, from his jumping on his hind legs for an ear scratch, from his begging for food.

Her dad put the leash on Mouse. He put on his rancher jacket and slung the carry-on over his shoulder.

Then he went right up to her, took her hand—which she struggled to pull away, but he held fast—and said, "Jeannie, this thing, this TV thing, maybe it's because you have no faith in people. You have to trust them. Enough to love and get hurt and to love again. To trust in people, even when they're . . . what's that word you've always used?" He paused for a minute to think, waiting for Jeannie's help. When none came, he continued, "Ach, who the hell cares. Whatever you call them, you'll be surprised how they'll rise to the occasion.

I'm nobody, I know, to give advice. Just your loser of a dad. But all I want from you is one thing: let yourself love. Then you'll see how forgiving you can be."

Then he opened the door, picked up his suitcase and Mouse's leash, said, "Come on, Mouse," and was gone.

"Turkeys," she said out loud. *Turkey. That's how all of this began.*

Late Night Swimming

The water felt especially cold tonight. Even after six laps, when her body should've easily acclimated to the temperature, her skin prickled, her muscles steeled, her heart beat hard against the chill.

Fuck all these men, she thought as her left arm rose out of the water, her head turning to the left to get a mouthful of air. She saw Tommy at the fountain, felt the disappointment deep in her chest, and lost her rhythm, taking a few strokes to get back in synch. She heard her dad's words, his criticism, saw him walk out the door with Mouse, and her arm slammed down forcefully against the surface of the water. But it was when she saw Moss's face and registered his disappointment in *her,* she had to stop, regain her equilibrium, breaststroke to the edge of the pool, catch her breath. She lifted her goggles onto her head and wiped her eyes, the salt of her tears commingling with the chlorine of the pool.

Fuck them all.

She leaned against the side of the pool, her legs out before her, her back supported by the tiled edge. The lummox in the lane left of hers was churning the water with his sloppy kicks. The woman in the lane to the right was wearing a silly pink tie-dye-printed cap, but swimming like an Olympian, fast and strong, a woman to beat. Two men in tiny Speedos were standing at the pool's edge over by the ladder and talking too loudly, their annoying voices echoing off the tiled walls. *Shut up. Shut the hell up* was what Jeannie wanted to say out loud.

She put her goggles back on, watching the pink cap soar through the water. *I'm going to kick her ass,* Jeannie thought. She squatted down low and pushed off, the water rushing against her ears. It took only a couple of laps for the tears to stop, for her to hit her stride, and fall into the trance-like rhythm of the strokes, her body sleek and swift and sure in the water. With each lap she gained on the pink cap, closing the distance between them to only a few feet. As Jeannie caught up to her competition and inched past her, her heart pumping wildly, her muscles aching from the strain, the woman in the pink cap sped up, not ceding the lead so easily. *Get out of my way,* Jeannie thought, pushing ahead, taking fewer breaths the way racers do, her shoulders arching out of the water, pulling her forward. Until, finally, they were neck and neck.

But her brain was doing the crawl and her heart the side-stroke. The thought of Moss looking at her the way he had, of him losing interest in her, of her not being up to his standards, held her back. She slowed, but the pink cap raced on. Through the blur of blue water she saw the woman's feet flutter past her, and Jeannie pulled her head out to watch her reach the edge. The woman stopped and stood, looking back at Jeannie with a satisfied grin. She took off her cap to reveal a short shock of platinum hair and Jeannie realized she couldn't have been older than twenty-two, if that, a good fifteen years younger than Jeannie. The younger woman hopped up and out of the pool and Jeannie watched her strong legs, without even the hint of a dimple, take her back into the dressing room.

Jeannie, who believed she would be twenty-two forever, was not. She wasn't even really "young" anymore, and she could see forty coming upon her all too quickly, like a head-on accident. Growing older was not, in and of itself, something that normally bothered Jeannie. But growing older full of disappointment scared the shit out of her.

She reached the edge of the pool and stopped, her chest heaving, her breath heavy. She took off her goggles and her cap, letting her hair fall, shaking it out. *No,* she thought, she was not going to be the cliché, the woman who is afraid of turning forty, still single and alone. *No, I am not that woman.* Jeannie was and always would be the spirited, independent woman who had *chosen* to wait for love, who *chose* singlehood over settling for some lame guy. So maybe she wouldn't have kids. It wasn't like kids were always on her mind; it was just that *not* having them hadn't been an option. And maybe she wouldn't ever find the love of her life. Or maybe she would, maybe she already had.

And it hit her then what was really upsetting her. The fear, the sadness, rose in her until it squeezed her throat and blinded her eyes. Finally she had met a man who might be the one to really love, who she could see building a life with. Nothing could have scared her more. Except one thing: losing him.

But then came that familiar old strut of pride: losing herself would be worse. Men had come and gone throughout her life. And perhaps, that was how it was meant to be. Moss wouldn't be the last of them.

Screw him. Screw his double standards and his self-righteous bullshit. I have a plan. And I will not waver. There was a gnawing in her gut that this plan of hers may not be a hundred percent thought out, but *what the hell is?* She couldn't wimp out now, not when there was so much at stake.

Gimme a V for Vigilante

Well, good, she thought the next morning. For the first time in a long time, she'd get to read the newspaper however she chose, without having to wait for her dad to finish. It was sitting on the kitchen counter, opened to the section that most interested her—the Metro section, the news about her own city. And right there were several stories that unnerved her. *Oh shit,* she thought.

Outbreaks of vigilantism had been reported across the tristate area. It was like a virus, the bug passing from one person to another until the entire landscape was infected with rash acts.

Trenton, New Jersey A man, 42, on a commuter train to New York City was annoyed by the woman, 26, sitting next to him, who was talking loudly on her cell phone. In response, he began to read his *New York Times* out loud, at the top of his lungs. A fight broke out and the train was held at the station for an hour as police were called in to end the dispute. Two people were sent to the hospital for injuries.

Great Neck, Long Island A man, 48, driving home from the hardware store on a rainy night was being tailgated by a black SUV, making him nervous every time he stopped for a light. Then it happened: at the intersection of Lakeville and Old Mill, the car rear-ended him. He was relieved to find that the only damage was a slight dent in his bumper. But he held up his hand and yelled at the woman at the wheel, "Stop! Do not move! Don't even think about going until I am down the street, out of your sight!"

Whether it was the tone of his voice, the anger in his face, or the hammer he wielded in a threatening manner, the woman did exactly as she was instructed and sat there, creating a traffic jam that clogged the main thoroughfare for an hour.

Greenwich Village, New York City After witnessing a 10-pound shih tzu relieving itself on the sidewalk in front of his turn-of-the-century town house, a 58-year-old man picked up the dog's poop and smeared it on the back of the dog's owner, a 20-year-old NYU student. "Yeah, I did it," the man said. "I'm sick of people not picking up after their dogs. And if I don't do something, who will?" The pre-law student filed an assault charge.

Norwalk, Connecticut Two middle-aged moms were arrested for affixing bumper stickers on over 30 Hummers throughout southern Connecticut. The bumper stickers read HONK IF YOU THINK I'M AN ASSHOLE.

Upper Nyack, New York When a woman, 33, spotted a perfectly able-bodied man walking to his car, which was parked in a blue space reserved for the disabled at Costco, she drove her car behind it to block him in and phoned the police on her cell. She wouldn't leave until the police arrived and the man was properly ticketed.

Scarsdale, New York A woman, 38, riding her bicycle on the sidewalk, took a dangerous spill when a young mother and her

8-year-old son were almost run over. "Ride in the street!" the mother was heard to have yelled, before she threw a stick in the bicycle's spokes, sending the rider up and over the handle-bars.

The one thing all the stories had in common was that the vigilante in each and every case shouted, "Caught ya!" after intercepting the bad behavior.

Jeannie put the paper down and looked out her window on the river below. It was catching on. People were finally taking matters of rude behavior into their own hands. Jeannie should have been thrilled.

The phone began to ring but she didn't pick it up. Harry left a message on the machine. Joseph too. They were look-ing for her, asking her to get into the studio.

By the time she got there it was mayhem, the phones going crazy, the staff running ragged. But there was no Luce, no Harry, no Moss. Only Joseph checking the gear and pack-ing it up for their next foray into the city.

"Hey, you," said Jeannie. "Where is everybody?"

"Well, Harry and Moss are in a meeting with Luce. That's all I know."

"Moss is meeting with Luce? That's weird."

"Maybe she's getting her own show. She looks really good on TV." He must've seen Jeannie's face, because he quickly added, "But I doubt it, just kidding."

Then Luce was there, in the studio, picking up her papers, her notebook, her bag.

Jeannie followed her. "Luce, what's going on? What're you doing?"

Luce was moving so fast, her head down, that it took a moment for Jeannie to see that she had been crying. Her eyes were swollen, her nose was red.

"Luce! Talk to me!"

Luce turned to Jeannie, pivoting on one foot, her ponytail flying, her stomach protruding from her black sweater set, her face enraged. "Talk to you? I should talk to you? As you would say, go you-know-what yourself!"

Jeannie had never heard Luce utter those non–swear words, had never seen her so upset. "What's happened?" she asked softly.

"Are you kidding me?"

"Luce—"

"Shut up, Jeannie, shut up. This stupid show. This mean, nasty, ugly show. You don't get it, do you? You're hurting people. You could get hurt yourself."

Now Jeannie was on the defensive. Why was everybody after her? This was exactly what she'd wanted. This show was working. "But look at the reports in the *Times*. It's growing, this vigilante *Caught Ya!* campaign. It's what we've worked so hard for." She noticed the clock and realized they didn't have much time before the show would begin. "But we need to get ready. Can we talk more about this later?"

Luce said, "No, Jeannie. There is no 'later.' I have definitely outlived my uselessness here. I'm off *Sterling Behavior*, off *Caught Ya!*, out of your life."

"You can't quit! How do we do the show without you? How do I—"

"You're very good without me." She put on her Burberry trench, flung her bag over her shoulder, and walked out, down the hall.

Luce. She could not imagine it—life, anything—without

her. It was as if there were an inverse relationship between her star rising and her love life of all kinds—paternal, fraternal, romantic—dwindling to nothing.

But there was a show to do, and tonight's would be a doozie. She had planned this one carefully, with the help of Tommy's friend at the City Desk of the *Times*, who put her in touch with a contact at the State Department of Transportation. Instead of submitting the idea to Harry, as usual, for his okay, she'd slipped him a different one that easily got by him and that bitch in Standards and Practices whose hackles were up over Jeannie's prank of posting the names and addresses of bad guys on air.

But now, without Luce, it would be a little more complicated. They'd have to start the show live from the street, and when it was time to cut to the approved tape, they'd preempt it with the live feed of Jeannie and Joseph on the highway. And by then it would be too late.

CAUGHT YA!

JEANNIE: *Tonight we're on the Long Island Expressway, parked here on the shoulder between exits thirty-eight and thirty-nine. Without naming names, I was able to arrange a change in some of the electronic digital signs out here to see if drivers are really watching the road and not talking on their cell phones as they drive. I'm here with Joseph—*

JOSEPH: *Jeannie, did you know that distractions like eating while driving, or kids in the back seat, or cell phones account for the majority of traffic accidents?*

JEANNIE: *I'm not surprised. And tonight's Caught Ya! is going to deal with just that. Can you show our viewers what the sign says now?*

JOSEPH: *It says, "We see you! You're talking on your cell phone!"*

JEANNIE: *And at the next exit is another sign that says, "If you're on your cell phone, you could kill someone." And at the one after, there's another sign that says, "Hey, you there, on your cell phone! You're being followed." And there are at least three more down the road We'll be driving down there, so you'll see it all. The last sign? Well, you'll see when we get there. Let's get in the car, Joseph, and drive on down. See how people are reacting.*

Nightmare on the LIE

With the car driving slowly in the right lane for the next few miles, Joseph was shooting with the mini-DV camera. He was able to catch drivers using handheld cell phones in at least half the cars they passed. Jeannie was taking notes and speaking into her mike, and a helicopter was filming and reporting to them from above. It took only a few minutes for the signs to take effect. First they saw several drivers put their cell phones down. Then traffic started to slow.

"Joseph, come in," said a voice coming over the scratchy receiver that was hooked up to the helicopter. "You've got an accident at sign number five. Looks like several cars involved."

Number five was the last sign. It said, "The guy talking on his cell phone just got creamed." "Let's get up there," Jeannie said to her driver, who got on the shoulder and sped the few miles to the scene. Traffic was at a total standstill, horns were being honked, people were getting out of their cars and yelling on the expressway.

God, this was a dream, something so perfect she couldn't have planned it.

When they got there, they saw a several-car pileup and heard a woman screaming, "My baby! Someone help my son! My boy! Help me!"

Jeannie broke out in a sweat and could hear her own heartbeat throbbing in her ears. Her driver pulled over. "Come on, let's go!" she yelled, and ran through the cars, Joseph following her and carrying the equipment.

And there was the car, its rear passenger door bashed in, with a boy inside crying. He was unable to move. "Let's get him out," Jeannie yelled.

The woman, his mother, looked at Jeannie and the camera and knew immediately who she was. "Don't you touch him. Don't you dare come any closer. This is all because of you. You and your stupid irresponsible prank. What were you thinking?"

Before Jeannie could react, she heard sirens and turned to see an ambulance and a fire truck coming up the shoulder. Finally they reached them, and when the jaws of life chewed their way into the skin of the car, they reached the boy. The EMS guys got him out, put him on a stretcher, and loaded him into the ambulance, his mother sitting by his side.

The EMS driver told Jeannie that the boy was being taken to Long Island Jewish. She said to the mom, "I'm so sorry. I hope he's okay. Please let me—"

"Shame on you," the mom said. "Shame on you."

Over and Out

Jeannie and Joseph followed the ambulance to the hospital and waited. The boy was lucky to have only a broken leg and was released a few hours later. But to Jeannie, it was catastrophic. How could she not have realized that she was an idiot to have been so caught up in the excitement of *Caught Ya!* and her need to prove herself that she risked lives and, literally, limbs? The electronic signs had proved to be more of a distraction than the cell phones.

When they got back to the studio, they were updated on the damage. Five cars involved in the accident, thousands of dollars in repairs. But because traffic had been moving so slowly, only a child's leg had been broken. It was a miracle, everyone agreed, that nobody had been killed.

Jeannie was summoned to Moss's office. He was standing facing his photo on the wall, his back to her. Harry was sitting in one of the leather chairs, glowering at her. "Close the door," Moss said softly.

She did. And then he turned to face her. He looked tired, worn, sad. His eyes bore into hers; his disappointment tore open her chest.

"Jeannie," he said, so softly she could barely hear him. "Someone could've been killed. You could've been hurt."

"You consciously deceived me and everybody on the show," said Harry. "After all the years, after everything we've—"

"What were you thinking?" asked Moss.

"I—"

"Don't answer. I'll tell you: you weren't. Besides the fines we face from the FCC, and the lawsuit that is sure to come from the family and every other car involved in the accident, which we'll deal with, there's you. I am very disappointed. I'm certain I don't have to say that. What happened to caring about others? At the very minimum, to being concerned for their safety and yours? This was a very stupid prank, Jeannie."

"Maybe if you'd been around . . ." She couldn't believe she'd said that.

"Bullshit. Your judgment should've been around. Of course, Harry and I have to shoulder some of the responsibility as well, as your bosses. But, Jeannie. Christ. What happened to you? Where was your heart?"

Jeannie couldn't answer, couldn't look at him.

"Needless to say, we have to let you go. We'll have your severance check messengered to you in the morning. Better to pack up your things now."

She looked up at him and at Harry now, pleading. "Not Joseph too, are you? He'll still have a job?"

Harry just shook his head, looking down at the floor.

Moss said, "Now you're concerned for him? Where was that concern before you dragged him into this?"

She looked at him and realized what she was losing here today. Fuck the job. It was Harry and their years together. Even bigger, it was Moss. Funny how in a moment like this, when you're blown to bits and wiping your guts off the floor, something is illuminated and you have clarity.

He looked at her. She had tears in her eyes and now they were running down her cheek; she made no move whatsoever to hide them, and all he wanted to do was wipe them away, hold her, and tell her it would be okay. But he was angry and he had a right to be. So when she turned to walk out, there wasn't even a good-bye.

In her cubicle, she packed her things in a couple of shopping bags she had under her desk and threw away all the shit accumulated over the years there. How could this tiny space hold so much?

Tommy, Can You Feel Me?

She took a taxi to Tommy's, looking, hoping for . . . what, she wasn't sure anymore. When he opened the door, she walked in and slumped on his couch.

"I'll be with you in a minute," he said, and went back to his laptop, which was on his dining table. "I have this story that has to be filed—"

"I got fired. A kid got hurt."

"I just need five minutes, and I'm all yours."

"What are you working on anyway?"

"Part of my new stay-in-New-York-to-be-with-Jeannie-gig. And fuck the show. They're idiots. You'll find something else."

"I'm the idiot. Acting with no compunction about hurting someone, as long as it's for the cause. Shit, that kid was hurt. He could've been seriously—"

"But he wasn't. Listen, we all make mistakes, Jeannie. We all walk that fine line between right and wrong."

"Oh, come on. So you've forgotten to hold a door for someone. Maybe walked in before letting people out. Been a little rude to a waiter. And kept a library book or two. That stuff is nothing compared to this."

"Jeannie," he said, getting up and coming to sit with her on the couch, taking her hands in his, their knees touching. "You're so naïve. These people don't matter. Who are they anyway? Just fodder for your show."

"They're you and me."

"No, they're not. They're nothing, Jeannie," he said, and got up and walked back to his computer. "You and me, Jeannie, we're of an entirely different species."

Jeannie was furious now, both at herself and at Tommy. Tommy, her old best friend. Had they stayed friends, they probably would've been friends forever. But once you cross the line into intimacy, it's as if you fall into the deep cellar of a person's soul, and you learn the secrets of what they store there.

She got up and walked around Tommy's chair, and saw over his shoulder what he'd been writing. It was an article from Uganda. Dated tomorrow.

At first she didn't understand. So she read it again. And then it became clear: Tommy was writing as if he were there, while sitting in his comfortable Upper East Side apartment here. She shook her head. "What's this? You haven't been away in the last month. Are you finishing a story you began there?" She felt dizzy, the floor rolling beneath her feet, the walls swaying.

He turned around in his chair and faced her, held her legs. "I'm doing this for you. For us."

She paused, thinking, figuring it out. "This is why you wouldn't leave your apartment for days. So you wouldn't be seen."

"They wouldn't give it to me. I wanted to stay, they're making me go, and I'm not going."

"You're pretending to be there."

"Listen, nobody knows the place better than I do. I'm not stealing, I'm not plagiarizing. Just inventing a little, nothing important, just a detail, saying I'm there when I'm here. It's like a white lie."

How could she not have seen this coming? She'd wanted this relationship so badly that she ignored every warning. The waiter air scribble, his treatment of her doorman, his insensitivity to Luce, his general disrespect of others. *If he can* steal library books, who knows, *he could do almost anything*, that caller had said. *That guy's working with a broken moral compass*, he'd said. But Luce had put it best: *Nobody is worth losing yourself over.*

She walked to the couch, picked up her mauled bag, and put it over her shoulder.

"Oh, don't tell me you're pissed," he said.

She went to the door.

"Don't go," he said. "This is nothing. Really. I can give you the names of ten journalists who've done worse. Come on, Jeannie. Get off your high goddamn horse and stop judging me. Stop judging yourself for that matter."

For once in her life, she had absolutely nothing to say. She turned to look at him and then walked out the door.

Unconditional Love

For so many days she lost count, Jeannie stayed in her apartment alone. She ventured out once to go to the deli for milk, to Morgan's for some fruit and veggies, and to Socrates for a chicken souvlaki. And one other time she picked up some meatballs at Gigino. It was a vibrant spring out there, full of sunlight and new growth, but in her apartment it was cold and dreary and lonely.

Jeannie had brought this upon herself. She had lost her two best friends, her job, her dad, and her dog within a few weeks. Even Moss, who she had to admit had hurt her most with his soft voice, his anger, his ice-cold brevity, and that whole "Where was your heart?" thing; she had lost him too.

She had hurt a kid from a nice family who would spend the next two months in a cast sitting in a wheelchair, and then on crutches. Sure, she had taught them a lesson, but at what price? This idea of going out and actually showing people the error of their ways had started out so promisingly, and had so quickly become a nightmare.

She missed Mouse at that moment, someone to pet and cuddle with, someone who needed her and depended on her. She thought of him pooping in the house, eating on all fours off the kitchen counter, chewing her panties, and how he'd learned to stop some of that lousy behavior. *Perhaps,* she thought, as she snuggled up tighter, pulling her old plaid flannel robe up over her shoulders and tightening the belt, drawing her knees toward her chest, *perhaps, like in the dog training manuals, like I learned living with Mouse, you can't change behavior by berating, yelling, punishing, hitting.* Perhaps, as with a dog who looks to you for love and guidance, when you reward his good behavior, that behavior will be repeated. And repeated. Until it becomes a habit. Not an original notion, she knew; in fact, it was so stupidly obvious that she called herself a dickwad in her mind.

And it made her think of Luce. Of everyone she'd lost, it was Luce whose loss she felt the most, who she missed the most.

Fuck this shit. Fuck this stupid shit, she thought.

She got up, threw her suede jacket on over her robe, slipped her feet into her Fryes, grabbed the bag that reminded her of Mouse every time she put it over her shoulder, and went out the door.

Luce let her in. But not a hug, not even a perfunctory air kiss was issued between the two. Luce didn't even say a word until Jeannie threw her jacket on the couch and then sat down. Luce sat in the big chair across from her.

"You're in your pajamas."

"I know. For days now. Where's Spike?"

"Hello? It's six in the morning. So keep your voice down."

"I'm sorry, I . . . ," she whispered. Luce was in sweatpants and a tank top that fit tightly over her pregnant stomach. She looked beautiful.

Luce snorted. "I am still really mad at you. I want you to know—"

"I know, I—"

"Shut up. Let me finish," Luce said.

"Okay. But I—"

"Shut up! I'm talking to you. You're not talking until I have said what I need to say. Otherwise—"

"Hey, I'm the one—"

"Shut up, would you? Just let me speak." She glared at Jeannie, and Jeannie did that silly childhood gesture of zipping her lips closed. "Okay. You are the most important person in my life, except for Spike, of course. But love, Jeannie, even yours and mine, is not unconditional, I've learned. Or wait," she said, thinking aloud, "maybe you never stop loving, but if a person hurts you so, or is bad to you, bad *for* you, love isn't enough. Yes, that's it. Just because love is unconditional, it isn't always enough. You see what I'm trying to say? I'm—"

"Yeah, I think—"

"*Shut up!*"

"But you asked—"

"It's a rhetorical question. No talking until I say so!" She got up from her chair and started to pace back and forth, her arms moving like the rotors of a helicopter. Then she stopped, turned, and looked at her friend head-on. "You really hurt me. When your show, your success, became more important than our friendship."

Jeannie raised her hand, as if in elementary school.

"Yes?" Luce said. "You may speak."

"You hurt me too. Not telling me about your pregnancy. Me!"

"Ssssh!"

"Sorry."

"I know that hurt, and I was wrong. I will never not tell you anything again."

"Me neither. What an asshole I was. Am. Nothing is more important to me than you."

"But what about Tommy?"

Jeannie shook her head as tears welled in her eyes. "It really hurts. Not losing the boyfriend, losing the friend. A really, really good friend. I'm going to miss him. The him I knew before I knew the real him." Jeannie laughed. "You know what I mean."

Luce laughed too, and stroked Jeannie's hair.

"You know, he was lying, faking his work," Jeannie continued. "He said he was doing it for me, but who would do something like that in the name of love?"

"Love does wacky things to people."

Jeannie shook her head. "Like pretending you don't see the person for who he is."

"Or hoping you're wrong. Or hoping you can change him."

"Or yourself. Hoping you can come to accept things that you don't respect about him."

"You're to be commended for trying," she said, as she sat down next to Jeannie on the couch. "You softy, you."

"But I dumped him. He really is a—"

"A dickwad?"

Jeannie, for the first time maybe ever, said nothing. Then she laughed and hugged Luce, and her tears spilled onto Luce's shoulder. Luce cried too. And then she pulled back.

"And then your stupid show!"

"I know," Jeannie said. "It's over."

"I heard. Harry called. Joseph too. And even Moss. He's worried about you."

"Tell him to bite me," Jeannie said.

Luce laughed. "I think he'd like to, you know."

"You think?" asked Jeannie. She thought of their walk around the pond up there in Central Park, of his washing her hands in the women's bathroom, of the light in his eyes as he looked at the photo of the forest canopy in his office, of his smile that wrecked her every time.

"How can you not see it? The way he looks at you."

"He fired me!"

"And not a moment too soon. Thank god for him. It was a good idea that went too far."

"No, it was a lousy idea. A shitty idea. But there might be a good idea deep down in it."

And the two friends talked until Spike woke up, sending them out to Three Guys on Madison for breakfast, Luce in her sweats and sneakers and Jeannie in her flannel robe, PJs, and boots, sitting in a booth in the back. They laughed as they recounted the history of *Sterling Behavior*, of Luce's wedding, of so many things that it took hours. Jeannie told Luce how she dumped Tommy. Luce walked Jeannie through every tiny detail of her pregnancy. And they knew, when it was time for them to go home, that their friendship was intact, and would stay that way for years to come, if not forever.

And the next day, when Jeannie received the call that her dad was in the hospital, that he'd had a heart attack, the first and only person she called—from the taxi as it made its way to JFK—was Luce.

Not One Stunning Stewardess
Bitch in Sight

The flight was packed. Jeannie was lucky, during this spring vacation week, to have gotten a seat at the last minute. She was stuck in a middle seat, way in the back, but she was grateful, even with a mom and her baby on one side of her, a big brawny teen listening to his iPod on the other. With her dad on her mind and her heart filled with Luce and Moss, for once she didn't care that the baby was crying or that she could hear some angry rap playing out of the kid's headphones. Because this flight, this packed, noisy flight, rocked Jeannie's world.

All that happened was this: an older man with horn-rimmed glasses, wearing a dark blue velour jogging suit, who should've checked his suitcase because it was obviously way overstuffed, was having trouble getting it into the overhead bin. He shoved and pushed, and finally put it down in frustration. Then a younger man, a big guy with long sideburns who clearly spent time at the gym and had been canoodling with the girl sitting next to him, got up out of his seat and helped him nudge it into the bin, and together, they eventually succeeded. The first man thanked him with a smile and a handshake. A loud talker, who Jeannie could hear three rows away, was approached by a flight attendant, who leaned over and whispered something in his ear. He immediately lowered his voice with a laugh, without argument. And then, to top it all off, a woman agreed to change seats—from an aisle to a middle!—so that a couple could sit together.

Maybe it was the vacation spirit. Maybe it was just that the flight was so damned crowded that people knew it was in their power to make the next six hours heaven or hell. Maybe it was just a combination of timing, generosity, and luck. Maybe it was simply about a change in Jeannie's perspective: with her dad very ill, she might've been less concerned with the little things that normally she had the luxury to obsess about. Or perhaps, for the first time, she was experiencing her life as half-full instead of half-empty. There wasn't one stunning stewardess bitch in sight.

Whatever it was, it gave Jeannie a reason to smile and let out a sigh. Treat a dog nicely, with love and affection, and he will learn. *We're all like Pavlov's dog, hungry for gestures of kindness,* Jeannie thought. So is it possible that kindness could, if repeated over and over, beget kindness?

"Duh!" Jeannie said out loud, with a shake of her head.

And the young woman in the seat next to her with the baby, who had finally fallen asleep, turned and whispered, "Totally."

Luce to the Rescue

"I just thought you'd want to know," Luce said.

"I'm glad you called. She's got a good friend in you, you know that."

"I just wish she weren't alone out there. And the doctor said I shouldn't fly right now."

"What about Tommy? Or is he somewhere in Africa?"

"I don't know where he is and I wouldn't call him if I did. Jeannie and he, well . . ."

"Not another word. You don't have to ask. I think you know that. When it comes to Jeannie . . . though I'm not sure she'll want to see me."

"Trust me. She will."

"You know what? I don't care one way or the other. She's got me coming, whether she likes it or not."

Finally, Words Spoken

"Dad. You awake?"

"You think I'd miss this? A visit from you? You flew?"

"Yeah, and are—"

"—your arms tired."

Jeannie smiled, though her eyes were dark with concern. Her dad smiled back as best he could. His skin was pale, flaccid.

"Did they feed you?" he asked. "They never feed you on the plane anymore."

"I bought a sandwich at the airport."

"Egg salad?"

"With muenster."

"With mustard!"

She took his hand. It was frail, cool. She held it and her dad turned his head to her.

He searched her eyes, trying to read her. "What?"

"What what?"

"How's the show?" he asked.

"Oh god, Dad, I don't know what happened. It was terrible. There was a wreck, a kid got hurt . . ." The tears rolled down her cheeks. She reached over to his bedside table, looking for a tissue. "You can't get a tissue in this place? We're in the hospital, for god's sake!"

"Here, use this." He feebly handed her his sleeve.

She shook her head and *tsk*ed, and went into the bathroom that was right off the room.

"I read about it, you know," her dad said as loudly as he could. "He's going to be okay, the paper said."

Then she was back with a wad of paper in her hand and took her place on the chair beside him. "Yeah, but . . ." She stopped herself and blew her nose.

"And you?"

"I'll find something."

"I know you will."

"You were right."

"I know. But sometimes you have to experience something yourself before you can learn it. Doesn't help to be told."

They sat in silence for a few minutes, one of those long, deep silences where nothing and so much is said.

"What?" her dad finally asked.

"What what?" she asked.

"So now's as good a time as any."

"For what?" she said.

"There ain't much time left. You might as well say it. Whatever it is you've wanted to say to me all these years that you thought you couldn't."

Again there was a silence. The sun shone through the window and the shadows of the eucalyptus leaves were mottled on the wall. Jeannie swallowed and fought back tears that burned like embers behind her eyes.

"Dad. I have nothing—"

"You're angry with me. I was a terrible father."

There it was, out on the table. There was no way she could sidestep it now. "Yeah, I was. And you were." She looked down at his hand in hers, then up to his eyes, which were unusually small, black and liquid, the whites yellowed from age and illness. She gulped. This was too hard. But this was maybe her last chance, and she sure didn't want to blow it. "There was only one thing I wanted from you, Pop, my whole life."

"Your whole long thirty-something life," he repeated, smiling.

"I wanted you to love me." Her eyes filled with tears. "Was that so hard?"

"It was a questioning time. I was the black sheep, a gypsy."

"Fuck that gypsy thing. Gypsies had kids and loved them."

"I just didn't know how. Your mom—"

"You're going to die blaming Mom?"

"I was about to say, before I was so rudely interrupted, that your mom was a good mom. It's just that her Joni Mitchell thing put me over the edge," he said with a smile. "I mean, how many times a day can you listen to 'moons and Junes and Ferris wheels' and all that shit and not want to kill somebody?"

Jeannie smiled but she couldn't answer. One of the tears she was working so hard to keep back found its way onto her cheek. She quickly wiped it away.

It took time to get these words out: "So why did you leave?"

"I couldn't live in that house anymore. Not with all those people. Listen, I was no angel; I couldn't live anywhere for long."

"So why didn't you take me? Or at least come see me enough to be sure I was okay?"

"Weren't you okay? I'll kill—"

"Of course, no, that's not the issue." She was amused by the idea of him punching out someone for her.

"I couldn't take you. I had little money, no home, a job now and then when I needed money for the home I didn't have. You had your mother. You had the house. School, friends. Me? I had bupkis."

"Yeah. And why is that, exactly?"

"For me, it was the dream. That's the whole thing, the kit and caboodle. It was all about chasing something—a life, a woman, a place—I probably was never going to find. But I wasn't going to let that stop me. Not your pop."

"You never thought of achieving something? Of having a career and a family—"

"I did. I had you."

"But you didn't feel responsible for me. Like being sure I had what I needed, or taking me to a play or a ball game, like being there for my birthdays or graduations or saving for college."

"I don't know, Jeannie."

She was angry now. There was no way she could stop it. "And what about doing something of value yourself, and feeling accomplished? Or just making a living, like everybody else?"

"I guess I didn't want to be like everybody else. No. I'm sorry, but I didn't see that for myself. I saw ocean beaches and strolling, eating a plate of oysters, a Danish, and fishing, watching the sunrise. That's your pop. Simple. Nothing more. I told you: I am a bum."

"I don't understand it," Jeannie confessed, shaking her head.

"But this I do feel strongly about: I love you, baby, I just want you to be happy. Forgive your dying old dad and be happy. You only have one shot. Don't waste it because of me. Or your mom."

"I can't tell you much, Dad, except this: for the first time in my life I don't want to kill anyone. Or fix anyone. Or change anyone. I don't even want to tell taxi drivers which way to go. Or cell phone–users to shut up."

"That's a start."

"But I'd be a hell of a lot happier if you'd come home with me and that stinker of a dog of yours. How about it? Where is that Mouse, anyway? Is someone—"

"He's okay. But he hasn't been the same since he left New York. The old lady next door is taking care of him."

"So come home with me and bring him. I miss him chewing my panties."

"No thanks. I'm good right here. How could I leave Nurse Ratched?"

She looked up to see a cute young nurse, short in stature, with big eyes and long blond hair, enter the room with a skip and a jump, like a little whirlwind of life force. "Hey, Lou, how you doing today? Missed you last night." She began to check his vitals.

"She's Nurse Ratched?" Jeannie had doubts.

"Did he call me that? That is such a cliché, Lou. I'm the nurse of your dreams."

Her dad smiled at the nurse, and Jeannie knew he was in good hands and was right to want to stay exactly where he was.

Then, out of her peripheral vision, Jeannie saw another figure appear in the door, and she looked up expecting the doctor doing his rounds. But it wasn't the doctor, or another nurse, or an orderly, or anybody of the medical establishment.

It was Moss. He smiled at her and it shook her to her core. Her eyes filled once again to see him standing there, holding what looked like a miniature bonsai cypress tree in a flat rectangular dish, planted in dirt covered with tiny stones. He didn't say a word. But he was there.

"Look, it's Moss, carrying a tree on a plate."

"A redwood?" her dad asked.

"It's a cypress, Pop," answered Jeannie.

"Hard to fit a redwood in a little dish like this," said Moss.

"I would've preferred a redwood," her dad said.

"Me too," said Moss, with a smile at the old man and a look at Jeannie.

"Dad, this is Nicholas Moss. Used to be my boss. He fired me, actually."

"A brave man," said her dad, slowly lifting his hand for Moss to take.

"Honored to meet you, Mr.—"

"Lou."

"Lou. Anybody who is responsible for this person here"— he put an arm around Jeannie—"is the king of all brave men."

Jeannie's dad looked at her and held out his hand for her to hold. She took it and he said, "To love Jeannie, you don't need to be brave. A little crazy, maybe."

And she answered, "I don't know, Dad. And I know this is sappy, but I think to love anybody you need to be brave. And vice versa." Then she looked at Moss. His eyes were on her.

Lou saw the look that passed between the two of them and was pleased. "Enough of this Hallmark shit, okay? Get out of here, would you? Your old man is tired," he said. "I don't know what they're giving me, but it sure ain't amphetamines. You poisoning me, Ratched?"

The nurse laughed and tweaked Lou's arm.

"Okay, Dad." Jeannie got up and kissed him on his cheek. "I'll be here in the morning."

"And buy her some dinner, would you?" he said to Moss. "She's been on the hospital cafeteria diet and it's having a bad effect."

Moss came over to the bed and put the bonsai down on the table next to it. It looked delicate and lovely there amidst the Jell-O containers and the juice boxes and the kidney-shaped bedpan.

"See you tomorrow, Lou." Moss squeezed his arm.

"Take care of her, would you?"

"Christ, Dad."

"Hey, I'm sick. Be nice," he said to Jeannie. But then he looked at Moss and said, "She doesn't think she needs it— and I don't think she needs it, I *know* she needs it. It can't hurt, right?"

"You!" she said to her dad, and kissed him again.

"It'll be my pleasure," said Moss.

Moss and Jeannie walked in silence out of the hospital, which sat at the top of a hill, to her car, a rented Chevy Impala that was parked in the visitor parking lot below. It had gotten dark and cool, the night air scented with eucalyptus, the moon hanging low over the city. Moss had his hand on the small of Jeannie's back most of the way down the steep hill. When they got to the car, he held on to Jeannie's elbow and pulled her to face him.

"You came," said Jeannie. "I didn't even have to ask."

"If you had to ask, it wouldn't be . . ." His voice drifted off as he kissed her. "Jeannie," Moss said, pulling back, holding her face with his hand, pushing her hair back, away from her eyes, "the girl who called me a turkey. Here I am kissing her in a parking lot. And not a Hummer in sight."

She raised her hand to his cheek, his ear, held the back of his neck. He took that hand by the wrist and turned it to kiss it below her palm, his lips on her pulse. She noticed the string bracelet again. Taking hold of his arm, she fingered it gently. "Tell me. Why do you wear this?"

He laughed, looked at it. "I met this kid, I don't know, six years ago already. The daughter, about ten years old at the time, of a woman I was dating. It didn't work out, but that little girl, she was something. She gave it to me and made me promise I wouldn't take it off until, well . . ." He paused, and looked into Jeannie's dark eyes.

"Tell me," she said in a whisper.

"Until . . . I found somebody to love. In a big way. She was very specific," he said with a smile. "So I've never taken it off." A quick yank did it. "Until now." He put it in his pocket and sought Jeannie's reaction.

She looked at him, and there, in his eyes, was that sad, dreamy quality, that wealth of feeling.

He kissed her again, even longer this time, passionately. He held her against him as he leaned over her, arching her back, his arm supporting her at her waist. He felt her arms holding tight around him, felt as if she and he were a perfect fit. And then he said, "Face it, you're crazy about me."

She so wanted to shout a resounding, "Shut up. No way, I am not. Up yours. I'm simply doing the polite thing. How could I not kiss you when you're all over me like this?" But she didn't. She had found home in his arms. She kissed him soft and sweet and said, "Yes, I am. Go figure."

A Gift

Her dad seemed to have disintegrated overnight. She could see it the minute she walked into his room. There was a hush as the nurse checked his IV. Jeannie nodded to her and approached the bed, sat in the chair, took his hand in hers.

"Dad."

"Hey, honey." His voice was low, raspy.

"How're you feeling?"

"Not so good."

"Yeah, you look like shit."

He smiled. Her eyes filled.

"Stop that. No tears."

"Oh, Dad."

"I love you, little girl."

"I know."

"You do? Then that's it, then."

"What the hell does that mean?"

"Get me some water, would ya?"

She poured, she put the cup to his mouth, he drank.

"What I meant is, I'm done. As long as you know I love you. Now live your life."

"I love you too."

"You won't."

"Da-ad—"

"When I tell you what I got to tell you."

"Which is?"

"My will. I left you one thing."

"Let me guess."

"Love him, okay? He's that kind of dog. Needs lots of love. Like you, honey, like you."

Jeannie held her dad's arm and put her forehead down on it, his cool skin sweet against the wetness of her cheek. And she whispered the words she'd wanted to say to him so many times since she was a young child.

"Pop, please, stay with me."

Lou's Home

Lou Sterling died two days later and was buried in the veterans' cemetery near Vacaville. Afterward, Moss drove Jeannie to Mendocino and waited in a café on Main Street while Jeannie went alone, as she'd wanted, to Lou's ramshackle little house on Kasten, heading north, up the hill. Its back windows faced east, so the morning sun hit her when she walked through the door. As did Mouse, who pounced on Jeannie with the thrill and hunger of a mountain lion on his prey. She got down low so he could lick her face before turning over onto his back for a good chest scratching, which she gave him. She received some final instructions from Mrs. Mueller, the dog sitter, who would not take the money that Jeannie offered, saying that being with Mouse was the most fun she'd had in years. Jeannie thanked her and promised she'd let her watch Mouse if they were ever in the area, and Mrs. Mueller gave Mouse a good-bye kiss on his muzzle. *How this dog has changed,* Jeannie thought. From a panty-chewing, food-stealing mongrel to a sweet and loving panty-chewing, food-stealing soul. She couldn't help but recognize the transforming power of love.

The house smelled a little musty, but she was surprised to find it so nicely kept. It was clean and orderly. The furniture, probably from secondhand stores and garage sales, sparsely filled the living room, and a few generic pictures lined the walls. It was clear that the person who lived here had invested little time and money to make it his own.

From the window behind the couch a sliver of the ocean

could be seen past more houses and trees. In the front closet a few jackets hung from hangers, and gloves and cowboy hats sat on the shelf above. Several pairs of cowboy boots, a pair of muddy, worn work boots, and two pairs of old tennis shoes filled the shoe rack on the floor.

Then she inspected the small kitchen, with its yellow walls and mottled tan Formica, that held three pots, two fry pans, a mix-and-match group of bowls and plates, cutlery and glasses, a couple of towels. The fridge was almost empty except for two bottles of Corona, half a loaf of sliced whole-wheat bread, eggs, jam, butter, pickles, ketchup, mustard, mayo, and some mint chip ice cream in the freezer. The dining area was right off the kitchen with a small old wooden table and four chairs, and a window to the back yard, which couldn't have been more than a couple hundred square feet, with a metal-link fence that ran down the sides and along the back of the house.

The bathroom was pale green, like hospital scrubs. A light blue towel, frayed at the edges, hung on the rack. The medicine chest held the usual stuff. It seemed as if this house held no secrets, not even much of the texture of the person who lived there.

Then she went to the bedroom, which held a mattress and box spring sitting on the floor, covered with an old down comforter and an embroidered pillow that said IF A MAN YELLS IN A FOREST AND NO WOMAN IS THERE TO HEAR HIM, IS HE STILL WRONG? Jeannie laughed to herself at that; it was so her dad. She was glad to find one thing in his home that was.

A table next to the bed held an old lamp with a shade painted with flowers, and a pile of books on a variety of nonfiction subjects—from Abraham Lincoln to World War II, to Jerry Lewis, to earthquakes, to ancient Egypt—and some suspense novels too.

She checked the closet in the bedroom and found her dad's clothes hanging neatly on hangers, with his one pair of dress shoes, an old pair of black Florsheims, on the floor below. On the shelf above were some old, faded sheets, a couple towels, and an extra blanket.

All that was left was a small old chest of drawers that, upon Jeannie's perusal, contained underwear and socks in its top drawer, and pajamas and some T-shirts in its second. And then, when she opened the third drawer, her heart raced. It was filled with papers and clippings and envelopes and files. Perhaps this was the mother lode, the writings and clippings that would explain him to her. Maybe there were letters to him from her mom. Maybe there were secret papers, documents, deeds.

She pulled the drawer out, put it on the bed, and sat down next to it. Here, finally, he would be revealed to her. Why he left, why he so rarely returned, why he couldn't or wouldn't keep a job, have a family, set down roots. But all she found—stacked on top of one another, many yellowed from age, others wearing so thin their creases were faded and tearing, some in envelopes and some in files, as if her dad had made an attempt to organize them—were clippings from newspapers and magazines. She opened one and then another, then a dozen more. By then it was clear what this was: her dad's hope chest, so to speak. Destinations he dreamed of visiting. An article on camping in Bali, another on archaeological digs in Guatemala, on the north coast of Australia, several on the Arctic Circle, on Norway in winter, on the Orient Express, on India, Tibet, and Thailand. Articles about the Kalahari, about Fiji, about Baja. Brochures about horseback riding in Israel, river-rafting in Italy, spelunking in Switzerland.

This was her dad, right here in this splintered old drawer. The soul of a dreamer. A vagabond at heart. Afraid to stay, always yearning to go. But unable, because of his own limitations, to get himself there. Or maybe it wasn't as simple as that. Maybe he did harbor a secret that could explain why he was the way he was. Everybody has secrets of the heart, Jeannie knew, but she would never know his.

There, sitting on the edge of the bed, Jeannie realized that this was the very first time she had ever been in her father's house. Not just this house, but any home of his, ever. She felt a terrible sadness then. She loved him, just as she loved her mom, but now neither was here to forgive, to understand, to appreciate.

But just knowing she'd like to made her feel less alone.

She placed with care everything in the drawer into one of the boxes she had brought to pack up the house. And she left with Mouse and the box, and one last look over her shoulder into the home her dad had made for himself.

This box and its contents would be the only thing of her father's Jeannie saved. As she had after her mother's death years before, she gave everything away, except the one thing that would keep him close to her. Back then she'd saved her mom's suede, fringed coat, and now she saved her dad's carton of dreams.

Oh, and of course, there was Mouse.

Touching Heaven

The wind blew the hair that wasn't secured in her helmet away from Jeannie's face. It was salty and wet, the wind that blew in from the Pacific, which she could see as far as the horizon from her perch. She was glad she'd worn her down jacket today and zipped it up past her chin, pulling the collar up to cover her neck.

The tree swayed, shivered, and shook. Jeannie was afraid, holding so tightly to the trunk that she thought the rough bark would pierce her gloves. But the rope that tethered her to Moss held tight, and she knew, deeply and with conviction, that she was safe up here with him. *Funny how that works,* she thought. *Fear, like right and wrong, is so often relative.* One day you could be afraid of crossing the street, and then the next not afraid at all to sit a hundred feet up, hanging in a saddle from the branch of a California redwood, on the edge of a cliff that led to a rocky beach below.

She looked at him sitting in his harness as he hung from the branch, to the right, just above. He was busy with the ropes, looping one around his arm, elbow to hand and back, and then pulling the other tight, through the carabiner that connected them to each other. She smiled, thinking that she didn't need a rope to connect her to him. Theirs was a natural, permanent connection. This she knew deep in her bones.

"I can see it, you know."

"What?" he said. "What can you see?"

"Where we buried my dad."

Moss looked southeast over the treetops. Of course the cemetery was miles away, but he thought of the short ceremony on the hilly green lawn that was striped with rows of white headstones. They'd stood in the hot sun under a vivid, royal-blue sky. A rabbi had officiated, Jeannie had wept, Moss had held her, and Lou had gotten the burial he'd wanted. Through her tears Jeannie had made a joke about his funeral being the only thing she could think of that Lou had planned in advance. Moss looked over at Jeannie now, sitting in his tree, and he breathed in the strong scent of the redwood, feeling more lucky and proud and alive than he'd ever felt possible.

"And I can see where we threw my mom, years ago."

"Jeannie, you didn't throw your mom. You threw her ashes."

"Well, I can see the spot."

He looked at her and smiled. Then he looked out to the ocean. It was calm and wide and glistening in the midday sun. "Me too. I see it too."

She threw her head back, laughed, and caught sight through the branches above of a layer of clouds moving across the sky as if on a mission, briskly, in the direction of the wind. But there was a top layer of clouds that stood still, anchored, as a lovely, protective covering. *The sky*, she thought, *has room for them both at once: the wayward and the secure.*

Jeannie looked at Moss. He was beautiful, dangling there in the dimpled light, his equipment hanging from his belt, his eyes alive, his smile full of warmth. This was a happy man, here in the tree. He extended his arm toward her.

"How about it? Let's go a little higher," he said. "Come on. Reach for me."

And she did.

Evening News

A little more powder and Luce would be ready. The lighting always made her skin shine, which normally was a good thing, but on television it made her look like a bad imitation of herself at Madame Tussaud's.

Look at me, she thought, *I am huge.* She stroked her belly and the baby kicked, and then kicked again, as if responding to her touch.

"Three minutes." Stacy rapped on the door.

Luce stood up and looked at herself, smoothed her hair, pulled down her sweater over her skirt. *How lucky I am*, she thought. Out of the ashes of *Caught Ya!*, where her composure, intelligence, and the way the camera loved her got the attention of the head producer at NY1. She was now the anchor of *News All Evening*.

And she looked down at her stomach, stroked it, and felt more than lucky. This was what she'd been talking about when she asked Jeannie about the stars. This miracle. And all the other treasures of life. Like their friendship, and her love for a guy who owned Phillips screwdrivers in twelve different sizes.

STERLING BEHAVIOR

JEANNIE: *Good morning, everybody! This is Jeannie Sterling, and you're listening to* Sterling Behavior *on WBUZ Radio, 660 on your AM dial, on this gorgeously sunny and delicious Wednesday. That's right, this is the second week of our glorious new time slot . . . ten a.m. to one p.m., every day, Monday to Friday.*

JOSEPH: *Come on, Jeannie. Don't you miss the late-night slot just a little bit? I kind of dug it.*

JEANNIE: *You're a night owl. You thrive at night. I bet this new schedule of ours has really thrown you. Me, I don't miss one thing about it. Let's hear it for daytime. For waking up in the morning. For sleeping at night. For living like a normal person.*

JOSEPH: *But what about your loyal insomniacs, as you used to call them?*

JEANNIE: *I'm hoping they've gotten some Ambien and that they join us here each and every day.*

JOSEPH: *What about TV? Don't you just miss the excitement of it at all?*

JEANNIE: *Not one bit. I love radio, I was born for radio, the floating voice, the anonymity, the freedom. You can say what you want and not have to worry about your hair. But TV turned out to be Luce's thing, and I'm so happy that she's found a home there. All you loyal listeners out there, you can catch Luce tonight on NY1. And don't you just love this weather, Joseph? Spring is happening. You should see the park full of daffodils, the lushness, the bright greens, the ducks on the pond.*

JOSEPH: *You sound happy in your love shack up there overlooking the pond, living with Nicholas Moss, who happens to be the owner of this station. Your sordid little lovefest with the boss.*

JEANNIE: *Joseph, Joseph, Joseph. We weren't going to mention that. It reeks of nepotism. People will think that's the only reason I have this job. And we darn well know it's the only reason I have this job!*

JOSEPH: *Not true.*

JEANNIE: *Well, the truth is that the pond is a piece of the city so few people have seen. It's beautiful. Of course, you need someone special to show it to you. Like the boss. On a sunny day just like this.*

JOSEPH: *Perfect weather for a ride, and I don't mean on a bicycle. Can't wait to get out on my Harley and—*

JEANNIE: *Yeah, don't you just love life? You learn something new every day. Ugh. Don't you just hate treacly aphorisms? Even when they're true? I do like your T-shirt, however.*

JOSEPH: *It's my new favorite, thanks to you.*

JEANNIE: *I'm glad to see things change . . . and yet stay the same. Joseph's T-shirt says* POLITE NEW EFFING YORKER. *And it really says "effing," as in E-F-F-I-N-G. And you can get a T-shirt just like it by calling in during the next hour and letting us know of an act of kindness and respect you witnessed or perpetrated on another. Let's all hear it for humanity. It's about all we've got, when it comes down to it.*

Acknowledgments

Ellen Kaye and Liz Perle read, re-read and read again, offering wisdom, advice, and support along the way. Their friendship and insights mean the world to me.

Thank you to Corinne Netzer and Tom Spain who read very early on, and Patty Dann who read much later, all offering invaluable suggestions.

Thanks to the many friends who provided pet peeves, observations, and tales of rude behavior: Erin Kennedy-Florez, David List, Wendell (Wee Wee) Livingston, Cynthia Meyer, Denise Minnerly, Josephine Phillips, Michael Pollack, Karah Preiss, Bruce Saber, and Maureen Van Bloem. And much appreciation to the California Schnurs, particularly Adam, Zach, Emma, Alan, Jeff, and Ellen, who have more peeves than anybody deserves who live in the beautiful Bay Area.

Richard Preston's article, "Climbing the Redwoods," in the February 14 and 21 issue of *The New Yorker* provided inspiration. It led me to treeclimbing.com, the website of Tree Climbers International, which made me wish that I were more adventurous.

Craig Wilson, writer/editor/producer of CBS News, provided hilarious and pathetic details of the lifestyle of the night-shifter.

Thanks to Joey Reynolds and Myra Chanin of *The Joey Reynolds Show* who have not only had me on the show more than once, but gave me the opportunity to hover annoyingly over the shoulders of Jenna and Tony.

I am forever indebted to my agent Richard Pine, whose depth, guidance, instincts, humor, and ability to nudge gently set him above and apart. And thanks to Beth Davey, who is a font of enthusiasm and ideas.

My editor Greer Hendricks' brilliant hand and deepest heart is evident on every page of this book, making it worlds better than it would've ever been without her. Thanks to Judith Curr, Hannah Morrill, Kathleen Schmidt, Kim Curtin, Sarah Wright, Aja Pollock, Gary Urda, and the entire creative team at Atria.

Byron Preiss (1953–2005) heard the idea for this book before a word was written, and was immediately enthusiastic and brimming with ideas. His friendship is deeply missed.

My kids, Gabe and Miriam, deserve a medal, but please don't tell them that. They make me laugh and keep my Behavior-Cop-of-the-World Complex in control with one "Mom, just stop."

And finally, a huge thanks to my husband, Jerry, the handiest man I know, whose commitment to "do-it-yourself" knows no bounds. His patience and support sustain me, he's a helpful, critical reader, and he looks cute in a tool belt.